PORT
OF
EARTH™

179° 56' 39.4' X 0° 2' 46.2

MW01028569

PUBLISHED BY TOP COW PRODUCTIONS, INC.
LOS ANGELES

PORT OF EARTH™

179° 56′ 39.4′ X 0° 2′ 46.2

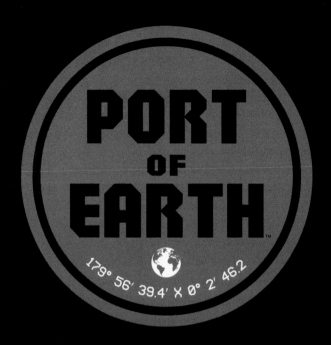

ZACK KAPLAN
Writer

ANDREA MUTTI
Artist

VLADIMIR POPOV
Colorist

TROY PETERI
Letterer

ELENA SALCEDO
Editor

For Top Cow Productions, Inc.

For Top Cow Productions, Inc.
Marc Silvestri - CEO
Matt Hawkins - President & COO
Elena Salcedo - Vice President of Operations
Henry Barajas - Director of Operations
Vincent Valentine - Production Manager
Dylan Gray - Marketing Director

IMAGE COMICS, INC.
Robert Kirkman—Chief Operating Officer
Erik Larsen—Chief Financial Officer
Todd McFarlane—President
Marc Silvestri—Chief Executive Officer
Jim Valentino—Vice President

Eric Stephenson—Publisher/Chief Creative Officer
Corey Hart—Director of Sales
Jeff Boison—Director of Publishing Planning & Book Trade Sales
Chris Ross—Director of Digital Sales
Jeff Stang—Director of Specialty Sales
Kat Salazar—Director of PR & Marketing
Drew Gill—Art Director
Heather Doornink—Production Director
Nicole Lapalme—Controller
IMAGECOMICS.COM

PORT OF EARTH, VOL. 2. First printing. September 2018. Published by Image Comics, Inc. Office of publication: 2701 NW Vaughn St., Suite 780, Portland, OR 97210.

ISBN: 978-1-5343-0848-0

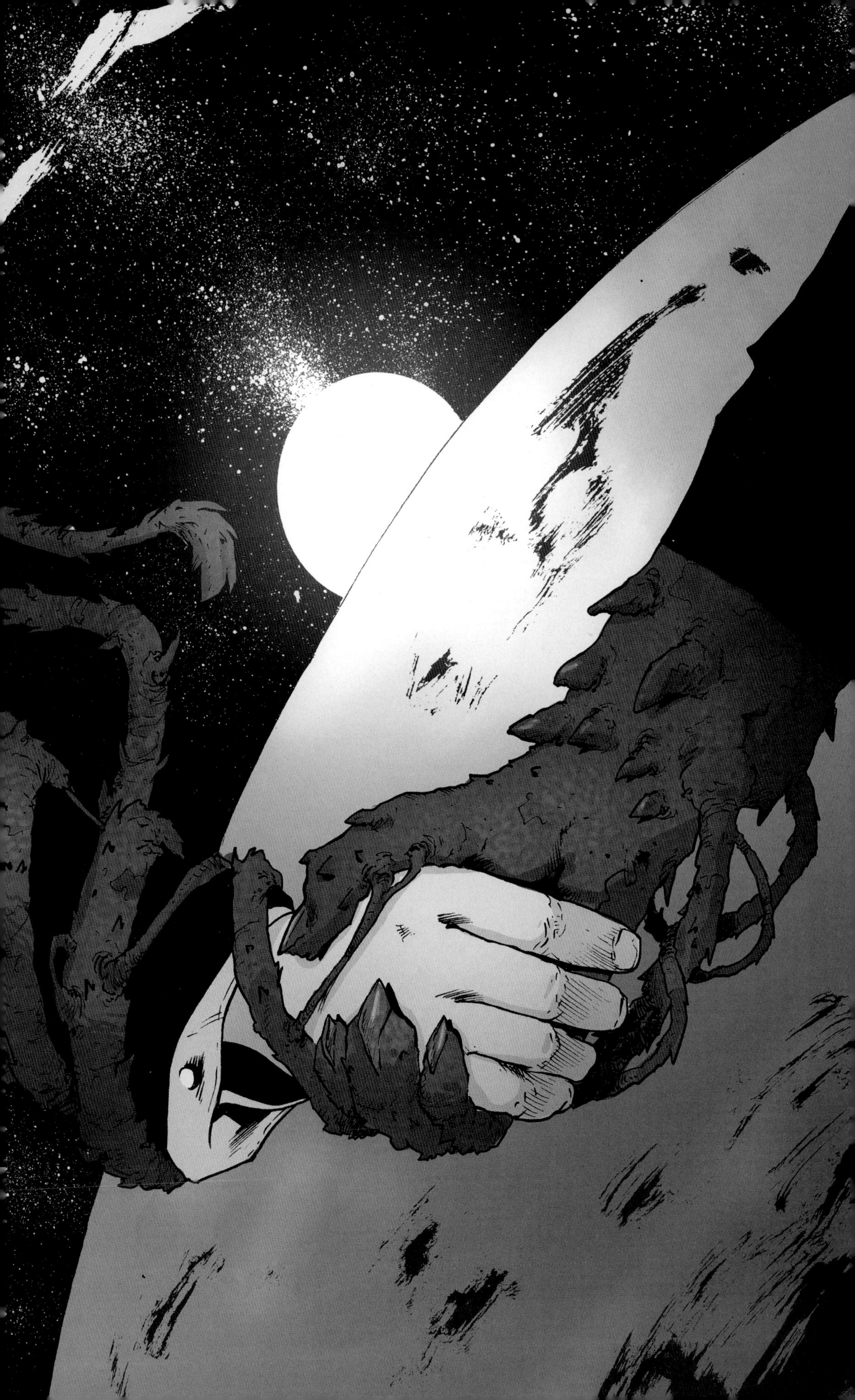

CHAPTER 5

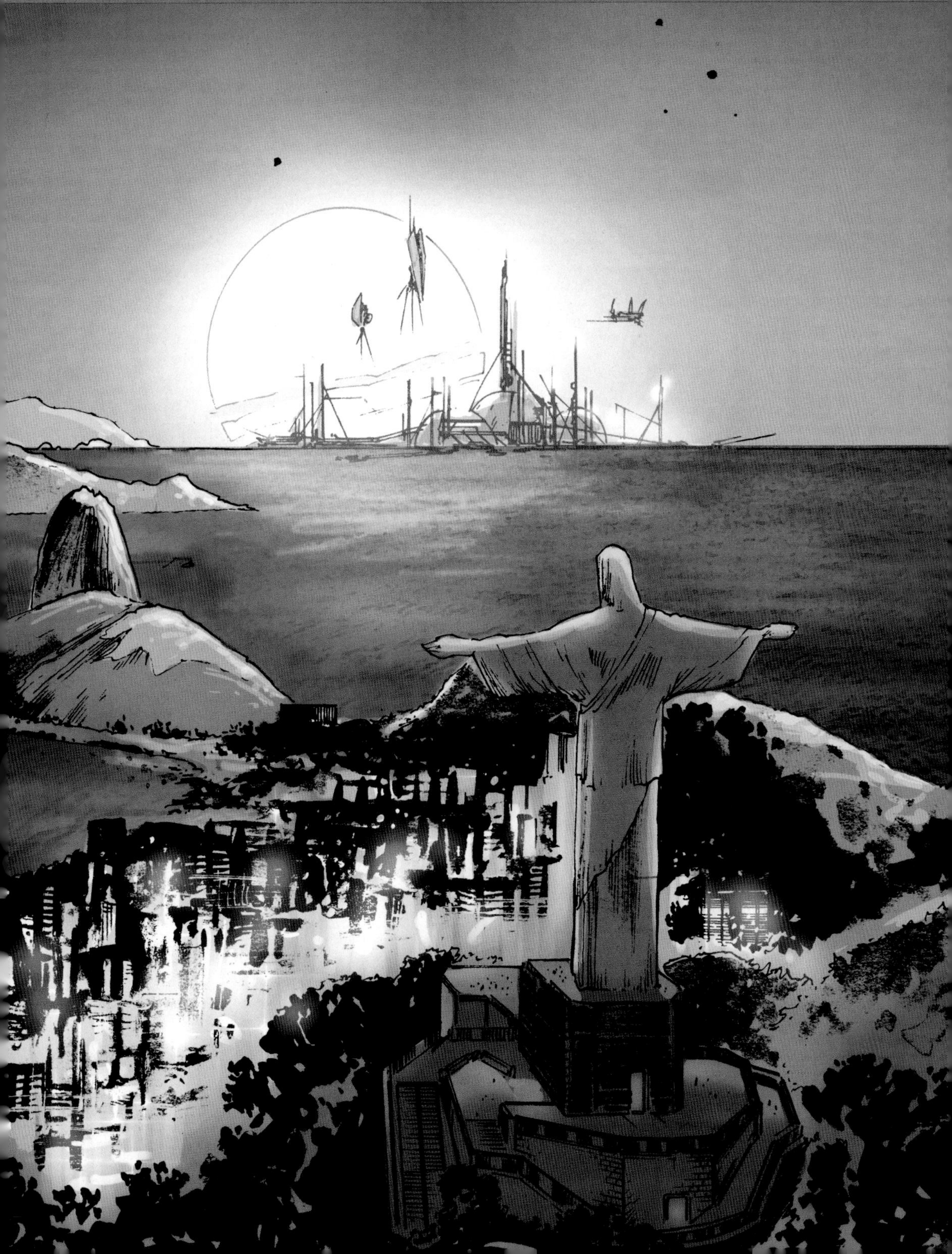

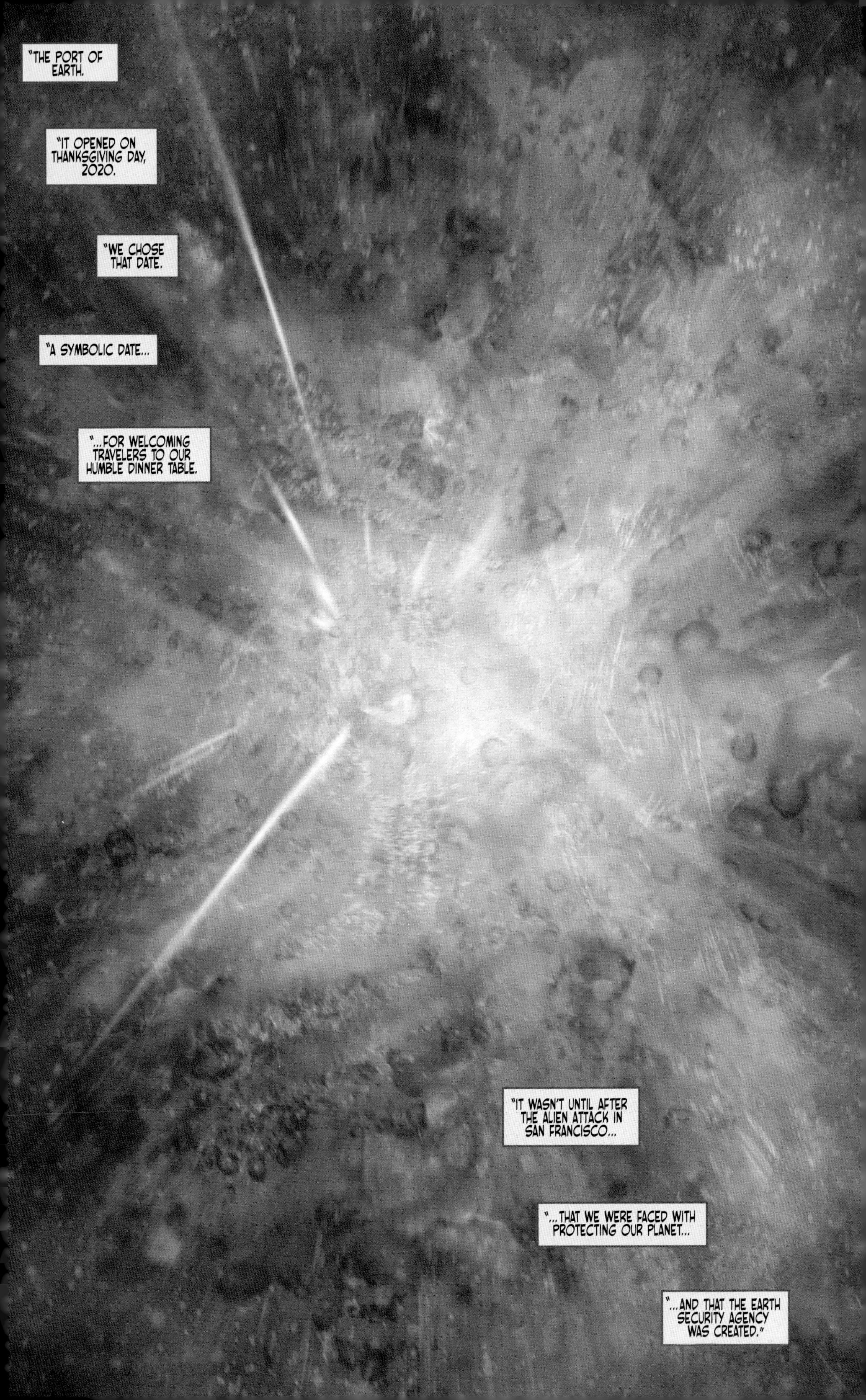
"THE PORT OF EARTH.
"IT OPENED ON THANKSGIVING DAY, 2020.
"WE CHOSE THAT DATE.
"A SYMBOLIC DATE...
"...FOR WELCOMING TRAVELERS TO OUR HUMBLE DINNER TABLE.
"IT WASN'T UNTIL AFTER THE ALIEN ATTACK IN SAN FRANCISCO...
"...THAT WE WERE FACED WITH PROTECTING OUR PLANET...
"...AND THAT THE EARTH SECURITY AGENCY WAS CREATED."

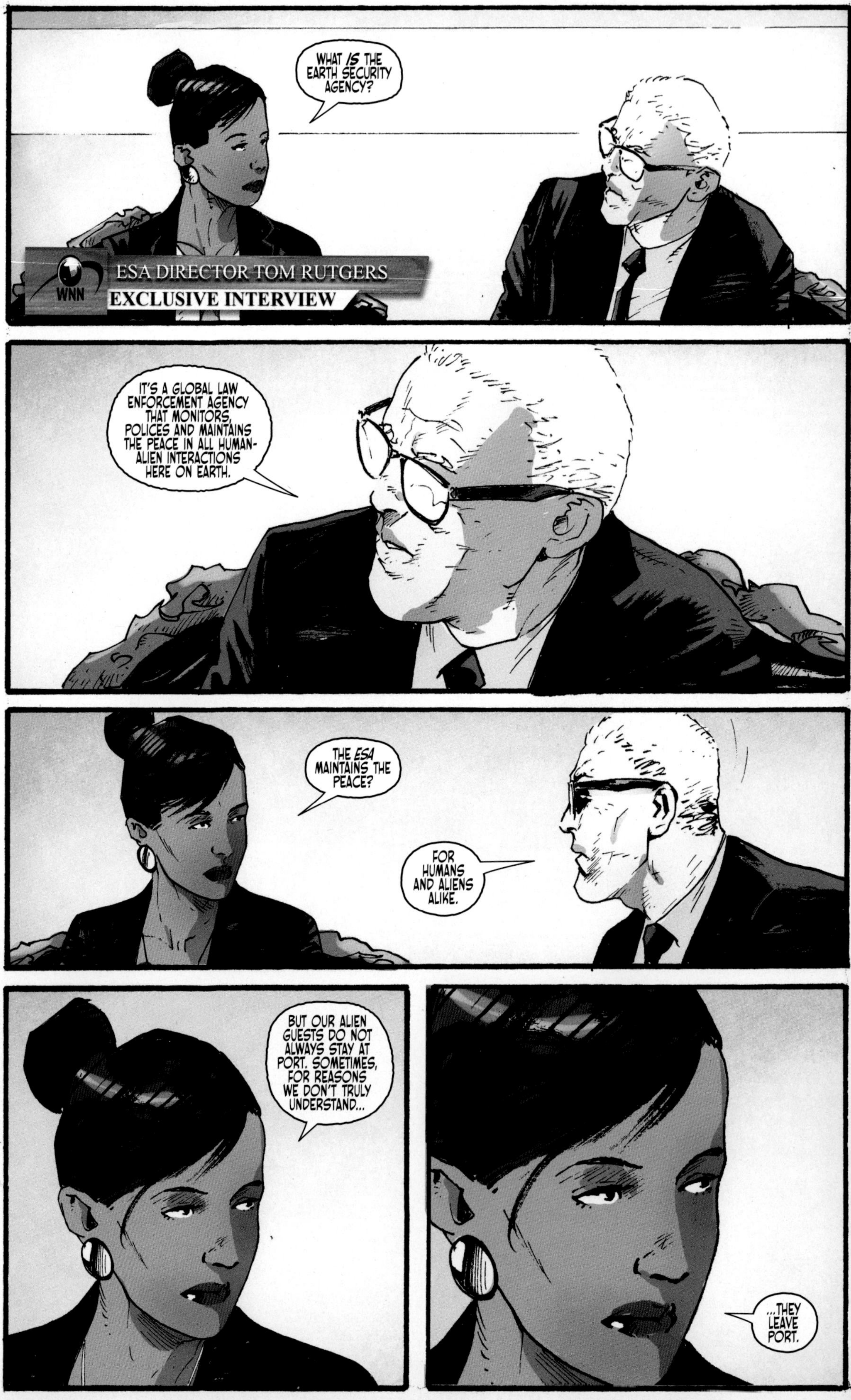
WHAT IS THE EARTH SECURITY AGENCY?
ESA DIRECTOR TOM RUTGERS
WNN
EXCLUSIVE INTERVIEW
IT'S A GLOBAL LAW ENFORCEMENT AGENCY THAT MONITORS, POLICES AND MAINTAINS THE PEACE IN ALL HUMAN-ALIEN INTERACTIONS HERE ON EARTH.
THE ESA MAINTAINS THE PEACE?
FOR HUMANS AND ALIENS ALIKE.
BUT OUR ALIEN GUESTS DO NOT ALWAYS STAY AT PORT. SOMETIMES, FOR REASONS WE DON'T TRULY UNDERSTAND...
...THEY LEAVE PORT.

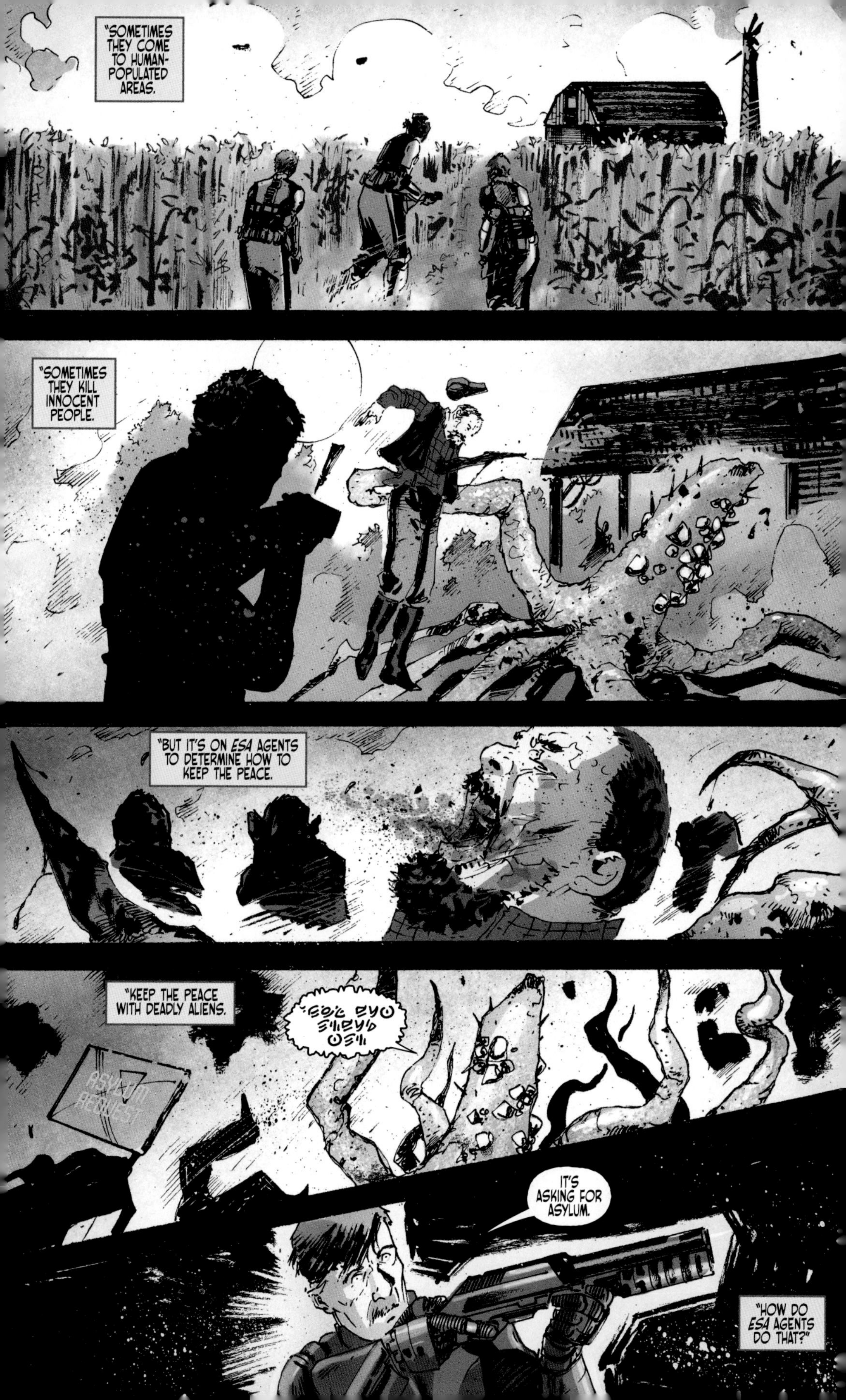
"SOMETIMES THEY COME TO HUMAN-POPULATED AREAS.
"SOMETIMES THEY KILL INNOCENT PEOPLE.
"BUT IT'S ON ESA AGENTS TO DETERMINE HOW TO KEEP THE PEACE.
"KEEP THE PEACE WITH DEADLY ALIENS.
ASYLUM REQUEST
IT'S ASKING FOR ASYLUM.
"HOW DO ESA AGENTS DO THAT?"

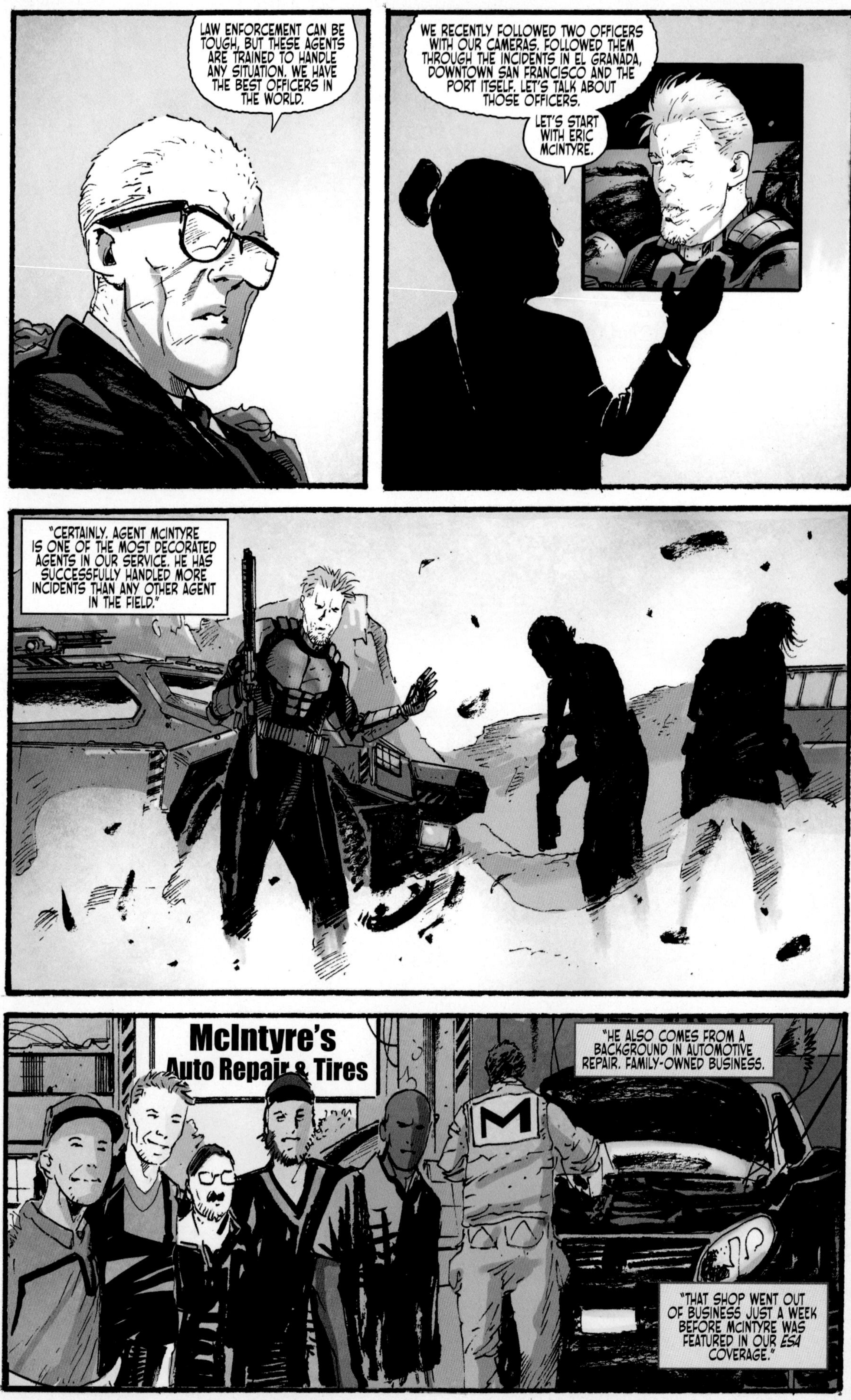
LAW ENFORCEMENT CAN BE TOUGH, BUT THESE AGENTS ARE TRAINED TO HANDLE ANY SITUATION. WE HAVE THE BEST OFFICERS IN THE WORLD.
WE RECENTLY FOLLOWED TWO OFFICERS WITH OUR CAMERAS. FOLLOWED THEM THROUGH THE INCIDENTS IN EL GRANADA, DOWNTOWN SAN FRANCISCO AND THE PORT ITSELF. LET'S TALK ABOUT THOSE OFFICERS.
LET'S START WITH ERIC McINTYRE.
"CERTAINLY. AGENT McINTYRE IS ONE OF THE MOST DECORATED AGENTS IN OUR SERVICE. HE HAS SUCCESSFULLY HANDLED MORE INCIDENTS THAN ANY OTHER AGENT IN THE FIELD."
McIntyre's
Auto Repair & Tires
"HE ALSO COMES FROM A BACKGROUND IN AUTOMOTIVE REPAIR. FAMILY-OWNED BUSINESS.
"THAT SHOP WENT OUT OF BUSINESS JUST A WEEK BEFORE McINTYRE WAS FEATURED IN OUR ESA COVERAGE."

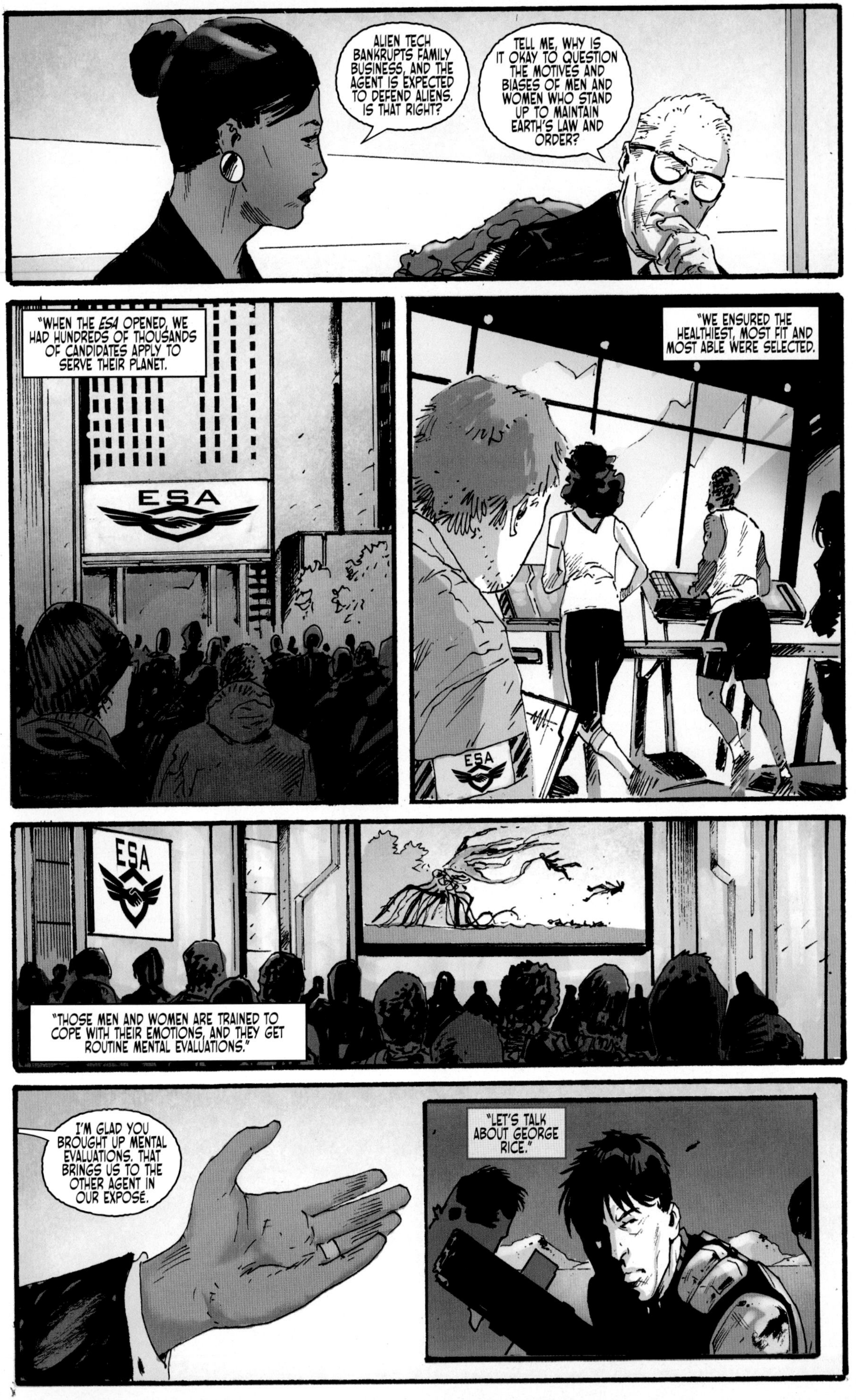
ALIEN TECH BANKRUPTS FAMILY BUSINESS, AND THE AGENT IS EXPECTED TO DEFEND ALIENS. IS THAT RIGHT?
TELL ME, WHY IS IT OKAY TO QUESTION THE MOTIVES AND BIASES OF MEN AND WOMEN WHO STAND UP TO MAINTAIN EARTH'S LAW AND ORDER?
"WHEN THE ESA OPENED, WE HAD HUNDREDS OF THOUSANDS OF CANDIDATES APPLY TO SERVE THEIR PLANET.
ESA
"WE ENSURED THE HEALTHIEST, MOST FIT AND MOST ABLE WERE SELECTED.
ESA
ESA
"THOSE MEN AND WOMEN ARE TRAINED TO COPE WITH THEIR EMOTIONS, AND THEY GET ROUTINE MENTAL EVALUATIONS."
I'M GLAD YOU BROUGHT UP MENTAL EVALUATIONS. THAT BRINGS US TO THE OTHER AGENT IN OUR EXPOSE.
"LET'S TALK ABOUT GEORGE RICE."

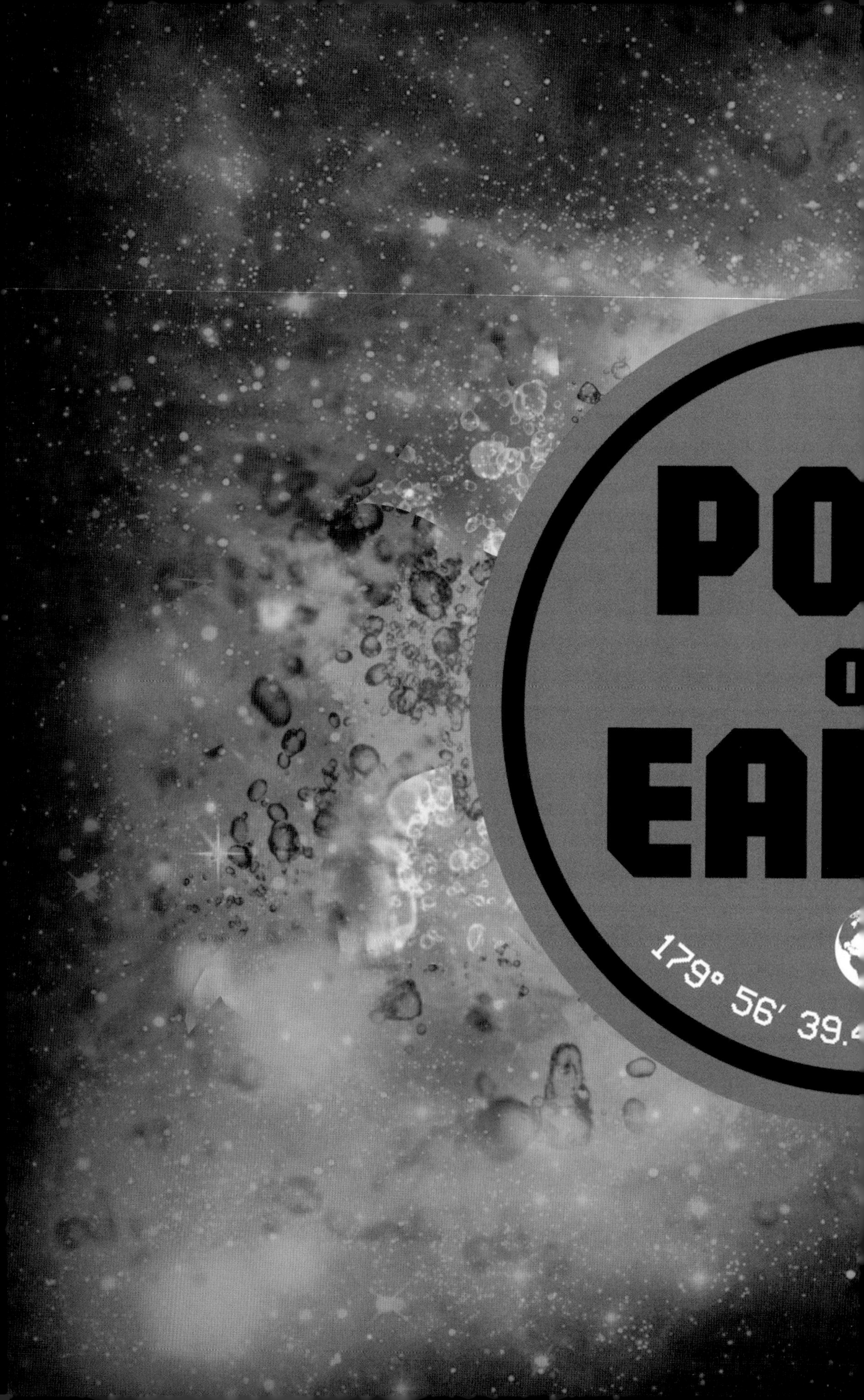

PO
O
EA

179° 56' 39.4

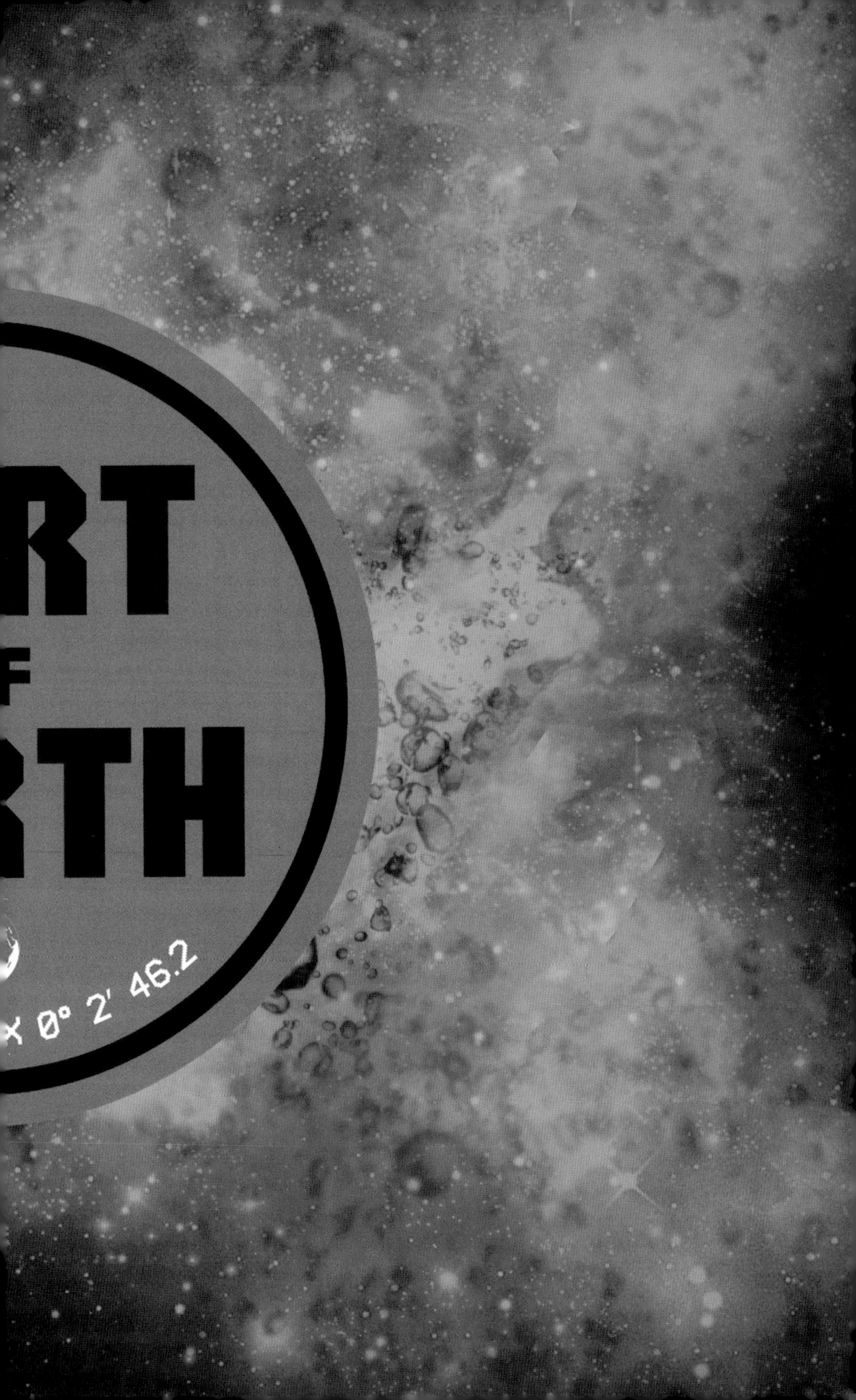
RT
F
RTH
X 0° 2′ 46.2

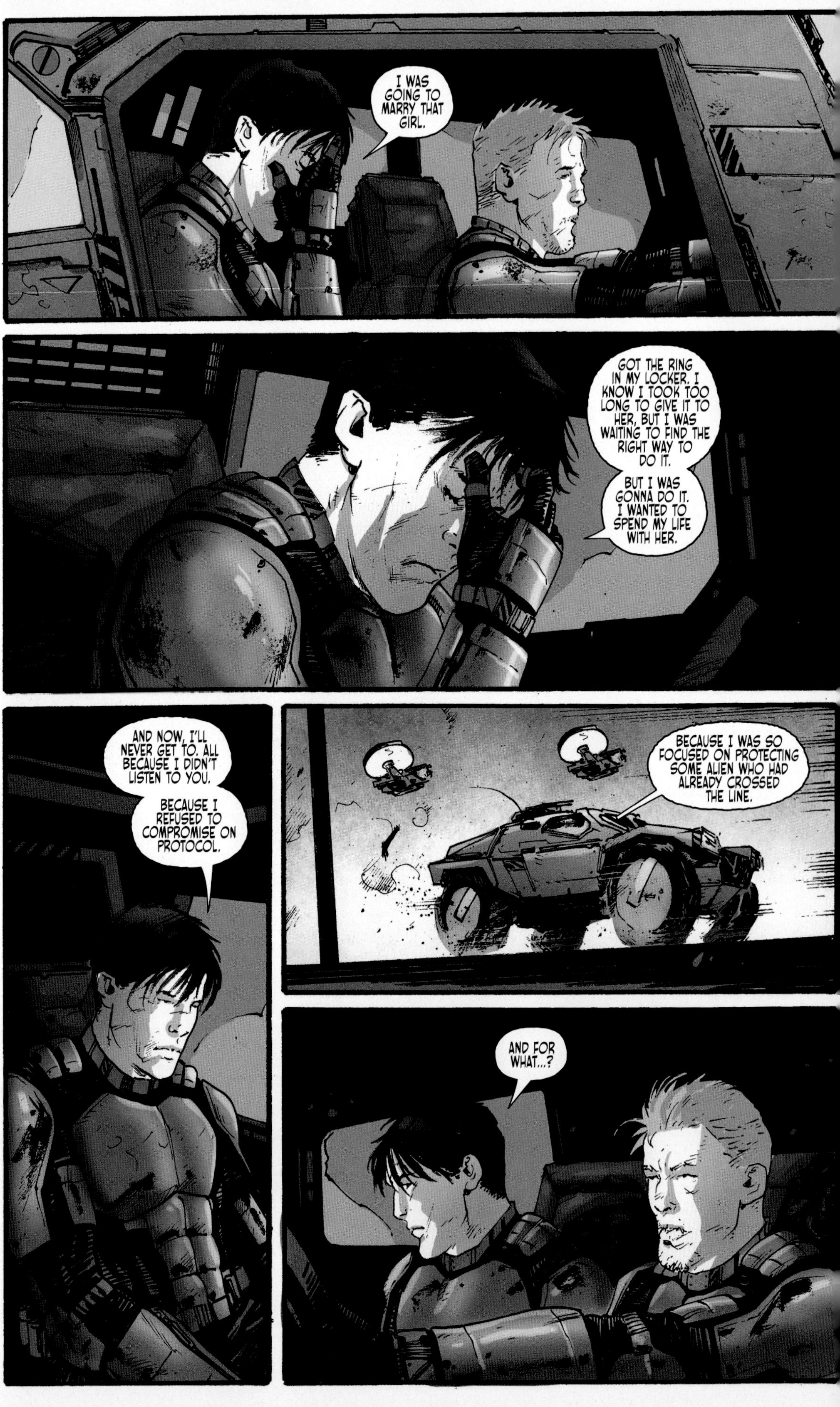
I WAS GOING TO MARRY THAT GIRL.
GOT THE RING IN MY LOCKER. I KNOW I TOOK TOO LONG TO GIVE IT TO HER, BUT I WAS WAITING TO FIND THE RIGHT WAY TO DO IT.
BUT I WAS GONNA DO IT. I WANTED TO SPEND MY LIFE WITH HER.
AND NOW, I'LL NEVER GET TO. ALL BECAUSE I DIDN'T LISTEN TO YOU.
BECAUSE I REFUSED TO COMPROMISE ON PROTOCOL.
BECAUSE I WAS SO FOCUSED ON PROTECTING SOME ALIEN WHO HAD ALREADY CROSSED THE LINE.
AND FOR WHAT...?

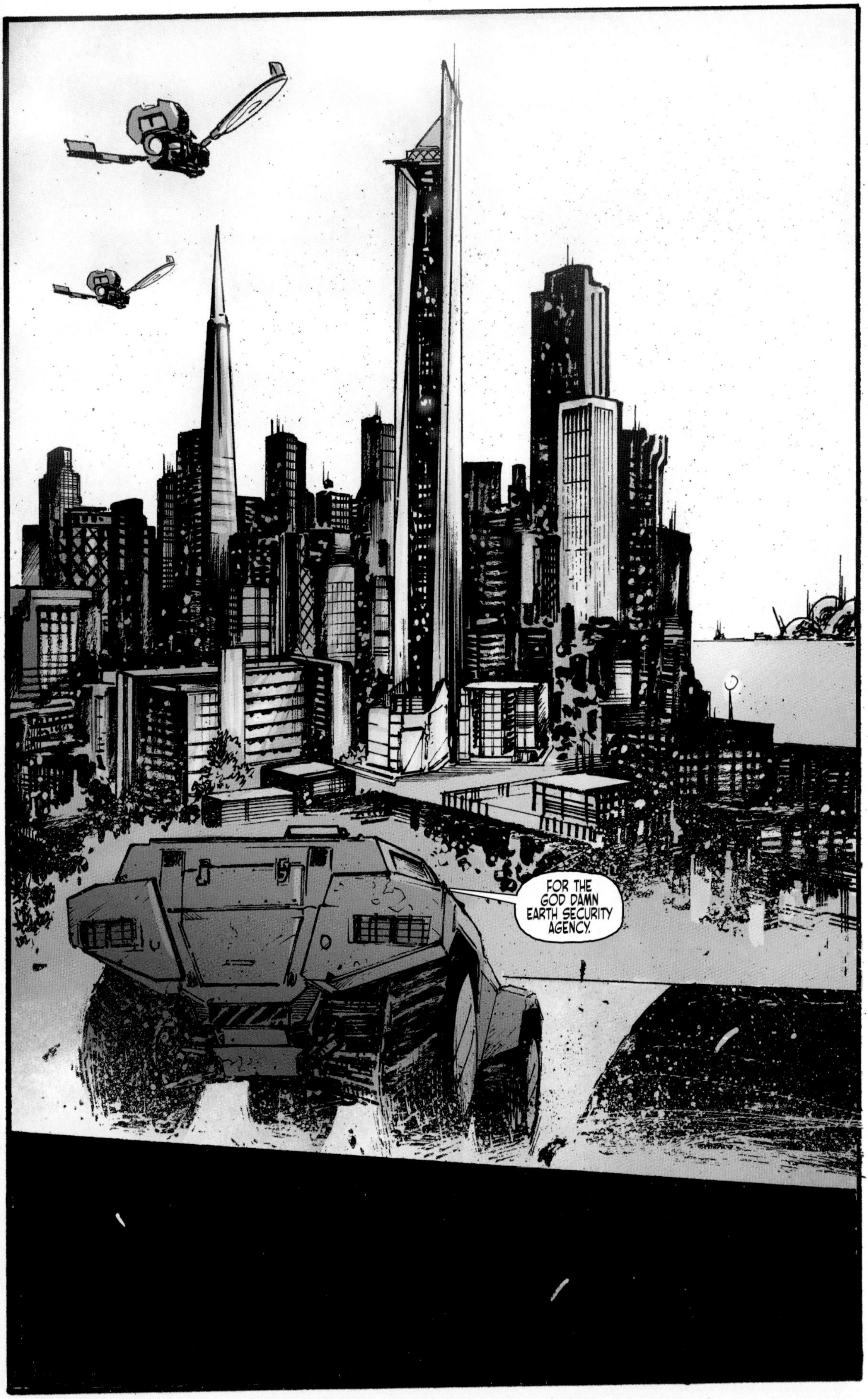
FOR THE GOD DAMN EARTH SECURITY AGENCY.

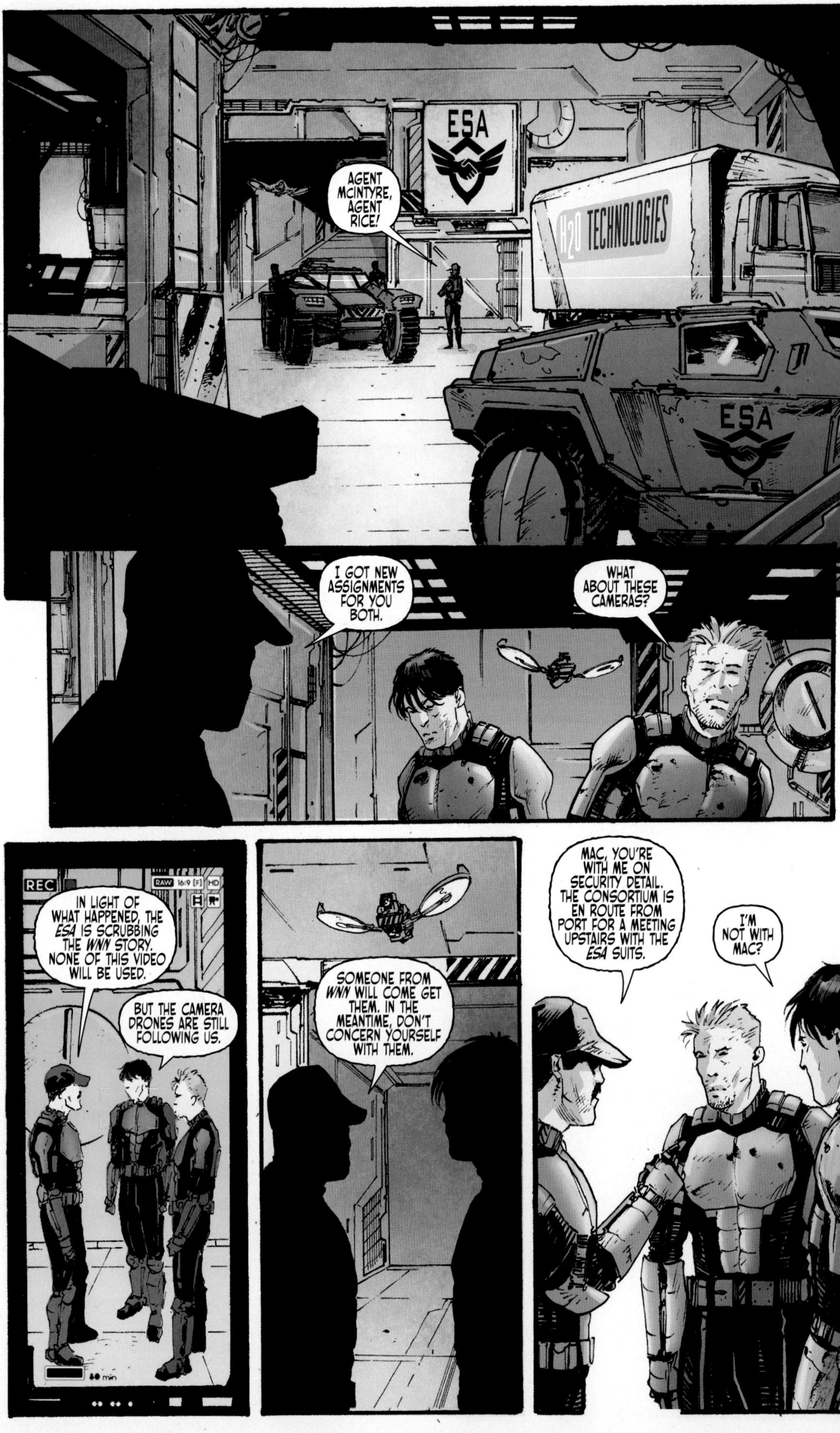

ESA
AGENT MCINTYRE, AGENT RICE!
H2O TECHNOLOGIES
ESA
I GOT NEW ASSIGNMENTS FOR YOU BOTH.
WHAT ABOUT THESE CAMERAS?
REC
RAW 16:9 [F] HD
IN LIGHT OF WHAT HAPPENED, THE *ESA* IS SCRUBBING THE *WNN* STORY. NONE OF THIS VIDEO WILL BE USED.
BUT THE CAMERA DRONES ARE STILL FOLLOWING US.
SOMEONE FROM *WNN* WILL COME GET THEM. IN THE MEANTIME, DON'T CONCERN YOURSELF WITH THEM.
MAC, YOU'RE WITH ME ON SECURITY DETAIL. THE CONSORTIUM IS EN ROUTE FROM PORT FOR A MEETING UPSTAIRS WITH THE *ESA* SUITS.
I'M NOT WITH MAC?

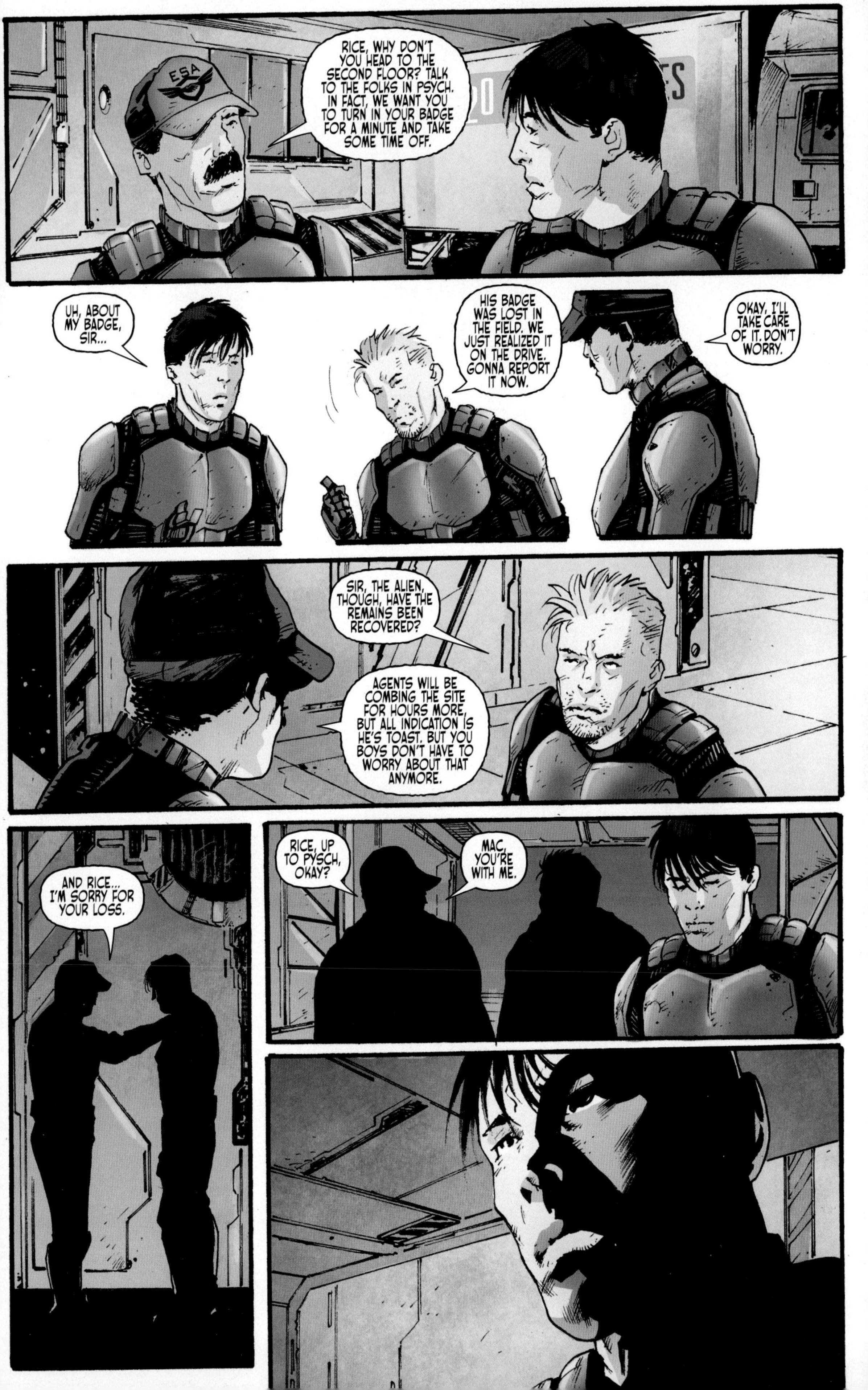
RICE, WHY DON'T YOU HEAD TO THE SECOND FLOOR? TALK TO THE FOLKS IN PSYCH. IN FACT, WE WANT YOU TO TURN IN YOUR BADGE FOR A MINUTE AND TAKE SOME TIME OFF.
UH, ABOUT MY BADGE, SIR...
HIS BADGE WAS LOST IN THE FIELD. WE JUST REALIZED IT ON THE DRIVE. GONNA REPORT IT NOW.
OKAY, I'LL TAKE CARE OF IT. DON'T WORRY.
SIR, THE ALIEN, THOUGH, HAVE THE REMAINS BEEN RECOVERED?
AGENTS WILL BE COMBING THE SITE FOR HOURS MORE, BUT ALL INDICATION IS HE'S TOAST. BUT YOU BOYS DON'T HAVE TO WORRY ABOUT THAT ANYMORE.
AND RICE... I'M SORRY FOR YOUR LOSS.
RICE, UP TO PYSCH, OKAY?
MAC, YOU'RE WITH ME.

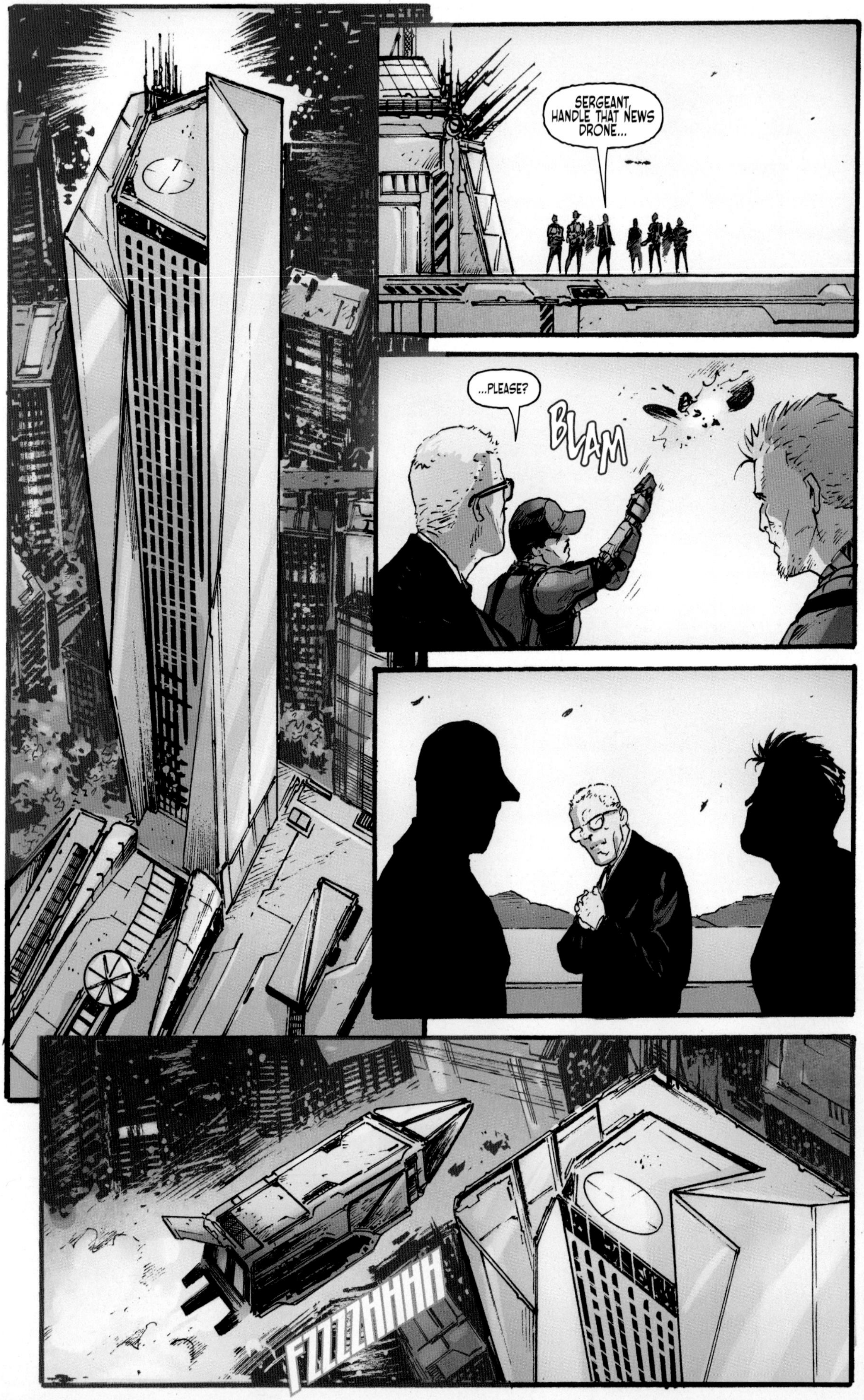
SERGEANT, HANDLE THAT NEWS DRONE...
...PLEASE?
BLAM
FZZZZHHHH

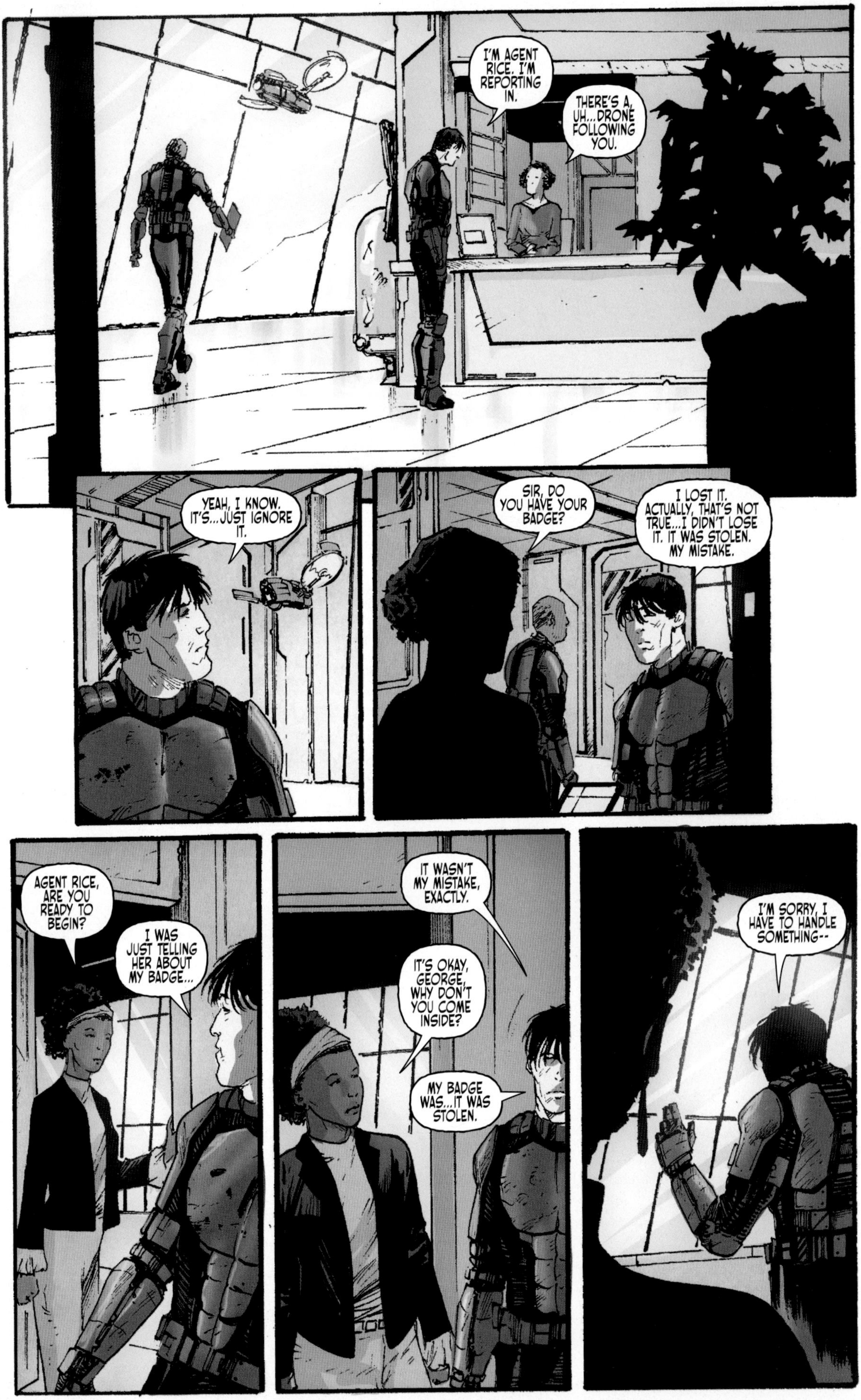

I'M AGENT RICE. I'M REPORTING IN.
THERE'S A, UH...DRONE FOLLOWING YOU.
YEAH, I KNOW. IT'S...JUST IGNORE IT.
SIR, DO YOU HAVE YOUR BADGE?
I LOST IT. ACTUALLY, THAT'S NOT TRUE...I DIDN'T LOSE IT. IT WAS STOLEN. MY MISTAKE.
AGENT RICE, ARE YOU READY TO BEGIN?
I WAS JUST TELLING HER ABOUT MY BADGE...
IT WASN'T MY MISTAKE, EXACTLY.
IT'S OKAY, GEORGE, WHY DON'T YOU COME INSIDE?
MY BADGE WAS...IT WAS STOLEN.
I'M SORRY, I HAVE TO HANDLE SOMETHING--

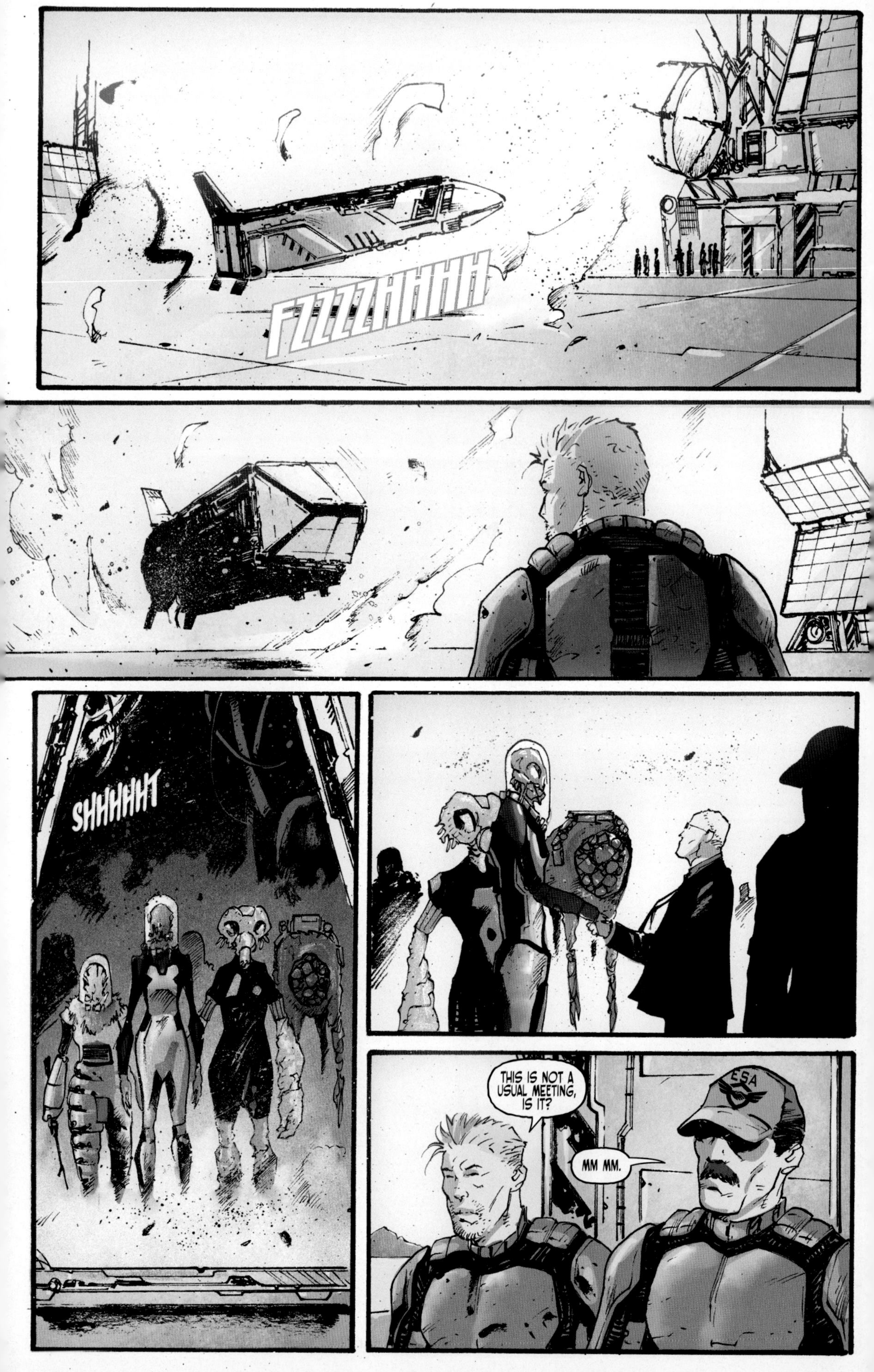
FZZZZHHHH
SHHHHHT
THIS IS NOT A USUAL MEETING, IS IT?
MM MM.
ESA

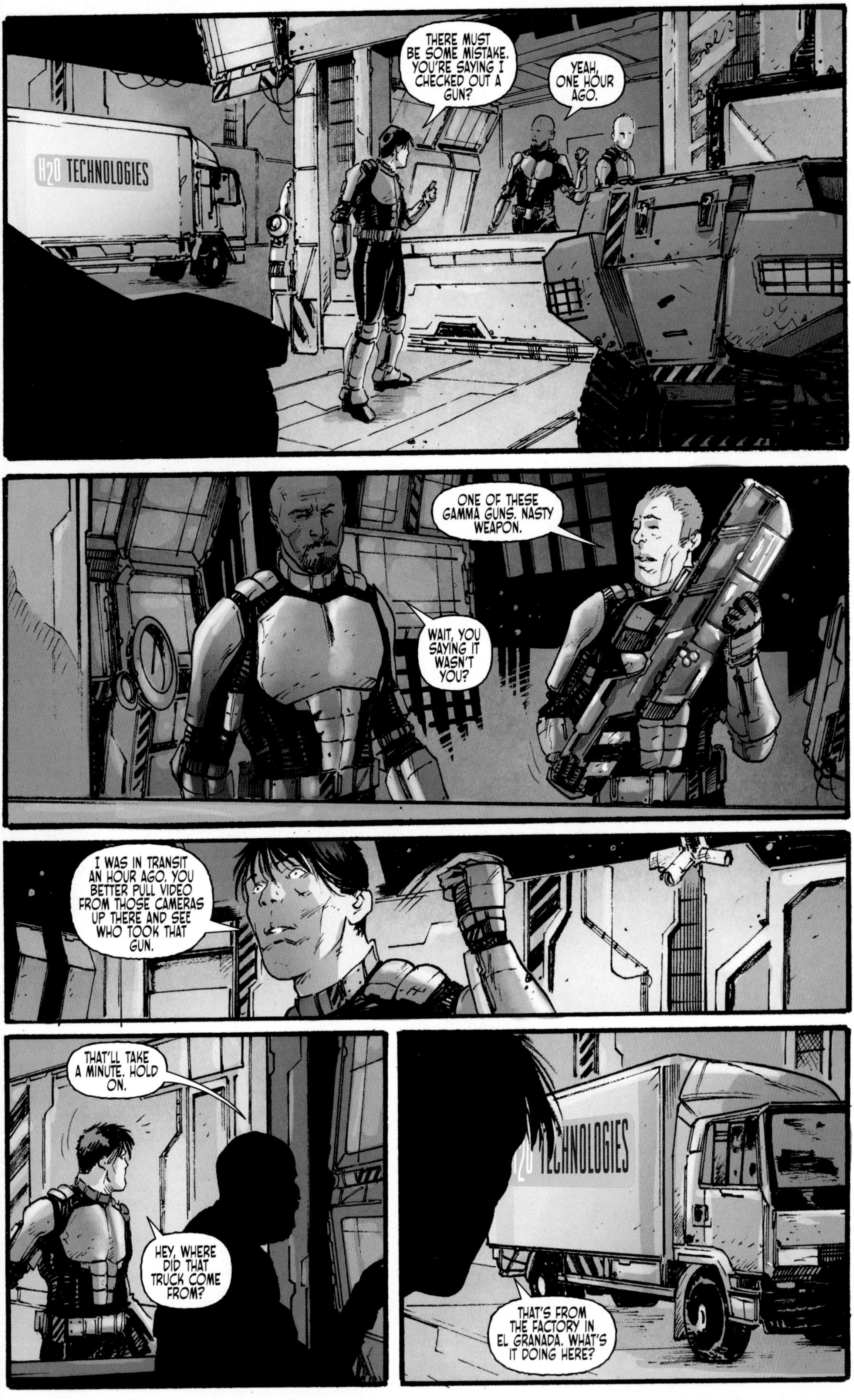
H2O TECHNOLOGIES
THERE MUST BE SOME MISTAKE. YOU'RE SAYING I CHECKED OUT A GUN?
YEAH, ONE HOUR AGO.
ONE OF THESE GAMMA GUNS. NASTY WEAPON.
WAIT, YOU SAYING IT WASN'T YOU?
I WAS IN TRANSIT AN HOUR AGO. YOU BETTER PULL VIDEO FROM THOSE CAMERAS UP THERE AND SEE WHO TOOK THAT GUN.
THAT'LL TAKE A MINUTE. HOLD ON.
HEY, WHERE DID THAT TRUCK COME FROM?
H2O TECHNOLOGIES
THAT'S FROM THE FACTORY IN EL GRANADA. WHAT'S IT DOING HERE?

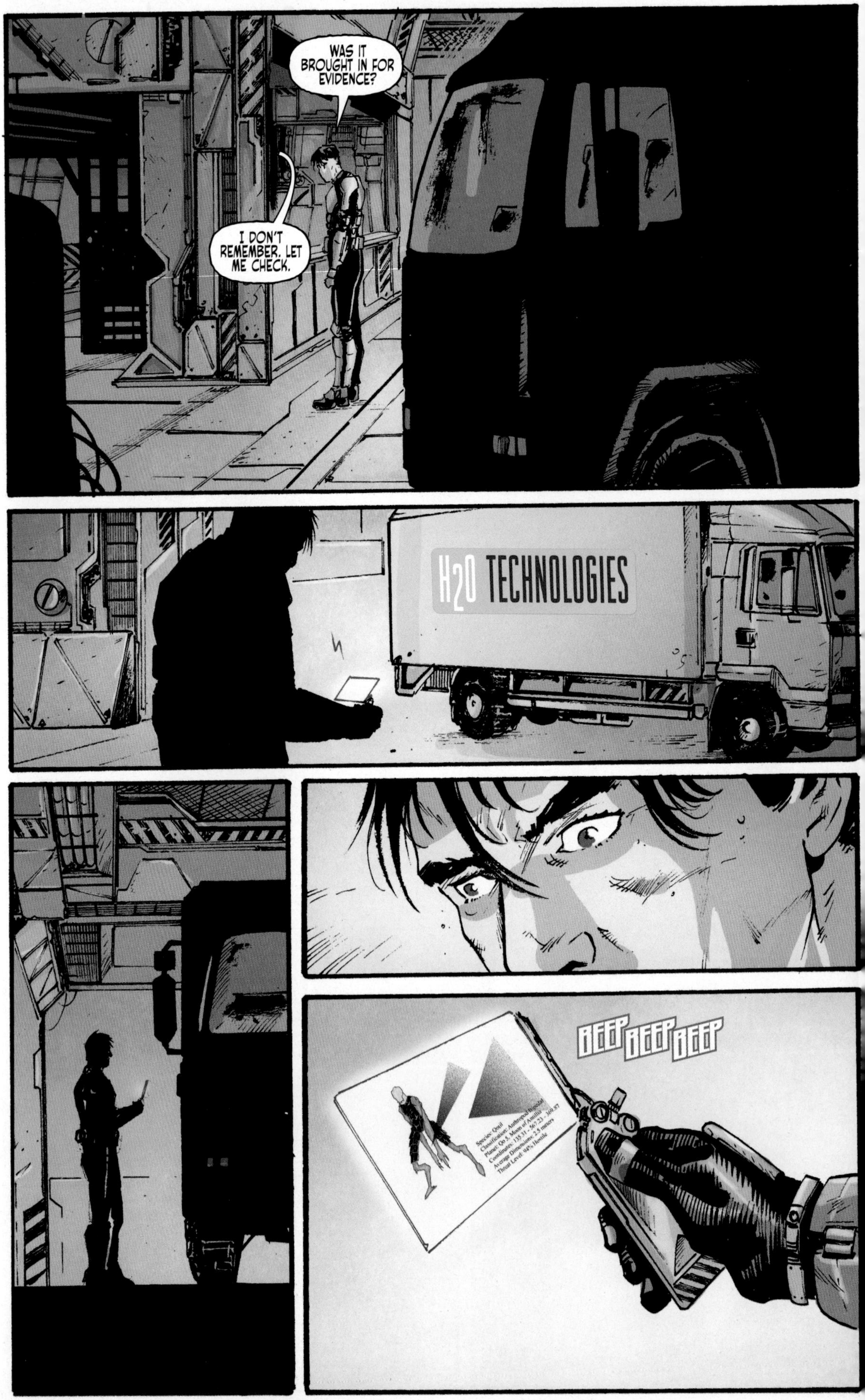
WAS IT BROUGHT IN FOR EVIDENCE?
I DON'T REMEMBER. LET ME CHECK.
H2O TECHNOLOGIES
BEEP BEEP BEEP
Species: Qoil
Classification: Anthropod Bipedal
Planet: Qo 5, Moon of Amillia
Coordinates: 135.31 - 567.23 - 369.87
Average Dimensions: 2.5 meters
Threat Level: 94% Hostile

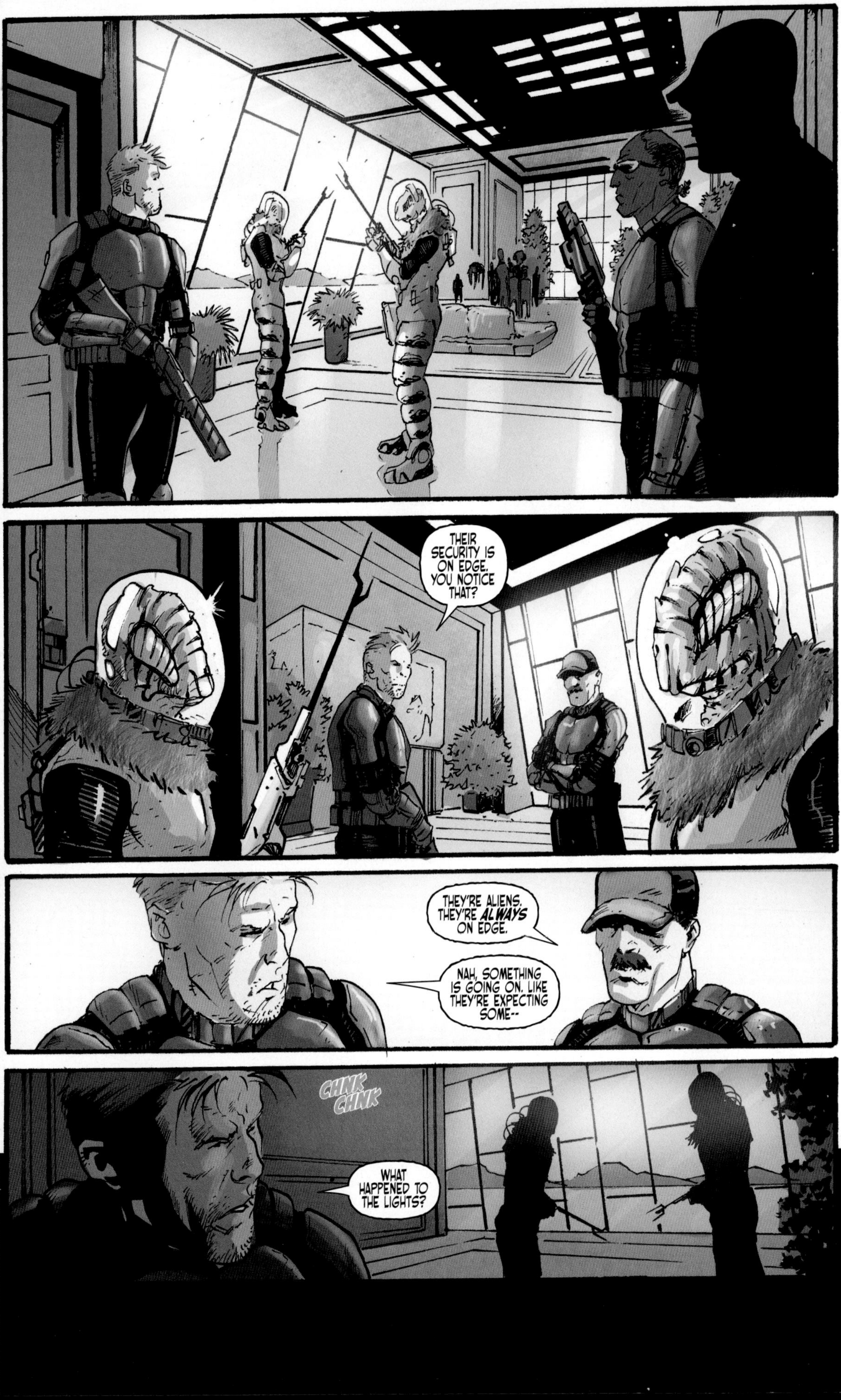
THEIR SECURITY IS ON EDGE. YOU NOTICE THAT?
THEY'RE ALIENS. THEY'RE ALWAYS ON EDGE.
NAH, SOMETHING IS GOING ON. LIKE THEY'RE EXPECTING SOME--
CHNK CHNK
WHAT HAPPENED TO THE LIGHTS?

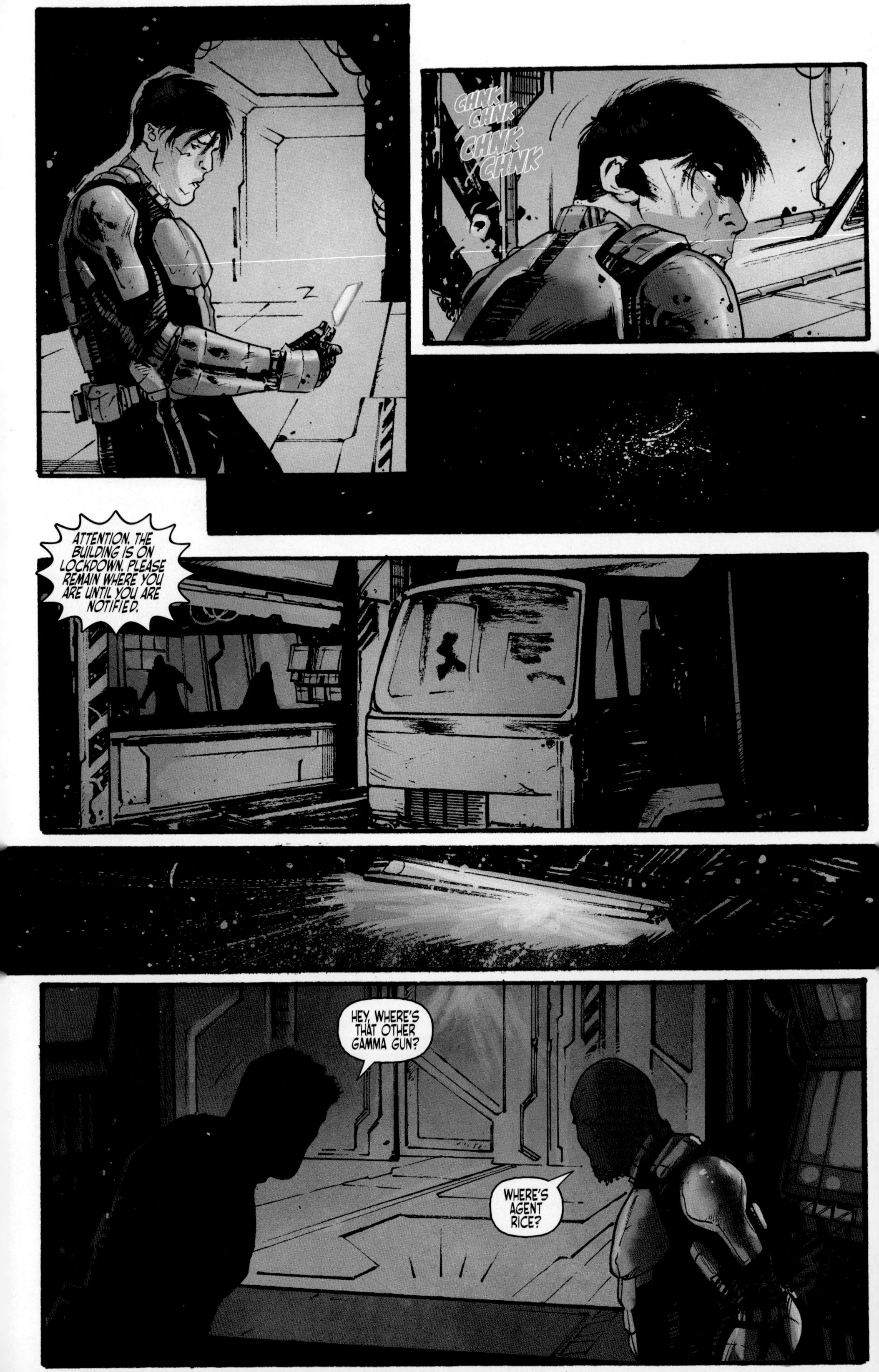
CHNK
CHNK
CHNK
CHNK
ATTENTION. THE BUILDING IS ON LOCKDOWN. PLEASE REMAIN WHERE YOU ARE UNTIL YOU ARE NOTIFIED.
HEY, WHERE'S THAT OTHER GAMMA GUN?
WHERE'S AGENT RICE?

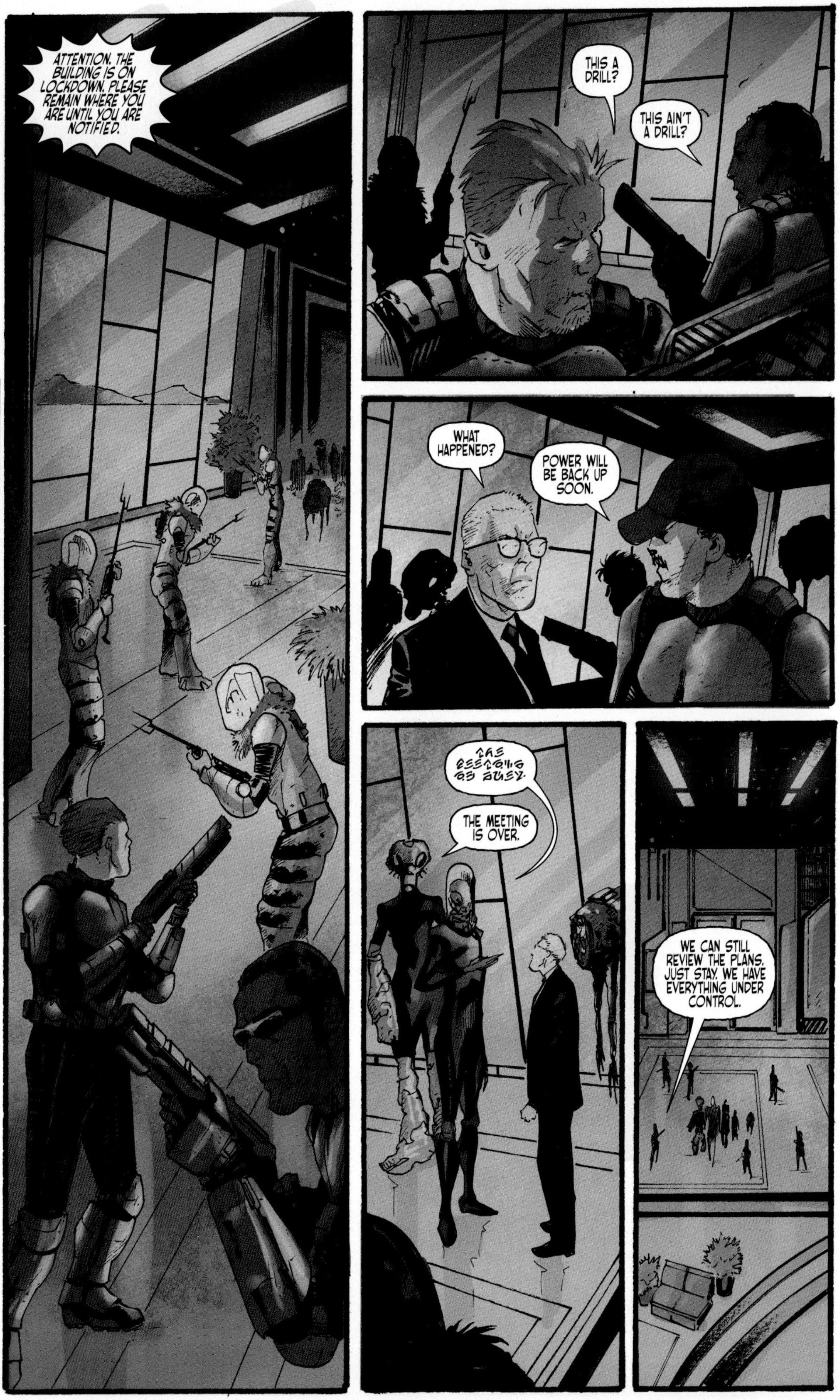
ATTENTION. THE BUILDING IS ON LOCKDOWN. PLEASE REMAIN WHERE YOU ARE UNTIL YOU ARE NOTIFIED.
THIS A DRILL?
THIS AIN'T A DRILL?
WHAT HAPPENED?
POWER WILL BE BACK UP SOON.
THE MEETING IS OVER.
WE CAN STILL REVIEW THE PLANS. JUST STAY. WE HAVE EVERYTHING UNDER CONTROL.

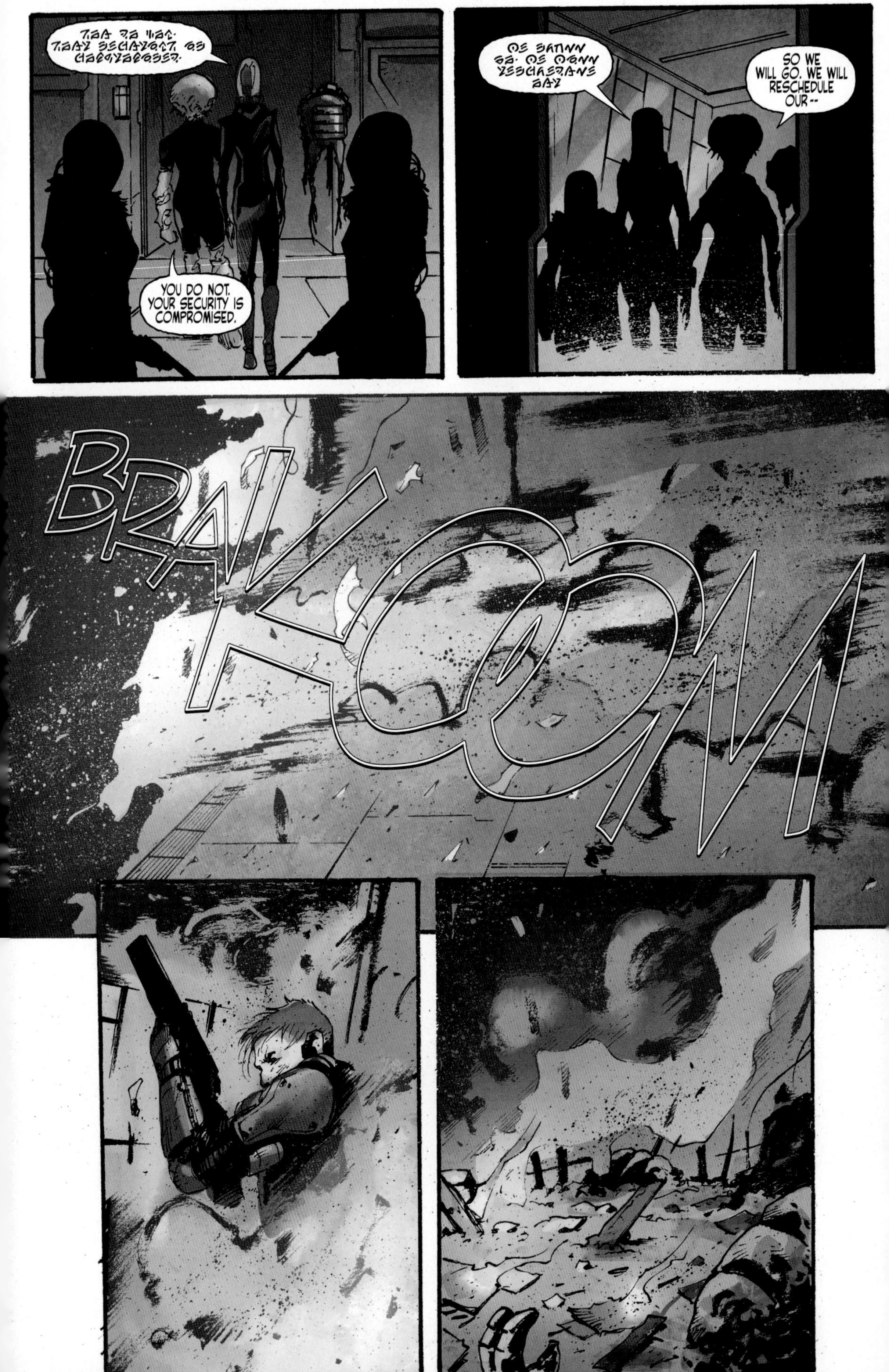
YOU DO NOT. YOUR SECURITY IS COMPROMISED.
SO WE WILL GO. WE WILL RESCHEDULE OUR--
BRAKOOM

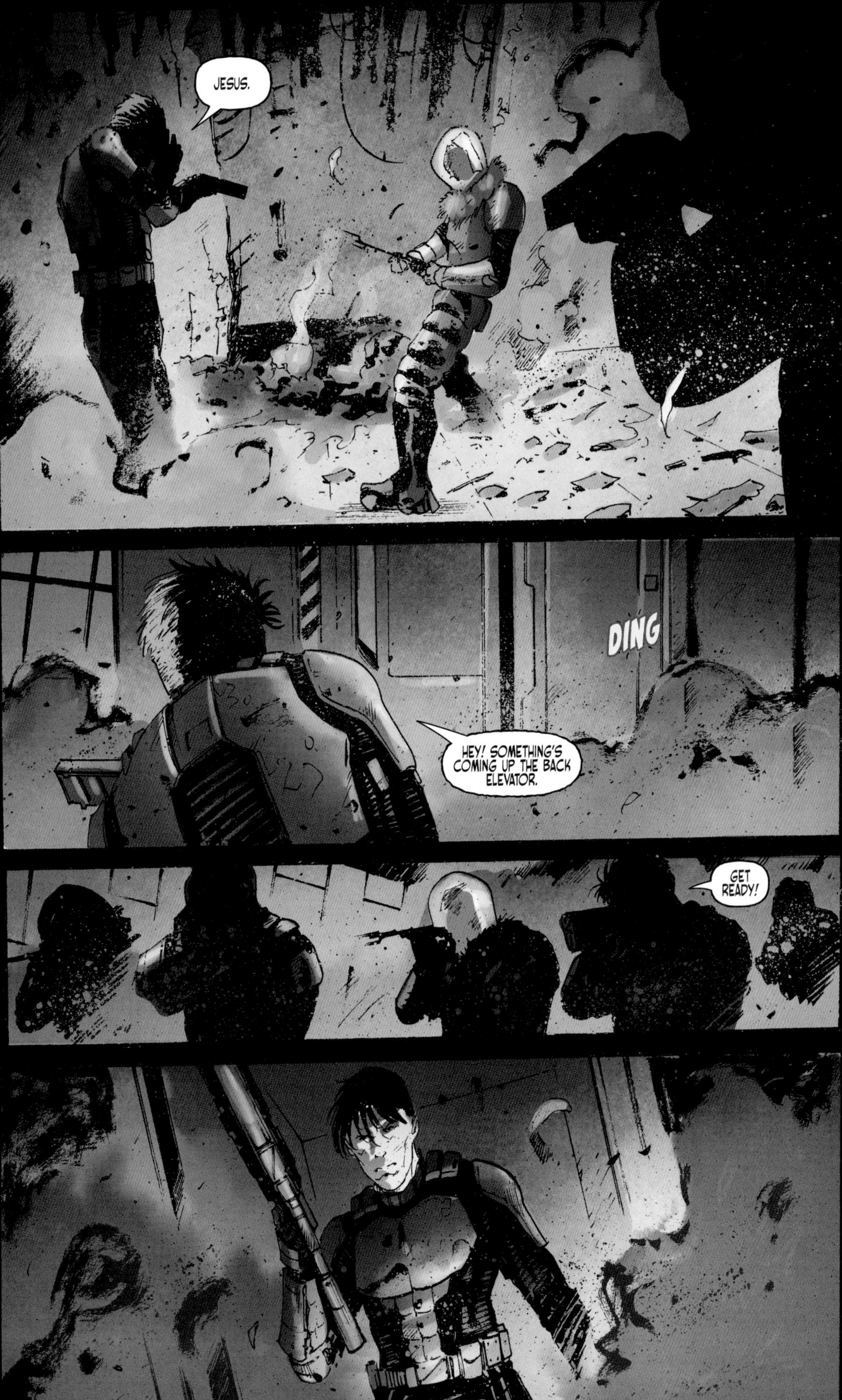

JESUS.
DING
HEY! SOMETHING'S COMING UP THE BACK ELEVATOR.
GET READY!

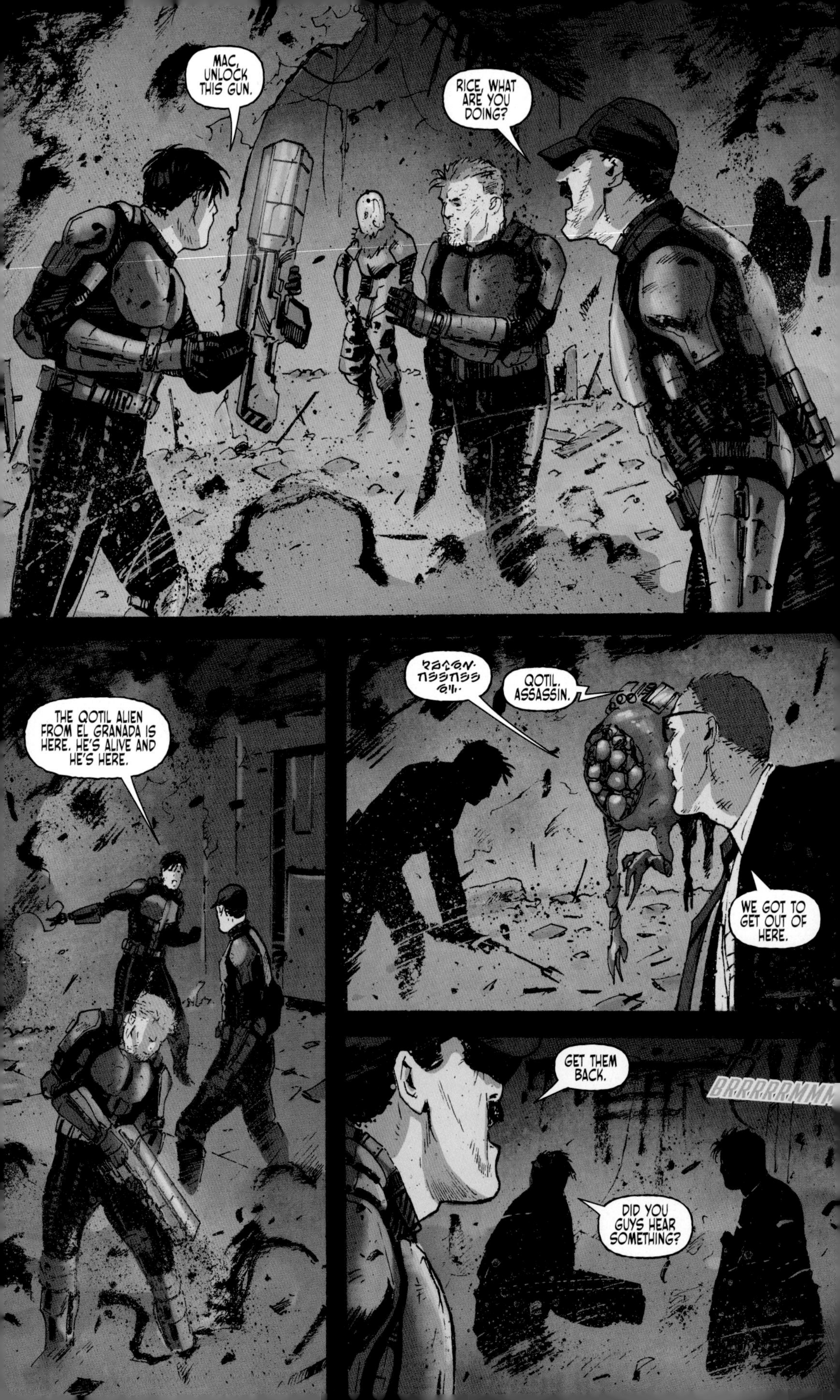
MAC, UNLOCK THIS GUN.
RICE, WHAT ARE YOU DOING?
THE QOTIL ALIEN FROM EL GRANADA IS HERE. HE'S ALIVE AND HE'S HERE.
QOTIL. ASSASSIN.
WE GOT TO GET OUT OF HERE.
GET THEM BACK.
BRRRRRMMM
DID YOU GUYS HEAR SOMETHING?

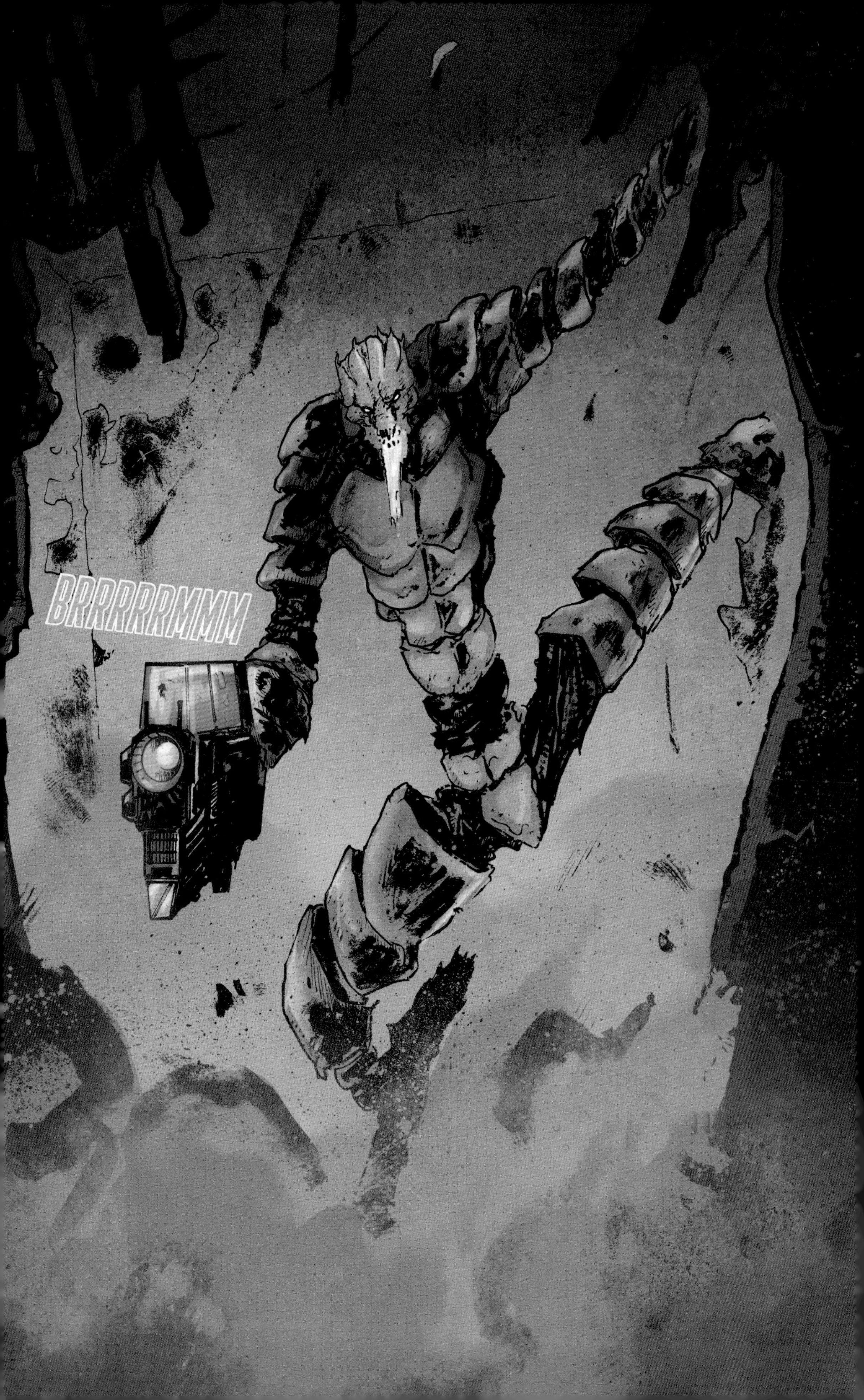
BRRRRRMMM

CHAPTER 6

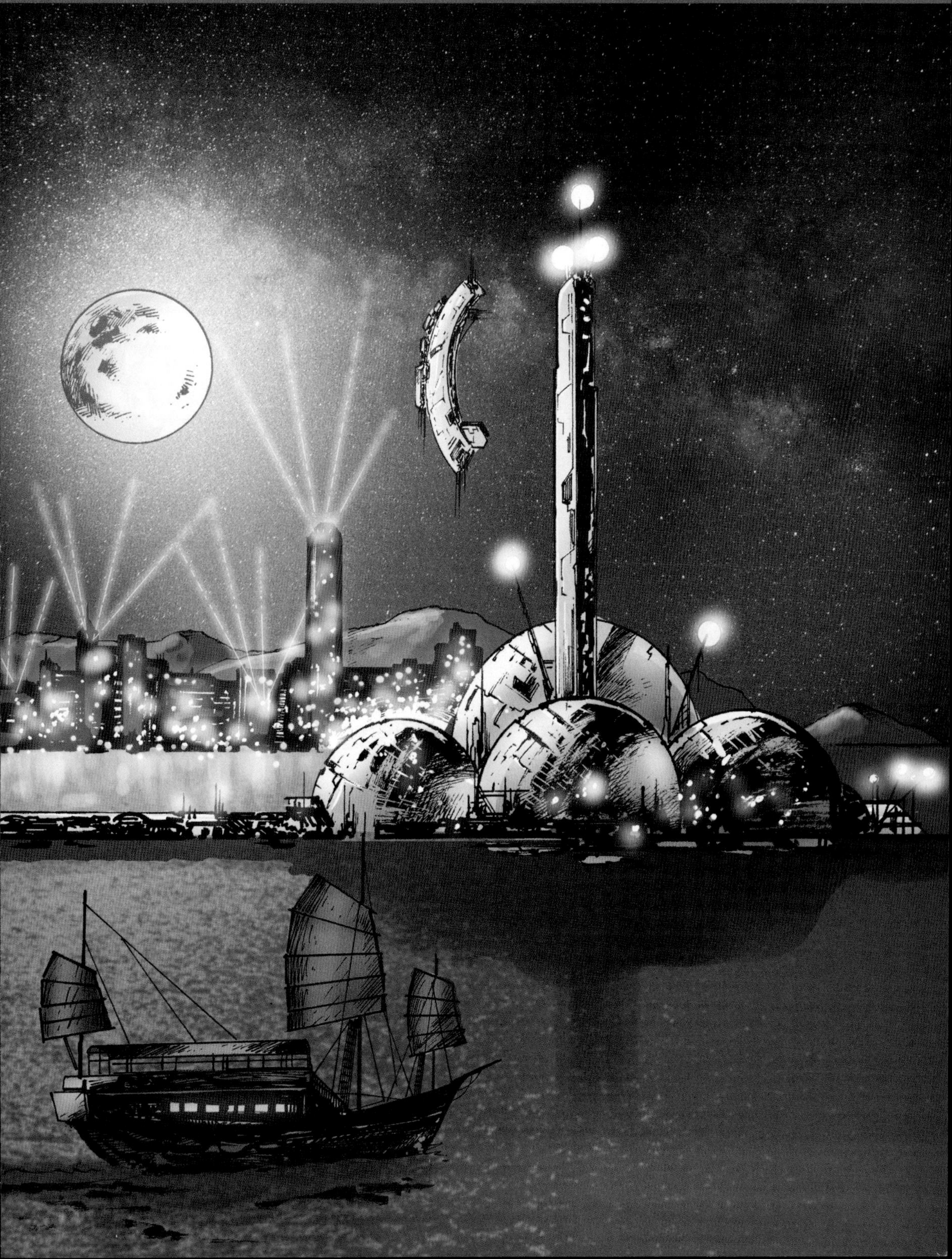

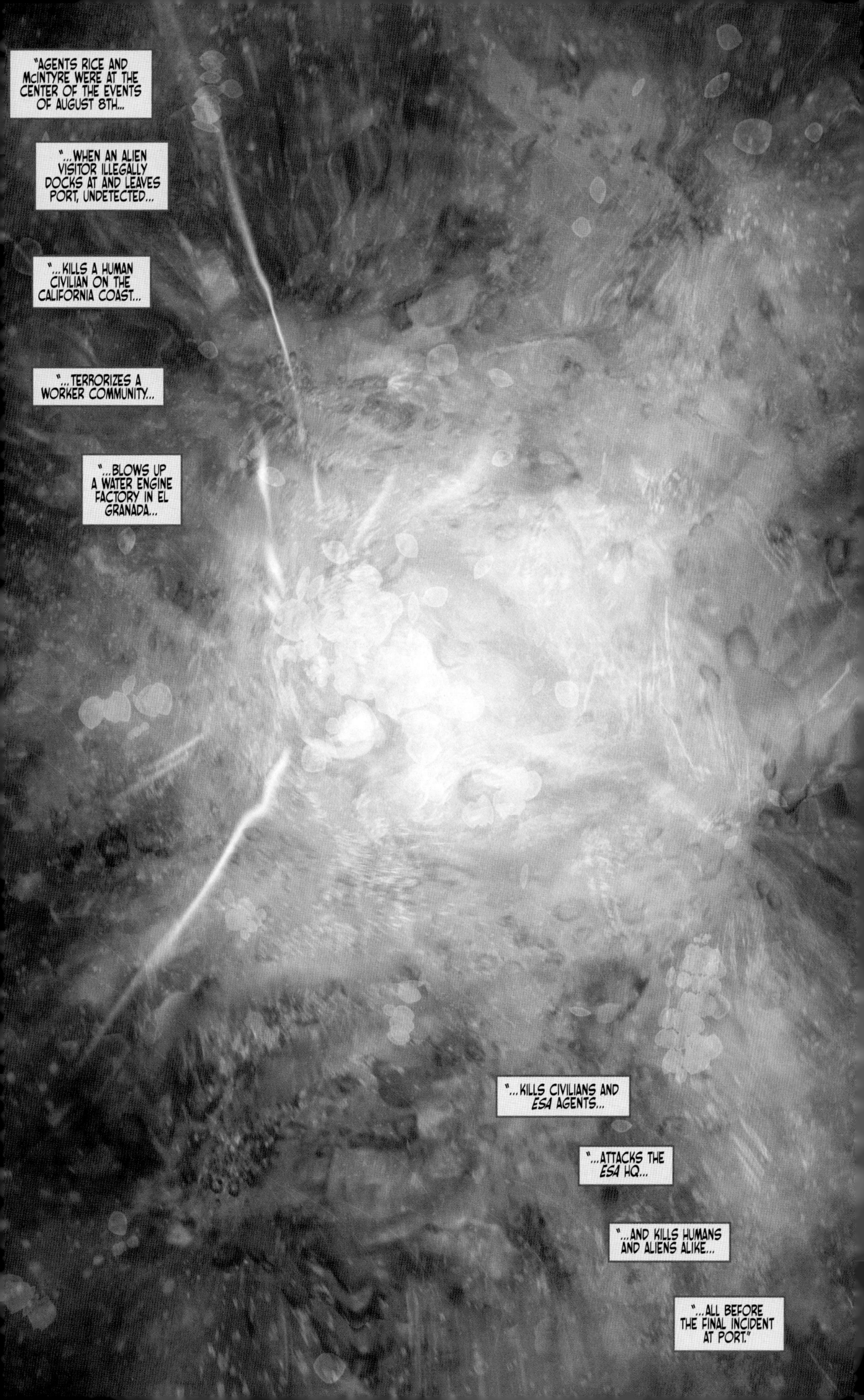
"AGENTS RICE AND McINTYRE WERE AT THE CENTER OF THE EVENTS OF AUGUST 8TH...
"...WHEN AN ALIEN VISITOR ILLEGALLY DOCKS AT AND LEAVES PORT, UNDETECTED...
"...KILLS A HUMAN CIVILIAN ON THE CALIFORNIA COAST...
"...TERRORIZES A WORKER COMMUNITY...
"...BLOWS UP A WATER ENGINE FACTORY IN EL GRANADA...
"...KILLS CIVILIANS AND *ESA* AGENTS...
"...ATTACKS THE *ESA* HQ...
"...AND KILLS HUMANS AND ALIENS ALIKE...
"...ALL BEFORE THE FINAL INCIDENT AT PORT."

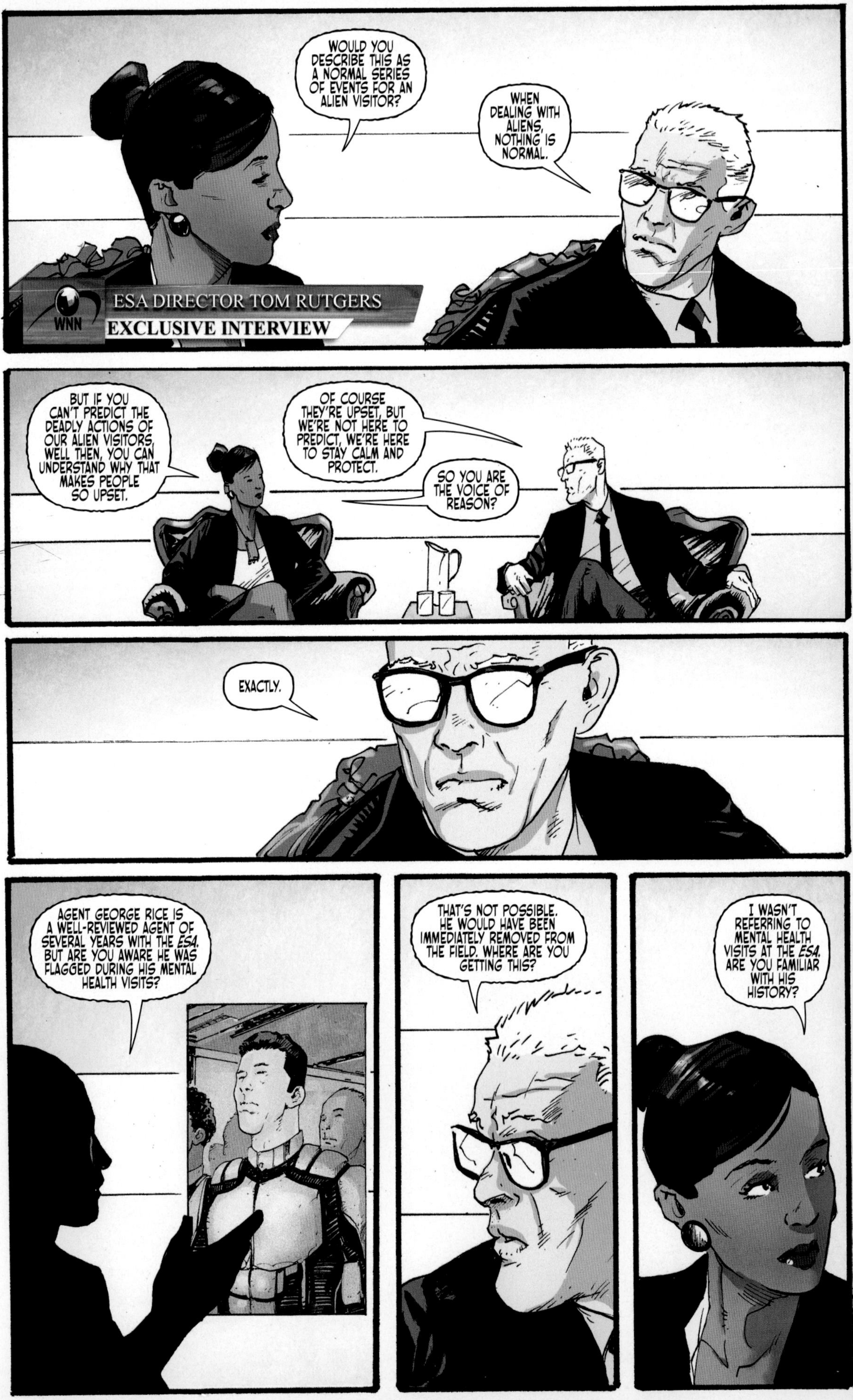
WOULD YOU DESCRIBE THIS AS A NORMAL SERIES OF EVENTS FOR AN ALIEN VISITOR?
WHEN DEALING WITH ALIENS, NOTHING IS NORMAL.
ESA DIRECTOR TOM RUTGERS
WNN
EXCLUSIVE INTERVIEW
BUT IF YOU CAN'T PREDICT THE DEADLY ACTIONS OF OUR ALIEN VISITORS, WELL THEN, YOU CAN UNDERSTAND WHY THAT MAKES PEOPLE SO UPSET.
OF COURSE THEY'RE UPSET, BUT WE'RE NOT HERE TO PREDICT, WE'RE HERE TO STAY CALM AND PROTECT.
SO YOU ARE THE VOICE OF REASON?
EXACTLY.
AGENT GEORGE RICE IS A WELL-REVIEWED AGENT OF SEVERAL YEARS WITH THE ESA. BUT ARE YOU AWARE HE WAS FLAGGED DURING HIS MENTAL HEALTH VISITS?
THAT'S NOT POSSIBLE. HE WOULD HAVE BEEN IMMEDIATELY REMOVED FROM THE FIELD. WHERE ARE YOU GETTING THIS?
I WASN'T REFERRING TO MENTAL HEALTH VISITS AT THE ESA. ARE YOU FAMILIAR WITH HIS HISTORY?

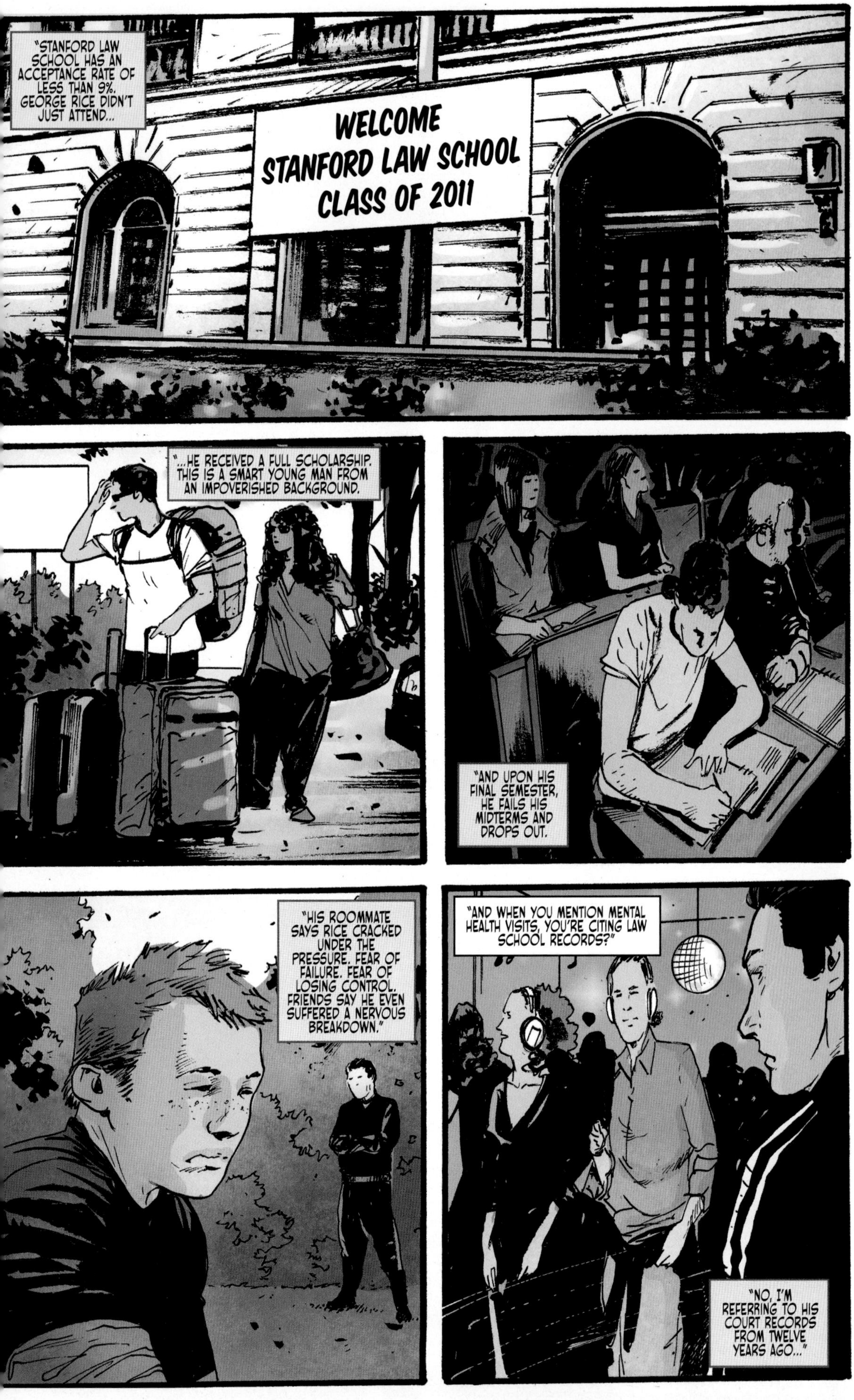
"STANFORD LAW SCHOOL HAS AN ACCEPTANCE RATE OF LESS THAN 9%. GEORGE RICE DIDN'T JUST ATTEND...
WELCOME STANFORD LAW SCHOOL CLASS OF 2011
"...HE RECEIVED A FULL SCHOLARSHIP. THIS IS A SMART YOUNG MAN FROM AN IMPOVERISHED BACKGROUND.
"AND UPON HIS FINAL SEMESTER, HE FAILS HIS MIDTERMS AND DROPS OUT.
"HIS ROOMMATE SAYS RICE CRACKED UNDER THE PRESSURE. FEAR OF FAILURE. FEAR OF LOSING CONTROL. FRIENDS SAY HE EVEN SUFFERED A NERVOUS BREAKDOWN."
"AND WHEN YOU MENTION MENTAL HEALTH VISITS, YOU'RE CITING LAW SCHOOL RECORDS?"
"NO, I'M REFERRING TO HIS COURT RECORDS FROM TWELVE YEARS AGO..."

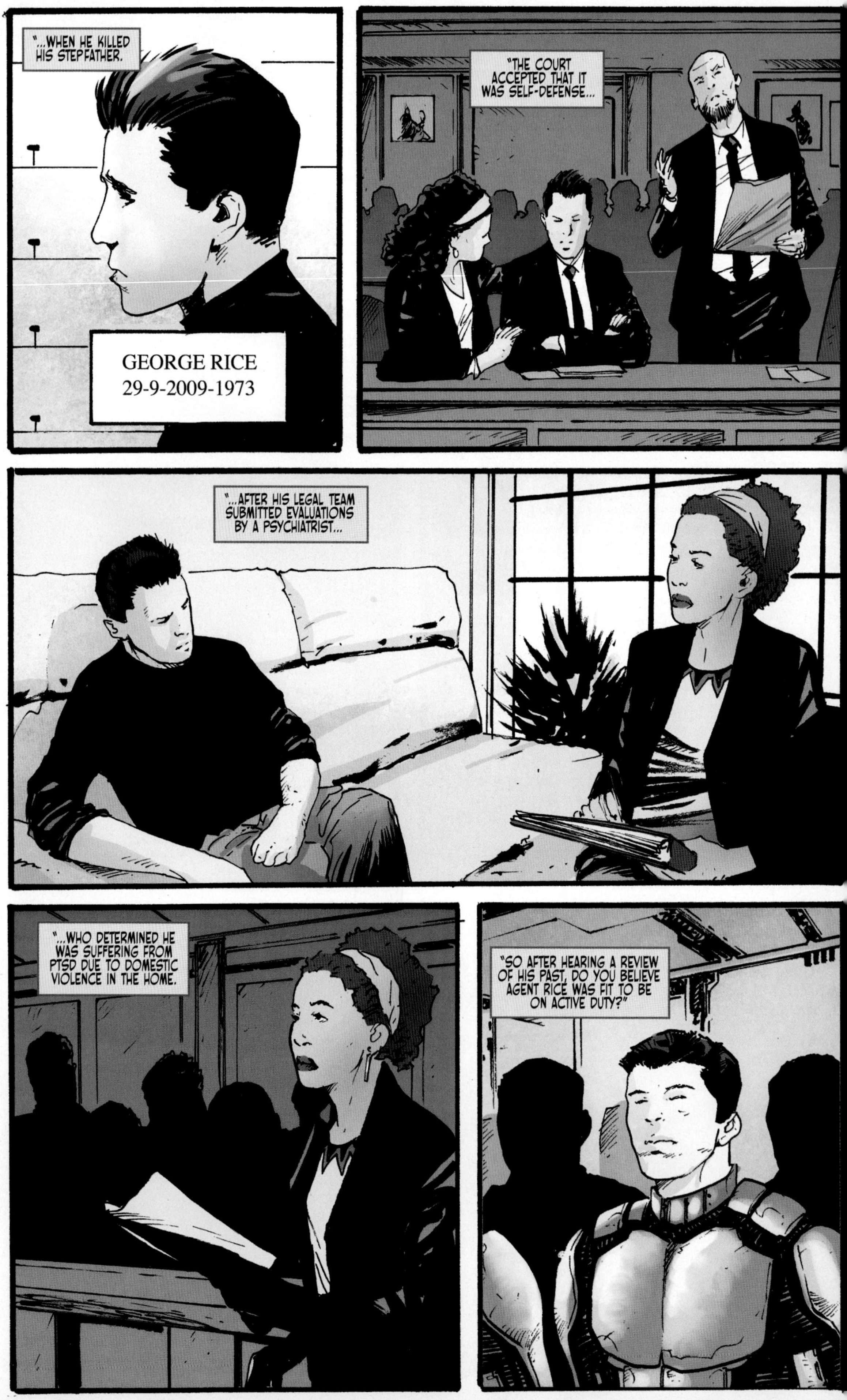

"...WHEN HE KILLED HIS STEPFATHER.
GEORGE RICE
29-9-2009-1973
"THE COURT ACCEPTED THAT IT WAS SELF-DEFENSE...
"...AFTER HIS LEGAL TEAM SUBMITTED EVALUATIONS BY A PSYCHIATRIST...
"...WHO DETERMINED HE WAS SUFFERING FROM PTSD DUE TO DOMESTIC VIOLENCE IN THE HOME.
"SO AFTER HEARING A REVIEW OF HIS PAST, DO YOU BELIEVE AGENT RICE WAS FIT TO BE ON ACTIVE DUTY?"

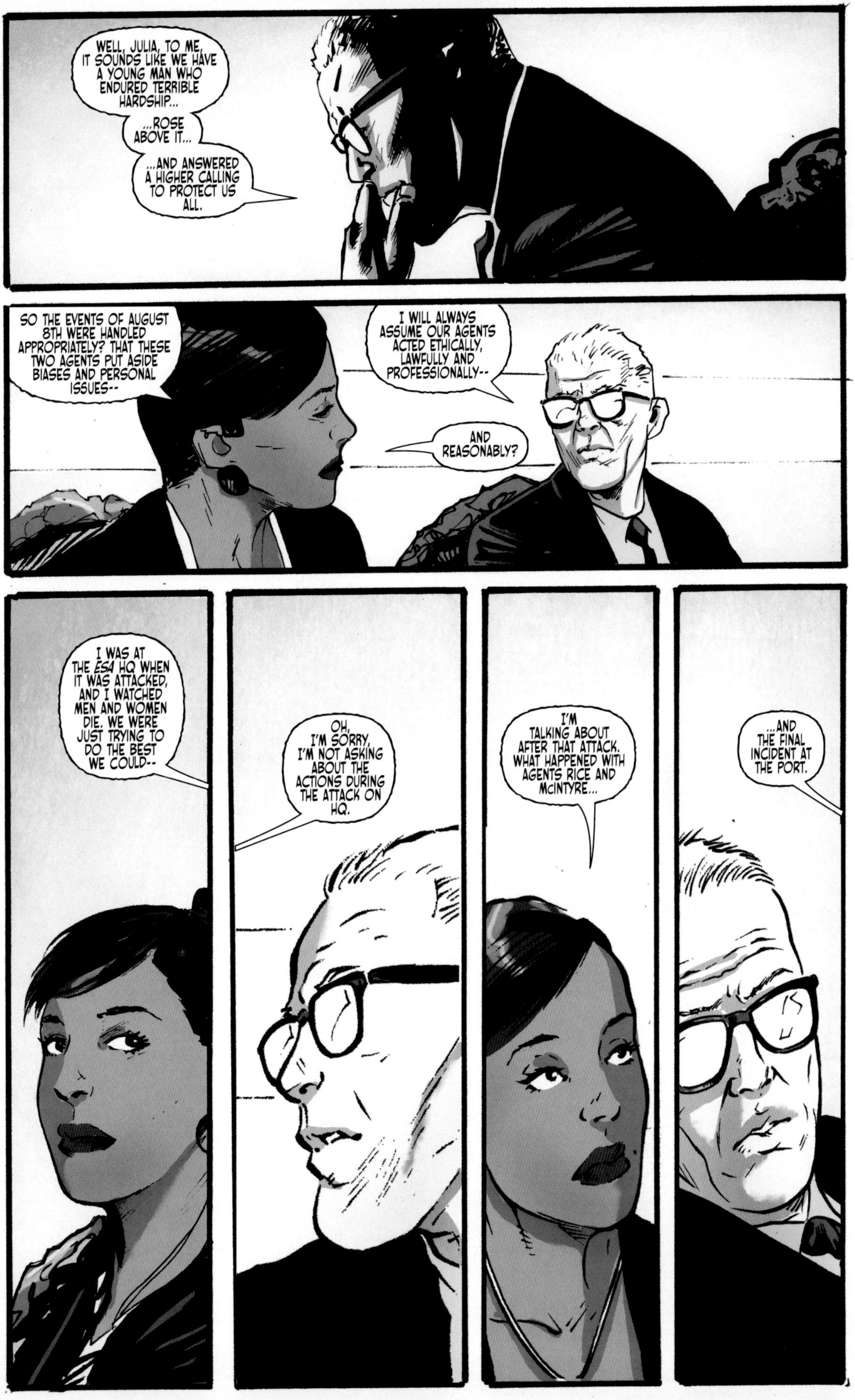
WELL, JULIA, TO ME, IT SOUNDS LIKE WE HAVE A YOUNG MAN WHO ENDURED TERRIBLE HARDSHIP...
...ROSE ABOVE IT...
...AND ANSWERED A HIGHER CALLING TO PROTECT US ALL.
SO THE EVENTS OF AUGUST 8TH WERE HANDLED APPROPRIATELY? THAT THESE TWO AGENTS PUT ASIDE BIASES AND PERSONAL ISSUES--
I WILL ALWAYS ASSUME OUR AGENTS ACTED ETHICALLY, LAWFULLY AND PROFESSIONALLY--
AND REASONABLY?
I WAS AT THE *ESA* HQ WHEN IT WAS ATTACKED, AND I WATCHED MEN AND WOMEN DIE. WE WERE JUST TRYING TO DO THE BEST WE COULD--
OH, I'M SORRY, I'M NOT ASKING ABOUT THE ACTIONS DURING THE ATTACK ON HQ.
I'M TALKING ABOUT AFTER THAT ATTACK. WHAT HAPPENED WITH AGENTS RICE AND McINTYRE...
...AND THE FINAL INCIDENT AT THE PORT.

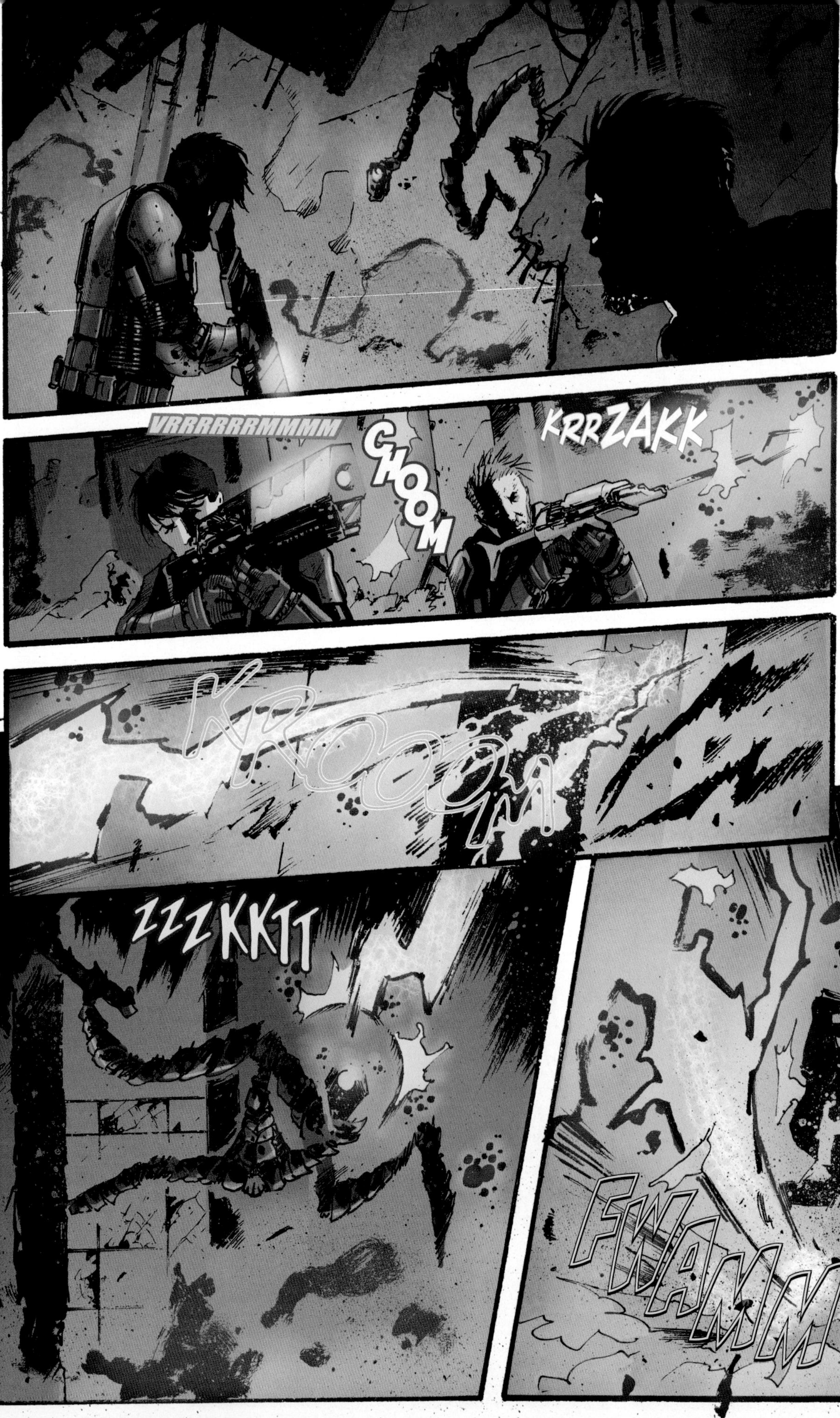
VRRRRRRMMMM
CHOOM
KRRZAKK
KROOOM
ZZZKKTT
FWAMM

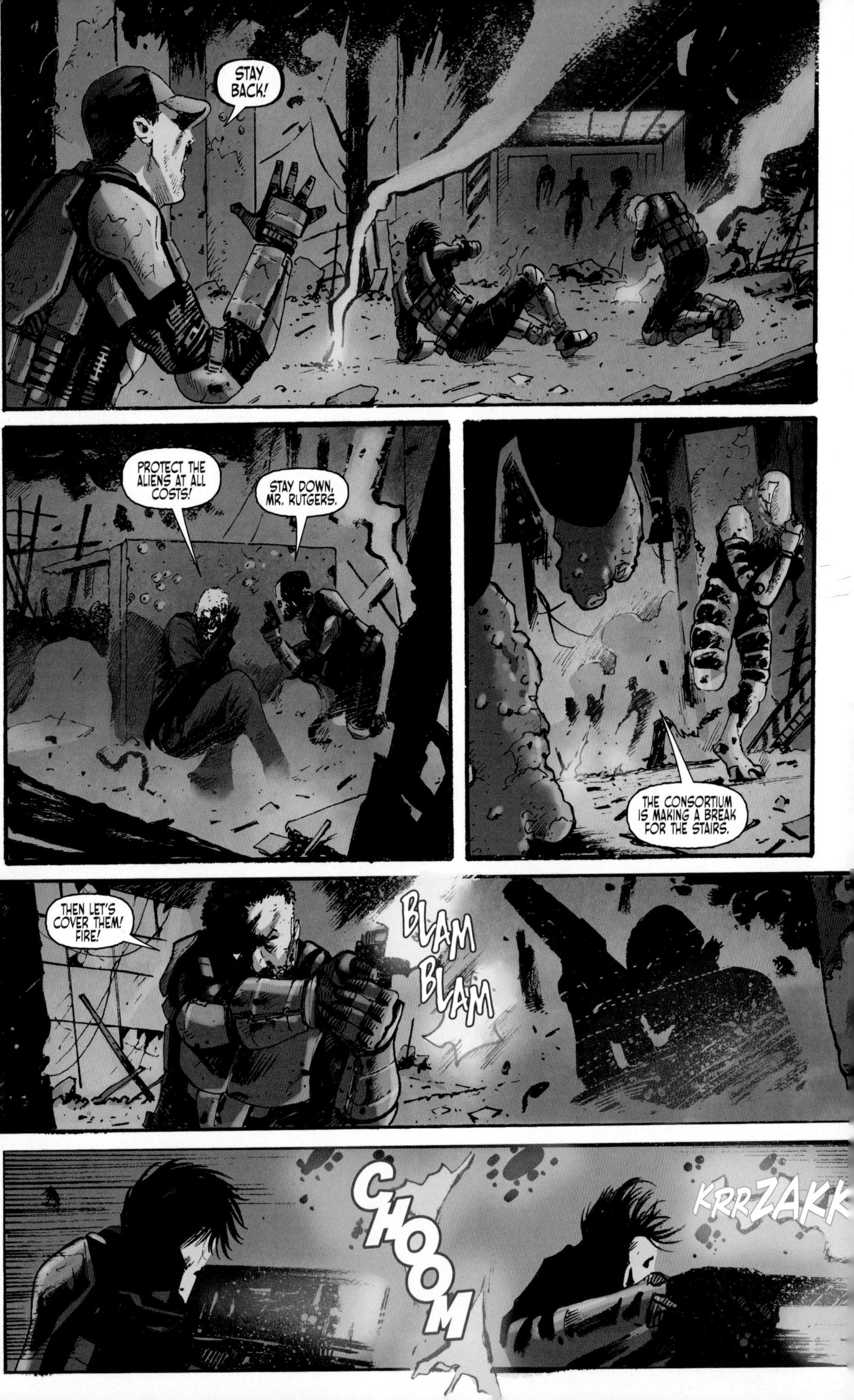
STAY BACK!
PROTECT THE ALIENS AT ALL COSTS!
STAY DOWN, MR. RUTGERS.
THE CONSORTIUM IS MAKING A BREAK FOR THE STAIRS.
THEN LET'S COVER THEM! FIRE!
BLAM
BLAM
CHOOM
KRRZAKK

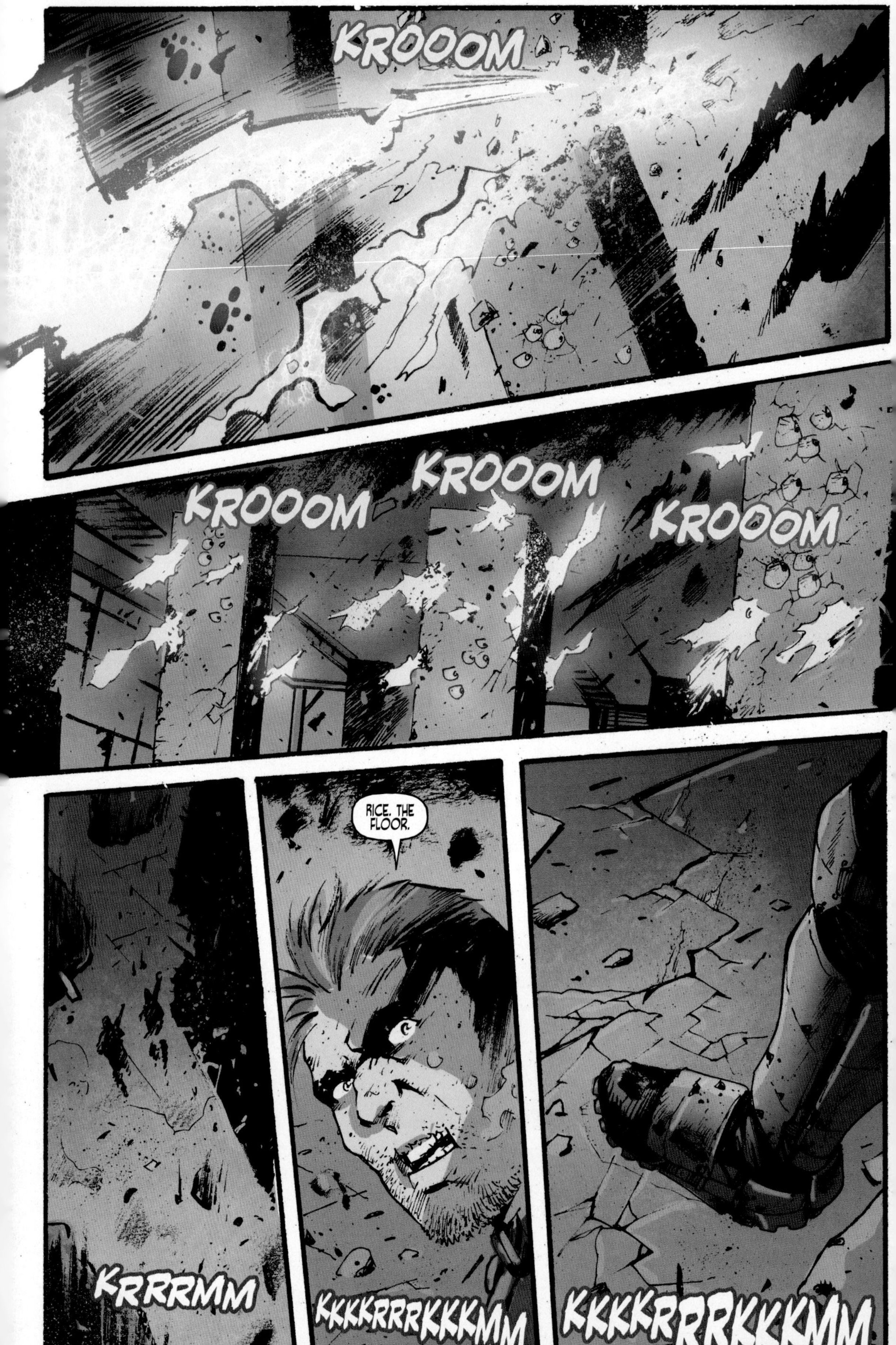
KROOOM
KROOOM
KROOOM
KROOOM
KRRRMM
RICE. THE FLOOR.
KKKKRRRKKKMM
KKKKRRRKKKMM

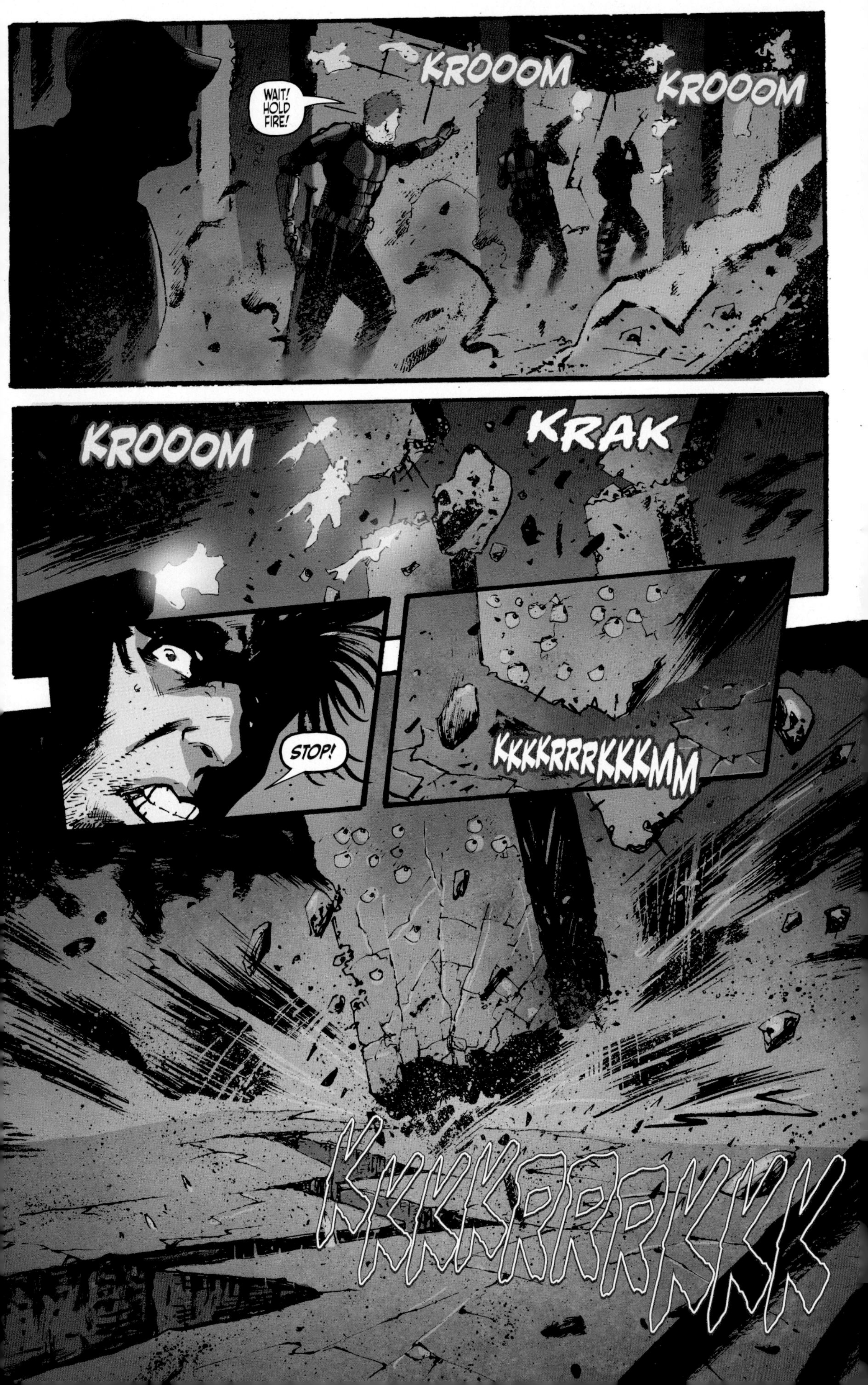
KROOOM
KROOOM
WAIT! HOLD FIRE!
KROOOM
KRAK
STOP!
KKKKRRRKKKMM
KKKKRRRKKK

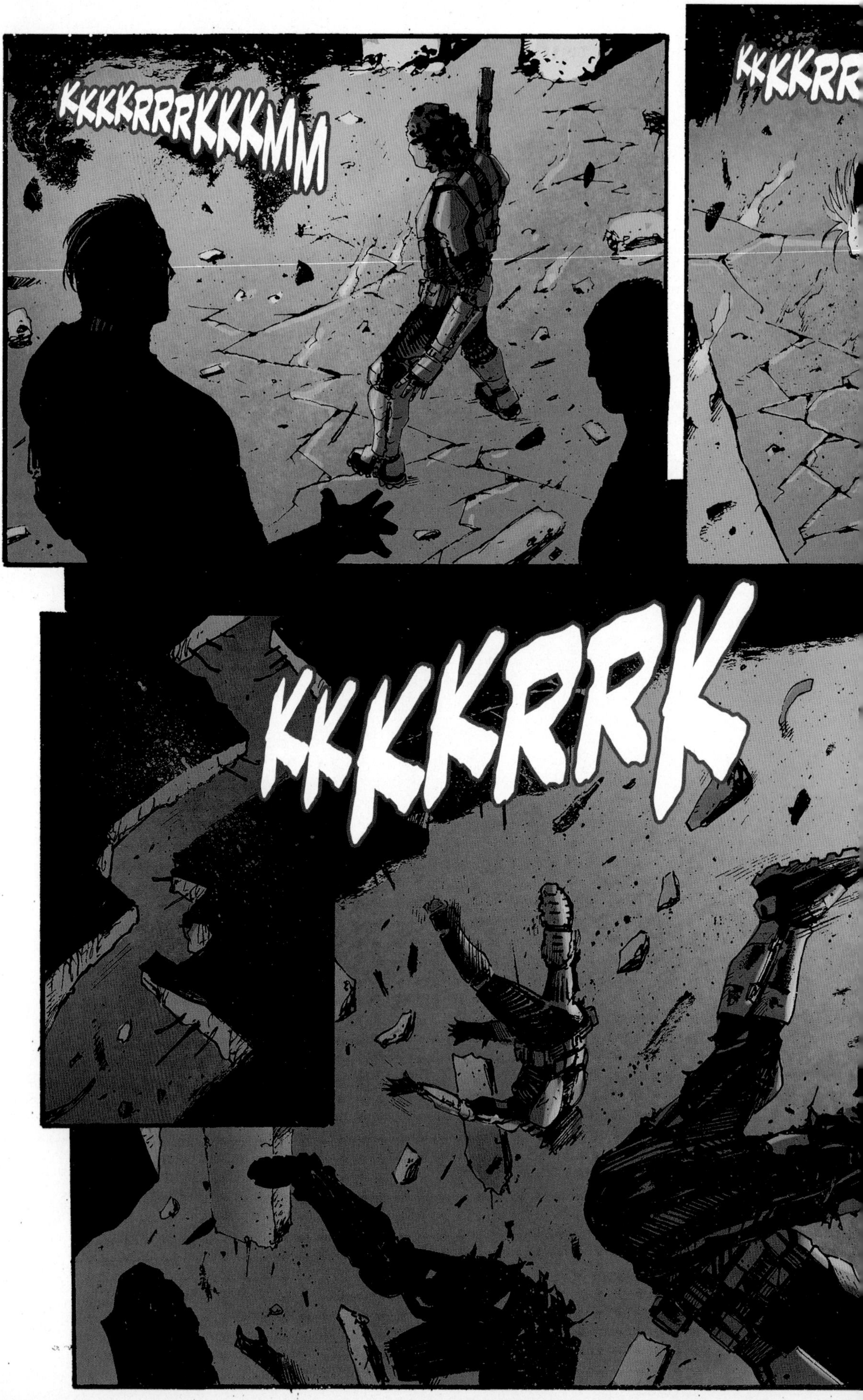
KKKKRRRKKKMM
KKKKRR
KKKKRRRK

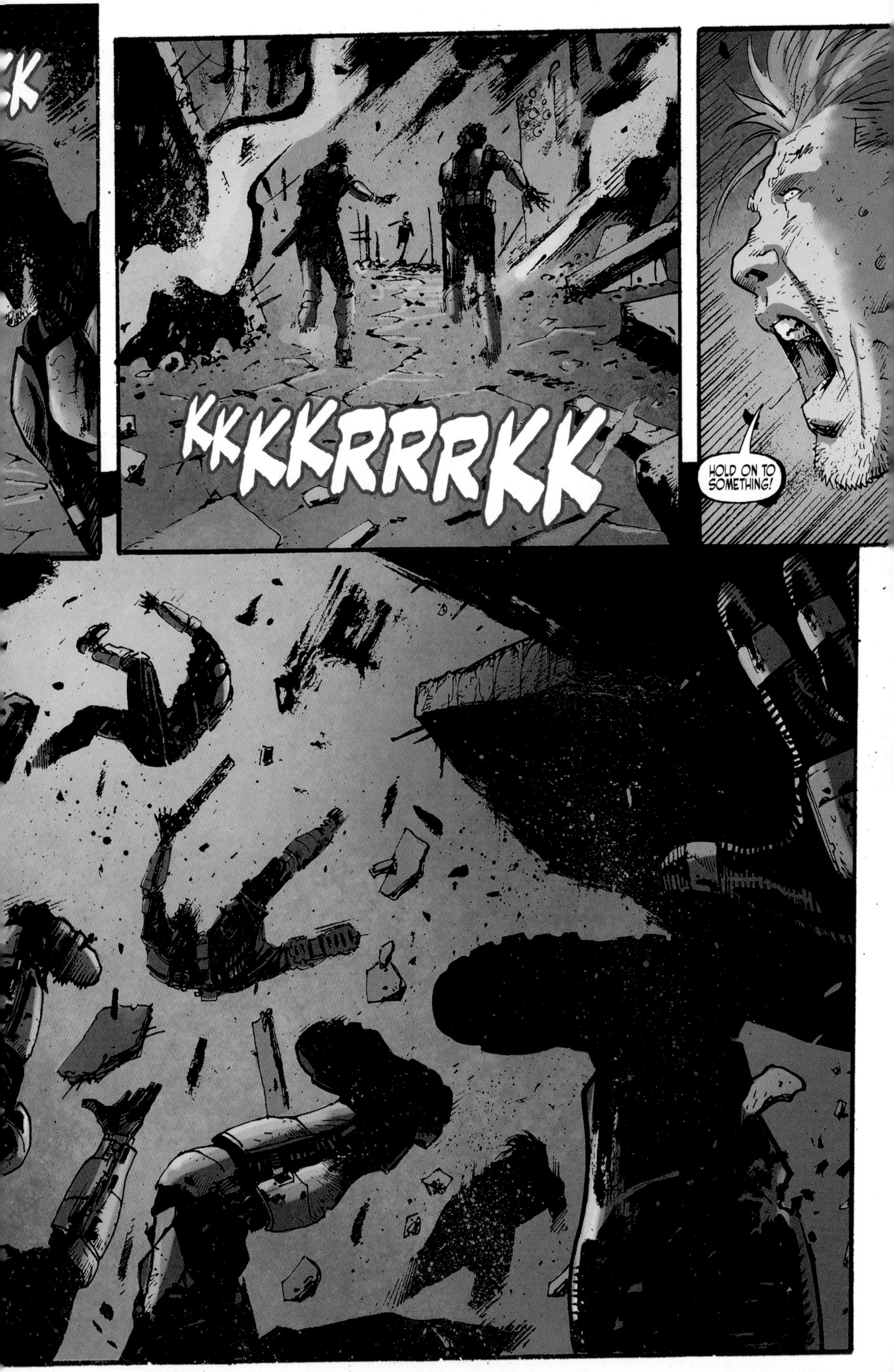
KK
KKKKRRRRKK
HOLD ON TO SOMETHING!

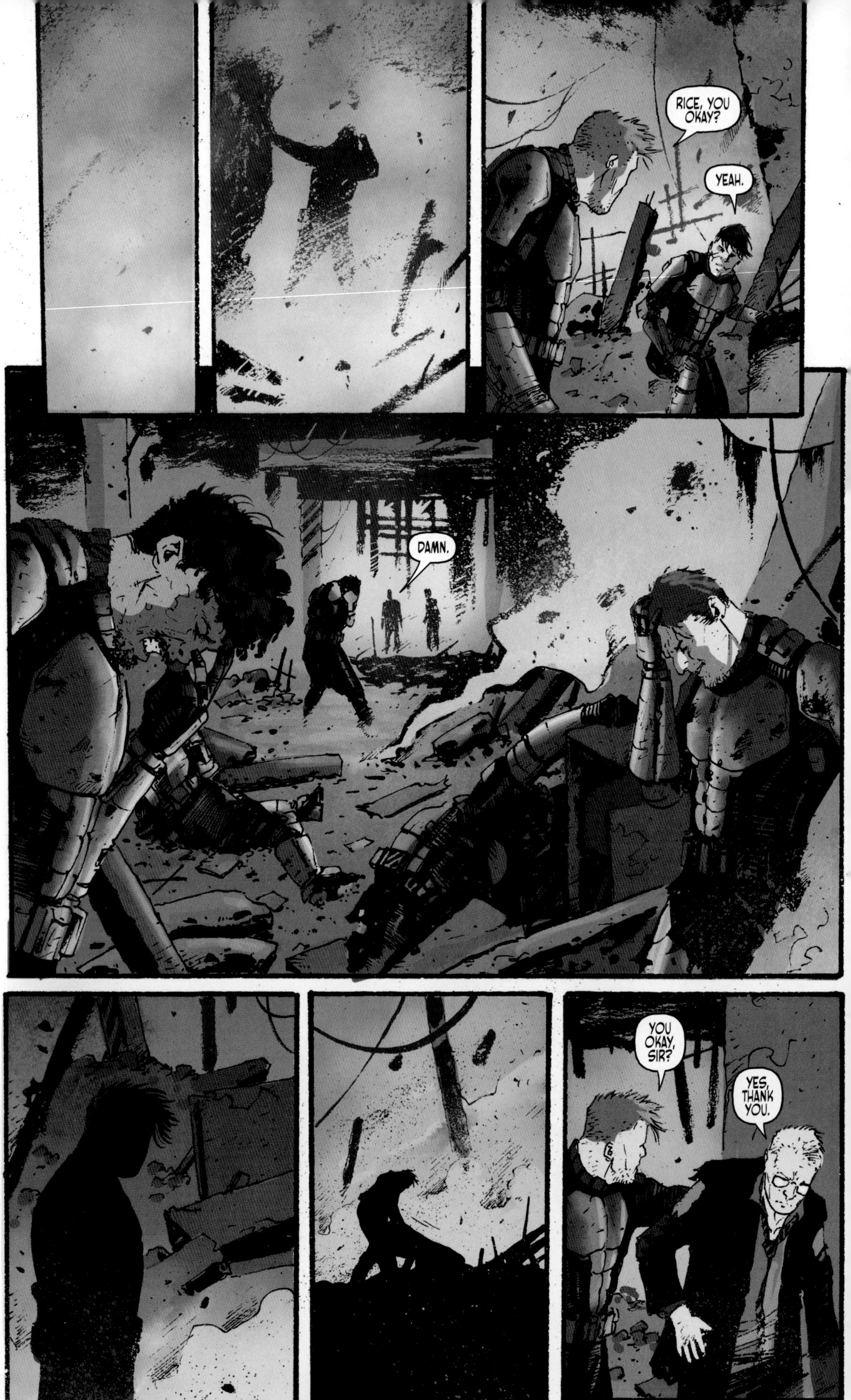
RICE, YOU OKAY?
YEAH.
DAMN.
YOU OKAY, SIR?
YES, THANK YOU.

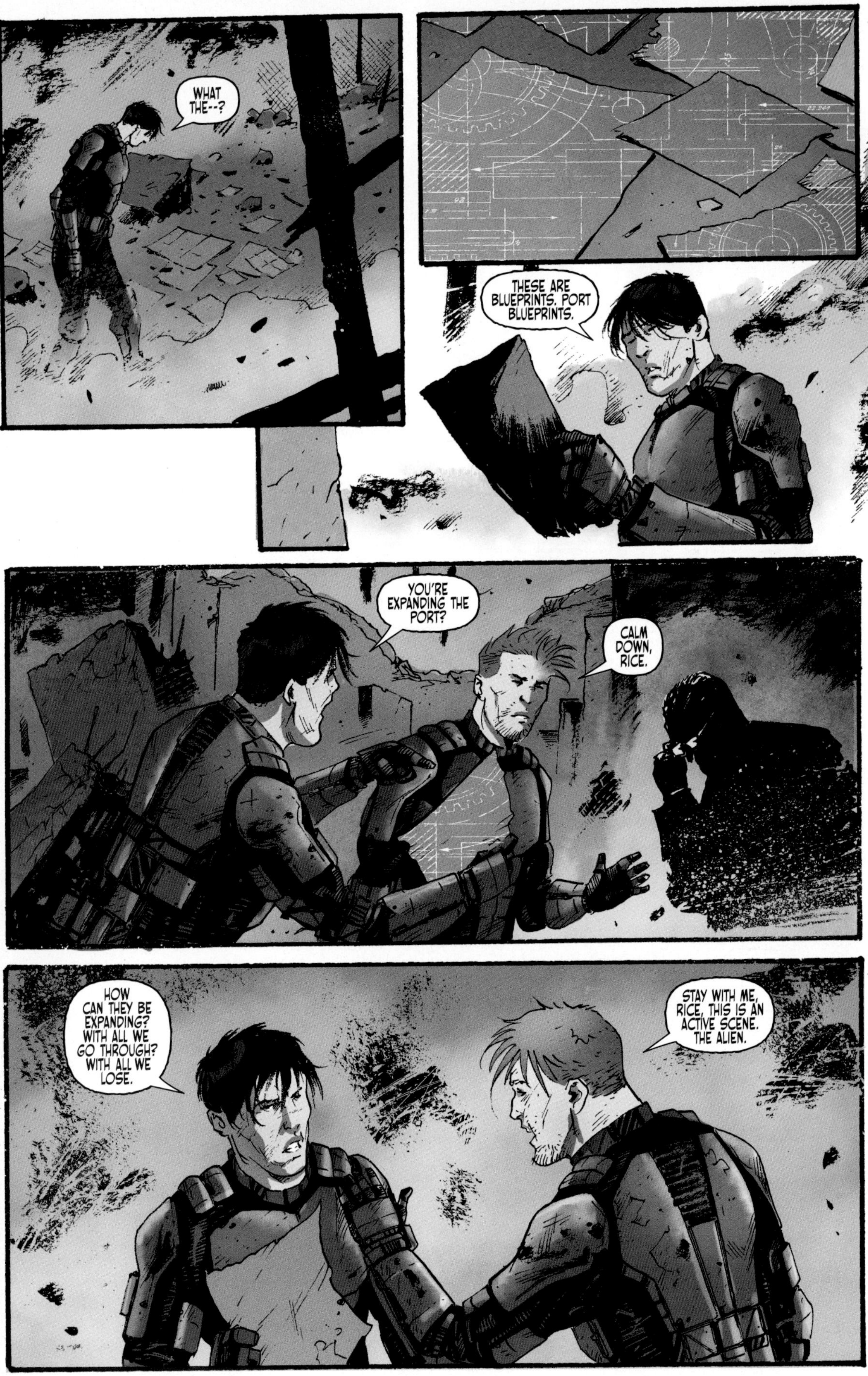
WHAT THE--?
THESE ARE BLUEPRINTS. PORT BLUEPRINTS.
YOU'RE EXPANDING THE PORT?
CALM DOWN, RICE.
HOW CAN THEY BE EXPANDING? WITH ALL WE GO THROUGH? WITH ALL WE LOSE.
STAY WITH ME, RICE, THIS IS AN ACTIVE SCENE. THE ALIEN.

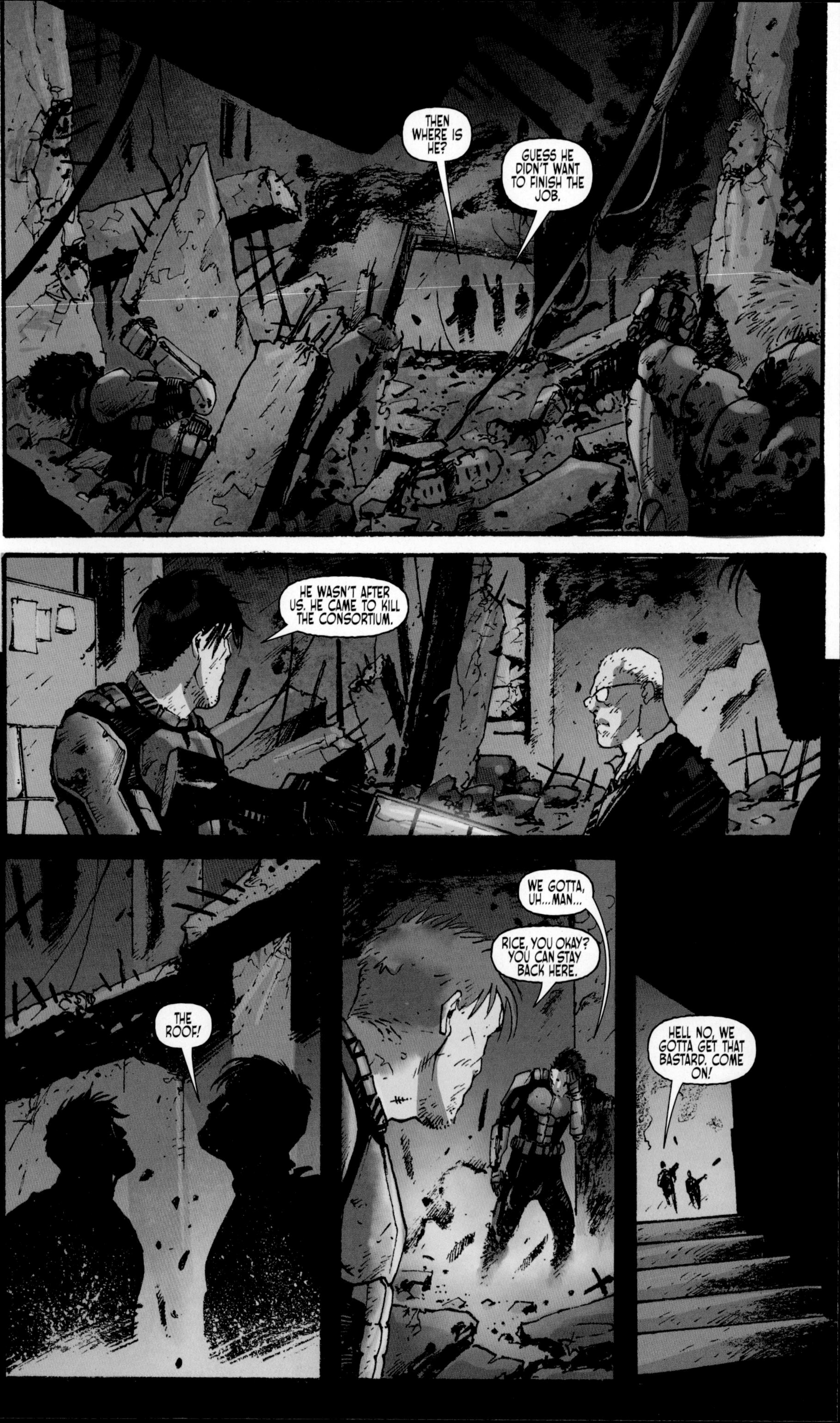
THEN WHERE IS HE?
GUESS HE DIDN'T WANT TO FINISH THE JOB.
HE WASN'T AFTER US. HE CAME TO KILL THE CONSORTIUM.
THE ROOF!
WE GOTTA, UH...MAN...
RICE, YOU OKAY? YOU CAN STAY BACK HERE.
HELL NO, WE GOTTA GET THAT BASTARD. COME ON!

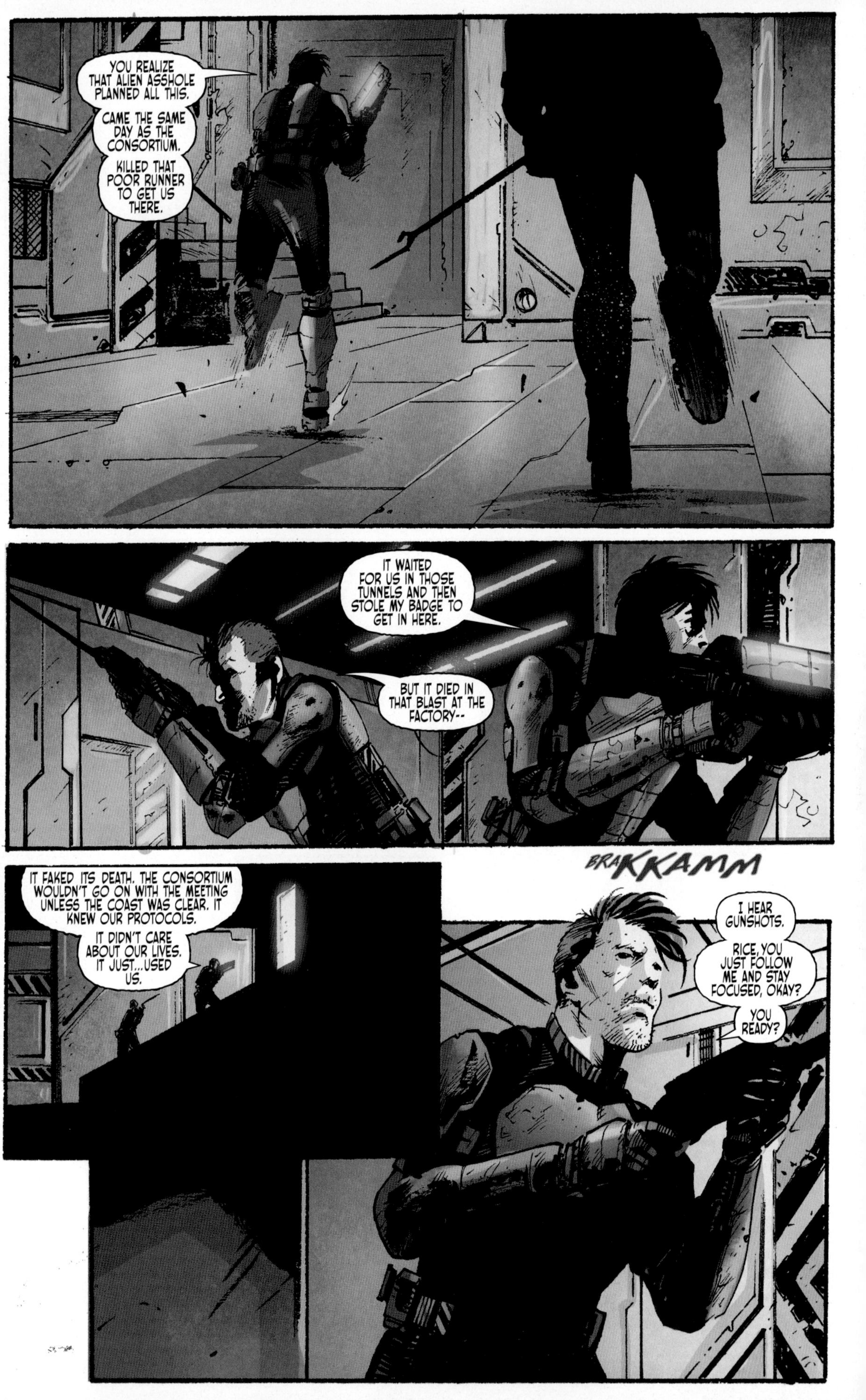
YOU REALIZE THAT ALIEN ASSHOLE PLANNED ALL THIS.
CAME THE SAME DAY AS THE CONSORTIUM.
KILLED THAT POOR RUNNER TO GET US THERE.
IT WAITED FOR US IN THOSE TUNNELS AND THEN STOLE MY BADGE TO GET IN HERE.
BUT IT DIED IN THAT BLAST AT THE FACTORY--
IT FAKED ITS DEATH. THE CONSORTIUM WOULDN'T GO ON WITH THE MEETING UNLESS THE COAST WAS CLEAR. IT KNEW OUR PROTOCOLS.
IT DIDN'T CARE ABOUT OUR LIVES. IT JUST...USED US.
BRAKKAMM
I HEAR GUNSHOTS.
RICE, YOU JUST FOLLOW ME AND STAY FOCUSED, OKAY?
YOU READY?

LET'S GO!
RICE, GET BACK!
VRRRRM
BRRRT BRRRRT
I GOT YOU, RICE!
HOLD ON.

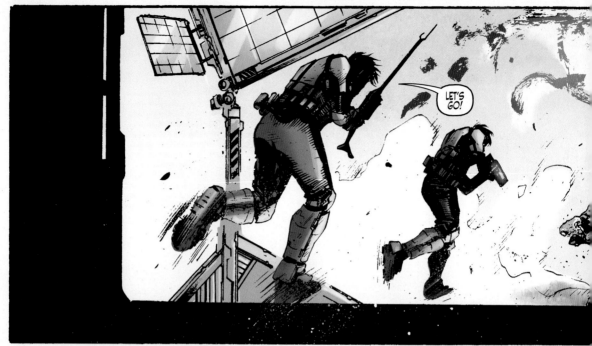

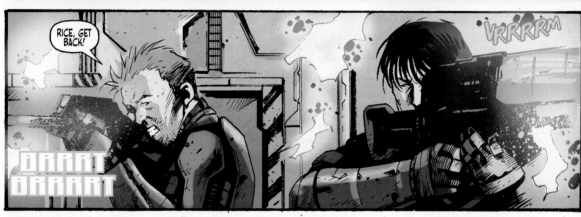

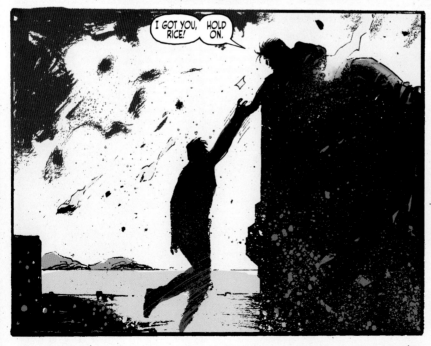

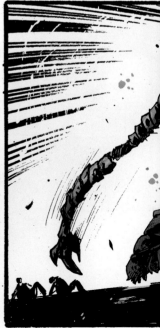

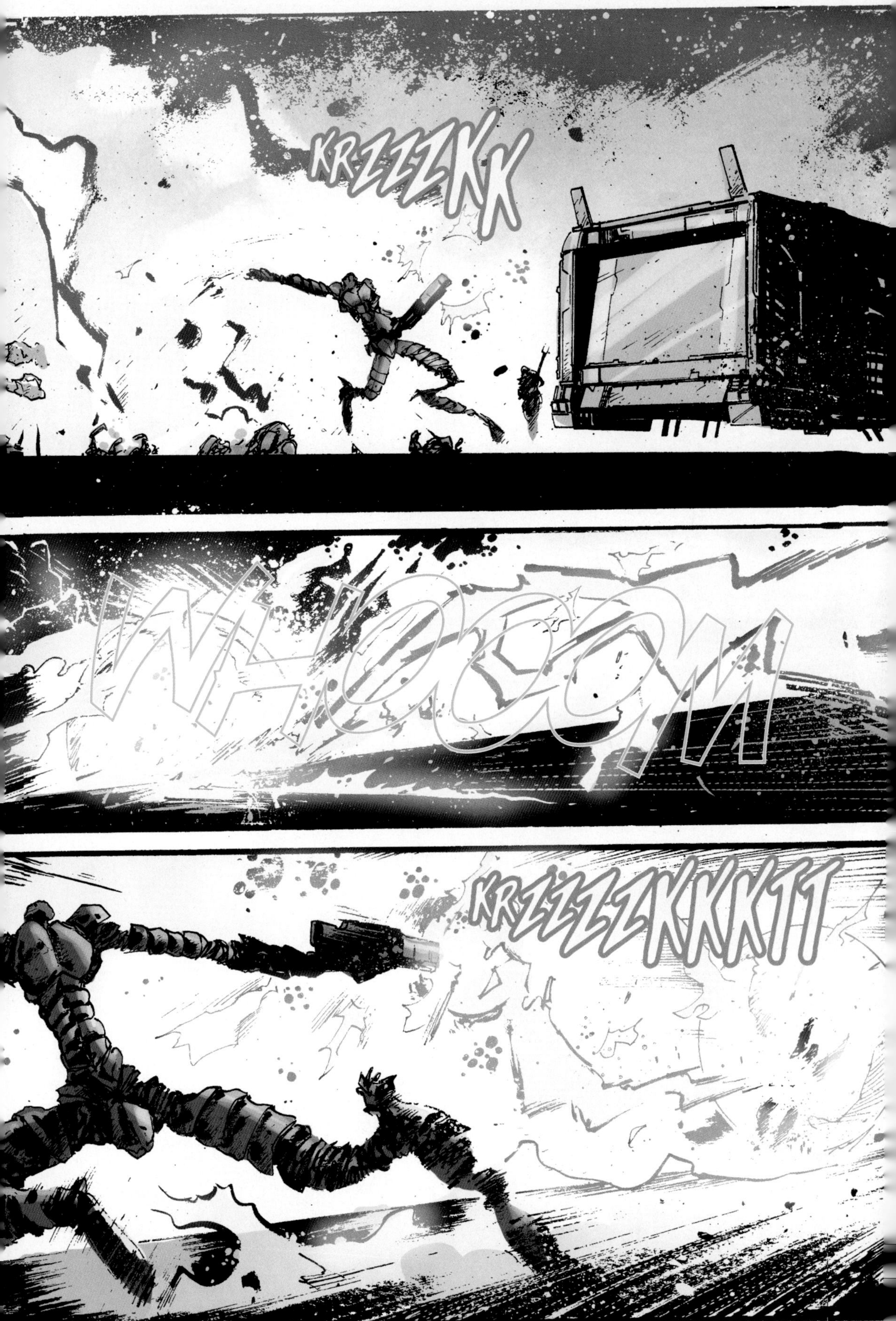
KRZZZKK
WHOOOM
KRZZZZKKKTT

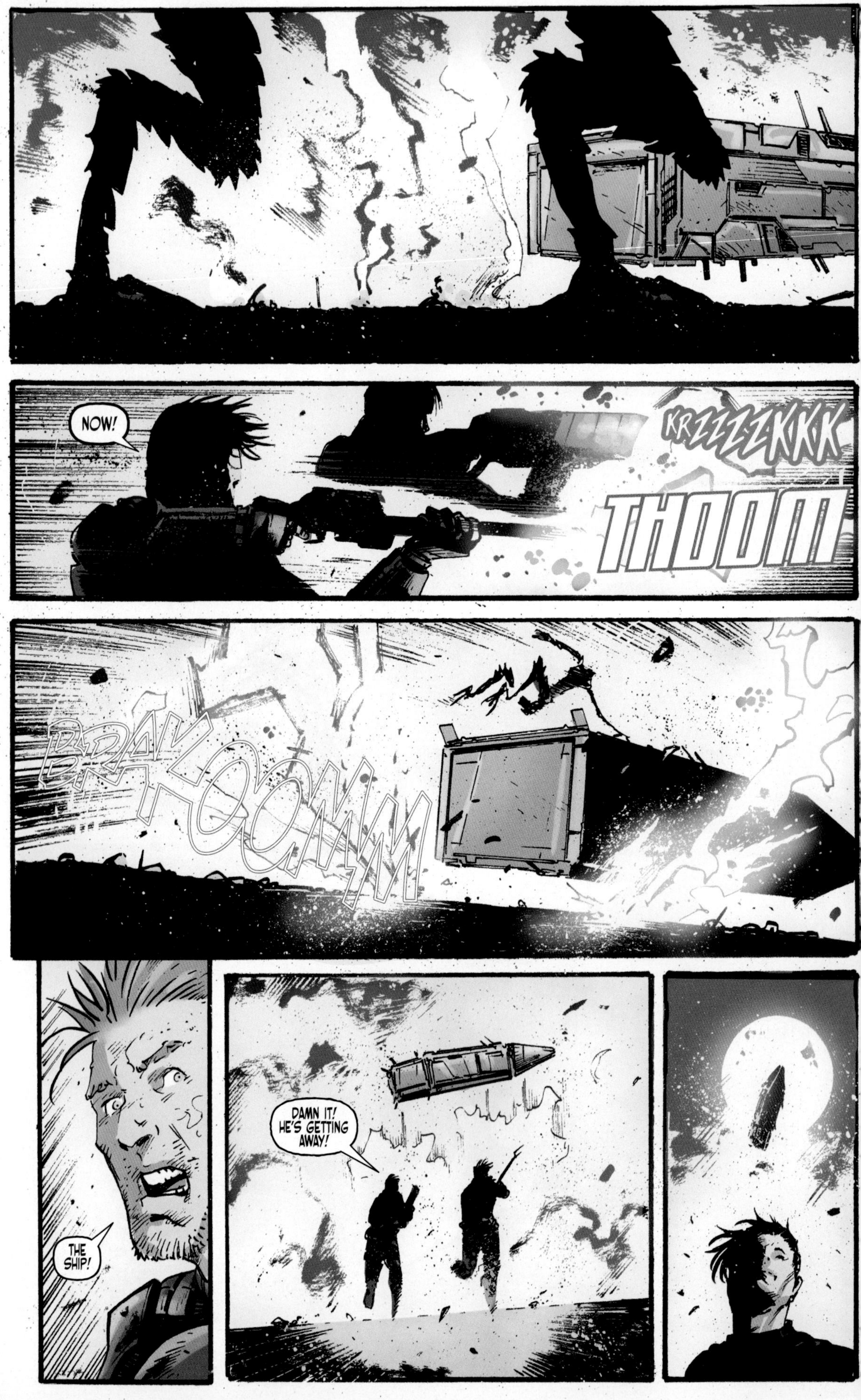
NOW!
KRZZZZKKK
THOOM
BRAKOOMM
THE SHIP!
DAMN IT! HE'S GETTING AWAY!

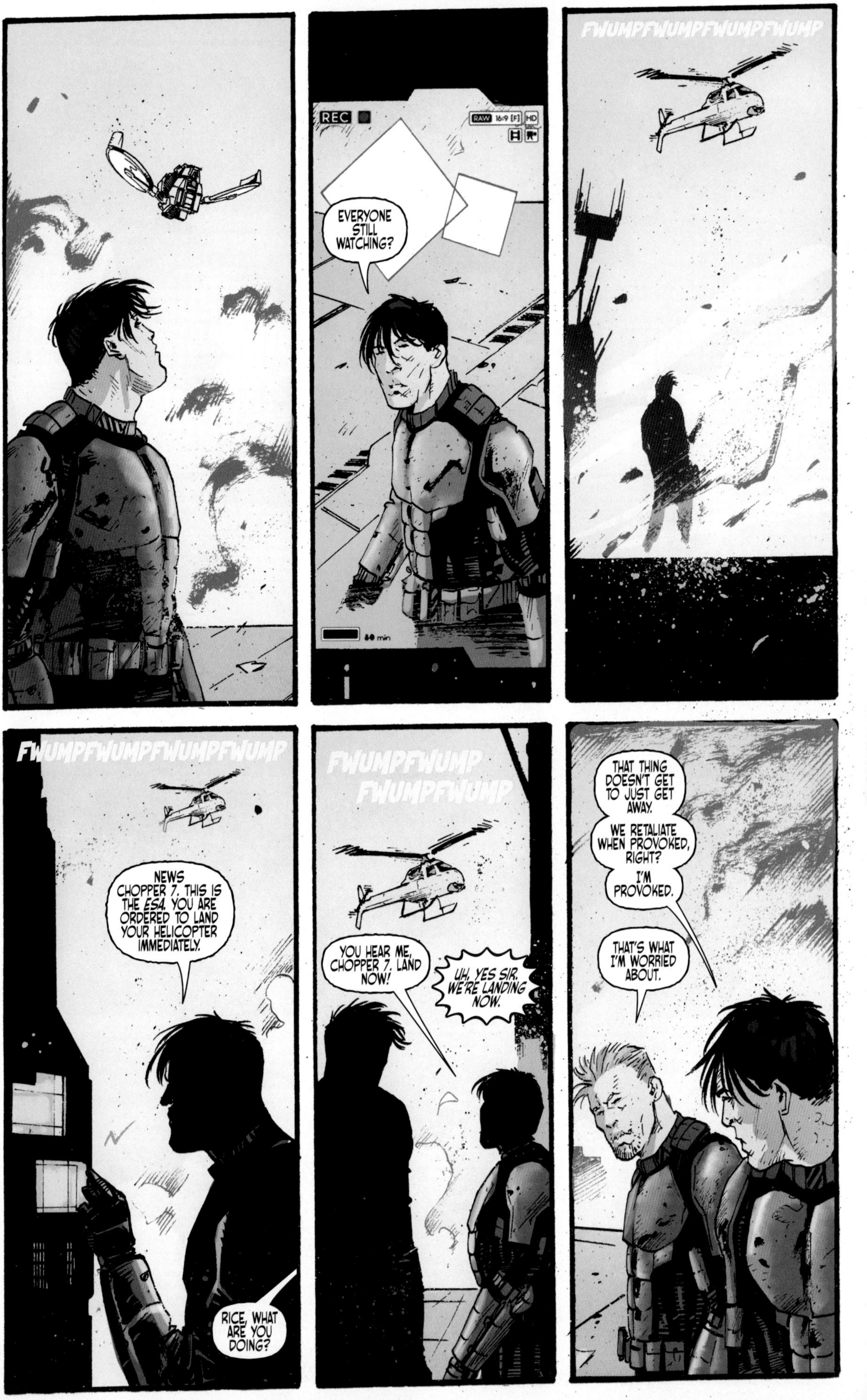
REC
RAW 16:9 [F] HD
EVERYONE STILL WATCHING?
FWUMPFWUMPFWUMPFWUMP
FWUMPFWUMPFWUMPFWUMP
NEWS CHOPPER 7. THIS IS THE ESA. YOU ARE ORDERED TO LAND YOUR HELICOPTER IMMEDIATELY.
RICE, WHAT ARE YOU DOING?
FWUMPFWUMP FWUMPFWUMP
YOU HEAR ME, CHOPPER 7. LAND NOW!
UH, YES SIR. WE'RE LANDING NOW.
THAT THING DOESN'T GET TO JUST GET AWAY.
WE RETALIATE WHEN PROVOKED, RIGHT?
I'M PROVOKED.
THAT'S WHAT I'M WORRIED ABOUT.

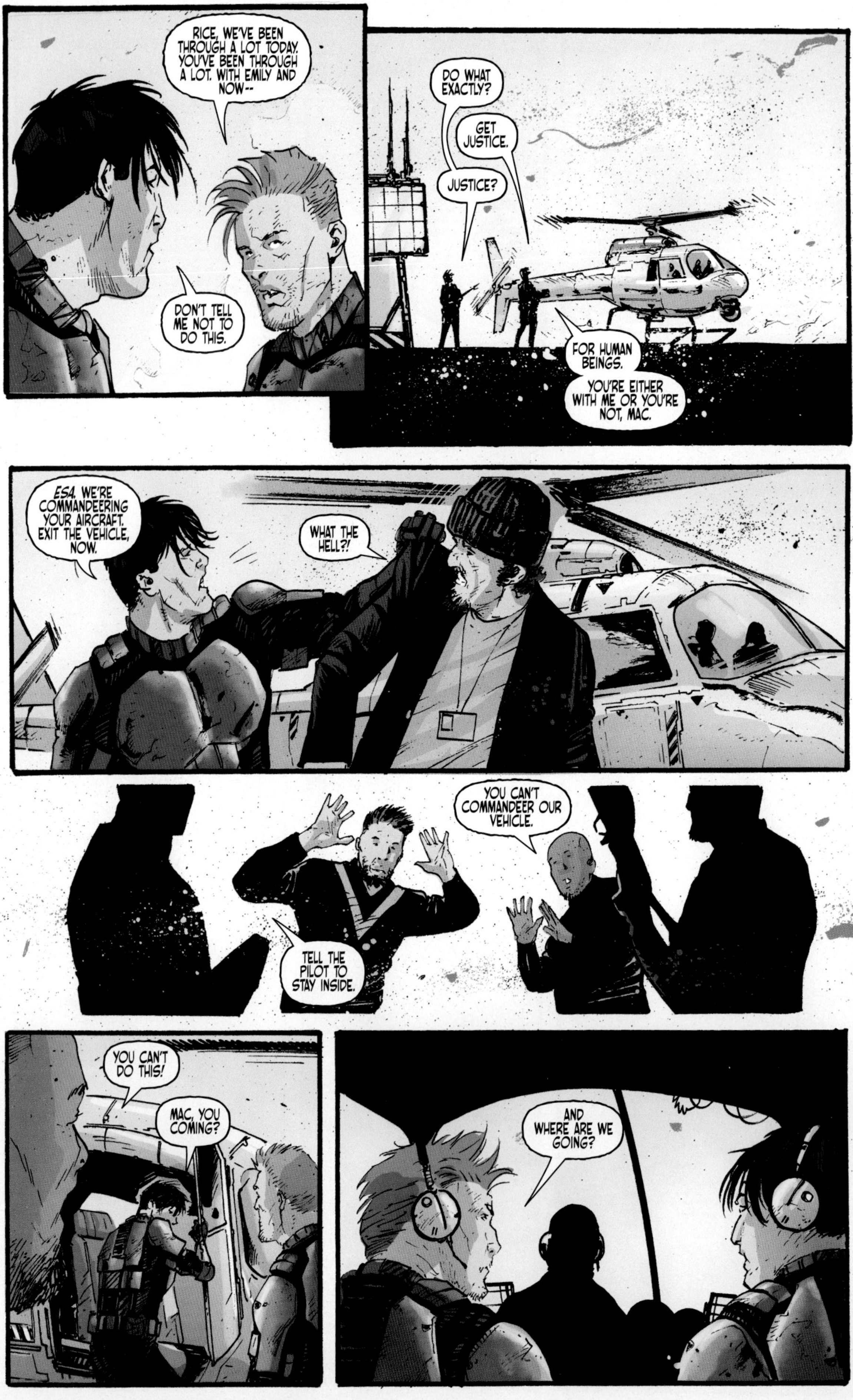
RICE, WE'VE BEEN THROUGH A LOT TODAY. YOU'VE BEEN THROUGH A LOT. WITH EMILY AND NOW--
DON'T TELL ME NOT TO DO THIS.
DO WHAT EXACTLY?
GET JUSTICE.
JUSTICE?
FOR HUMAN BEINGS.
YOU'RE EITHER WITH ME OR YOU'RE NOT, MAC.
ESA. WE'RE COMMANDEERING YOUR AIRCRAFT. EXIT THE VEHICLE, NOW.
WHAT THE HELL?!
YOU CAN'T COMMANDEER OUR VEHICLE.
TELL THE PILOT TO STAY INSIDE.
YOU CAN'T DO THIS!
MAC, YOU COMING?
AND WHERE ARE WE GOING?

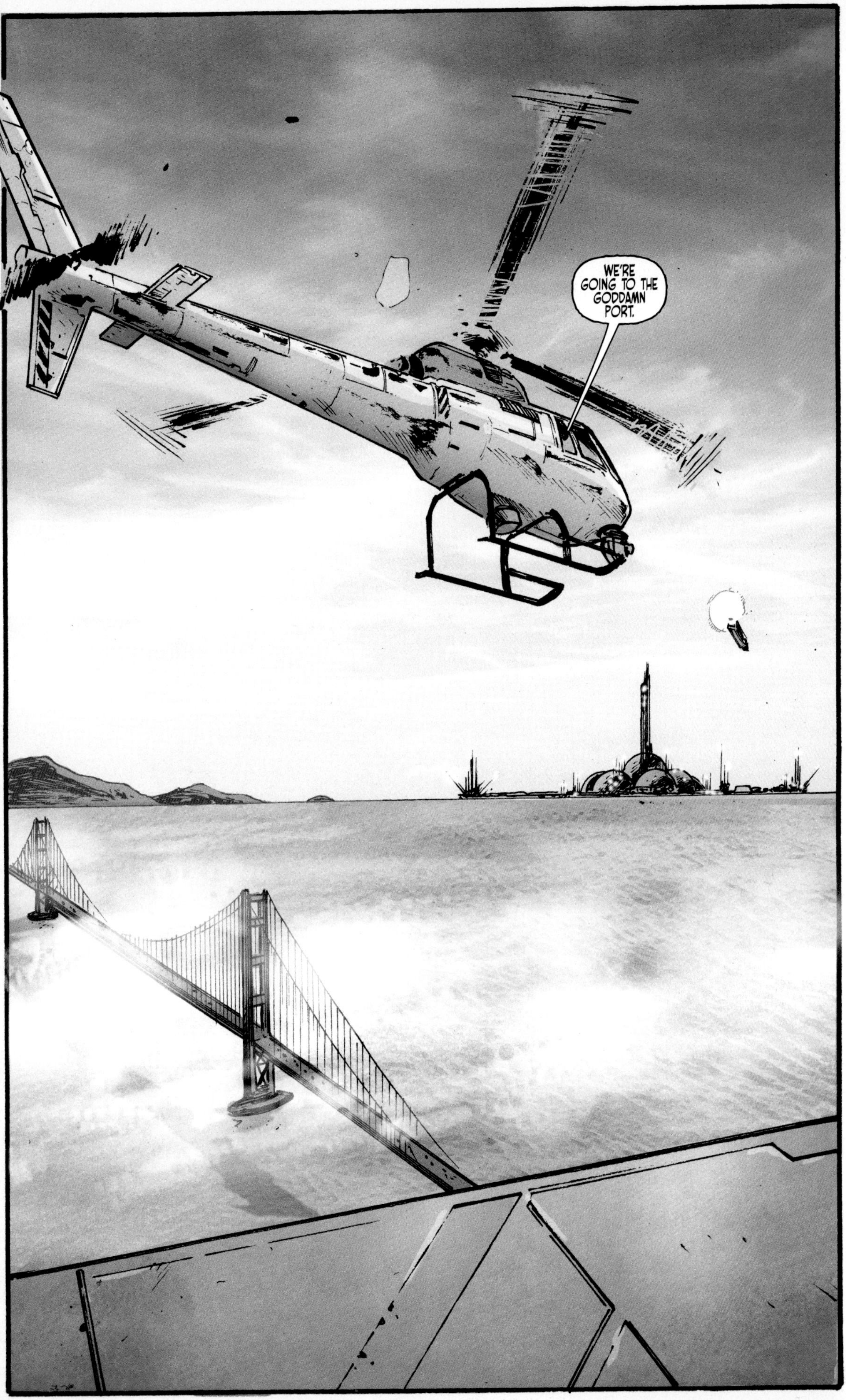
WE'RE GOING TO THE GODDAMN PORT.

CHAPTER 7

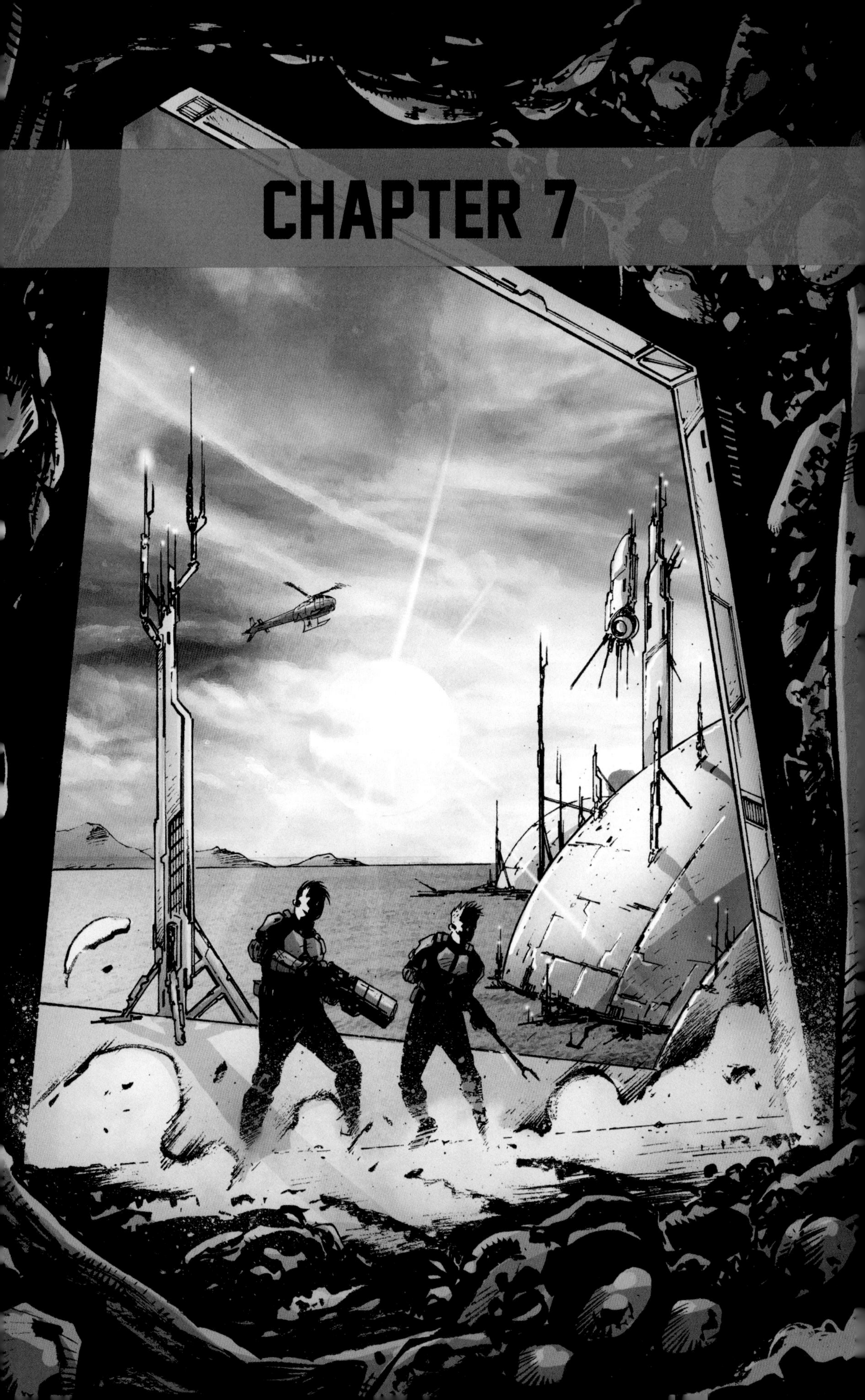

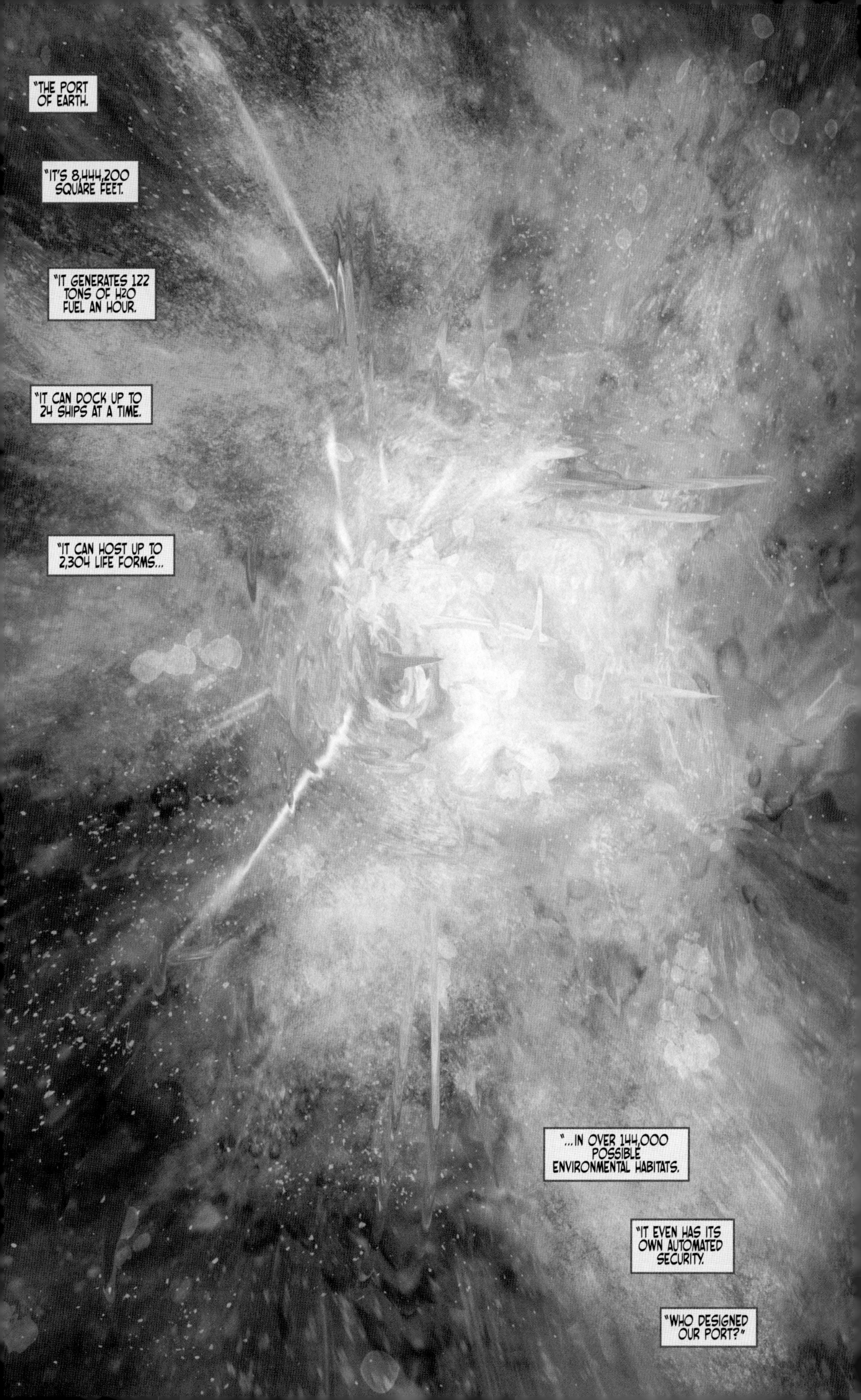
"THE PORT OF EARTH.
"IT'S 8,444,200 SQUARE FEET.
"IT GENERATES 122 TONS OF H2O FUEL AN HOUR.
"IT CAN DOCK UP TO 24 SHIPS AT A TIME.
"IT CAN HOST UP TO 2,304 LIFE FORMS...
"...IN OVER 144,000 POSSIBLE ENVIRONMENTAL HABITATS.
"IT EVEN HAS ITS OWN AUTOMATED SECURITY.
"WHO DESIGNED OUR PORT?"

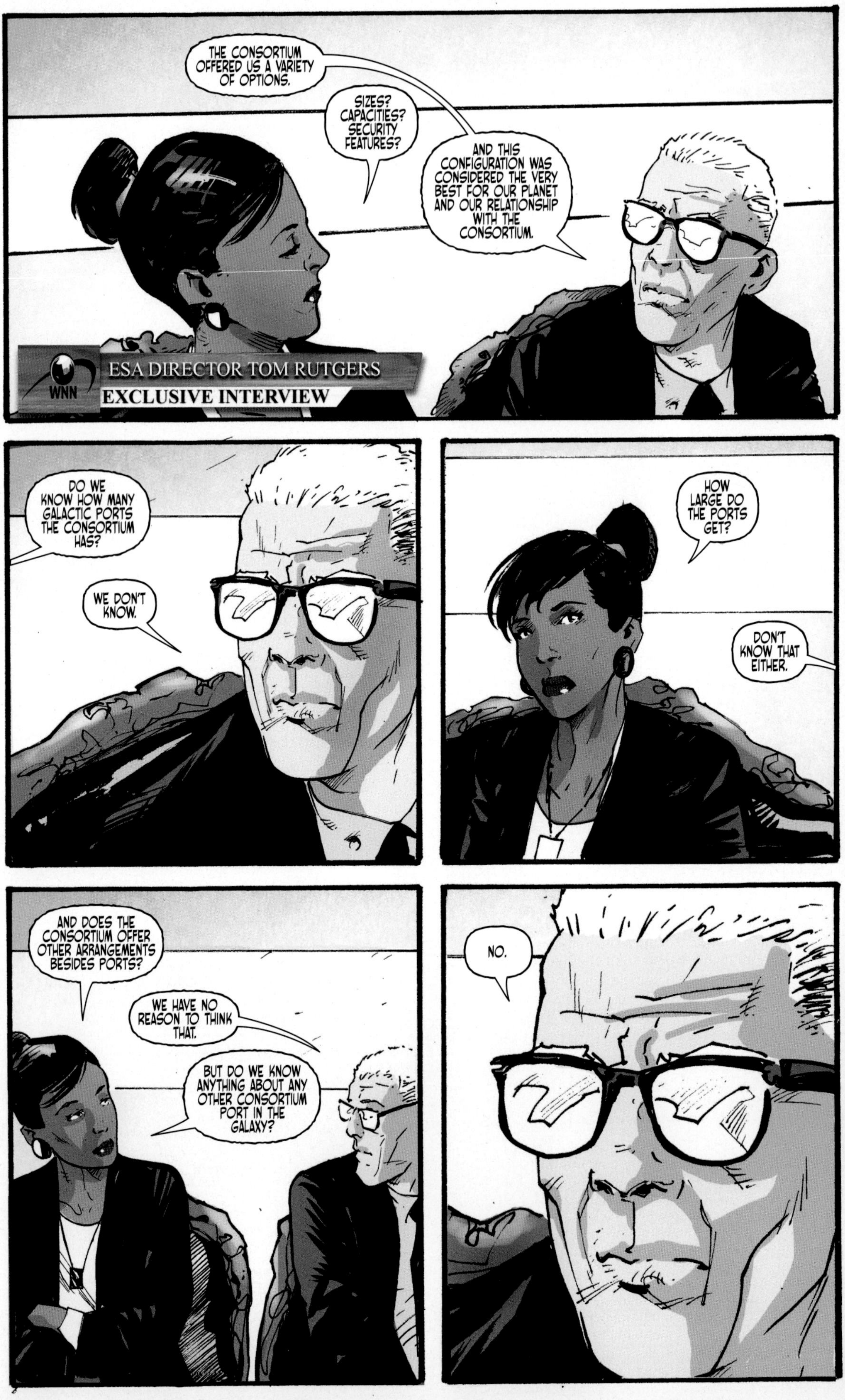
THE CONSORTIUM OFFERED US A VARIETY OF OPTIONS.
SIZES? CAPACITIES? SECURITY FEATURES?
AND THIS CONFIGURATION WAS CONSIDERED THE VERY BEST FOR OUR PLANET AND OUR RELATIONSHIP WITH THE CONSORTIUM.
WNN
ESA DIRECTOR TOM RUTGERS
EXCLUSIVE INTERVIEW
DO WE KNOW HOW MANY GALACTIC PORTS THE CONSORTIUM HAS?
WE DON'T KNOW.
HOW LARGE DO THE PORTS GET?
DON'T KNOW THAT EITHER.
AND DOES THE CONSORTIUM OFFER OTHER ARRANGEMENTS BESIDES PORTS?
WE HAVE NO REASON TO THINK THAT.
BUT DO WE KNOW ANYTHING ABOUT ANY OTHER CONSORTIUM PORT IN THE GALAXY?
NO.

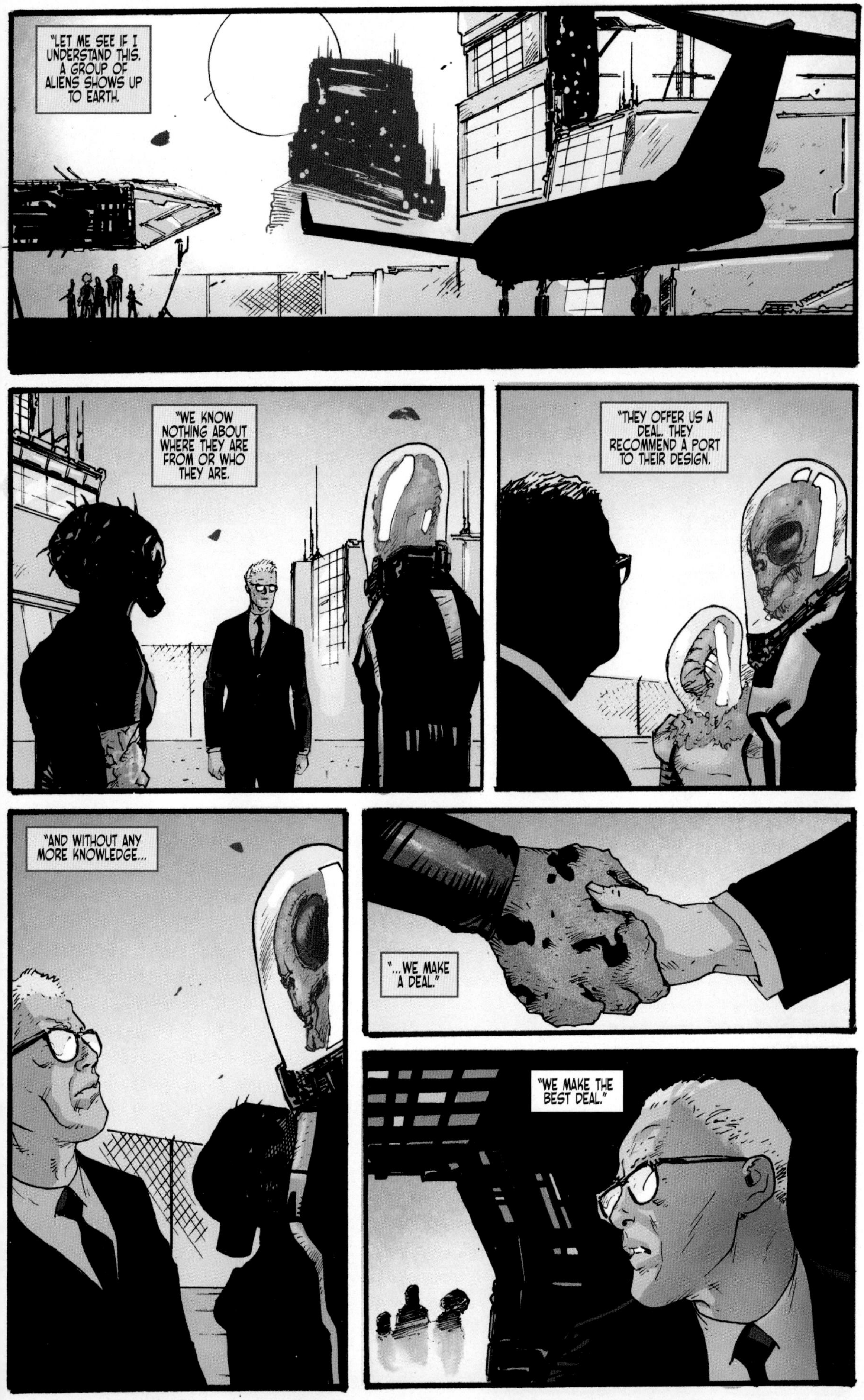
"LET ME SEE IF I UNDERSTAND THIS. A GROUP OF ALIENS SHOWS UP TO EARTH.
"WE KNOW NOTHING ABOUT WHERE THEY ARE FROM OR WHO THEY ARE.
"THEY OFFER US A DEAL. THEY RECOMMEND A PORT TO THEIR DESIGN.
"AND WITHOUT ANY MORE KNOWLEDGE...
"...WE MAKE A DEAL."
"WE MAKE THE BEST DEAL."

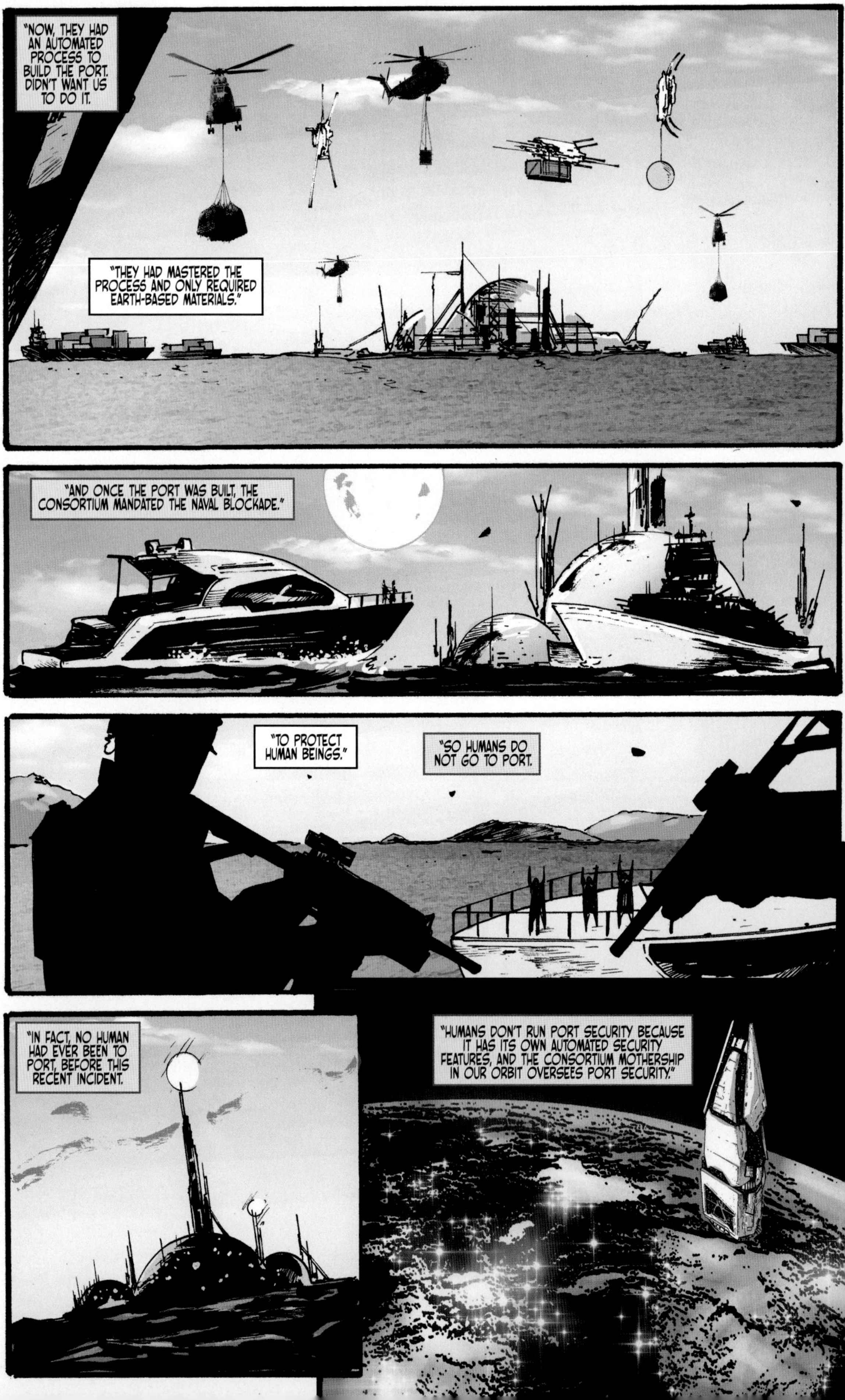
"NOW, THEY HAD AN AUTOMATED PROCESS TO BUILD THE PORT. DIDN'T WANT US TO DO IT.
"THEY HAD MASTERED THE PROCESS AND ONLY REQUIRED EARTH-BASED MATERIALS."
"AND ONCE THE PORT WAS BUILT, THE CONSORTIUM MANDATED THE NAVAL BLOCKADE."
"TO PROTECT HUMAN BEINGS."
"SO HUMANS DO NOT GO TO PORT.
"IN FACT, NO HUMAN HAD EVER BEEN TO PORT, BEFORE THIS RECENT INCIDENT.
"HUMANS DON'T RUN PORT SECURITY BECAUSE IT HAS ITS OWN AUTOMATED SECURITY FEATURES, AND THE CONSORTIUM MOTHERSHIP IN OUR ORBIT OVERSEES PORT SECURITY."

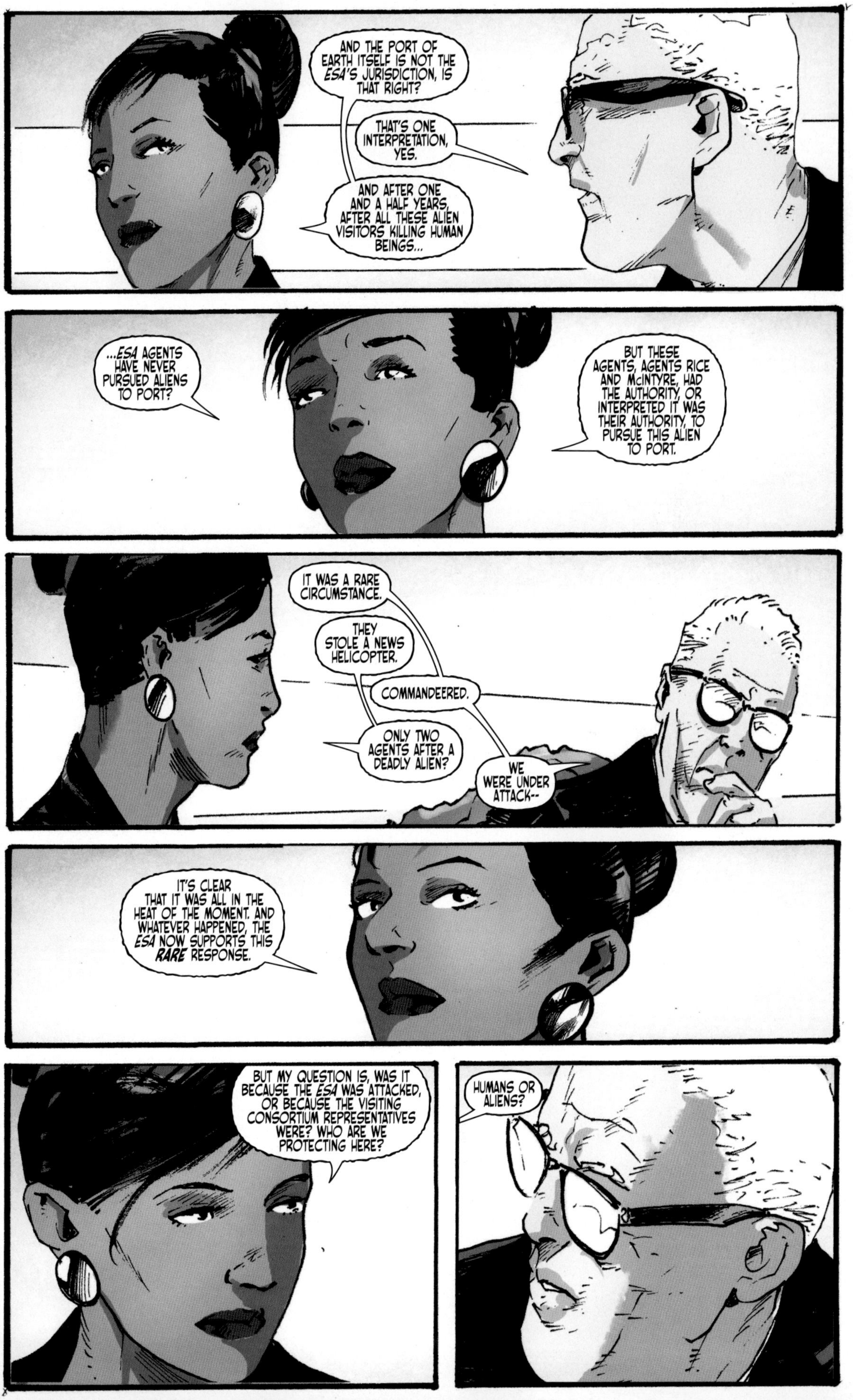
AND THE PORT OF EARTH ITSELF IS NOT THE *ESA*'S JURISDICTION, IS THAT RIGHT?
THAT'S ONE INTERPRETATION, YES.
AND AFTER ONE AND A HALF YEARS, AFTER ALL THESE ALIEN VISITORS KILLING HUMAN BEINGS...
...*ESA* AGENTS HAVE NEVER PURSUED ALIENS TO PORT?
BUT THESE AGENTS, AGENTS RICE AND McINTYRE, HAD THE AUTHORITY, OR INTERPRETED IT WAS THEIR AUTHORITY, TO PURSUE THIS ALIEN TO PORT.
IT WAS A RARE CIRCUMSTANCE.
THEY STOLE A NEWS HELICOPTER.
COMMANDEERED.
ONLY TWO AGENTS AFTER A DEADLY ALIEN?
WE WERE UNDER ATTACK--
IT'S CLEAR THAT IT WAS ALL IN THE HEAT OF THE MOMENT. AND WHATEVER HAPPENED, THE *ESA* NOW SUPPORTS THIS ***RARE*** RESPONSE.
BUT MY QUESTION IS, WAS IT BECAUSE THE *ESA* WAS ATTACKED, OR BECAUSE THE VISITING CONSORTIUM REPRESENTATIVES WERE? WHO ARE WE PROTECTING HERE?
HUMANS OR ALIENS?

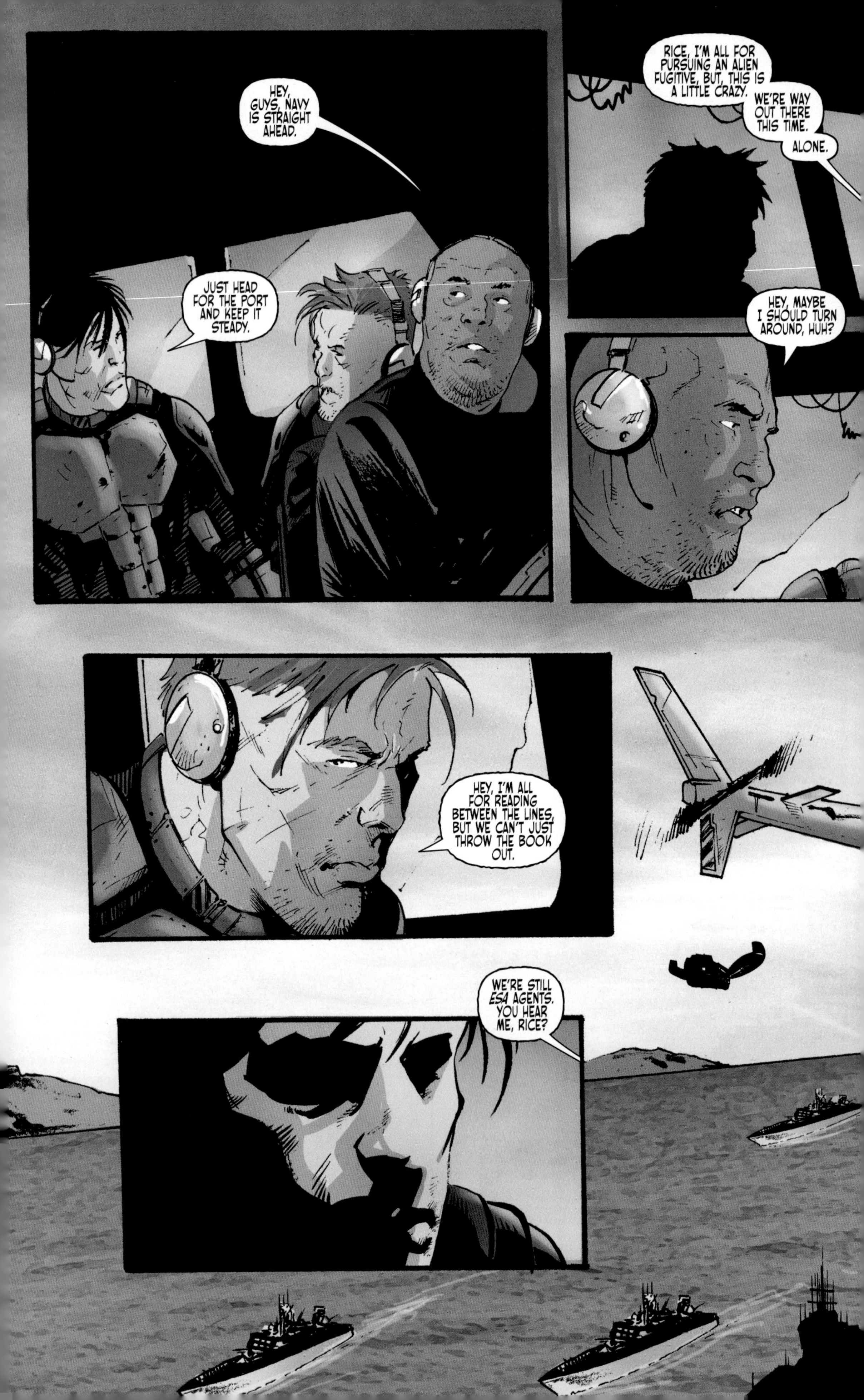
HEY, GUYS, NAVY IS STRAIGHT AHEAD.
JUST HEAD FOR THE PORT AND KEEP IT STEADY.
RICE, I'M ALL FOR PURSUING AN ALIEN FUGITIVE, BUT, THIS IS A LITTLE CRAZY.
WE'RE WAY OUT THERE THIS TIME.
ALONE.
HEY, MAYBE I SHOULD TURN AROUND, HUH?
HEY, I'M ALL FOR READING BETWEEN THE LINES, BUT WE CAN'T JUST THROW THE BOOK OUT.
WE'RE STILL *ESA* AGENTS. YOU HEAR ME, RICE?

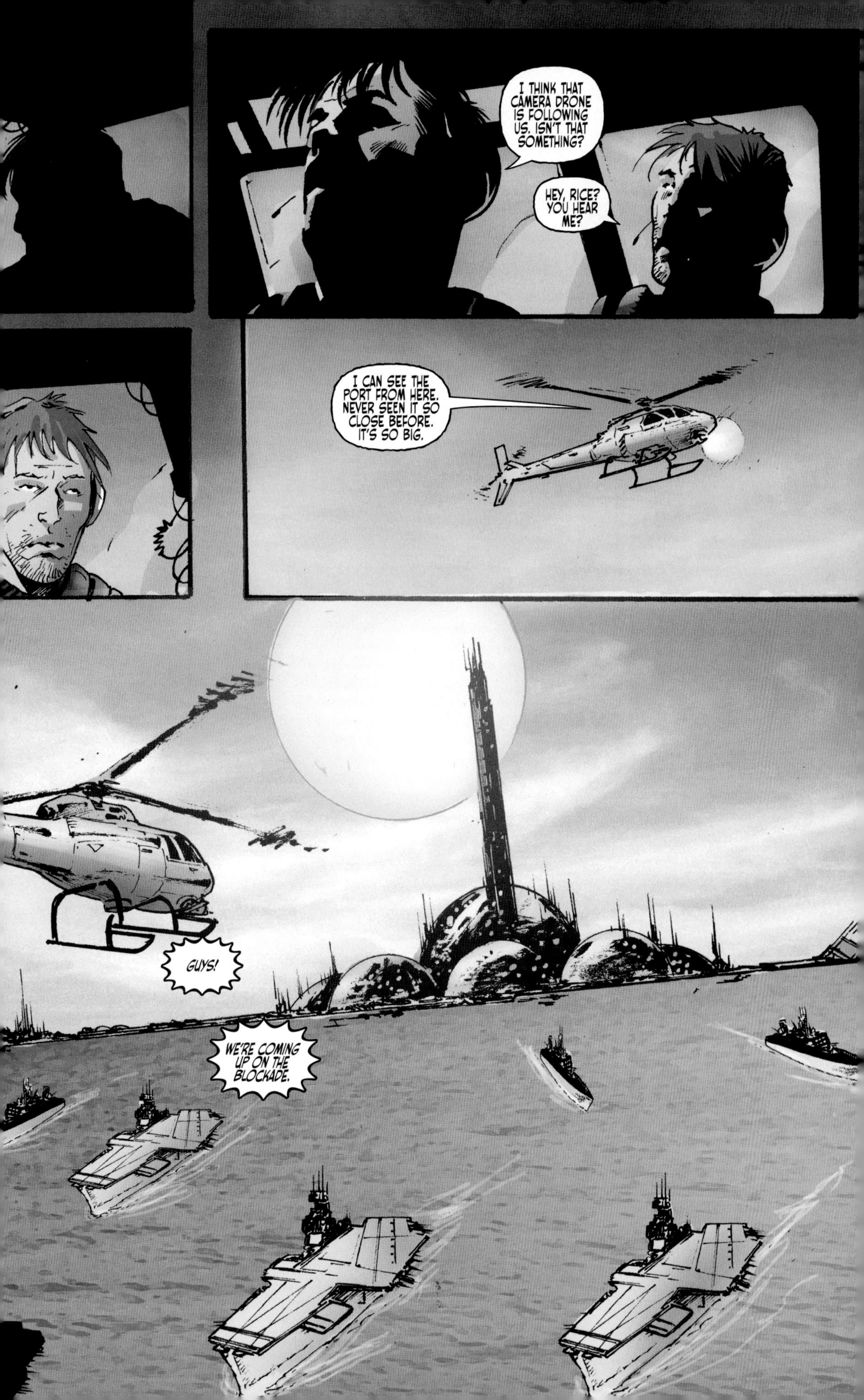
I THINK THAT CAMERA DRONE IS FOLLOWING US. ISN'T THAT SOMETHING?
HEY, RICE? YOU HEAR ME?
I CAN SEE THE PORT FROM HERE. NEVER SEEN IT SO CLOSE BEFORE. IT'S SO BIG.
GUYS!
WE'RE COMING UP ON THE BLOCKADE.

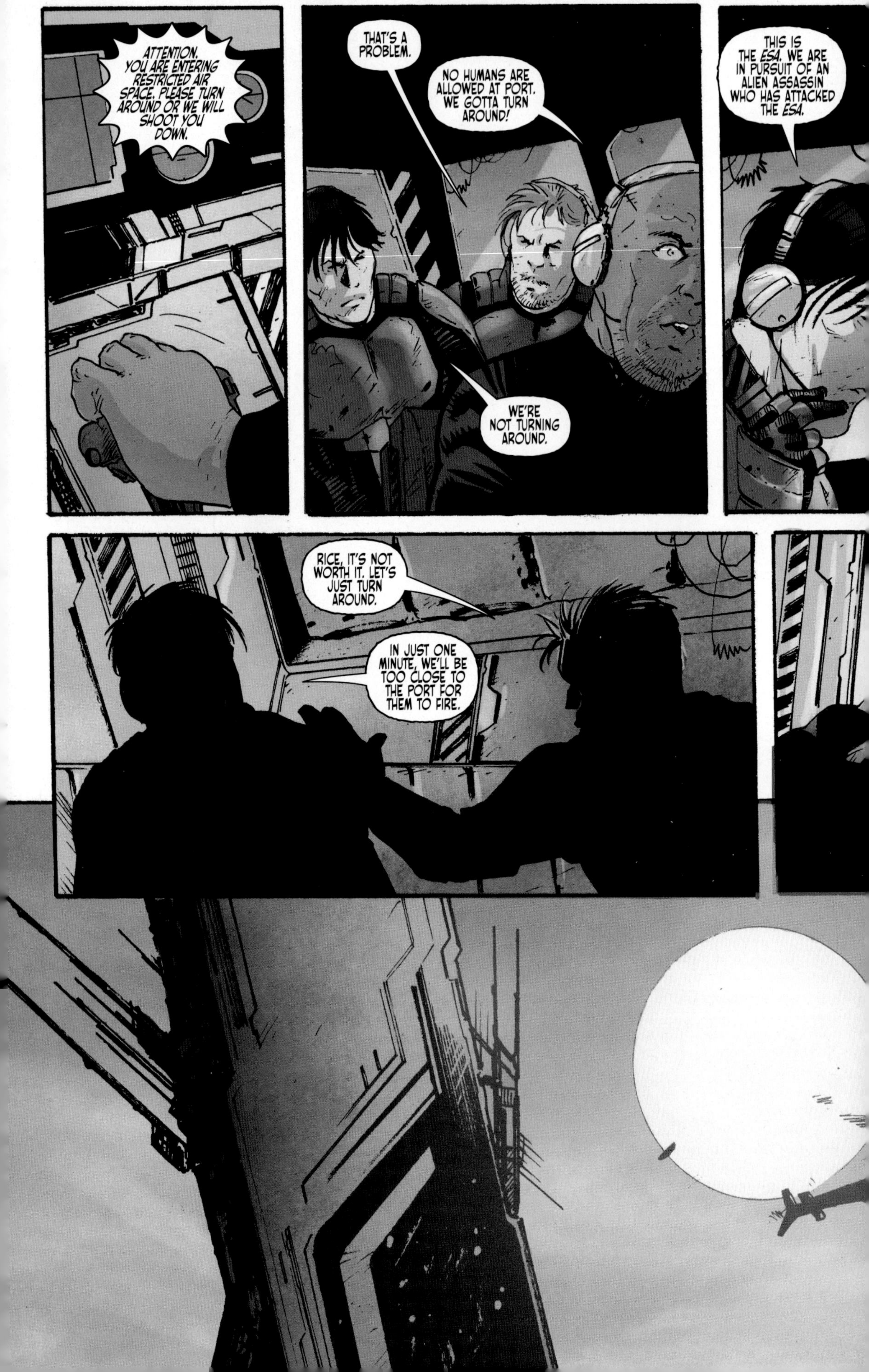
ATTENTION. YOU ARE ENTERING RESTRICTED AIR SPACE. PLEASE TURN AROUND OR WE WILL SHOOT YOU DOWN.
THAT'S A PROBLEM.
NO HUMANS ARE ALLOWED AT PORT. WE GOTTA TURN AROUND!
WE'RE NOT TURNING AROUND.
THIS IS THE ESA. WE ARE IN PURSUIT OF AN ALIEN ASSASSIN WHO HAS ATTACKED THE ESA.
RICE, IT'S NOT WORTH IT. LET'S JUST TURN AROUND.
IN JUST ONE MINUTE, WE'LL BE TOO CLOSE TO THE PORT FOR THEM TO FIRE.

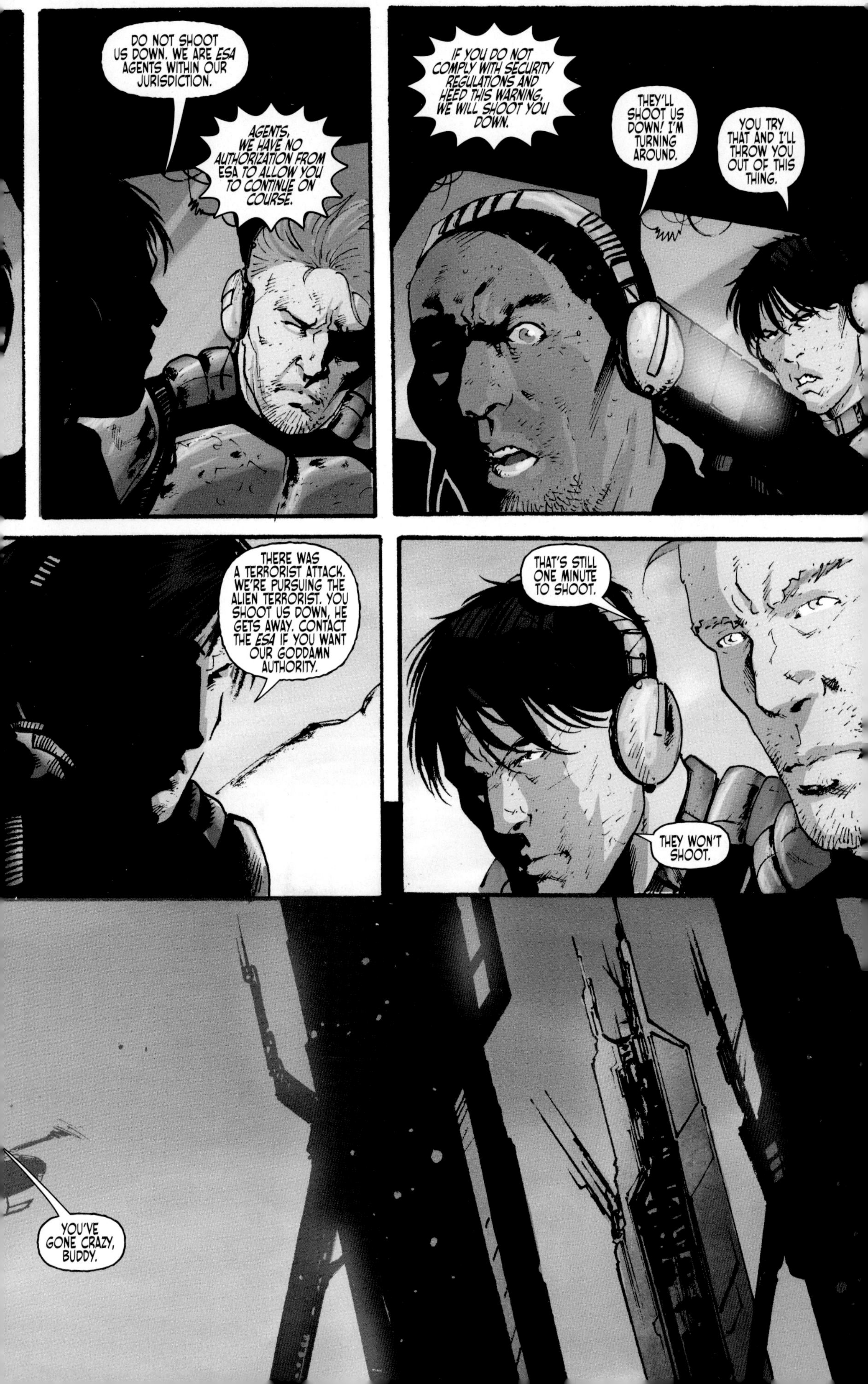

DO NOT SHOOT US DOWN. WE ARE ESA AGENTS WITHIN OUR JURISDICTION.
AGENTS, WE HAVE NO AUTHORIZATION FROM ESA TO ALLOW YOU TO CONTINUE ON COURSE.
IF YOU DO NOT COMPLY WITH SECURITY REGULATIONS AND HEED THIS WARNING, WE WILL SHOOT YOU DOWN.
THEY'LL SHOOT US DOWN! I'M TURNING AROUND.
YOU TRY THAT AND I'LL THROW YOU OUT OF THIS THING.
THERE WAS A TERRORIST ATTACK. WE'RE PURSUING THE ALIEN TERRORIST. YOU SHOOT US DOWN, HE GETS AWAY. CONTACT THE ESA IF YOU WANT OUR GODDAMN AUTHORITY.
THAT'S STILL ONE MINUTE TO SHOOT.
THEY WON'T SHOOT.
YOU'VE GONE CRAZY, BUDDY.

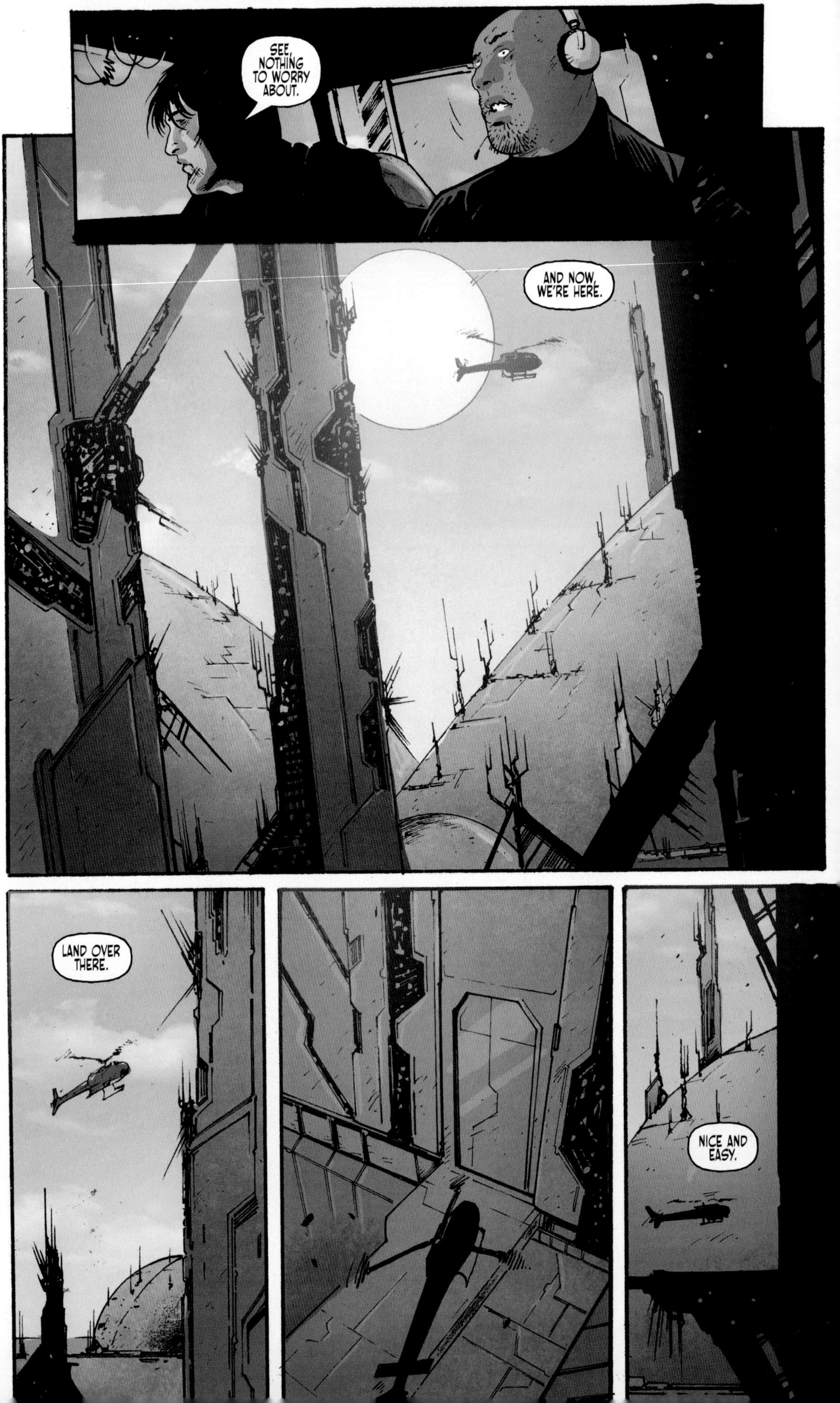
SEE, NOTHING TO WORRY ABOUT.
AND NOW, WE'RE HERE.
LAND OVER THERE.
NICE AND EASY.

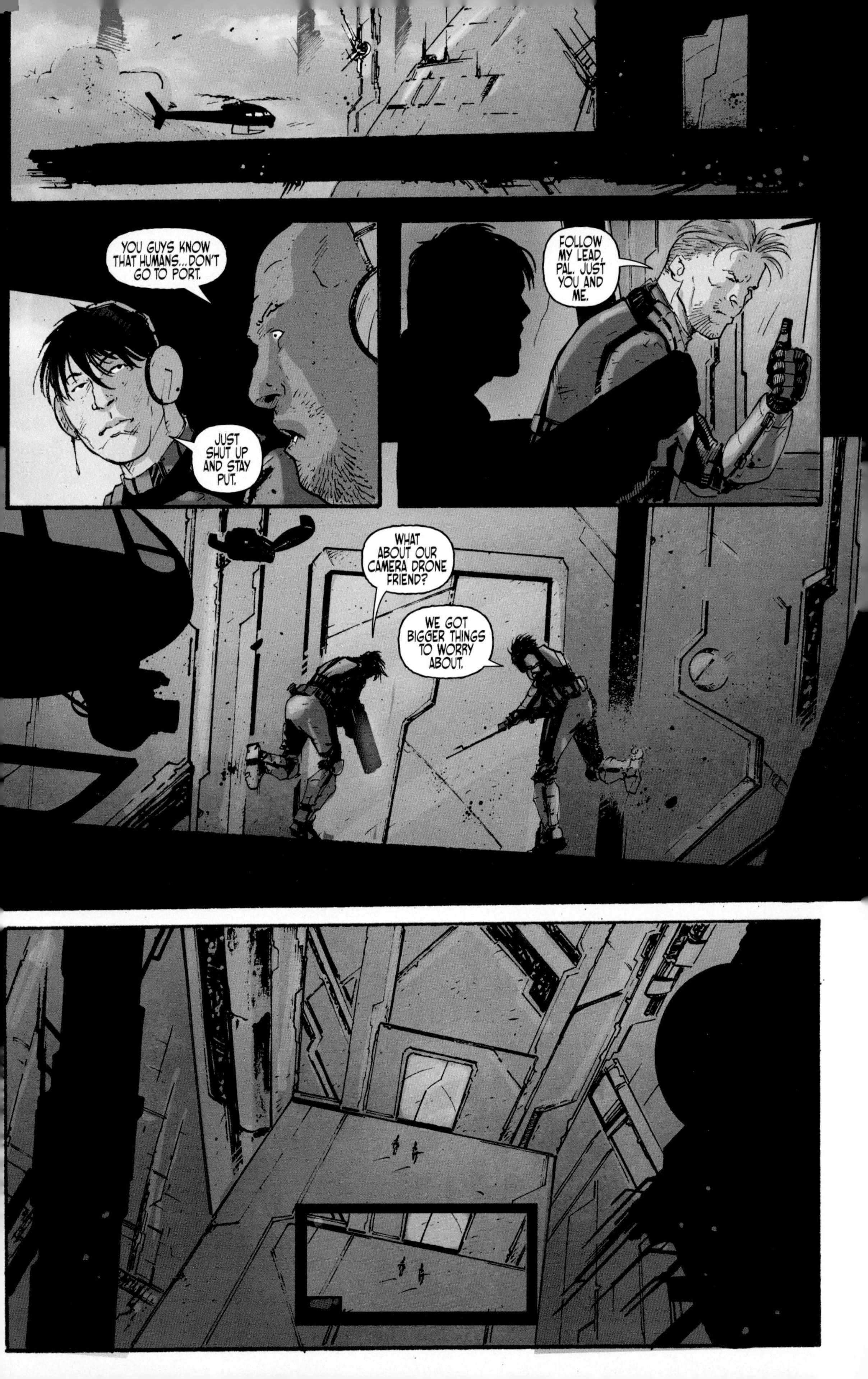
YOU GUYS KNOW THAT HUMANS...DON'T GO TO PORT.
JUST SHUT UP AND STAY PUT.
FOLLOW MY LEAD, PAL. JUST YOU AND ME.
WHAT ABOUT OUR CAMERA DRONE FRIEND?
WE GOT BIGGER THINGS TO WORRY ABOUT.

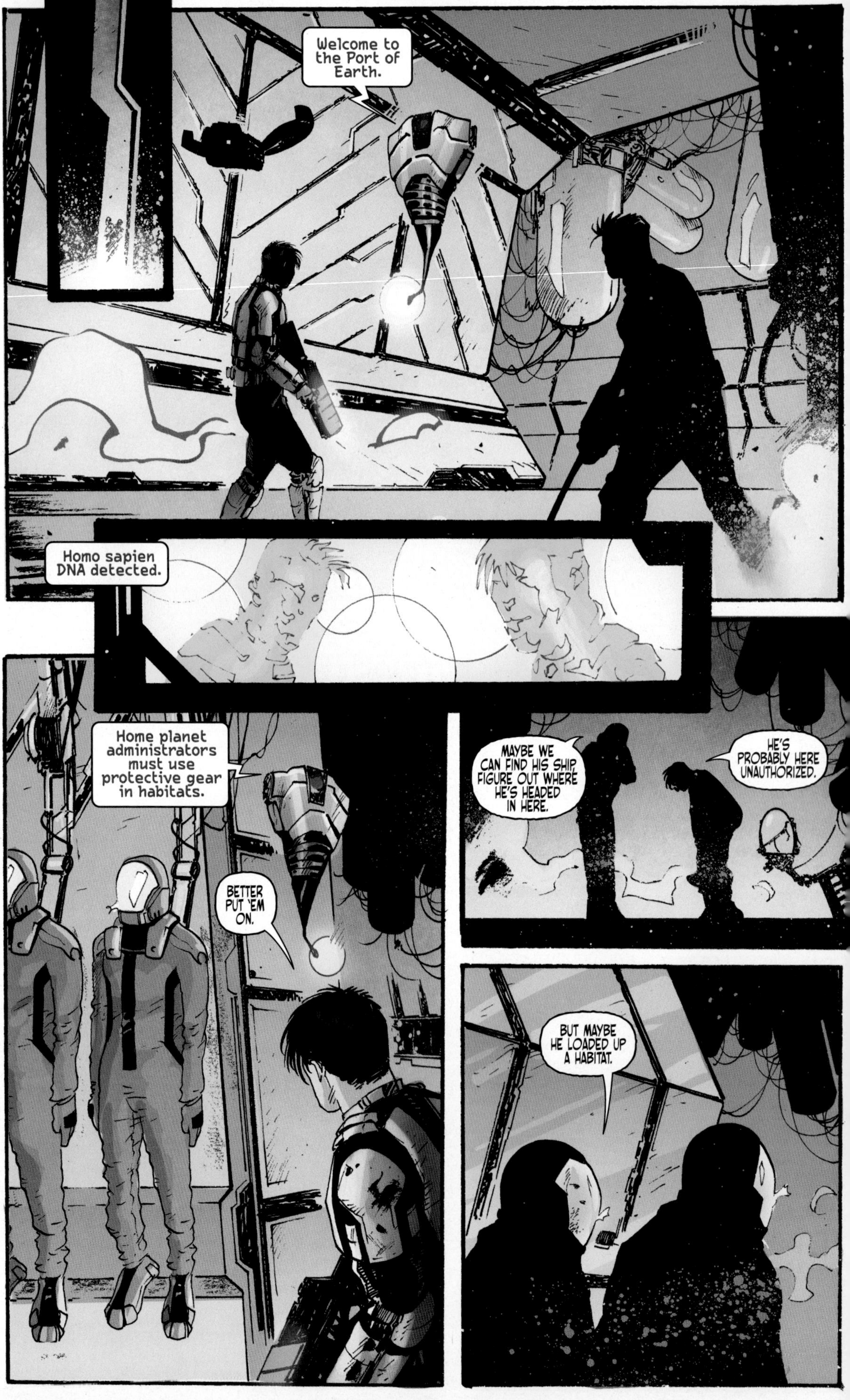
Welcome to the Port of Earth.
Homo sapien DNA detected.
Home planet administrators must use protective gear in habitats.
BETTER PUT 'EM ON.
MAYBE WE CAN FIND HIS SHIP FIGURE OUT WHERE HE'S HEADED IN HERE.
HE'S PROBABLY HERE UNAUTHORIZED.
BUT MAYBE HE LOADED UP A HABITAT.

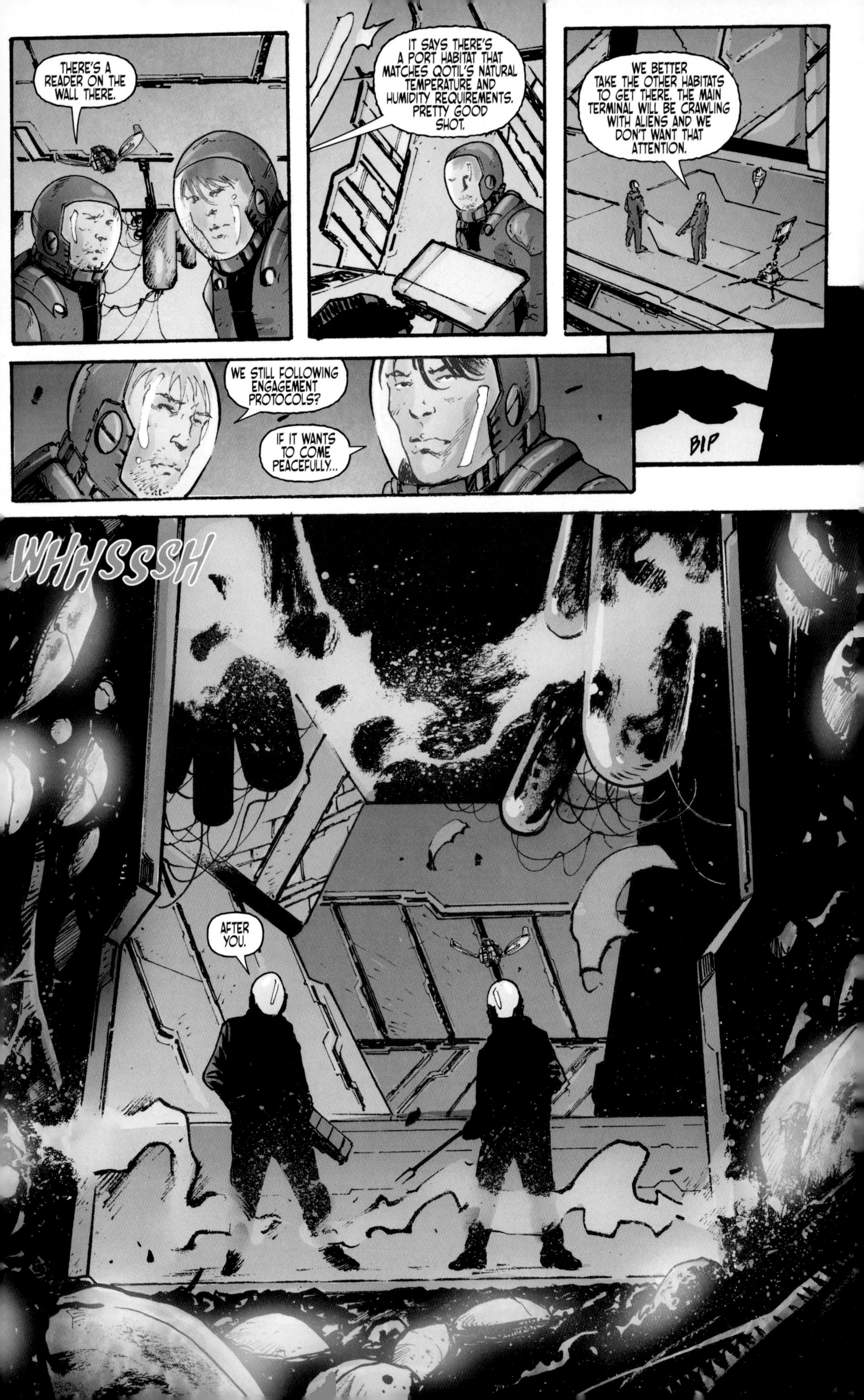
THERE'S A READER ON THE WALL THERE.
IT SAYS THERE'S A PORT HABITAT THAT MATCHES QOTIL'S NATURAL TEMPERATURE AND HUMIDITY REQUIREMENTS. PRETTY GOOD SHOT.
WE BETTER TAKE THE OTHER HABITATS TO GET THERE. THE MAIN TERMINAL WILL BE CRAWLING WITH ALIENS AND WE DON'T WANT THAT ATTENTION.
WE STILL FOLLOWING ENGAGEMENT PROTOCOLS?
IF IT WANTS TO COME PEACEFULLY...
BIP
WHHSSSH
AFTER YOU.

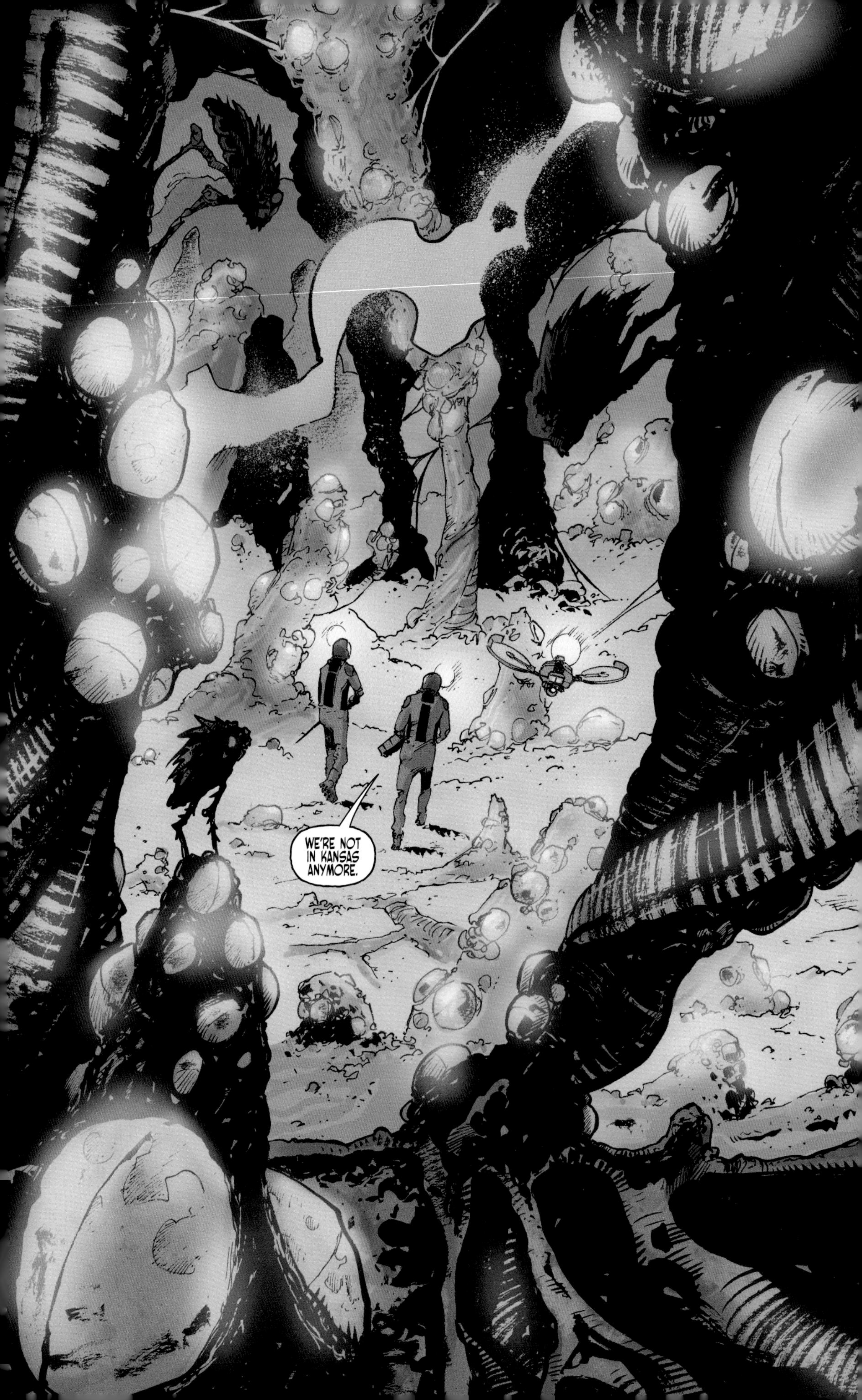
WE'RE NOT IN KANSAS ANYMORE.

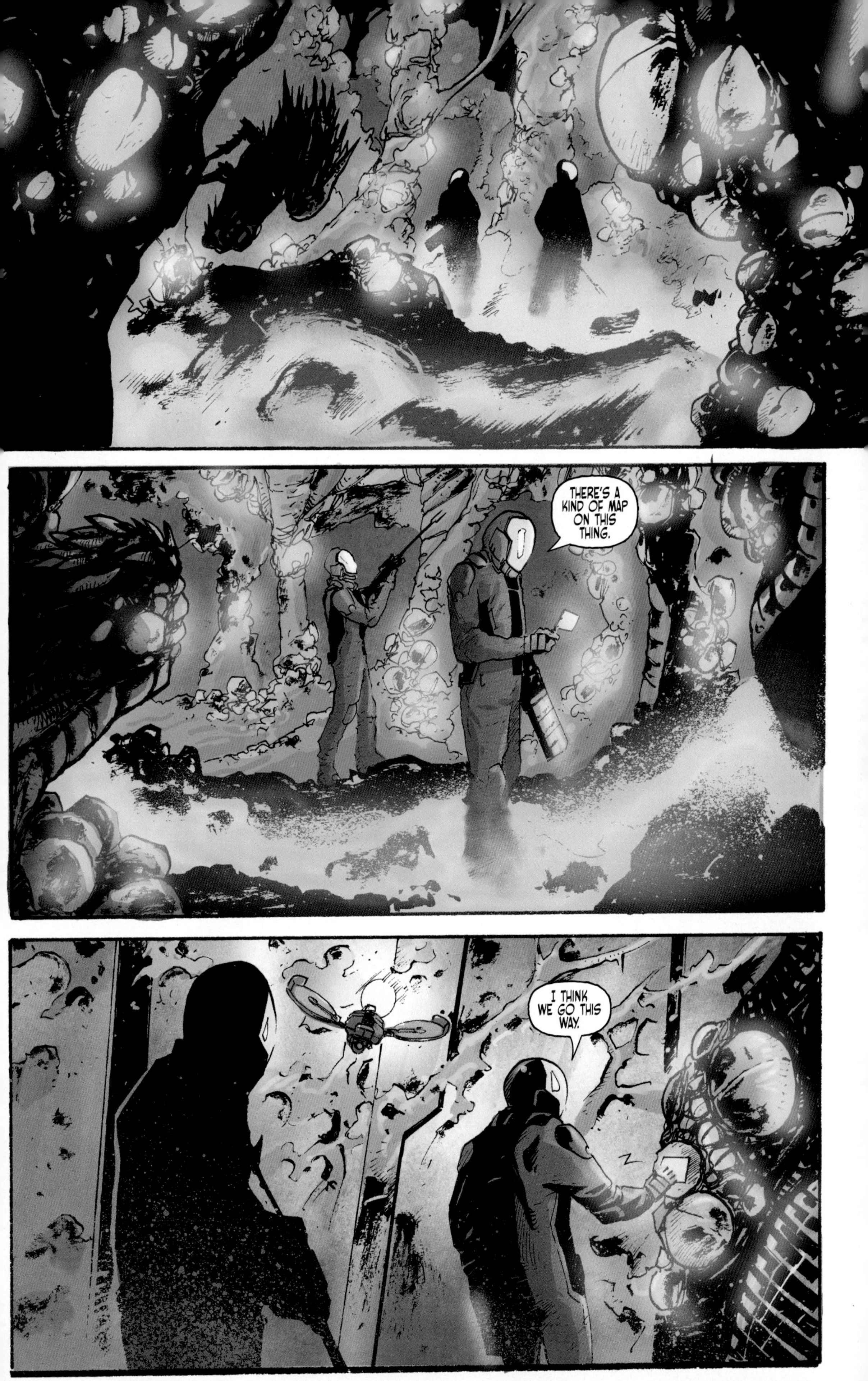
THERE'S A KIND OF MAP ON THIS THING.
I THINK WE GO THIS WAY.

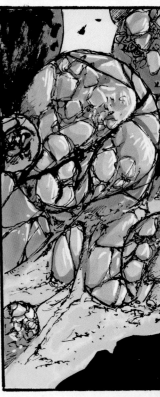

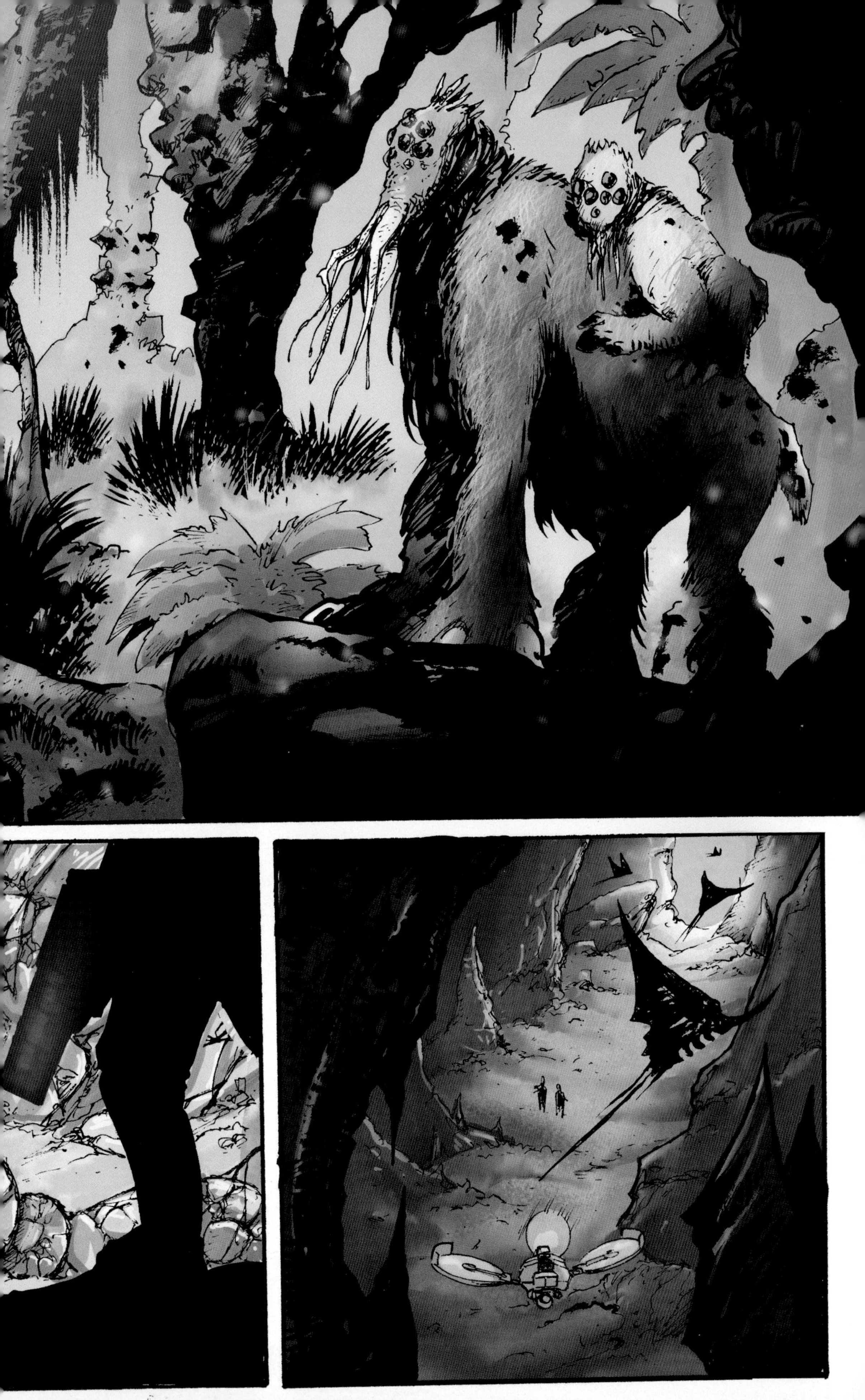

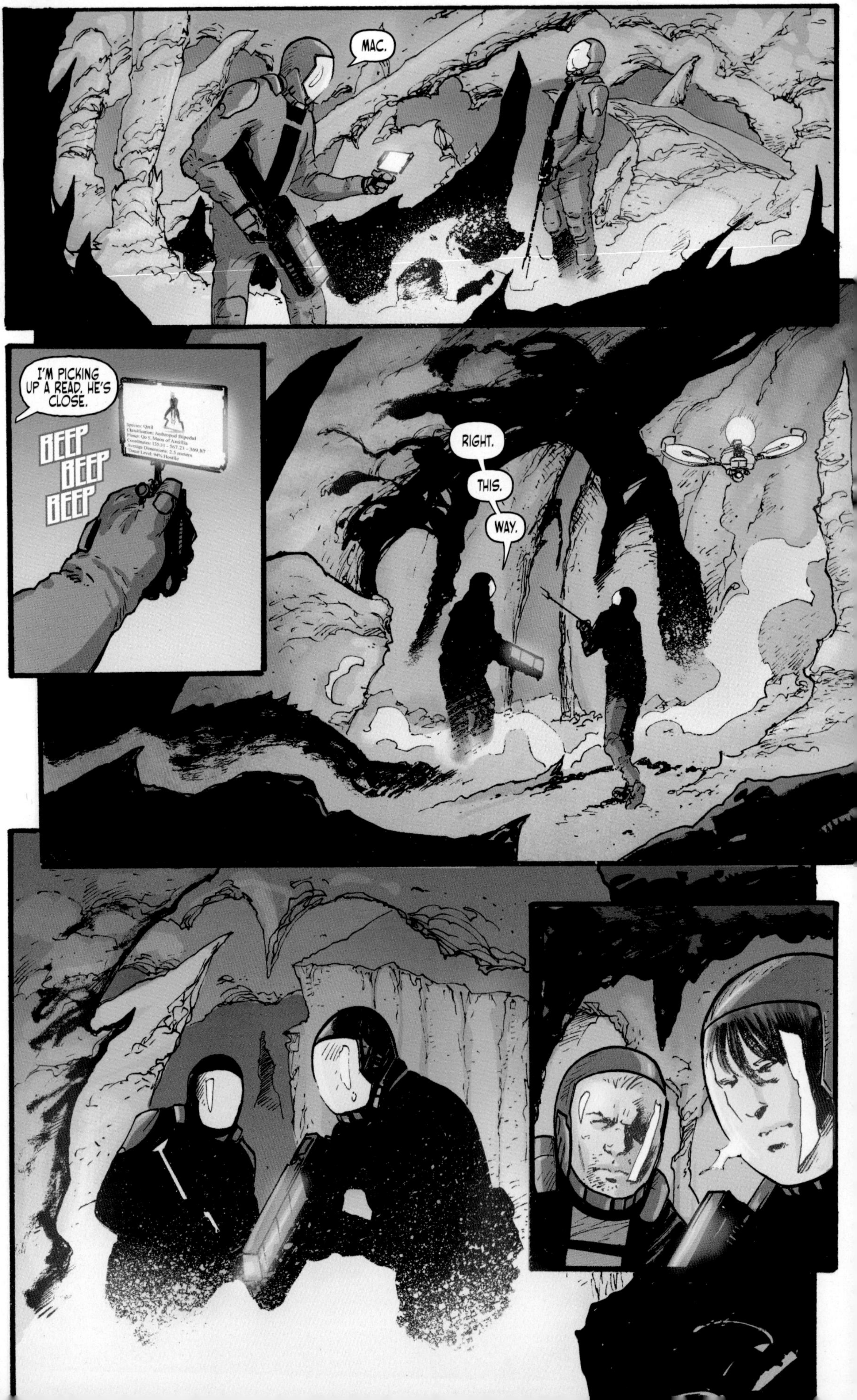
MAC.
I'M PICKING UP A READ. HE'S CLOSE.
Species: Qoril
Classification: Anthropod Bipedal
Planet: Qo 5, Moon of Antillia
Coordinates: 135.31 - 567.23 - 369.87
Average Dimensions: 2.5 meters
Threat Level: 94% Hostile
BEEP BEEP BEEP
RIGHT.
THIS.
WAY.

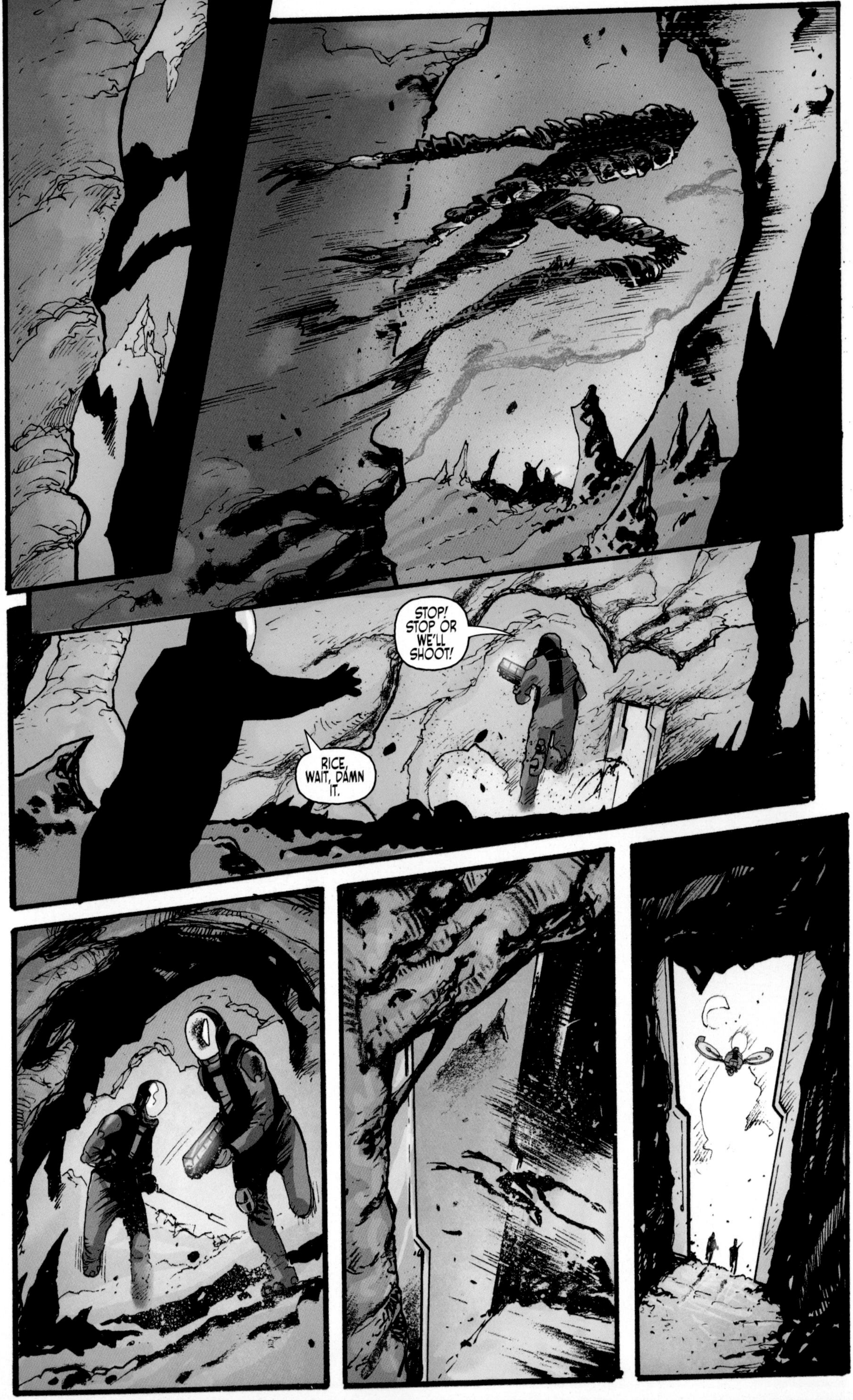
STOP! STOP OR WE'LL SHOOT!
RICE, WAIT, DAMN IT.

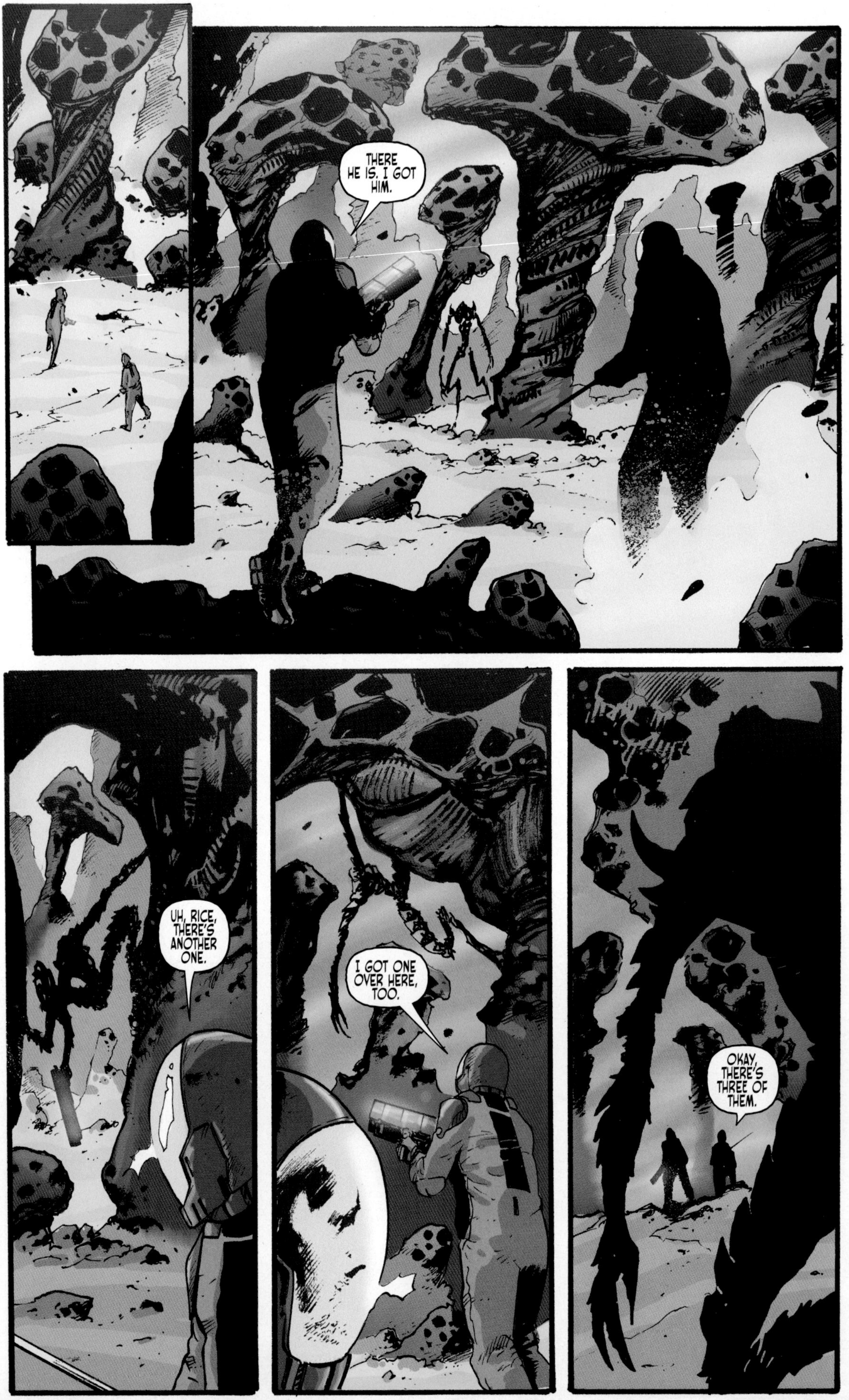
THERE HE IS. I GOT HIM.
UH, RICE, THERE'S ANOTHER ONE.
I GOT ONE OVER HERE, TOO.
OKAY, THERE'S THREE OF THEM.

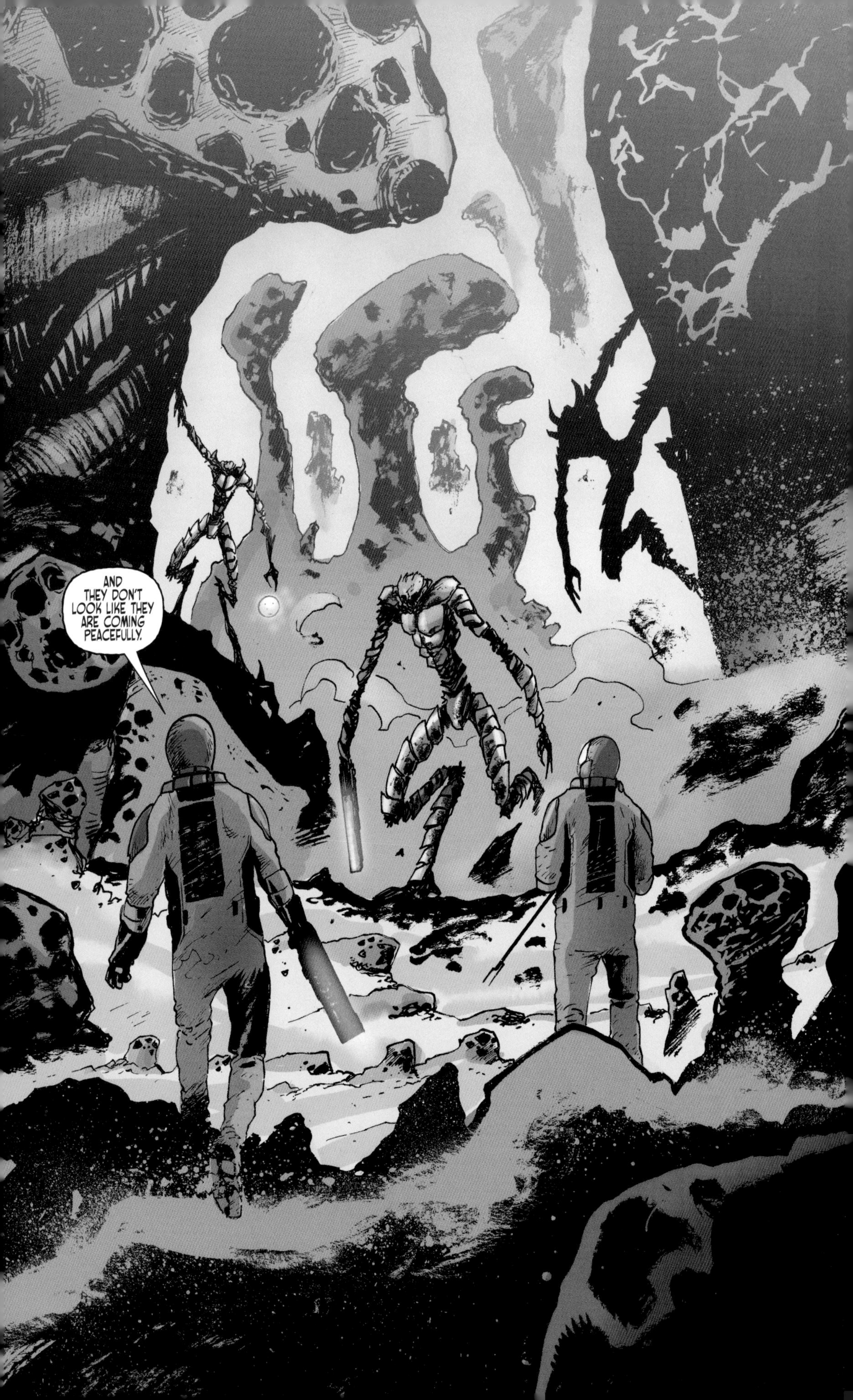
AND THEY DON'T LOOK LIKE THEY ARE COMING PEACEFULLY.

CHAPTER 8

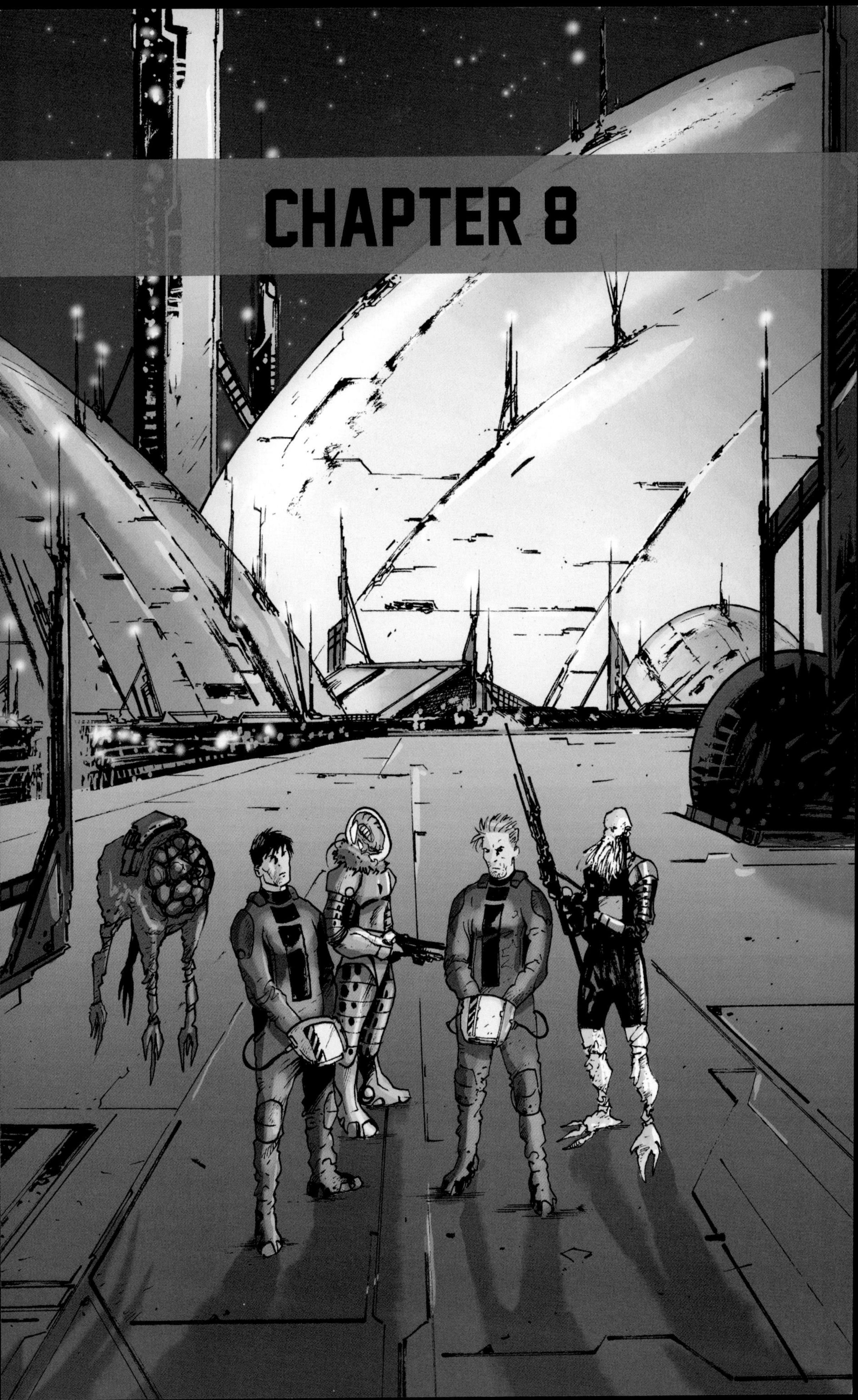

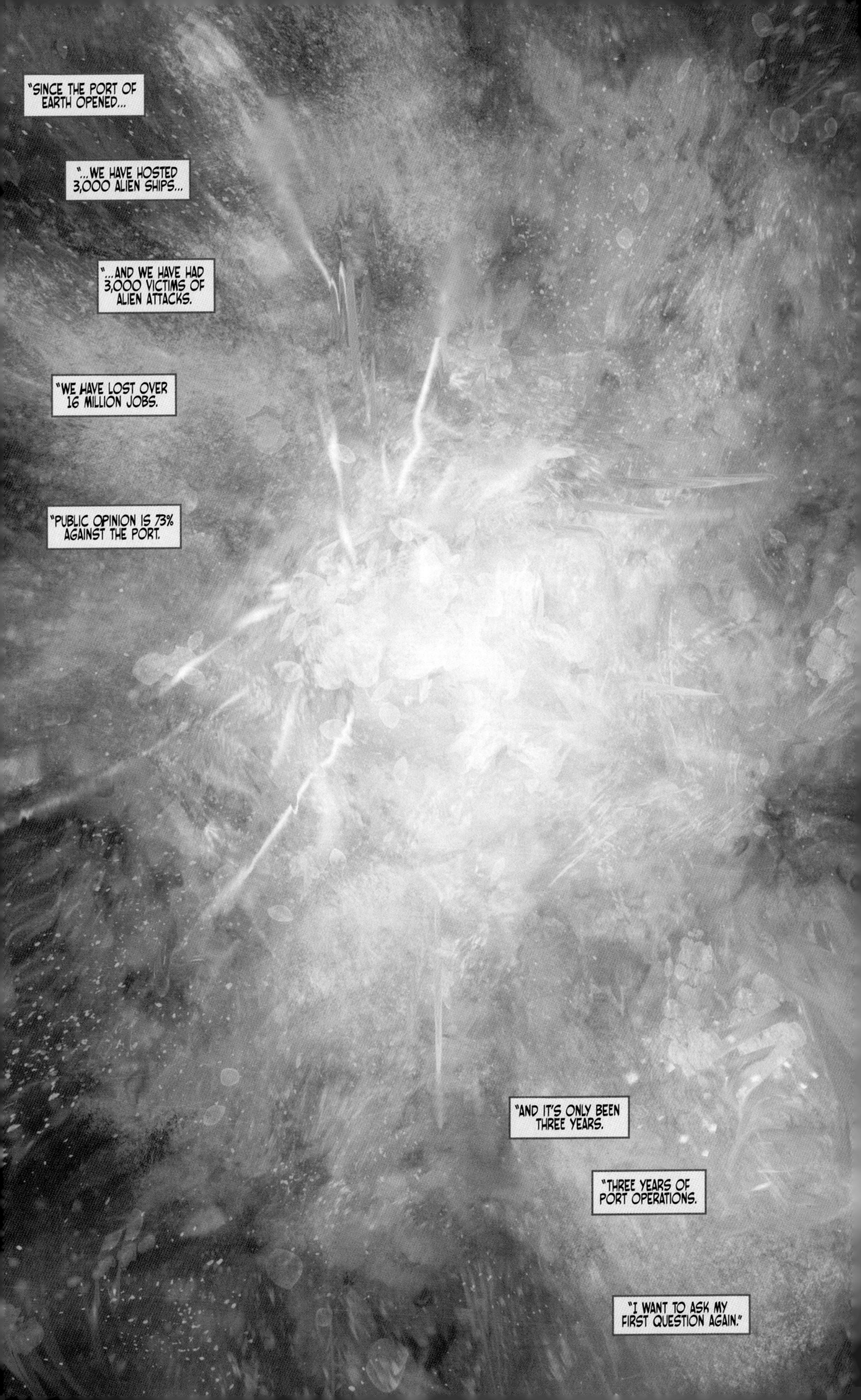
"SINCE THE PORT OF EARTH OPENED...
"...WE HAVE HOSTED 3,000 ALIEN SHIPS...
"...AND WE HAVE HAD 3,000 VICTIMS OF ALIEN ATTACKS.
"WE HAVE LOST OVER 16 MILLION JOBS.
"PUBLIC OPINION IS 73% AGAINST THE PORT.
"AND IT'S ONLY BEEN THREE YEARS.
"THREE YEARS OF PORT OPERATIONS.
"I WANT TO ASK MY FIRST QUESTION AGAIN."

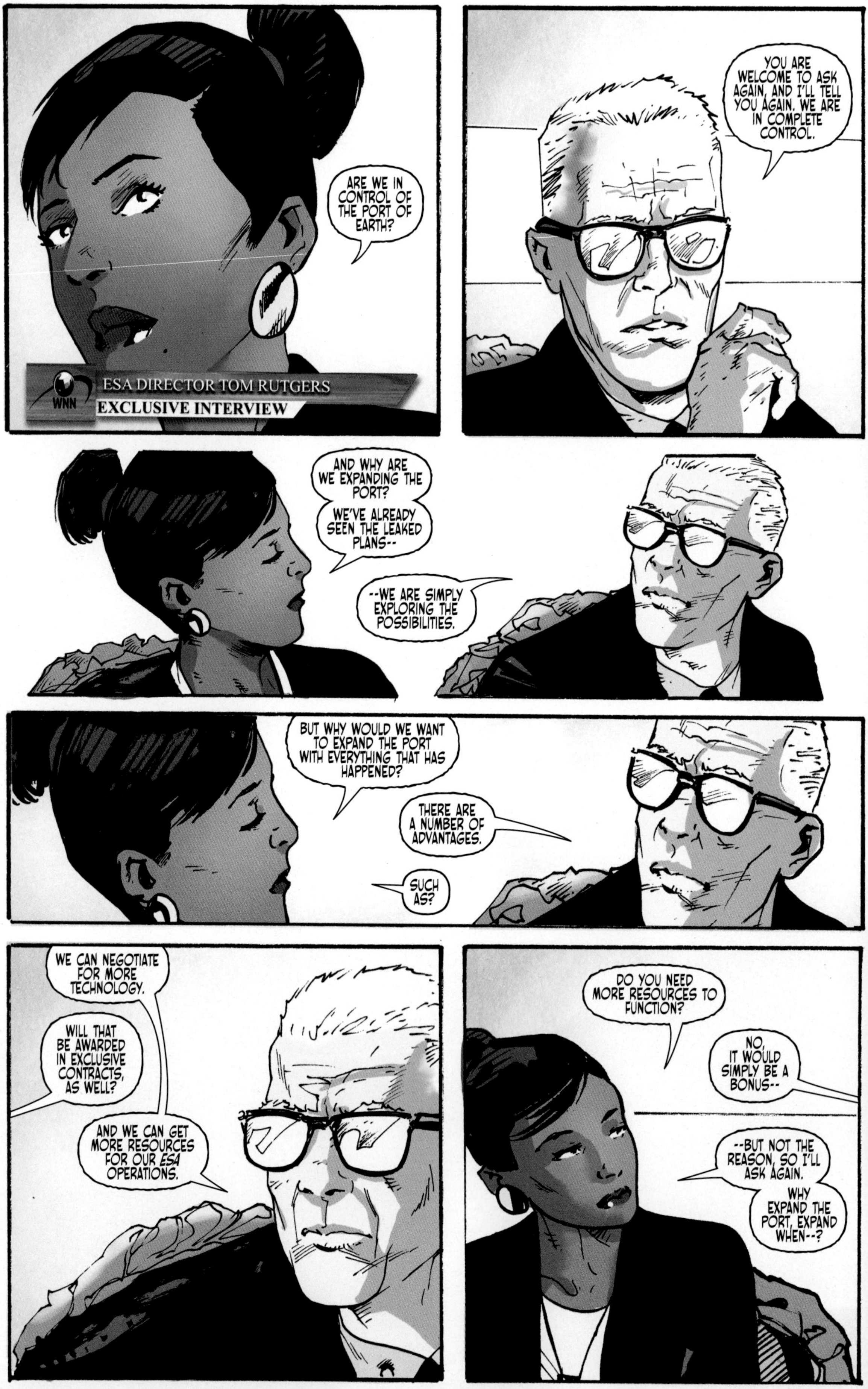

ARE WE IN CONTROL OF THE PORT OF EARTH?
ESA DIRECTOR TOM RUTGERS
WNN
EXCLUSIVE INTERVIEW
YOU ARE WELCOME TO ASK AGAIN, AND I'LL TELL YOU AGAIN. WE ARE IN COMPLETE CONTROL.
AND WHY ARE WE EXPANDING THE PORT?
WE'VE ALREADY SEEN THE LEAKED PLANS--
--WE ARE SIMPLY EXPLORING THE POSSIBILITIES.
BUT WHY WOULD WE WANT TO EXPAND THE PORT WITH EVERYTHING THAT HAS HAPPENED?
THERE ARE A NUMBER OF ADVANTAGES.
SUCH AS?
WE CAN NEGOTIATE FOR MORE TECHNOLOGY.
WILL THAT BE AWARDED IN EXCLUSIVE CONTRACTS, AS WELL?
AND WE CAN GET MORE RESOURCES FOR OUR ESA OPERATIONS.
DO YOU NEED MORE RESOURCES TO FUNCTION?
NO, IT WOULD SIMPLY BE A BONUS--
--BUT NOT THE REASON, SO I'LL ASK AGAIN.
WHY EXPAND THE PORT, EXPAND WHEN--?

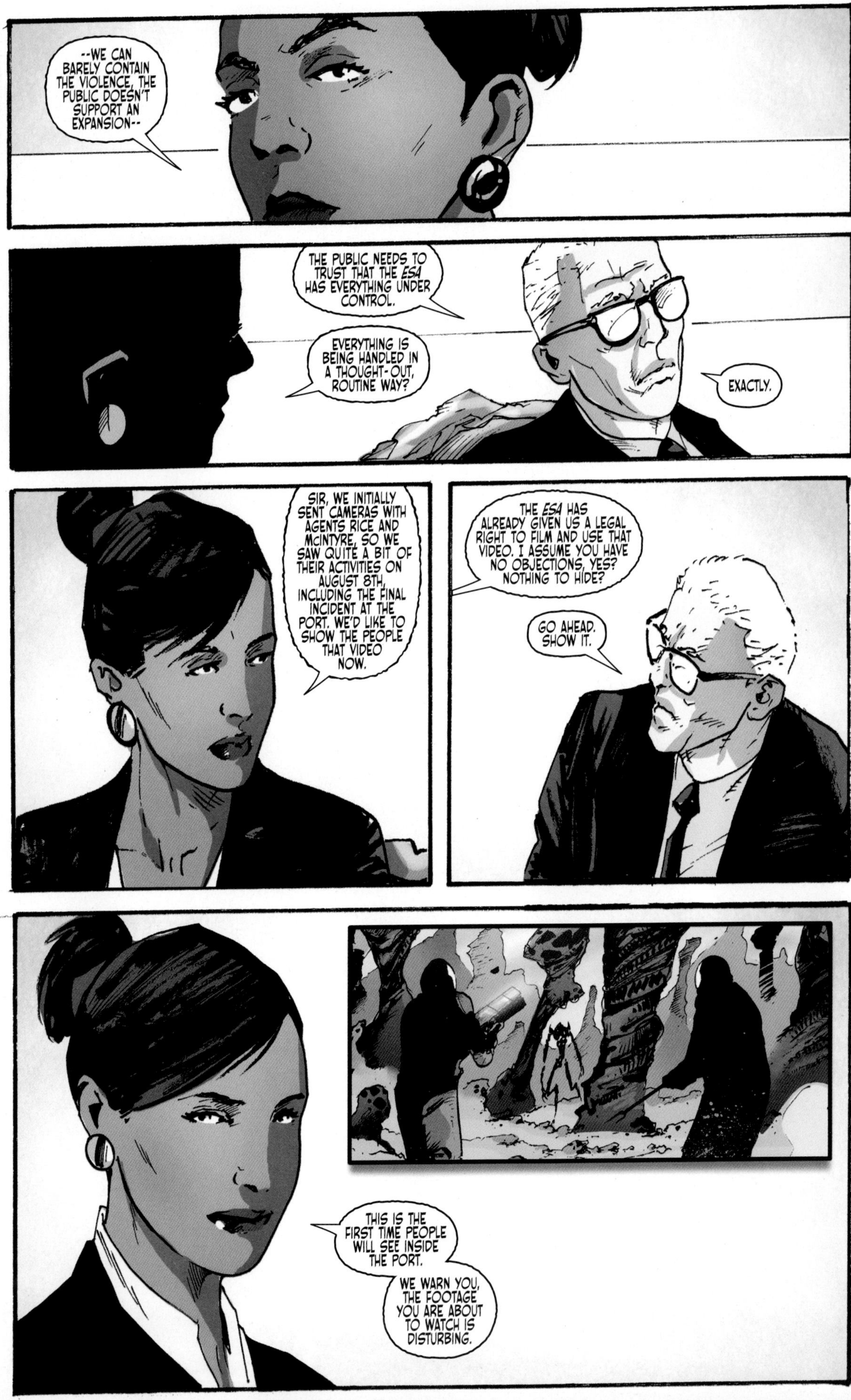
--WE CAN BARELY CONTAIN THE VIOLENCE, THE PUBLIC DOESN'T SUPPORT AN EXPANSION--
THE PUBLIC NEEDS TO TRUST THAT THE ESA HAS EVERYTHING UNDER CONTROL.
EVERYTHING IS BEING HANDLED IN A THOUGHT-OUT, ROUTINE WAY?
EXACTLY.
SIR, WE INITIALLY SENT CAMERAS WITH AGENTS RICE AND McINTYRE, SO WE SAW QUITE A BIT OF THEIR ACTIVITIES ON AUGUST 8TH, INCLUDING THE FINAL INCIDENT AT THE PORT. WE'D LIKE TO SHOW THE PEOPLE THAT VIDEO NOW.
THE ESA HAS ALREADY GIVEN US A LEGAL RIGHT TO FILM AND USE THAT VIDEO. I ASSUME YOU HAVE NO OBJECTIONS, YES? NOTHING TO HIDE?
GO AHEAD. SHOW IT.
THIS IS THE FIRST TIME PEOPLE WILL SEE INSIDE THE PORT.
WE WARN YOU, THE FOOTAGE YOU ARE ABOUT TO WATCH IS DISTURBING.

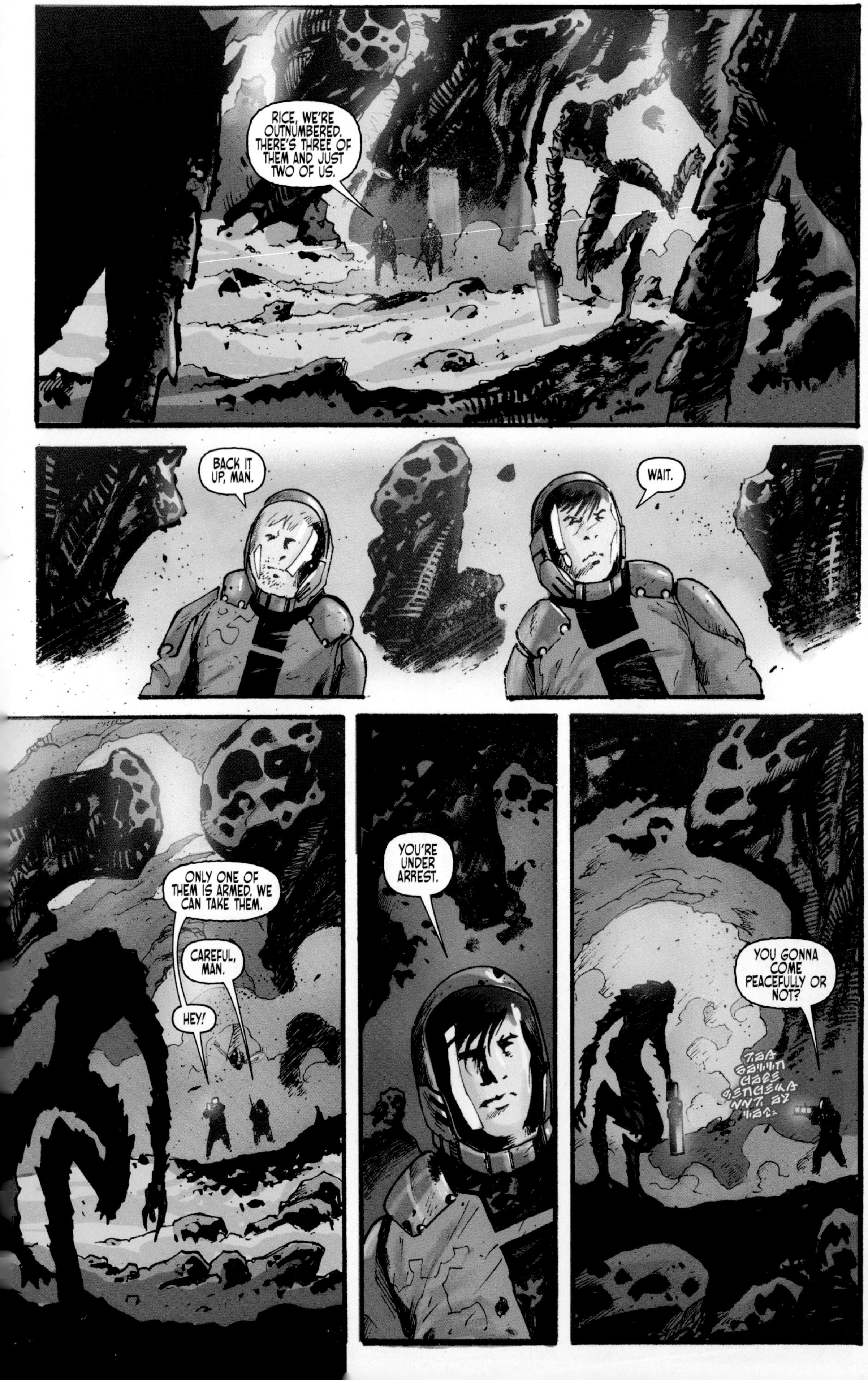
RICE, WE'RE OUTNUMBERED. THERE'S THREE OF THEM AND JUST TWO OF US.
BACK IT UP, MAN.
WAIT.
ONLY ONE OF THEM IS ARMED. WE CAN TAKE THEM.
CAREFUL, MAN.
HEY!
YOU'RE UNDER ARREST.
YOU GONNA COME PEACEFULLY OR NOT?

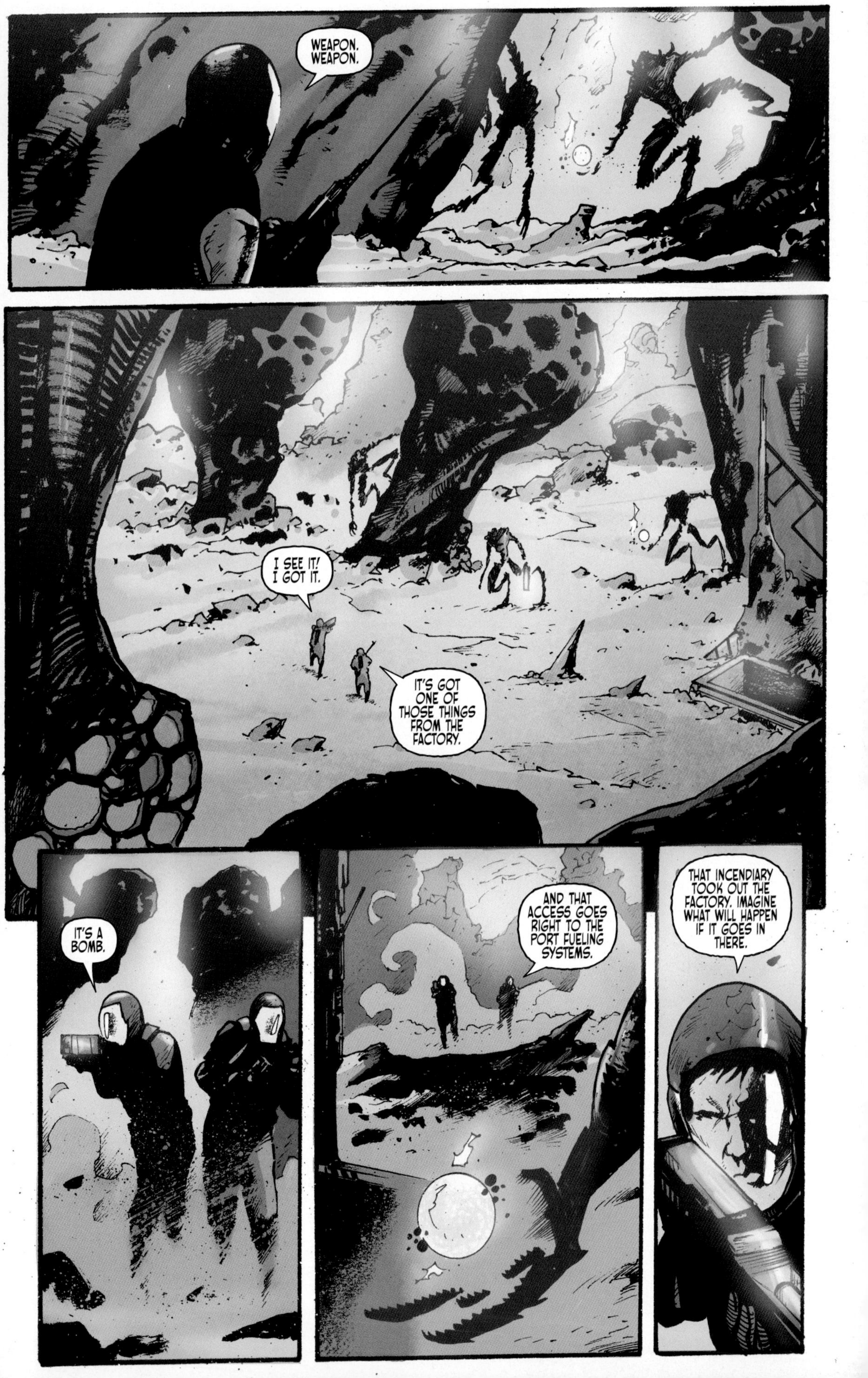
WEAPON. WEAPON.
I SEE IT! I GOT IT.
IT'S GOT ONE OF THOSE THINGS FROM THE FACTORY.
IT'S A BOMB.
AND THAT ACCESS GOES RIGHT TO THE PORT FUELING SYSTEMS.
THAT INCENDIARY TOOK OUT THE FACTORY. IMAGINE WHAT WILL HAPPEN IF IT GOES IN THERE.

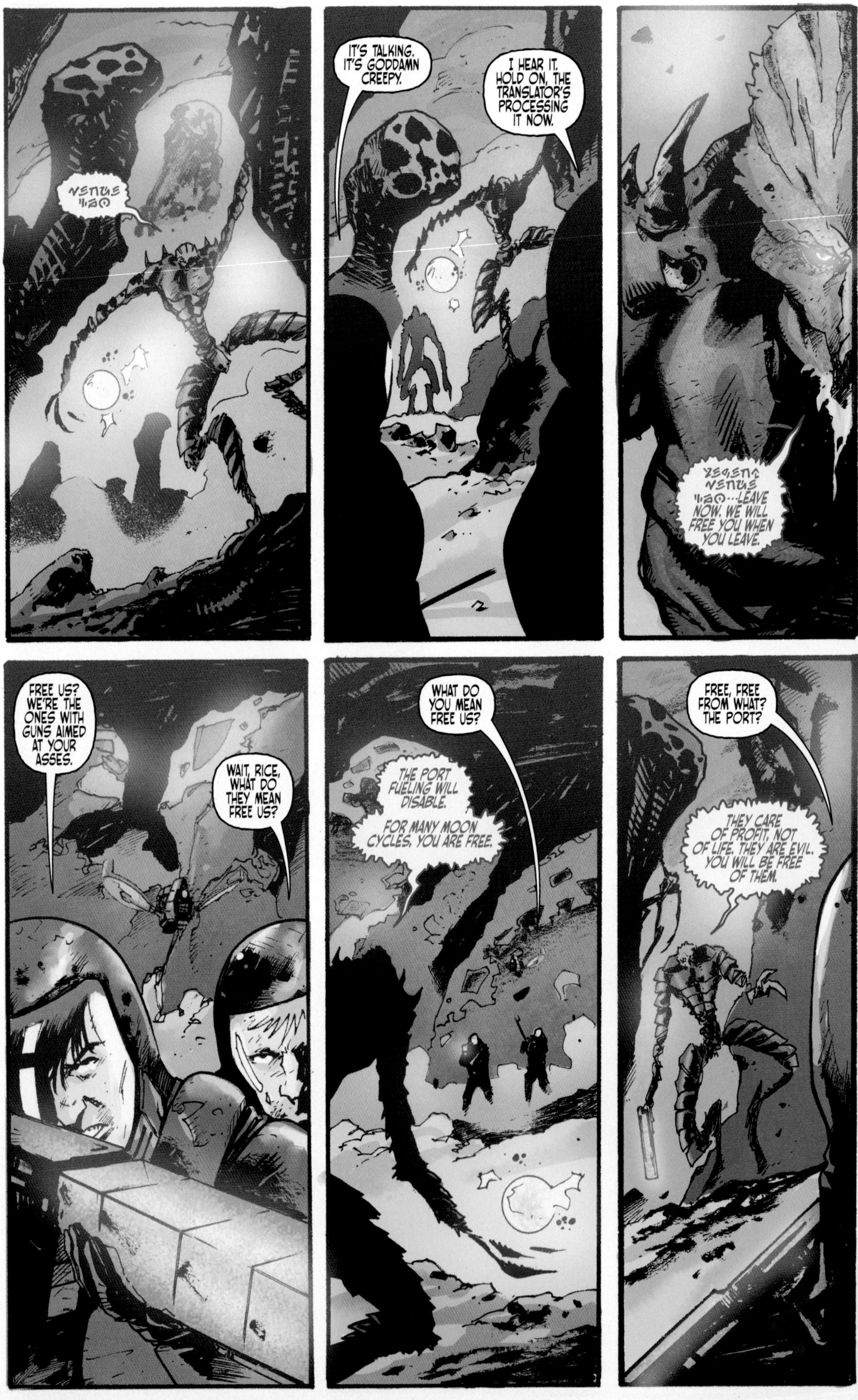
IT'S TALKING. IT'S GODDAMN CREEPY.
I HEAR IT. HOLD ON, THE TRANSLATOR'S PROCESSING IT NOW.
...LEAVE NOW. WE WILL FREE YOU WHEN YOU LEAVE.
FREE US? WE'RE THE ONES WITH GUNS AIMED AT YOUR ASSES.
WAIT, RICE, WHAT DO THEY MEAN FREE US?
WHAT DO YOU MEAN FREE US?
THE PORT FUELING WILL DISABLE.
FOR MANY MOON CYCLES, YOU ARE FREE.
FREE, FREE FROM WHAT? THE PORT?
THEY CARE OF PROFIT, NOT OF LIFE. THEY ARE EVIL. YOU WILL BE FREE OF THEM.

THEY'RE EVIL? YOU COME TO OUR HOME, KILL INNOCENT PEOPLE AND THEY'RE EVIL?

INNOCENTS DIE TO FREE YOU. KILL US AND THEY DIE FOR NOTHING.

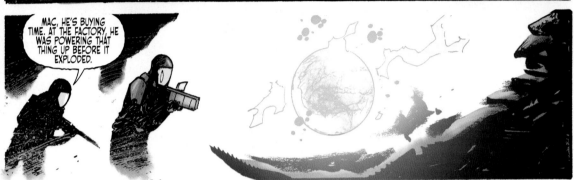

MAC, HE'S BUYING TIME. AT THE FACTORY, HE WAS POWERING THAT THING UP BEFORE IT EXPLODED.

THIS ONE ISN'T POWERED YET. I CAN STILL DROP HIM.

WE MUST HURRY. SOON THEY WILL NOT BE DISTRACTED. THIS IS YOUR TIME. HURRY.

WAIT, RICE.

WHAT DO YOU KNOW OF THE CONSORTIUM?

THEY CONTACT US WITH A DEAL. IT IS NOT A GOOD DEAL.

WHY? WHY NOT? WHAT HAPPENED?

OCCUPATION.

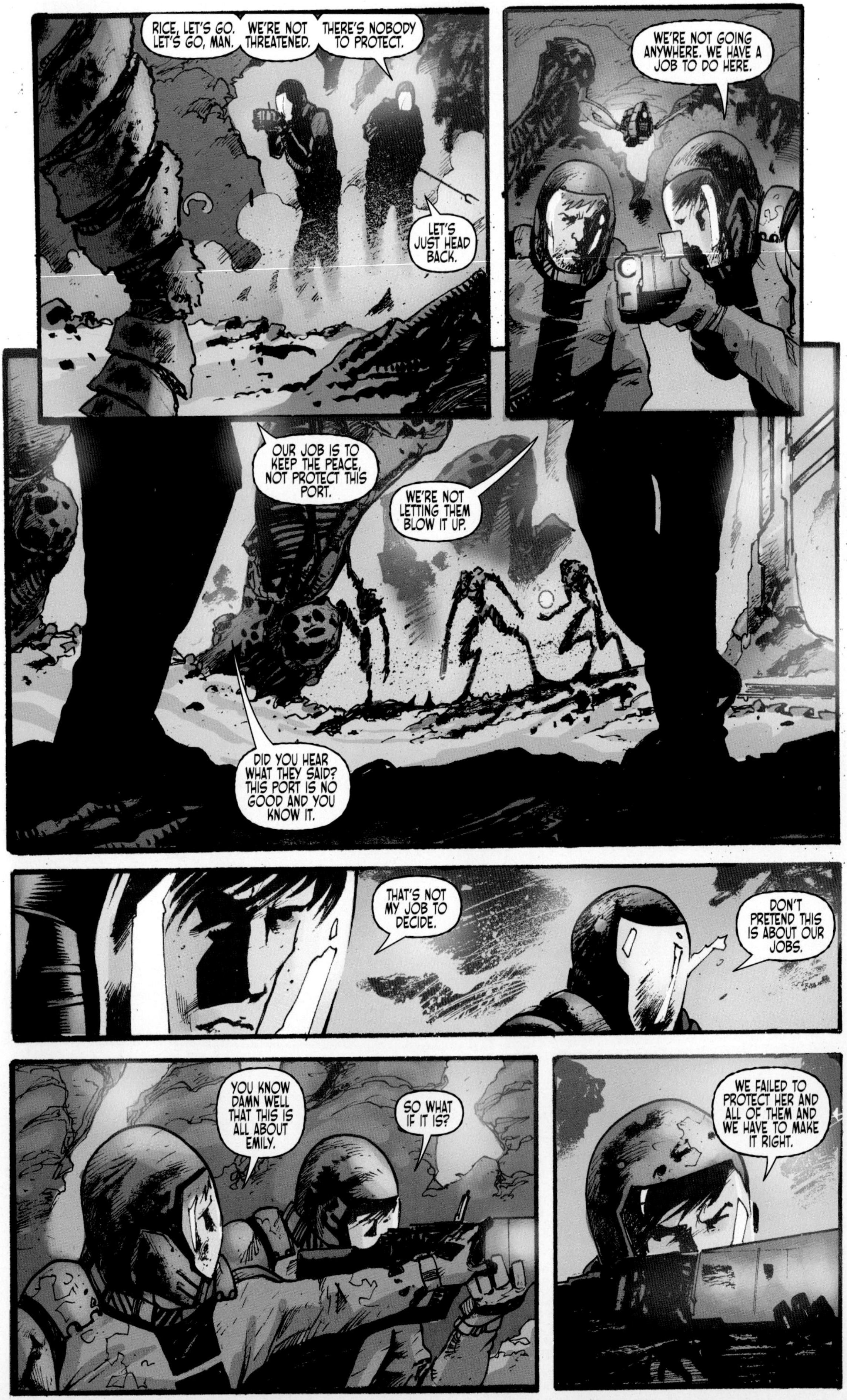
RICE, LET'S GO. LET'S GO, MAN.
WE'RE NOT THREATENED.
THERE'S NOBODY TO PROTECT.
LET'S JUST HEAD BACK.
WE'RE NOT GOING ANYWHERE. WE HAVE A JOB TO DO HERE.
OUR JOB IS TO KEEP THE PEACE, NOT PROTECT THIS PORT.
WE'RE NOT LETTING THEM BLOW IT UP.
DID YOU HEAR WHAT THEY SAID? THIS PORT IS NO GOOD AND YOU KNOW IT.
THAT'S NOT MY JOB TO DECIDE.
DON'T PRETEND THIS IS ABOUT OUR JOBS.
YOU KNOW DAMN WELL THAT THIS IS ALL ABOUT EMILY.
SO WHAT IF IT IS?
WE FAILED TO PROTECT HER AND ALL OF THEM AND WE HAVE TO MAKE IT RIGHT.

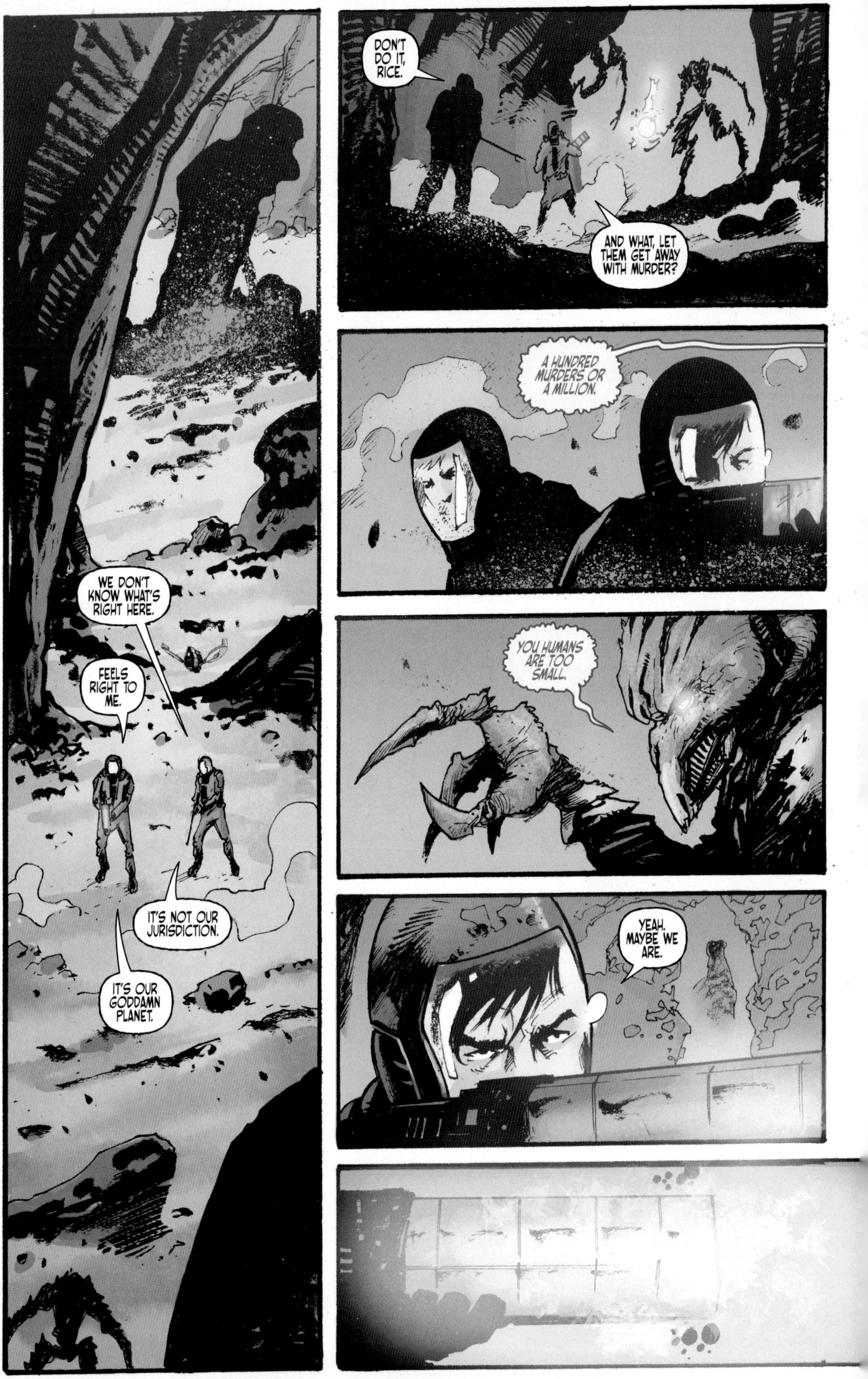
WE DON'T KNOW WHAT'S RIGHT HERE.
FEELS RIGHT TO ME.
IT'S NOT OUR JURISDICTION.
IT'S OUR GODDAMN PLANET.
DON'T DO IT, RICE.
AND WHAT, LET THEM GET AWAY WITH MURDER?
A HUNDRED MURDERS OR A MILLION.
YOU HUMANS ARE TOO SMALL.
YEAH. MAYBE WE ARE.

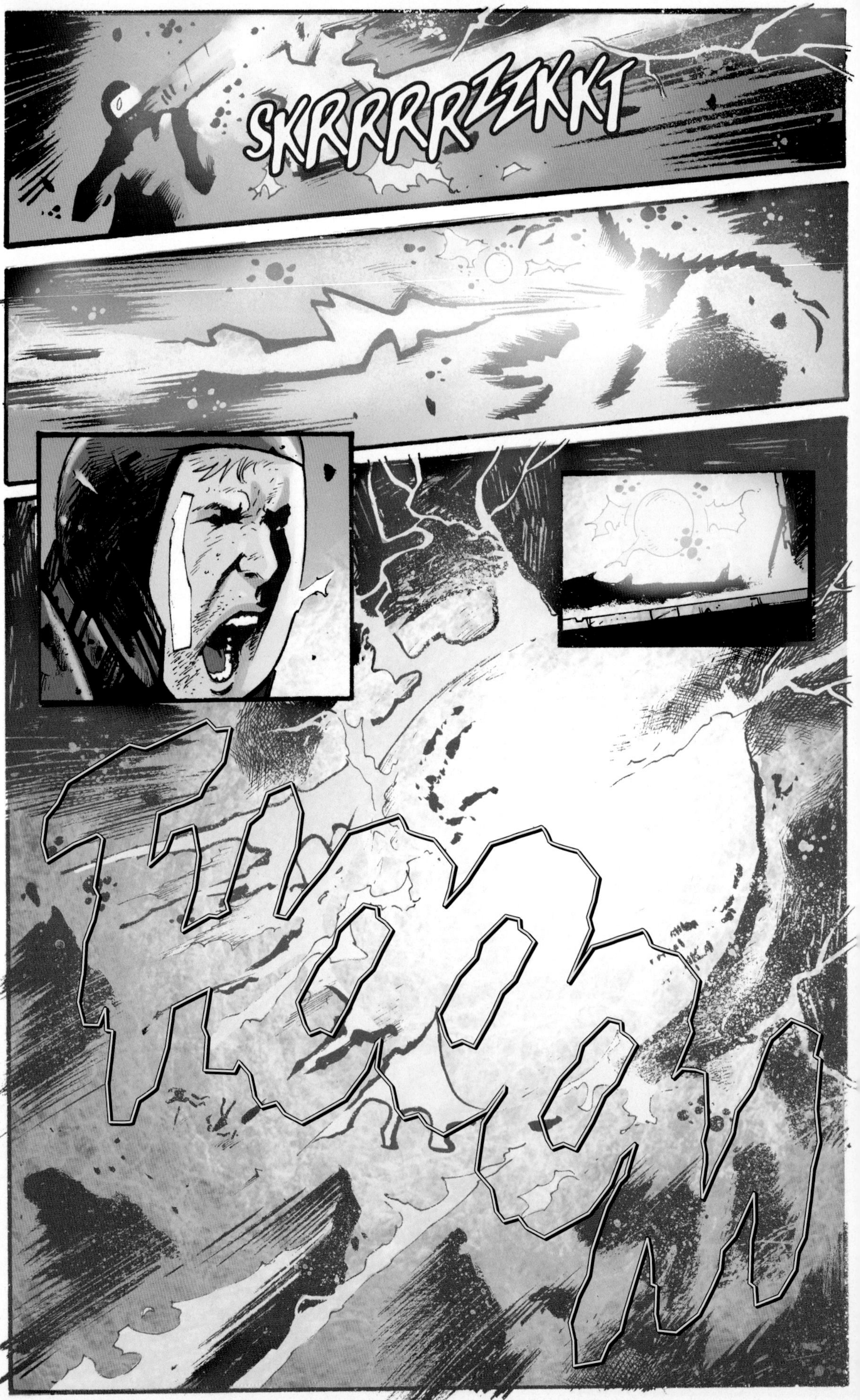
SKRRRRZZKKT
FWOOOM

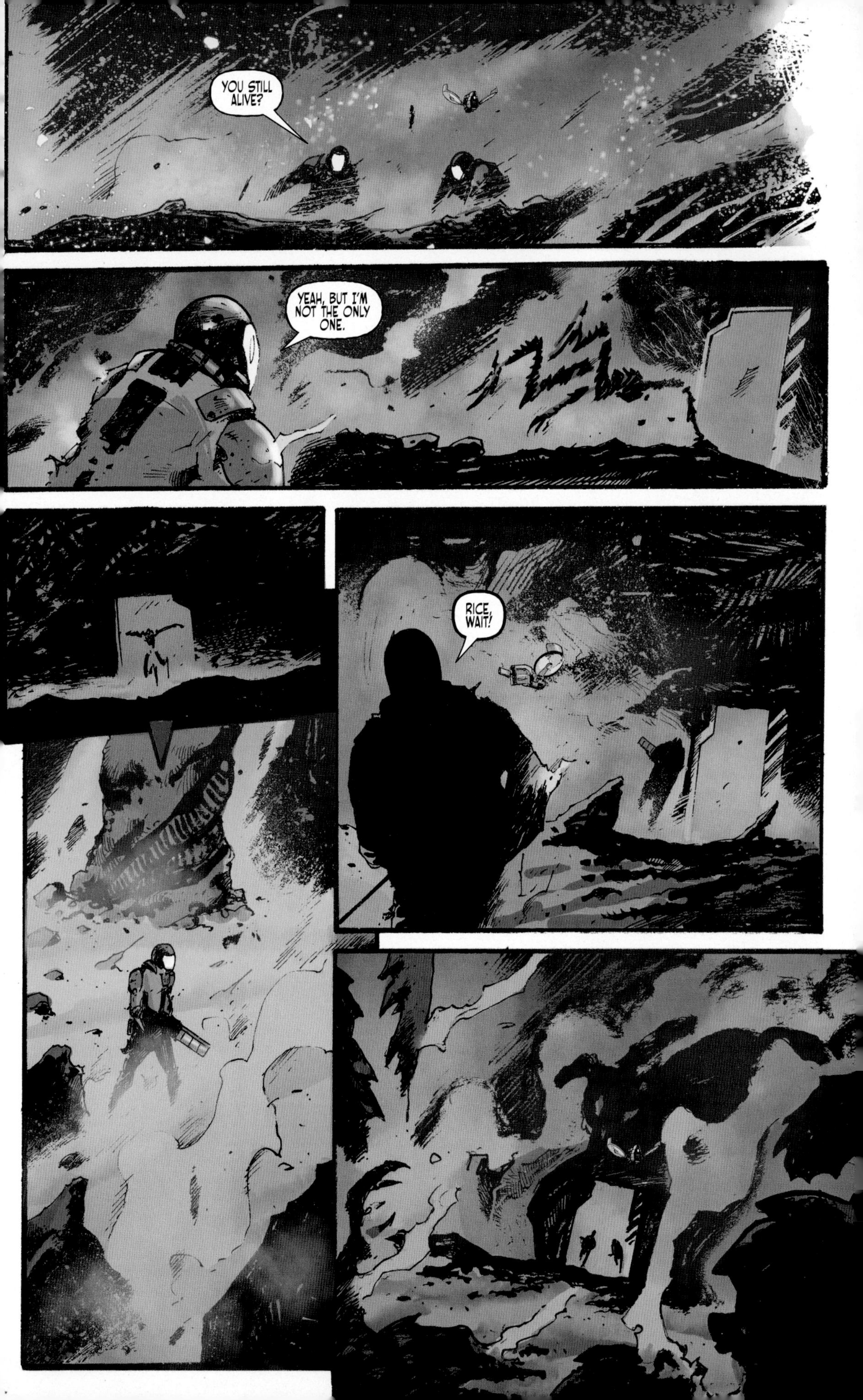
YOU STILL ALIVE?
YEAH, BUT I'M NOT THE ONLY ONE.
RICE, WAIT!

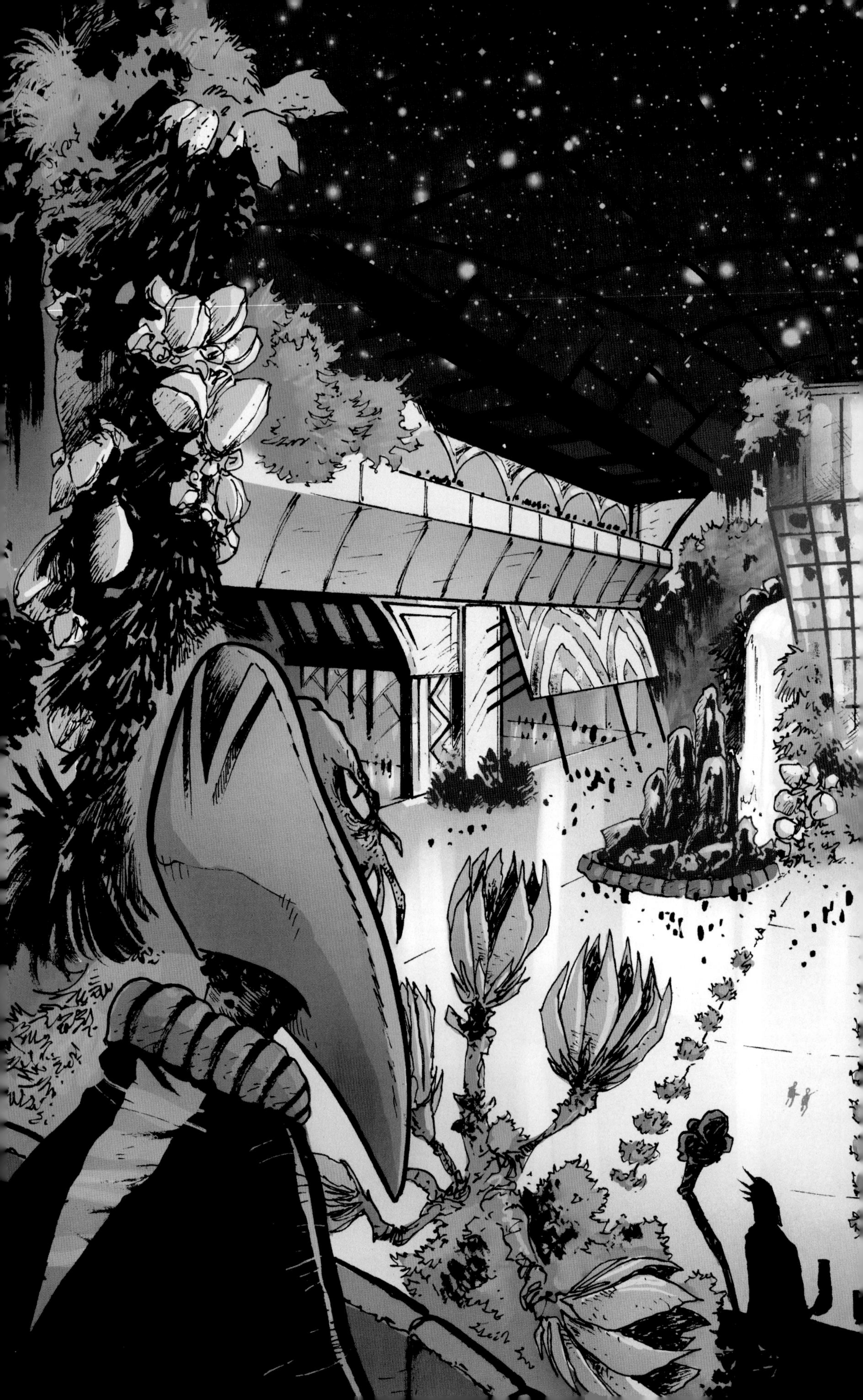

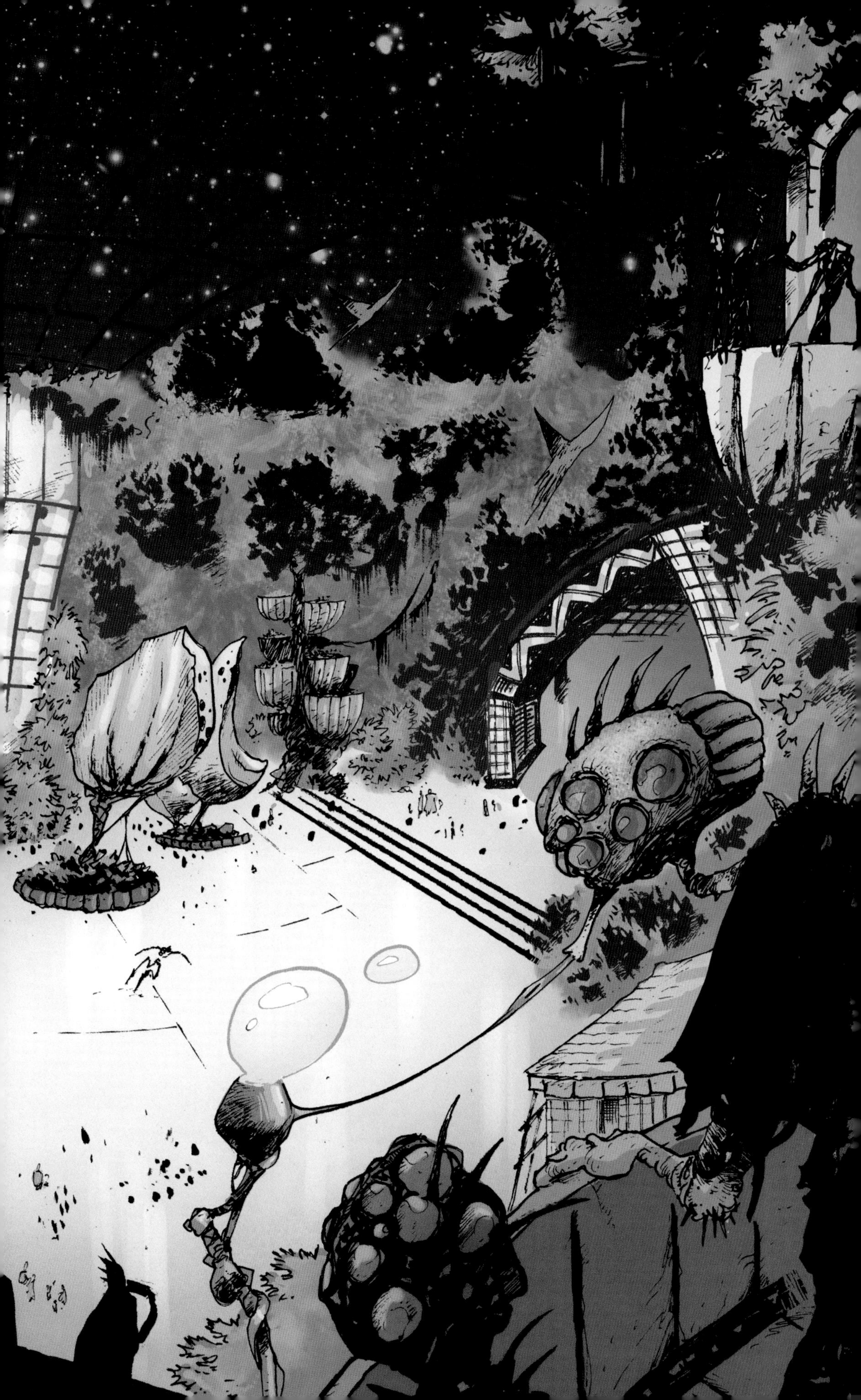

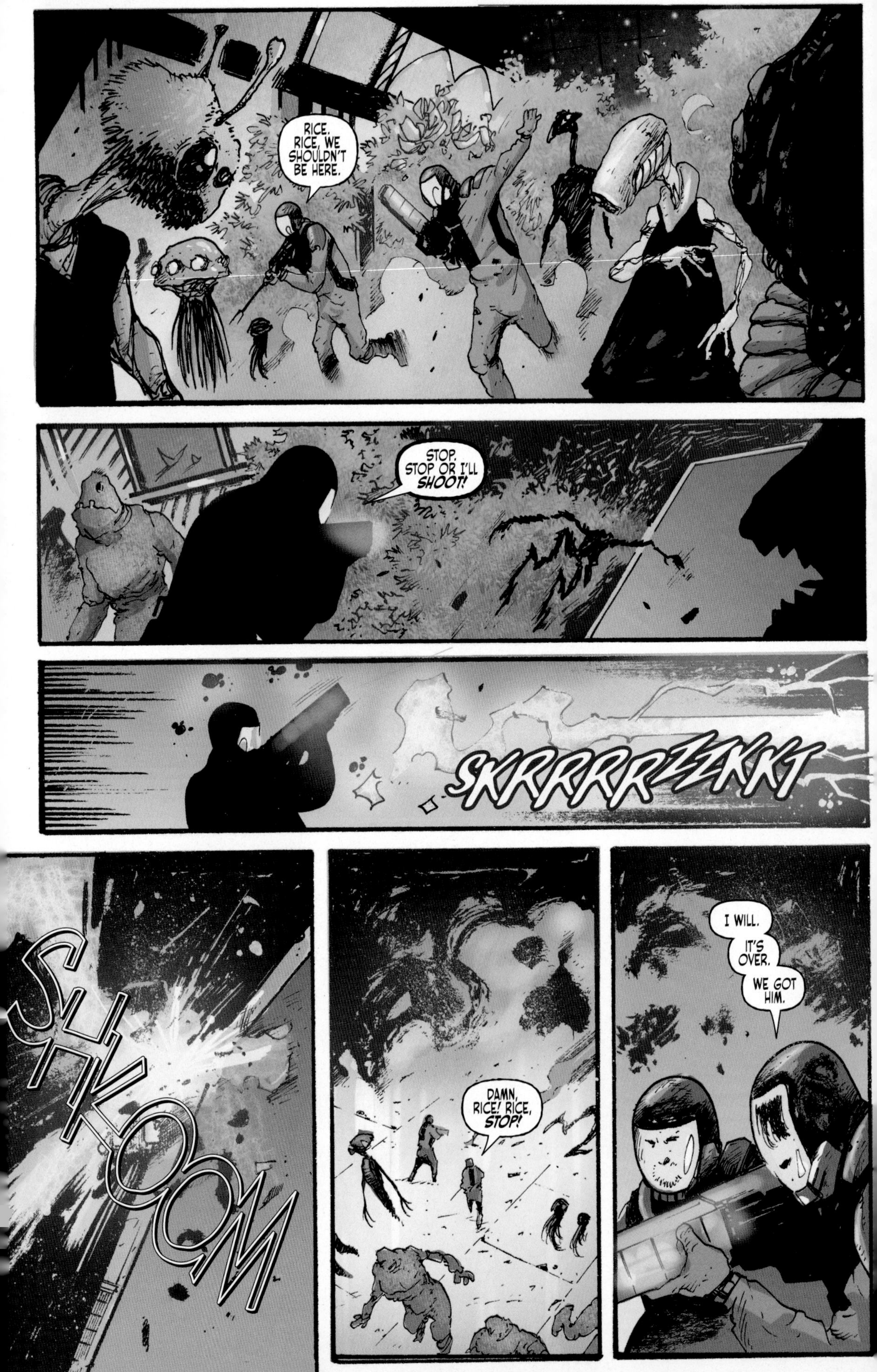
RICE. RICE, WE SHOULDN'T BE HERE.
STOP. STOP OR I'LL SHOOT!
SKRRRRRZZKKT
SHKOOM
DAMN, RICE! RICE, STOP!
I WILL.
IT'S OVER.
WE GOT HIM.

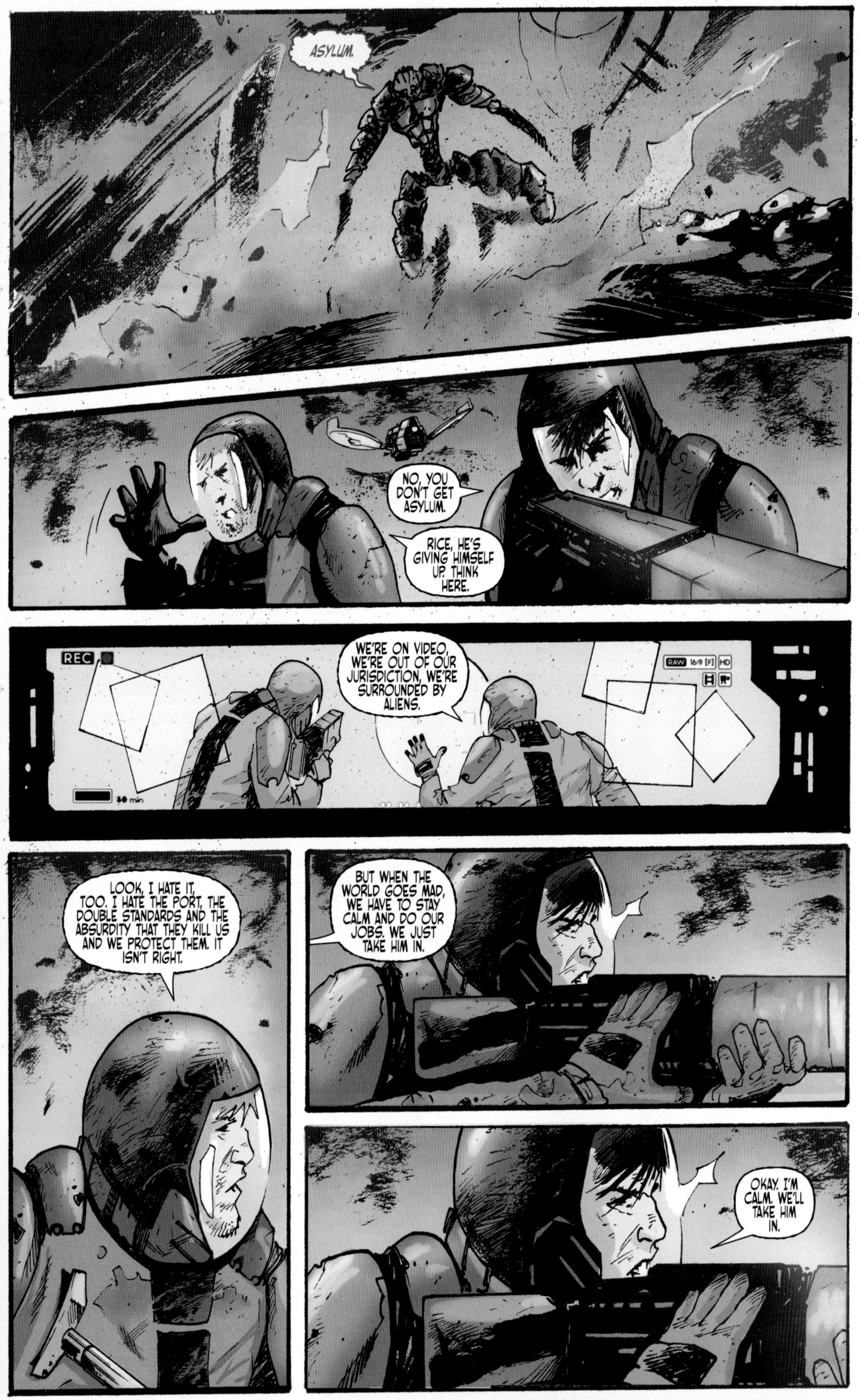
ASYLUM.
NO, YOU DON'T GET ASYLUM.
RICE, HE'S GIVING HIMSELF UP. THINK HERE.
REC
RAW 16:9 [F] HD
WE'RE ON VIDEO, WE'RE OUT OF OUR JURISDICTION, WE'RE SURROUNDED BY ALIENS.
LOOK, I HATE IT, TOO. I HATE THE PORT, THE DOUBLE STANDARDS AND THE ABSURDITY THAT THEY KILL US AND WE PROTECT THEM. IT ISN'T RIGHT.
BUT WHEN THE WORLD GOES MAD, WE HAVE TO STAY CALM AND DO OUR JOBS. WE JUST TAKE HIM IN.
OKAY. I'M CALM. WE'LL TAKE HIM IN.

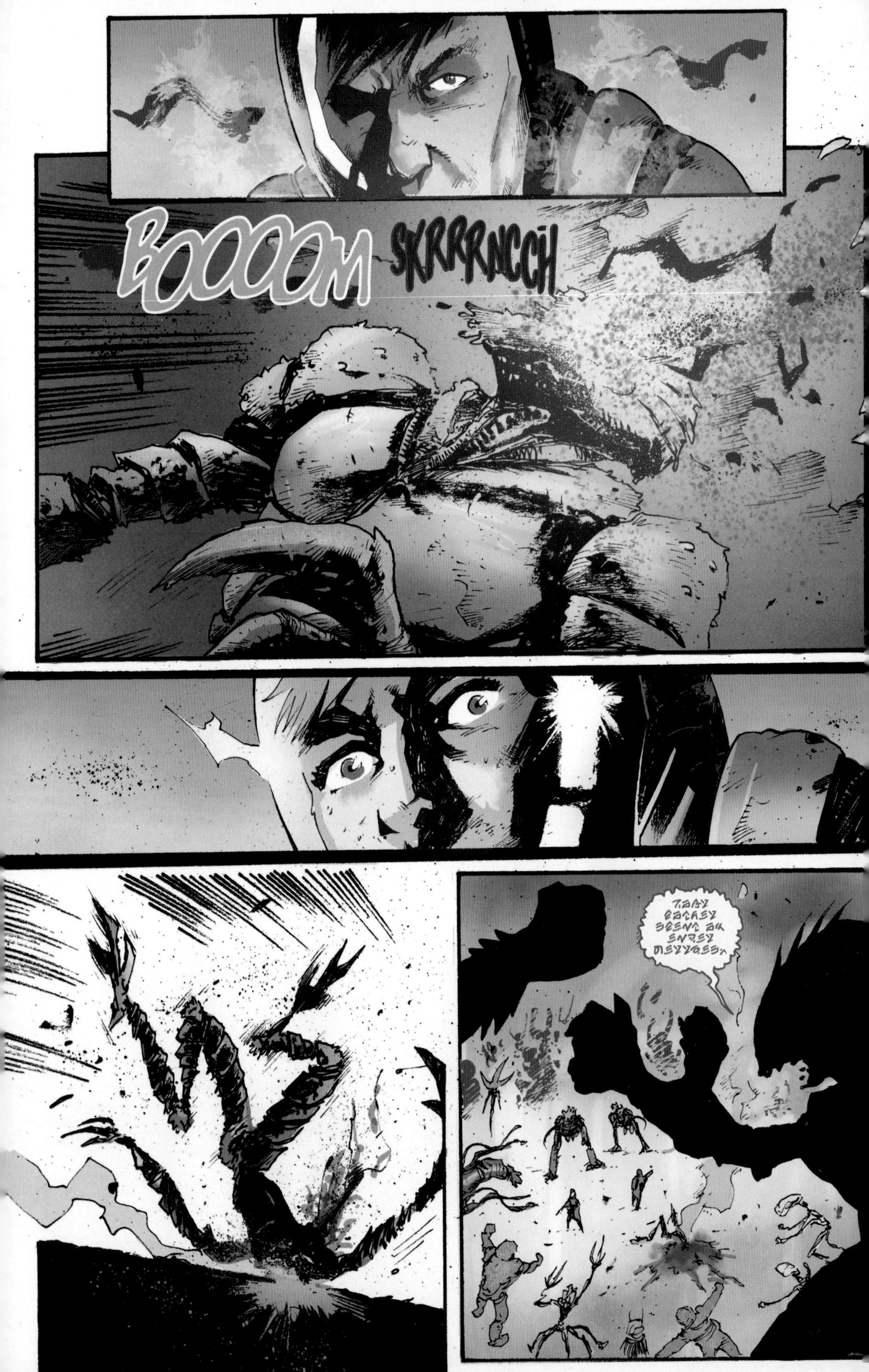
BOOOOM
SKRRRNCCH

BACK.
ALL OF YOU,
STAY BACK.

SKRRRKT

STOP!
STOP!

SKRRRKT

JESUS, RICE,
WHAT DID YOU
DO?

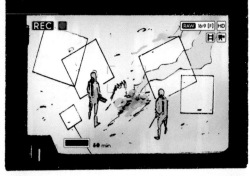

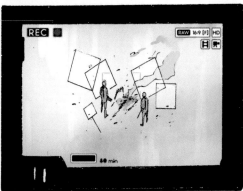

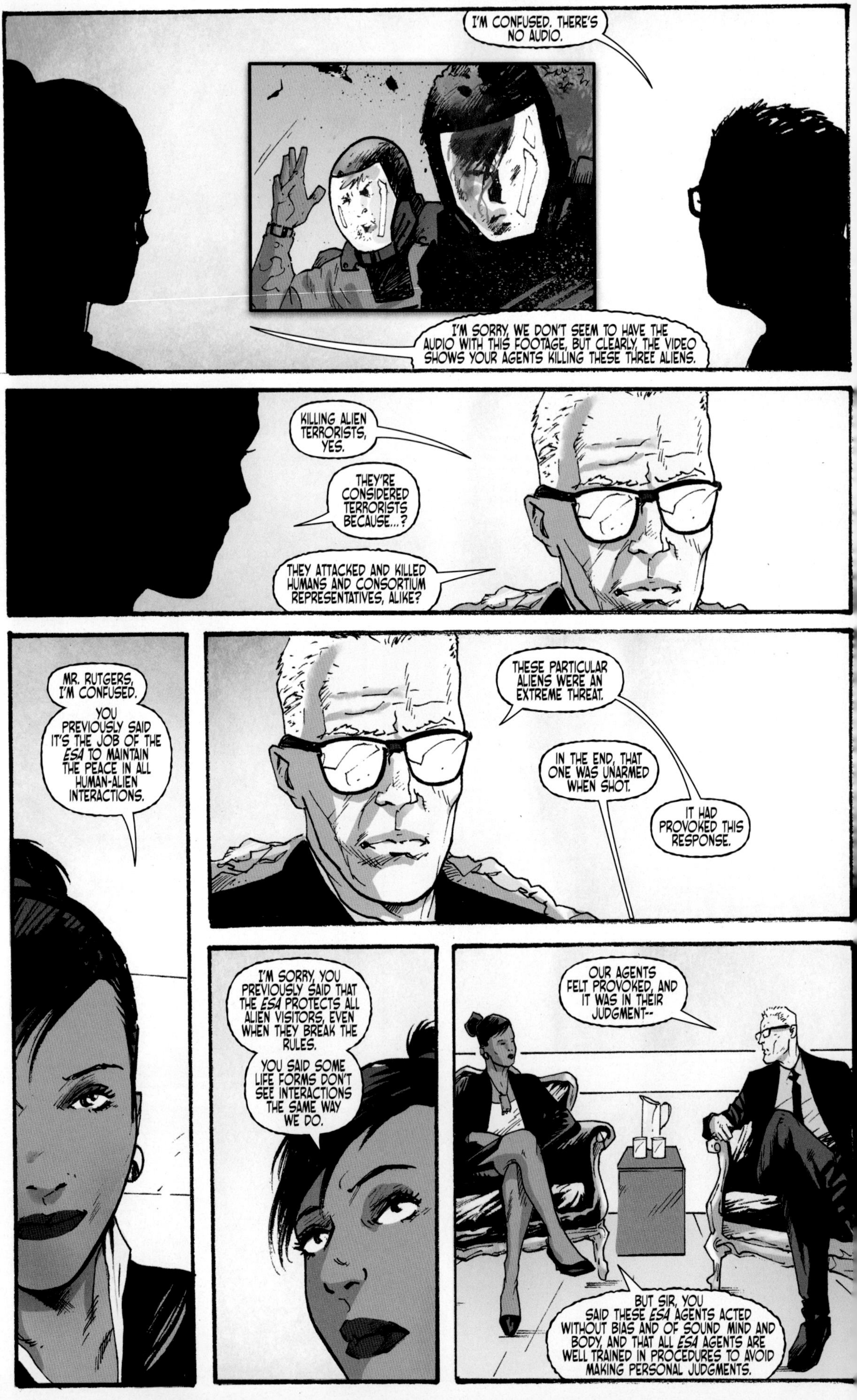

I'M CONFUSED. THERE'S NO AUDIO.
I'M SORRY, WE DON'T SEEM TO HAVE THE AUDIO WITH THIS FOOTAGE, BUT CLEARLY, THE VIDEO SHOWS YOUR AGENTS KILLING THESE THREE ALIENS.
KILLING ALIEN TERRORISTS, YES.
THEY'RE CONSIDERED TERRORISTS BECAUSE...?
THEY ATTACKED AND KILLED HUMANS AND CONSORTIUM REPRESENTATIVES, ALIKE?
MR. RUTGERS, I'M CONFUSED.
YOU PREVIOUSLY SAID IT'S THE JOB OF THE ESA TO MAINTAIN THE PEACE IN ALL HUMAN-ALIEN INTERACTIONS.
THESE PARTICULAR ALIENS WERE AN EXTREME THREAT.
IN THE END, THAT ONE WAS UNARMED WHEN SHOT.
IT HAD PROVOKED THIS RESPONSE.
I'M SORRY, YOU PREVIOUSLY SAID THAT THE ESA PROTECTS ALL ALIEN VISITORS, EVEN WHEN THEY BREAK THE RULES.
YOU SAID SOME LIFE FORMS DON'T SEE INTERACTIONS THE SAME WAY WE DO.
OUR AGENTS FELT PROVOKED, AND IT WAS IN THEIR JUDGMENT--
BUT SIR, YOU SAID THESE ESA AGENTS ACTED WITHOUT BIAS AND OF SOUND MIND AND BODY, AND THAT ALL ESA AGENTS ARE WELL TRAINED IN PROCEDURES TO AVOID MAKING PERSONAL JUDGMENTS.

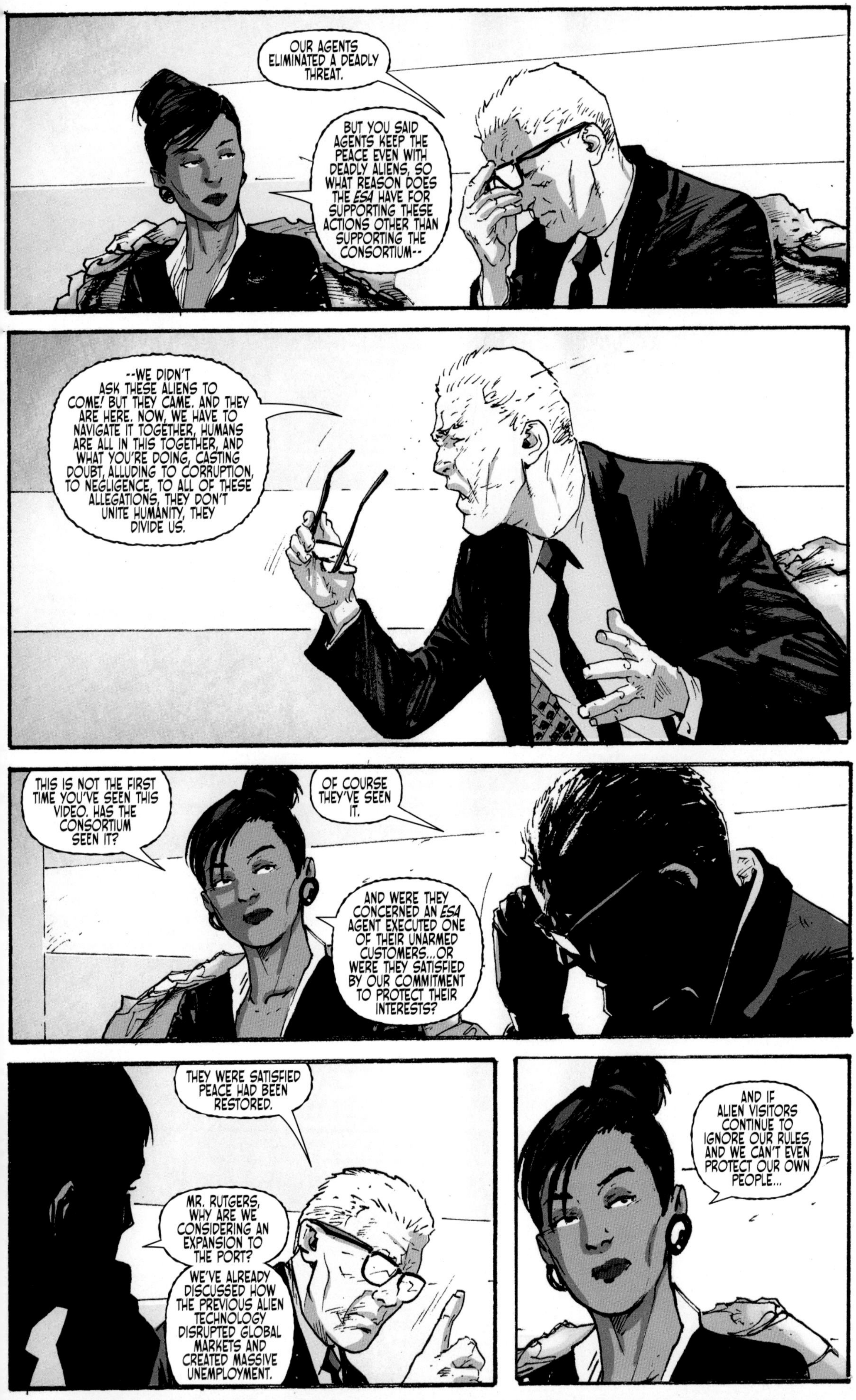
OUR AGENTS ELIMINATED A DEADLY THREAT.
BUT YOU SAID AGENTS KEEP THE PEACE EVEN WITH DEADLY ALIENS, SO WHAT REASON DOES THE ESA HAVE FOR SUPPORTING THESE ACTIONS OTHER THAN SUPPORTING THE CONSORTIUM--
--WE DIDN'T ASK THESE ALIENS TO COME! BUT THEY CAME. AND THEY ARE HERE. NOW, WE HAVE TO NAVIGATE IT TOGETHER, HUMANS ARE ALL IN THIS TOGETHER, AND WHAT YOU'RE DOING, CASTING DOUBT, ALLUDING TO CORRUPTION, TO NEGLIGENCE, TO ALL OF THESE ALLEGATIONS, THEY DON'T UNITE HUMANITY, THEY DIVIDE US.
THIS IS NOT THE FIRST TIME YOU'VE SEEN THIS VIDEO. HAS THE CONSORTIUM SEEN IT?
OF COURSE THEY'VE SEEN IT.
AND WERE THEY CONCERNED AN ESA AGENT EXECUTED ONE OF THEIR UNARMED CUSTOMERS...OR WERE THEY SATISFIED BY OUR COMMITMENT TO PROTECT THEIR INTERESTS?
THEY WERE SATISFIED PEACE HAD BEEN RESTORED.
MR. RUTGERS, WHY ARE WE CONSIDERING AN EXPANSION TO THE PORT?
WE'VE ALREADY DISCUSSED HOW THE PREVIOUS ALIEN TECHNOLOGY DISRUPTED GLOBAL MARKETS AND CREATED MASSIVE UNEMPLOYMENT.
AND IF ALIEN VISITORS CONTINUE TO IGNORE OUR RULES, AND WE CAN'T EVEN PROTECT OUR OWN PEOPLE...

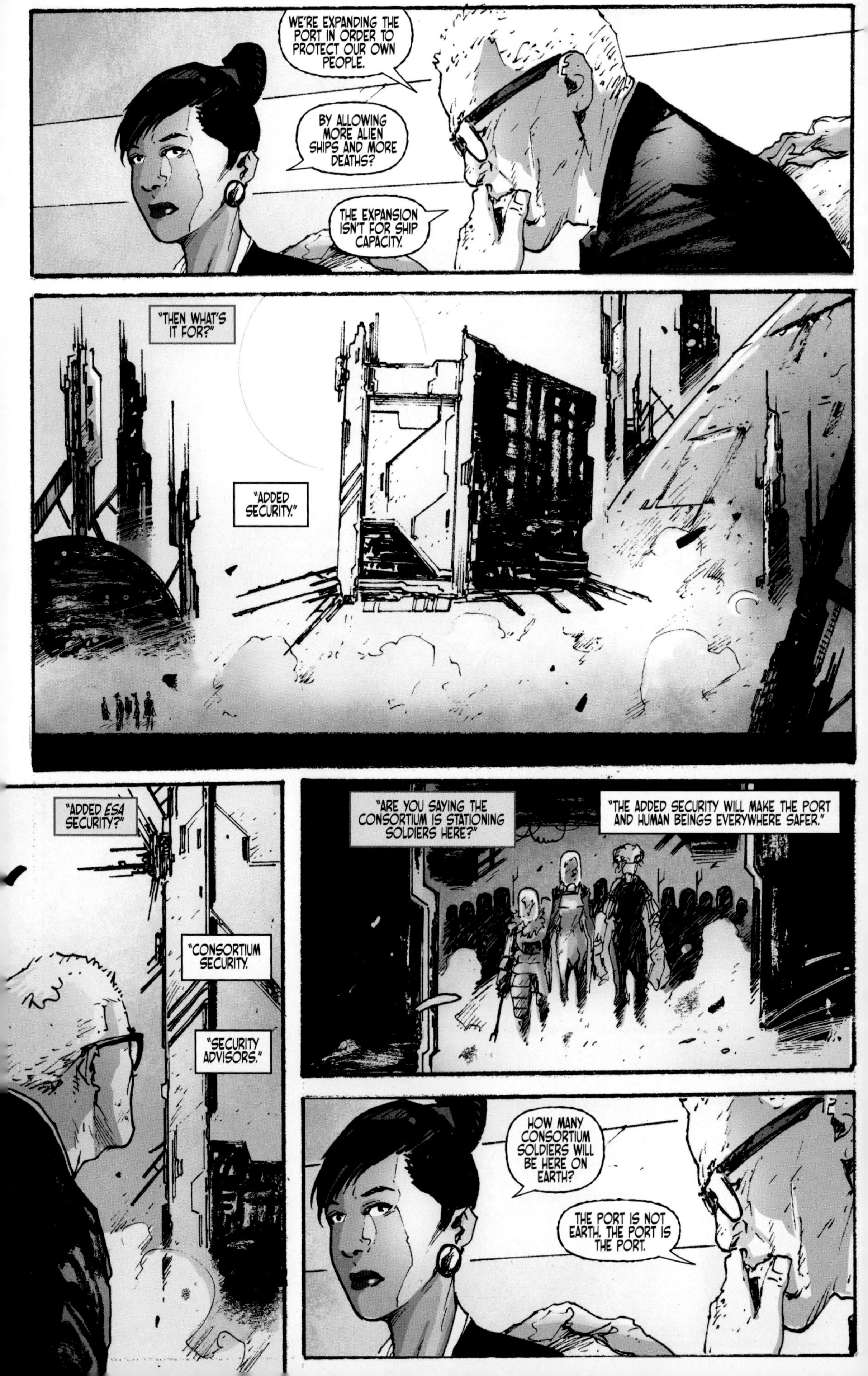
WE'RE EXPANDING THE PORT IN ORDER TO PROTECT OUR OWN PEOPLE.
BY ALLOWING MORE ALIEN SHIPS AND MORE DEATHS?
THE EXPANSION ISN'T FOR SHIP CAPACITY.
"THEN WHAT'S IT FOR?"
"ADDED SECURITY."
"ADDED *ESA* SECURITY?"
"CONSORTIUM SECURITY.
"SECURITY ADVISORS."
"ARE YOU SAYING THE CONSORTIUM IS STATIONING SOLDIERS HERE?"
"THE ADDED SECURITY WILL MAKE THE PORT AND HUMAN BEINGS EVERYWHERE SAFER."
HOW MANY CONSORTIUM SOLDIERS WILL BE HERE ON EARTH?
THE PORT IS NOT EARTH. THE PORT IS THE PORT.

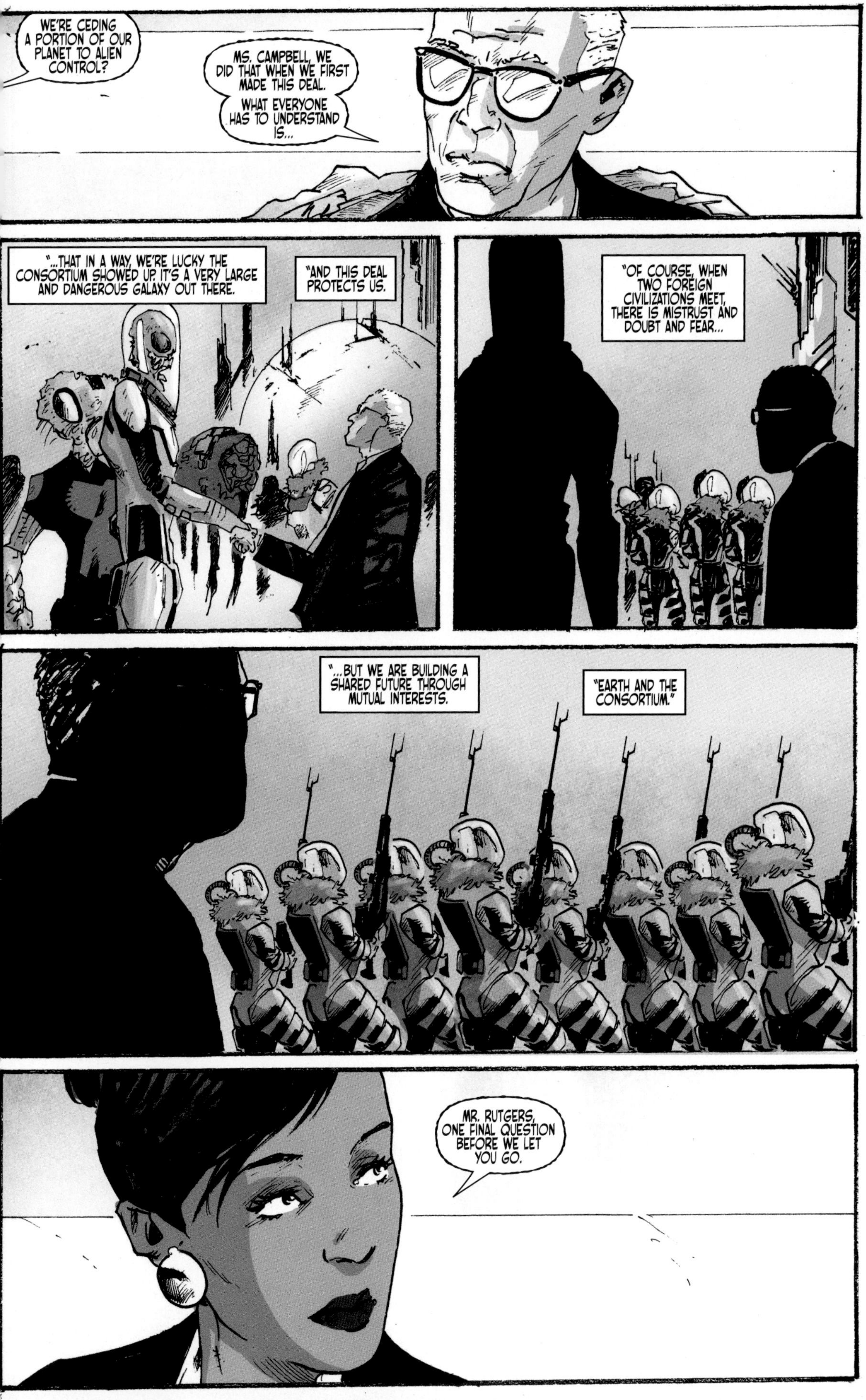
WE'RE CEDING A PORTION OF OUR PLANET TO ALIEN CONTROL?
MS. CAMPBELL, WE DID THAT WHEN WE FIRST MADE THIS DEAL.
WHAT EVERYONE HAS TO UNDERSTAND IS...
"...THAT IN A WAY, WE'RE LUCKY THE CONSORTIUM SHOWED UP. IT'S A VERY LARGE AND DANGEROUS GALAXY OUT THERE.
"AND THIS DEAL PROTECTS US.
"OF COURSE, WHEN TWO FOREIGN CIVILIZATIONS MEET, THERE IS MISTRUST AND DOUBT AND FEAR...
"...BUT WE ARE BUILDING A SHARED FUTURE THROUGH MUTUAL INTERESTS.
"EARTH AND THE CONSORTIUM."
MR. RUTGERS, ONE FINAL QUESTION BEFORE WE LET YOU GO.

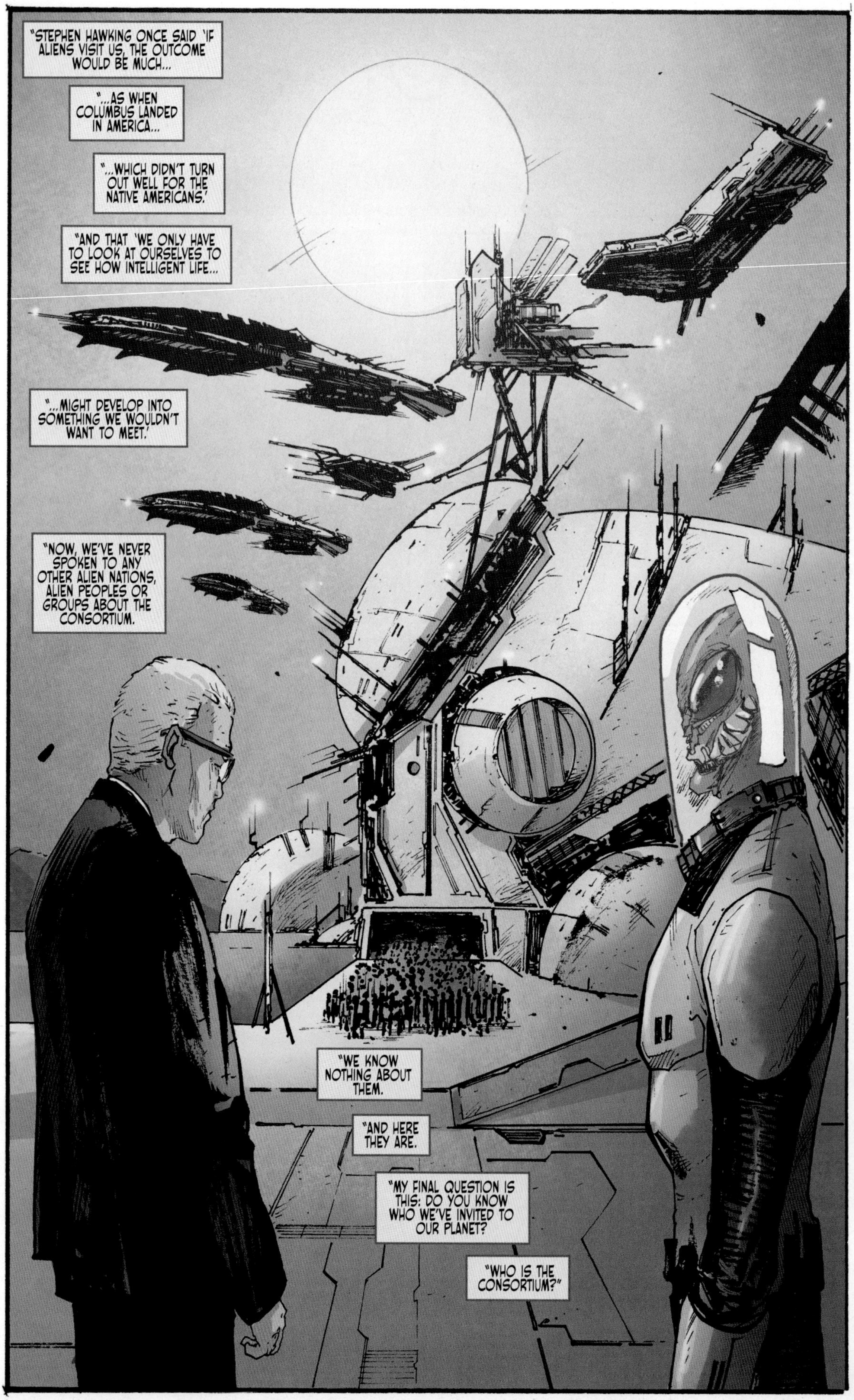
"STEPHEN HAWKING ONCE SAID 'IF ALIENS VISIT US, THE OUTCOME WOULD BE MUCH...
"...AS WHEN COLUMBUS LANDED IN AMERICA...
"...WHICH DIDN'T TURN OUT WELL FOR THE NATIVE AMERICANS.'
"AND THAT 'WE ONLY HAVE TO LOOK AT OURSELVES TO SEE HOW INTELLIGENT LIFE...
"...MIGHT DEVELOP INTO SOMETHING WE WOULDN'T WANT TO MEET.'
"NOW, WE'VE NEVER SPOKEN TO ANY OTHER ALIEN NATIONS, ALIEN PEOPLES OR GROUPS ABOUT THE CONSORTIUM.
"WE KNOW NOTHING ABOUT THEM.
"AND HERE THEY ARE.
"MY FINAL QUESTION IS THIS: DO YOU KNOW WHO WE'VE INVITED TO OUR PLANET?
"WHO IS THE CONSORTIUM?"

COVER GALLERY

ISSUE 5

ANDREA MUTTI
VLADIMIR POPOV

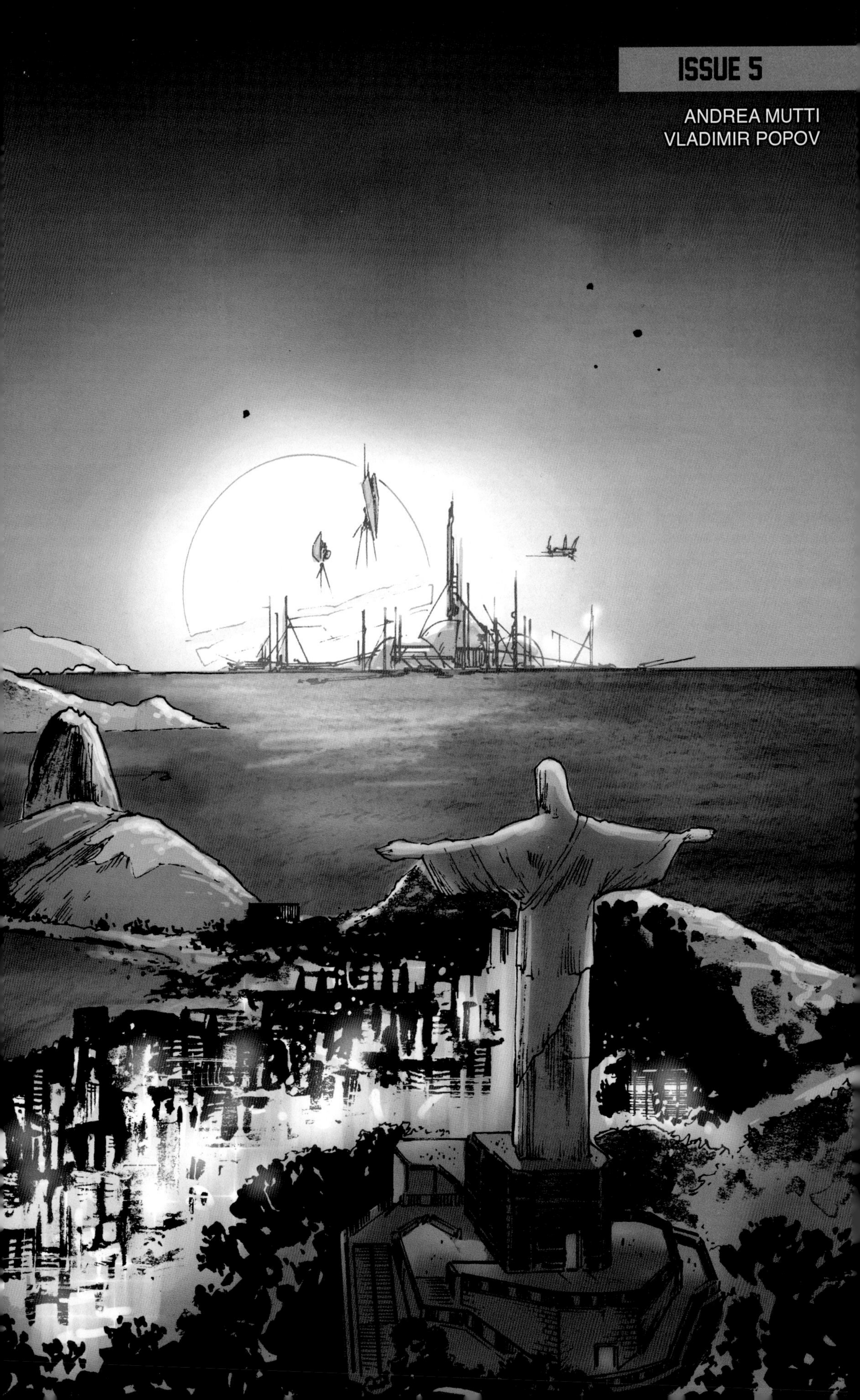

ANDREA MUTTI
VLADIMIR POPOV

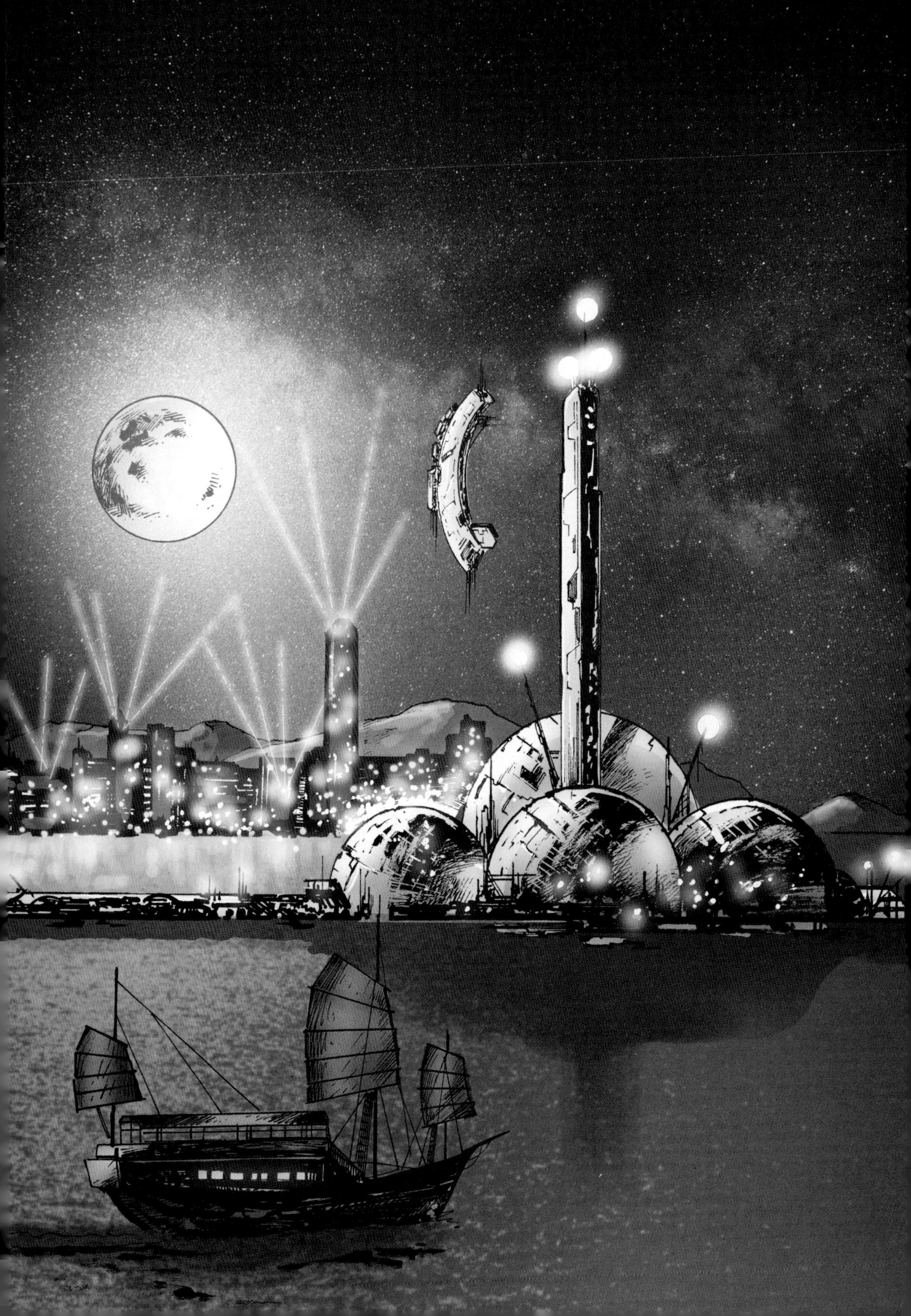

ISSUE 7

ANDREA MUTTI
VLADIMIR POPOV

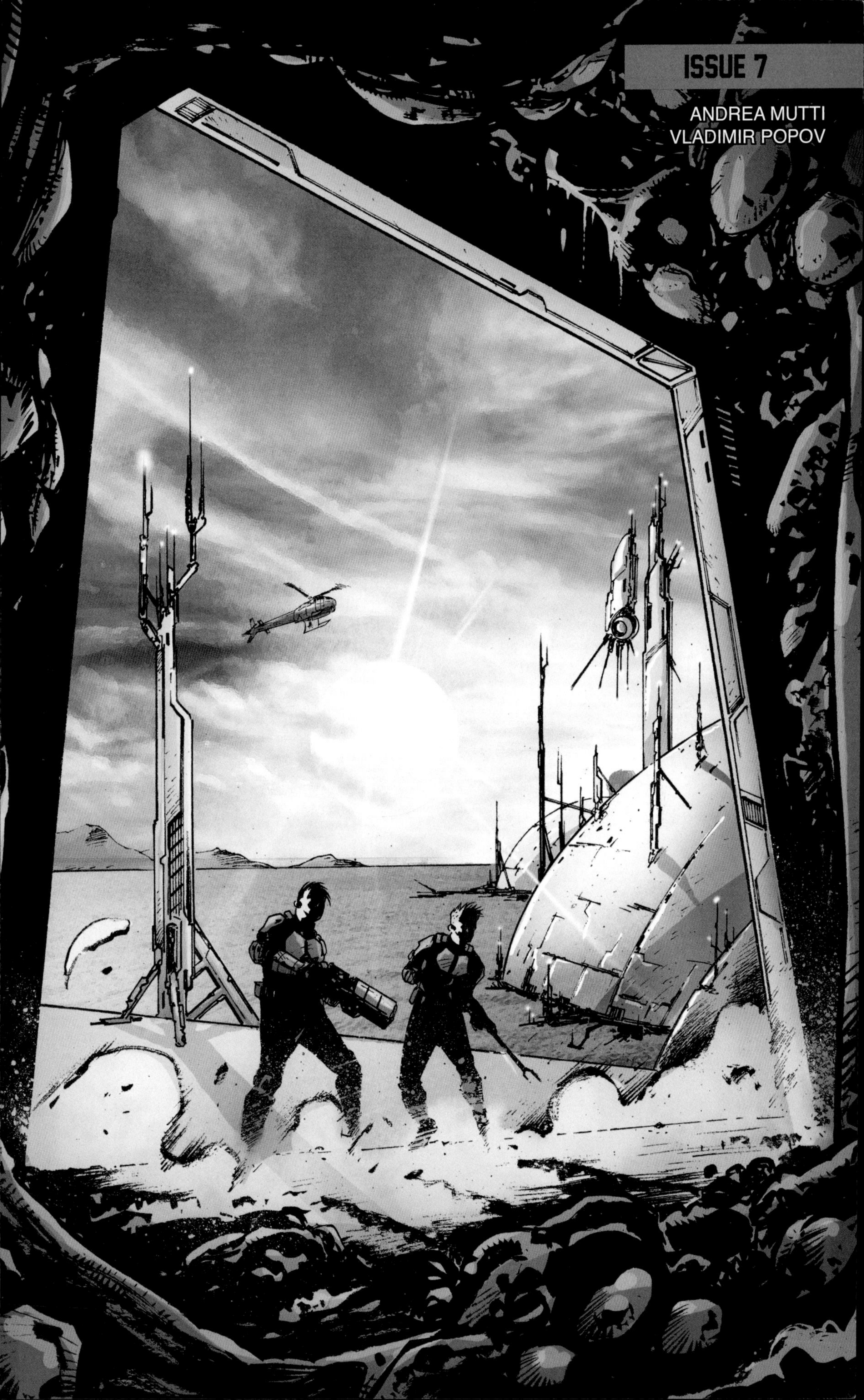

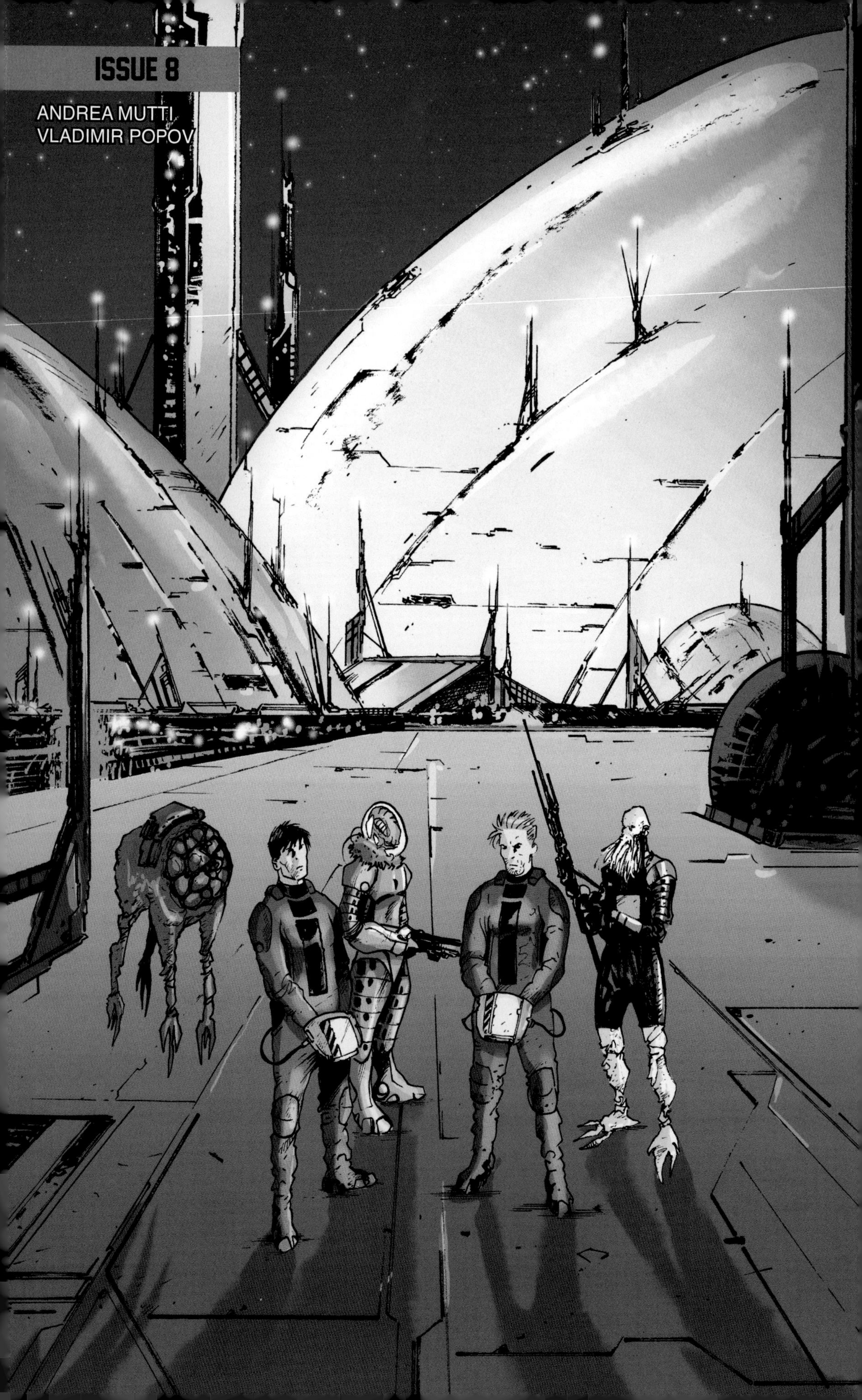
ISSUE 8
ANDREA MUTTI
VLADIMIR POPOV

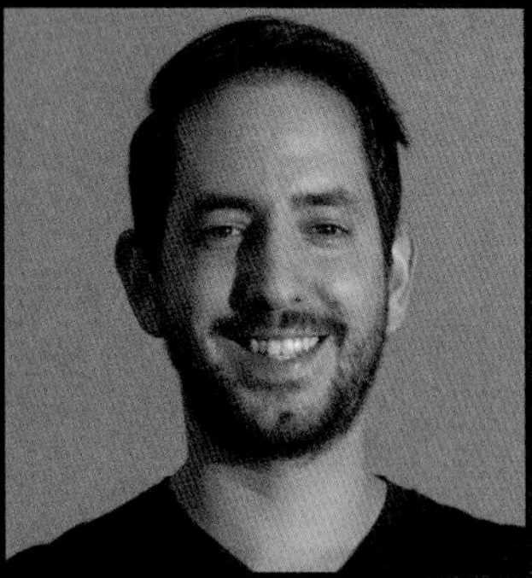

ZACK KAPLAN is a new comic book writer whose debut sci-fi series, ECLIPSE, exploded onto the scene in fall of 2016 to an amazing response and was quickly promoted from a mini to an ongoing series. Zack's sophomore comic effort, PORT OF EARTH, also published by Image Comics and Top Cow Productions, released November, 2017. Zack taught screenwriting at the International Academy of Film and TV, located in the Philippines, and he also writes film and television.

ANDREA MUTTI is an Italian artist that has worked in the comic book world for 25 years. He studied at the Comics School in Brescia and has worked with such publishers as Marvel, DC, Dark Horse, Vertigo, IDW, BOOM! Studios, Dynamite, Stela, Adaptive and many more European publishers like Glenat, Casterman, Soleil, Dargaud and Titan. He lives in Italy and you can learn more about his career at his website: www.andrearedmutti.com.

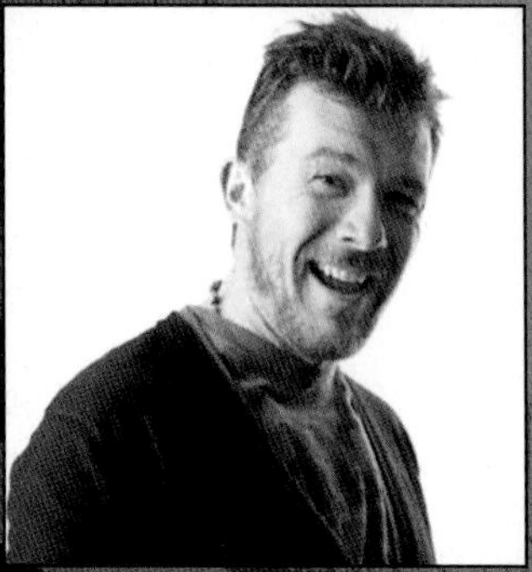

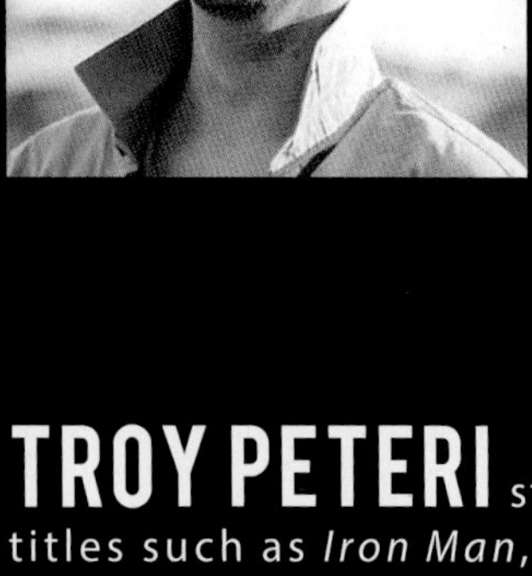

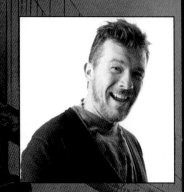

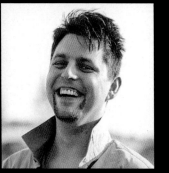

VLADIMIR POPOV is an European-based color artist who has worked for publishers such as Boom Studios, Dynamite, Stela, DoubleTake, Soleil (French) and others on high-profile titles such as Clive Barker's *Hellraiser & Next Testament*, *Robocop*, *Steed and Mrs Peel*, *Noir*, *Adventure Time* and *Maze Runner*. He has collaborated on creator-owned titles such as *Sand + Bone*, *Rome West*, *Control*, *The Returning*, *Darklight*, *Americatown* and *Freelancers*. He has MSC degree in computer sciences with major in digital art.

TROY PETERI started his career at Comicraft, lettering titles such as *Iron Man*, *Wolverine* and *Amazing Spider-Man*, among many others. He's been lettering roughly 97% of all Top Cow titles since 2005. In addition to Top Cow, he currently letters comics from multiple publishers and websites, such as Image Comics, Dynamite, and Archaia. He (along with co-writer Tom Martin and artist Dave Lanphear) is currently writing (and lettering) *Tales of Equinox*, a webcomic of his own creation for www.Thrillbent.com.

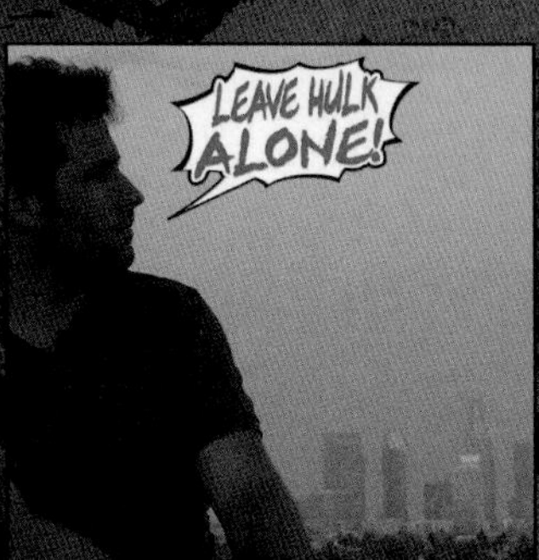
LEAVE HULK ALONE!

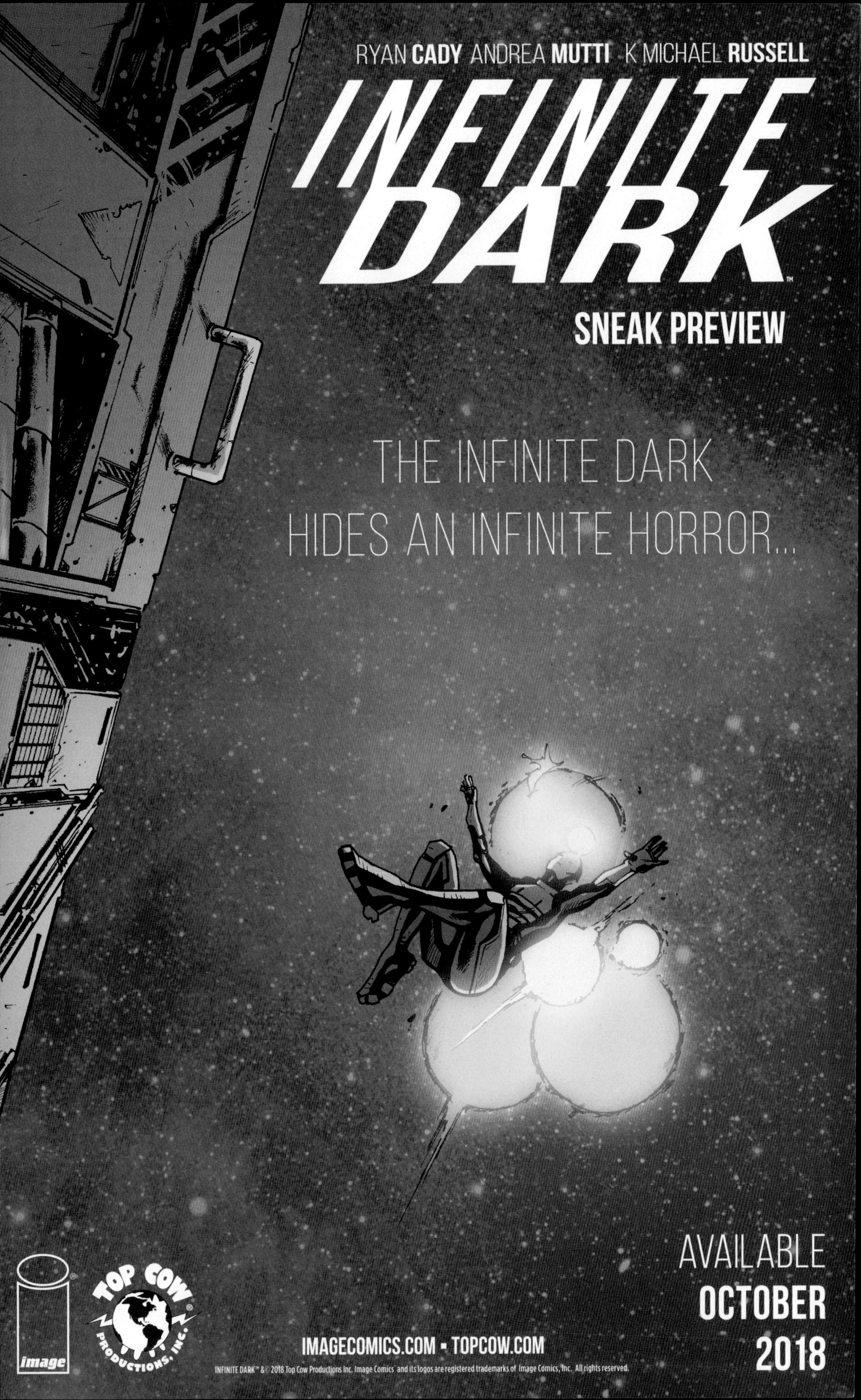
RYAN CADY ANDREA MUTTI K MICHAEL RUSSELL
INFINITE DARK™
SNEAK PREVIEW
THE INFINITE DARK
HIDES AN INFINITE HORROR...
AVAILABLE
OCTOBER
2018
IMAGECOMICS.COM - TOPCOW.COM
INFINITE DARK™ & © 2018 Top Cow Productions Inc. Image Comics and its logos are registered trademarks of Image Comics, Inc. All rights reserved.

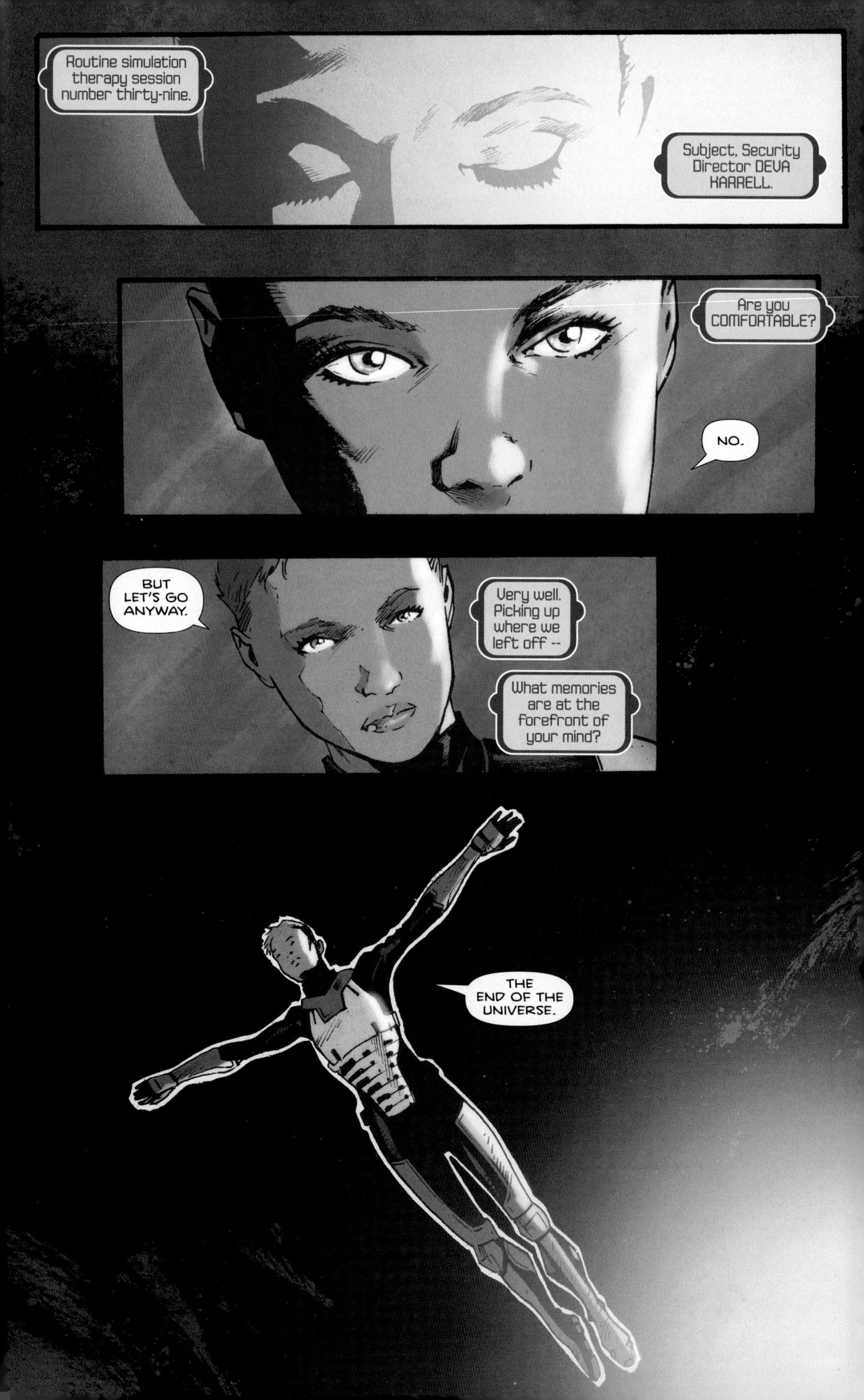
Routine simulation therapy session number thirty-nine.
Subject, Security Director DEVA KARRELL.
Are you COMFORTABLE?
NO.
BUT LET'S GO ANYWAY.
Very well. Picking up where we left off --
What memories are at the forefront of your mind?
THE END OF THE UNIVERSE.

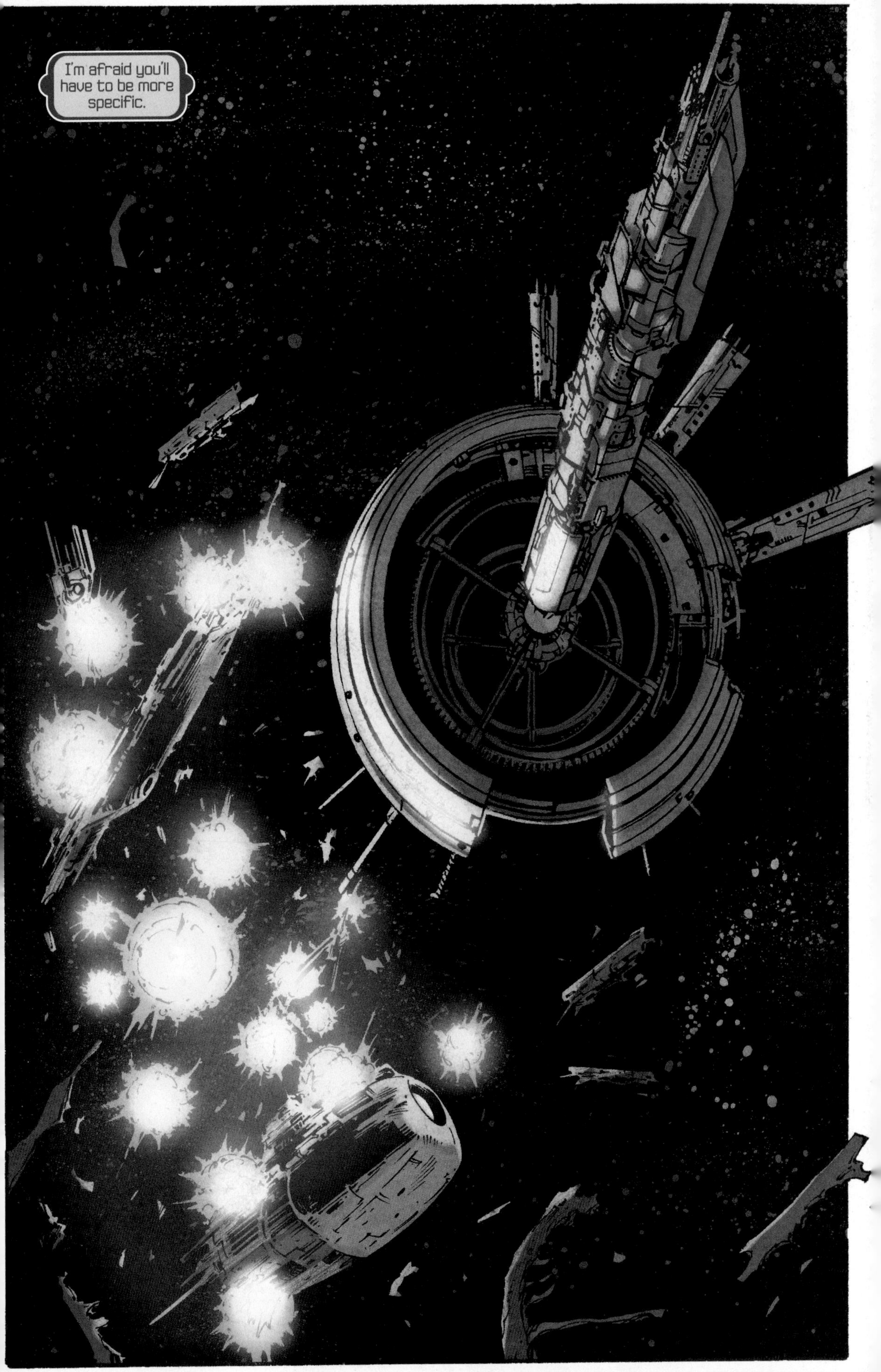
I'm afraid you'll have to be more specific.

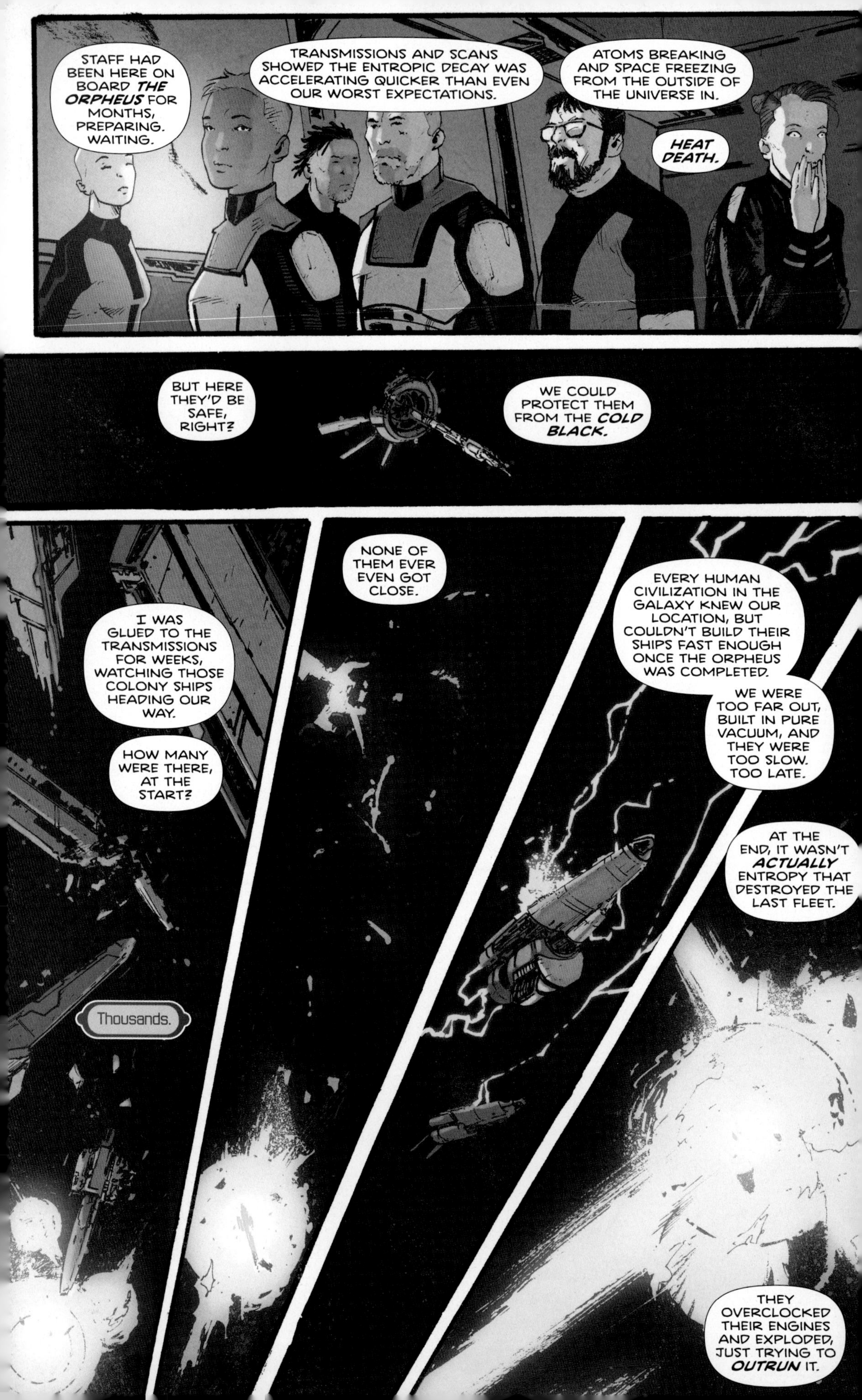
STAFF HAD BEEN HERE ON BOARD *THE ORPHEUS* FOR MONTHS, PREPARING. WAITING.
TRANSMISSIONS AND SCANS SHOWED THE ENTROPIC DECAY WAS ACCELERATING QUICKER THAN EVEN OUR WORST EXPECTATIONS.
ATOMS BREAKING AND SPACE FREEZING FROM THE OUTSIDE OF THE UNIVERSE IN.
HEAT DEATH.
BUT HERE THEY'D BE SAFE, RIGHT?
WE COULD PROTECT THEM FROM THE *COLD BLACK.*
I WAS GLUED TO THE TRANSMISSIONS FOR WEEKS, WATCHING THOSE COLONY SHIPS HEADING OUR WAY.
HOW MANY WERE THERE, AT THE START?
Thousands.
NONE OF THEM EVER EVEN GOT CLOSE.
EVERY HUMAN CIVILIZATION IN THE GALAXY KNEW OUR LOCATION, BUT COULDN'T BUILD THEIR SHIPS FAST ENOUGH ONCE THE ORPHEUS WAS COMPLETED.
WE WERE TOO FAR OUT, BUILT IN PURE VACUUM, AND THEY WERE TOO SLOW. TOO LATE.
AT THE END, IT WASN'T *ACTUALLY* ENTROPY THAT DESTROYED THE LAST FLEET.
THEY OVERCLOCKED THEIR ENGINES AND EXPLODED, JUST TRYING TO *OUTRUN* IT.

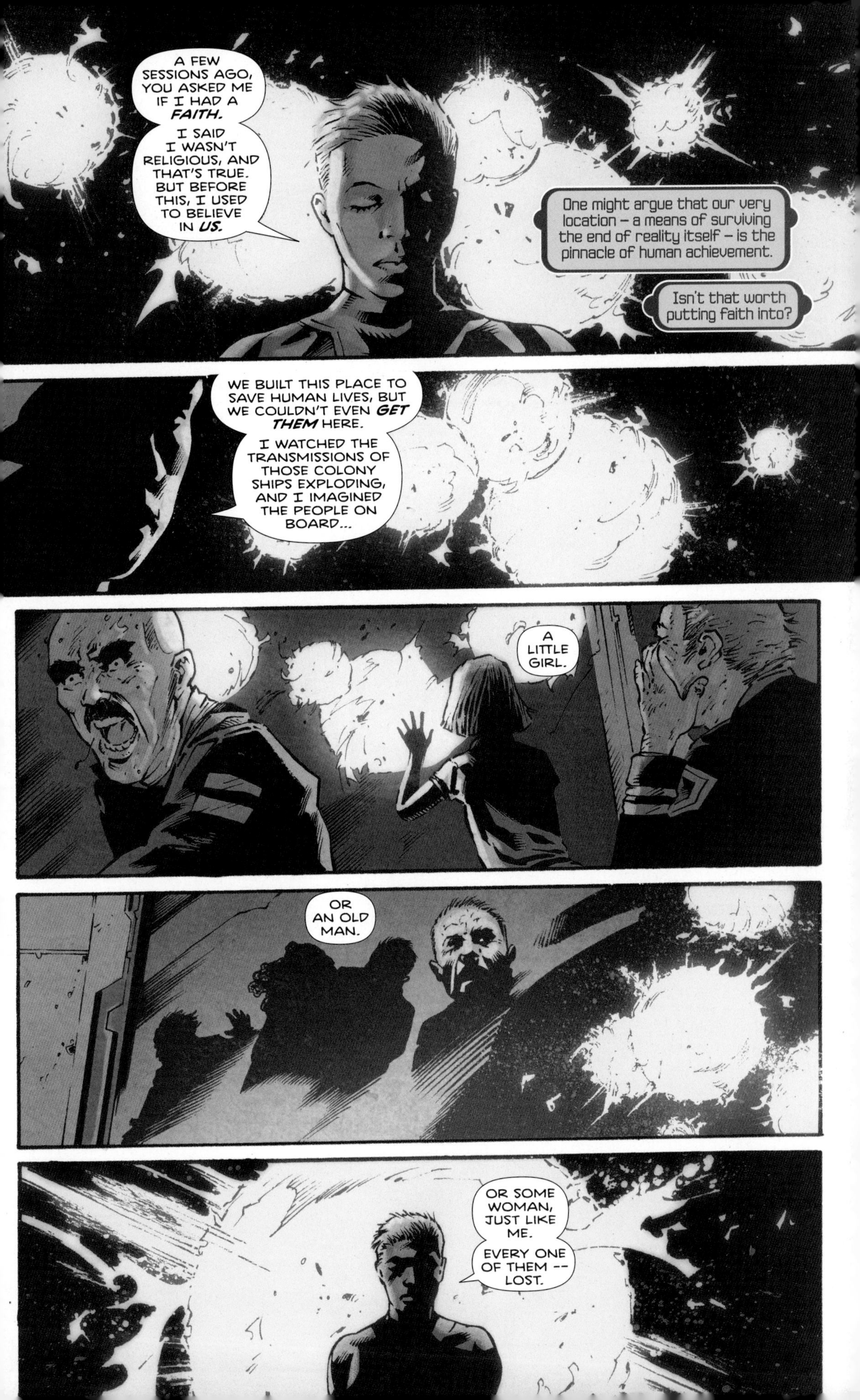
A FEW SESSIONS AGO, YOU ASKED ME IF I HAD A *FAITH.*
I SAID I WASN'T RELIGIOUS, AND THAT'S TRUE. BUT BEFORE THIS, I USED TO BELIEVE IN *US.*
One might argue that our very location – a means of surviving the end of reality itself – is the pinnacle of human achievement.
Isn't that worth putting faith into?
WE BUILT THIS PLACE TO SAVE HUMAN LIVES, BUT WE COULDN'T EVEN *GET THEM* HERE.
I WATCHED THE TRANSMISSIONS OF THOSE COLONY SHIPS EXPLODING, AND I IMAGINED THE PEOPLE ON BOARD...
A LITTLE GIRL.
OR AN OLD MAN.
OR SOME WOMAN, JUST LIKE ME.
EVERY ONE OF THEM -- LOST.

THIS DOESN'T FEEL LIKE AN ACHIEVEMENT TO ME. IT FEELS LIKE A TOMBSTONE.

I DON'T KNOW WHY I'M BEING SO #@&%ING MAUDLIN.

WE'RE FAILURES, NOT SAVIORS.

Begging your pardon, director, but in the two years since you've been in charge of this station's security, you've yet to result in anything I would consider FAILURE.

THANK YOU, SM1TH.

YOU'RE KIND, FOR A *VIRTUAL INTELLIGENCE* WHO'S PROBABLY FOCUSED ON TWENTY OTHER THINGS WHILE WE TALK.

TWENTY-SEVEN. And I've passed this session's report on to Dr. Chalos.

USUALLY YOU DON'T LIKE ME TO CUT THINGS THIS EARLY.

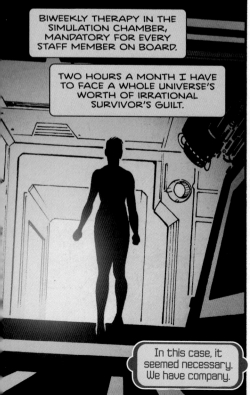

BIWEEKLY THERAPY IN THE SIMULATION CHAMBER, MANDATORY FOR EVERY STAFF MEMBER ON BOARD.

TWO HOURS A MONTH I HAVE TO FACE A WHOLE UNIVERSE'S WORTH OF IRRATIONAL SURVIVOR'S GUILT.

In this case, it seemed necessary. We have company.

MAYBE THAT'S THE POINT. UNLOAD ON THE A.I. AND NOT MY SUBORDINATES.

SEBASTIAN.

SORRY FOR INTERRUPTING, DIRECTOR.

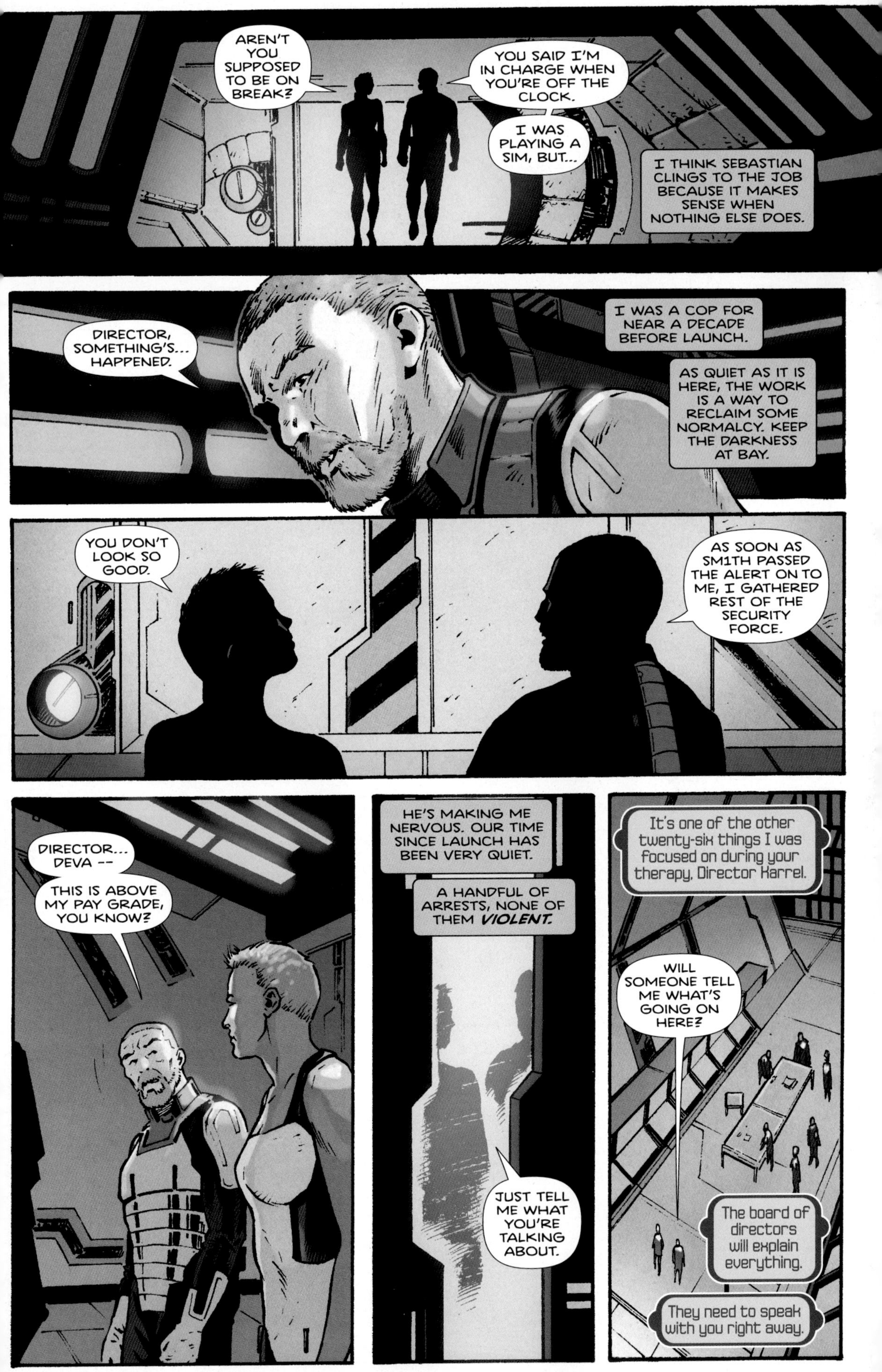
AREN'T YOU SUPPOSED TO BE ON BREAK?
YOU SAID I'M IN CHARGE WHEN YOU'RE OFF THE CLOCK.
I WAS PLAYING A SIM, BUT...
I THINK SEBASTIAN CLINGS TO THE JOB BECAUSE IT MAKES SENSE WHEN NOTHING ELSE DOES.
DIRECTOR, SOMETHING'S... HAPPENED.
I WAS A COP FOR NEAR A DECADE BEFORE LAUNCH.
AS QUIET AS IT IS HERE, THE WORK IS A WAY TO RECLAIM SOME NORMALCY. KEEP THE DARKNESS AT BAY.
YOU DON'T LOOK SO GOOD.
AS SOON AS SM1TH PASSED THE ALERT ON TO ME, I GATHERED REST OF THE SECURITY FORCE.
DIRECTOR... DEVA --
THIS IS ABOVE MY PAY GRADE, YOU KNOW?
HE'S MAKING ME NERVOUS. OUR TIME SINCE LAUNCH HAS BEEN VERY QUIET.
A HANDFUL OF ARRESTS, NONE OF THEM VIOLENT.
JUST TELL ME WHAT YOU'RE TALKING ABOUT.
It's one of the other twenty-six things I was focused on during your therapy, Director Harrel.
WILL SOMEONE TELL ME WHAT'S GOING ON HERE?
The board of directors will explain everything.
They need to speak with you right away.

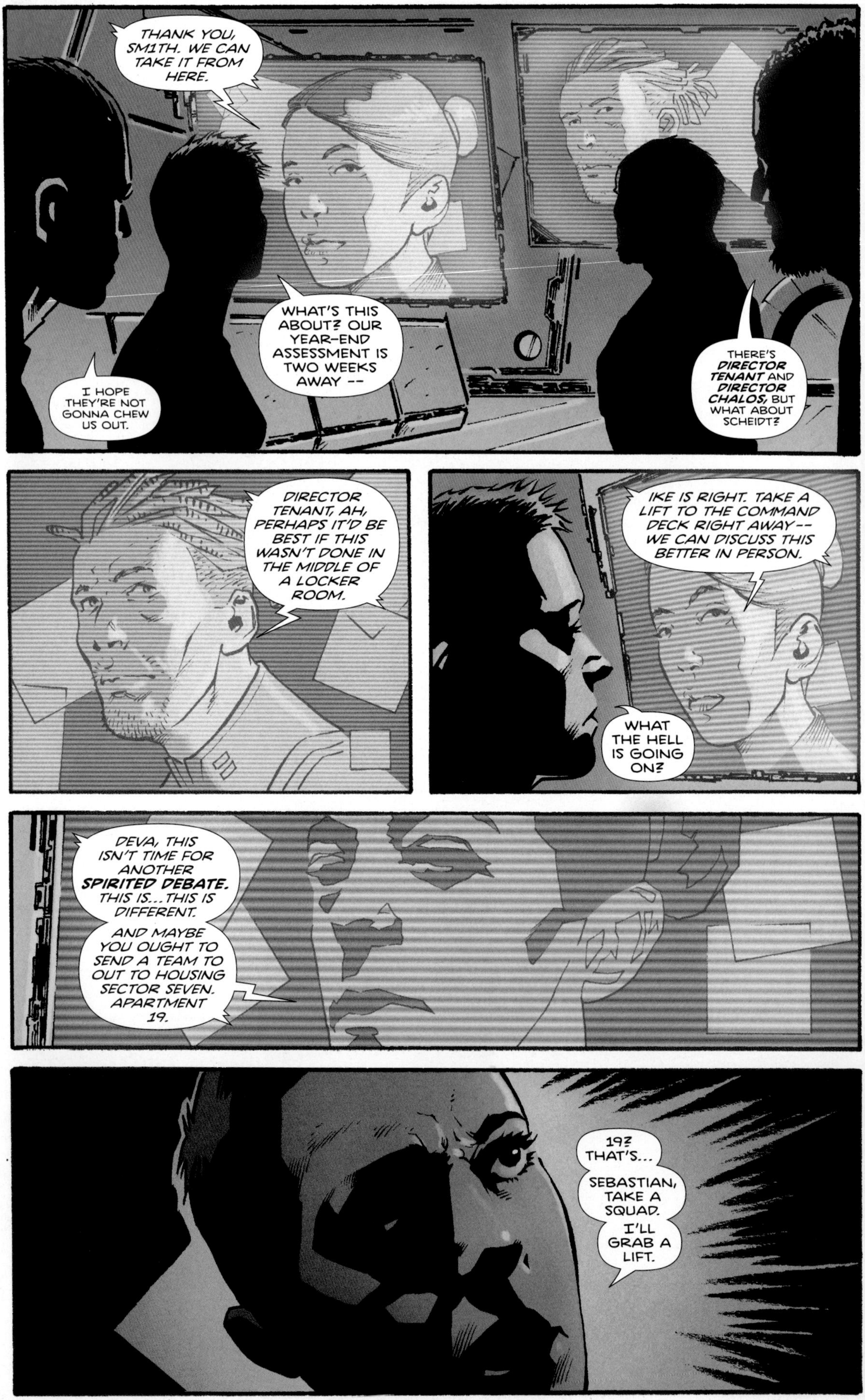
THANK YOU, SM1TH. WE CAN TAKE IT FROM HERE.
I HOPE THEY'RE NOT GONNA CHEW US OUT.
WHAT'S THIS ABOUT? OUR YEAR-END ASSESSMENT IS TWO WEEKS AWAY --
THERE'S DIRECTOR TENANT AND DIRECTOR CHALOS, BUT WHAT ABOUT SCHEIDT?
DIRECTOR TENANT, AH, PERHAPS IT'D BE BEST IF THIS WASN'T DONE IN THE MIDDLE OF A LOCKER ROOM.
IKE IS RIGHT. TAKE A LIFT TO THE COMMAND DECK RIGHT AWAY-- WE CAN DISCUSS THIS BETTER IN PERSON.
WHAT THE HELL IS GOING ON?
DEVA, THIS ISN'T TIME FOR ANOTHER SPIRITED DEBATE. THIS IS... THIS IS DIFFERENT.
AND MAYBE YOU OUGHT TO SEND A TEAM TO OUT TO HOUSING SECTOR SEVEN. APARTMENT 19.
19? THAT'S...
SEBASTIAN, TAKE A SQUAD.
I'LL GRAB A LIFT.

I READ ABOUT A MONUMENT BUILT LONG AGO--BACK ON EARTH, WHERE WE CAME FROM.

THERE WAS A MAN WHOSE WIFE DIED, AND IN HER HONOR, HE WANTED TO BUILD THE GRANDEST TOMB IN HISTORY.

AND HE DID.

BUT IN THE YEARS IT TOOK TO FINISH THE PERFECT TOMB, THE BODY HAD GONE MISSING. NO ONE COULD FIND IT, AND THE GREAT MAUSOLEUM REMAINED, AN EMPTY WONDER.

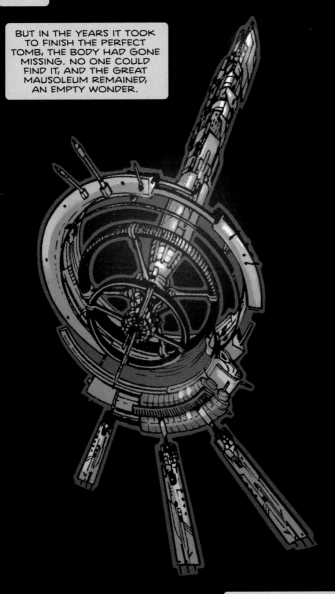

THAT'S WHAT THE ORPHEUS FEELS LIKE--HUMANITY'S PERFECT TOMB, OUTWITTING THE END OF ALL THINGS, THE ULTIMATE HABITAT...

BUT NO ONE ON BOARD BUT THE PEOPLE WHO *BUILT* IT LEFT TO APPRECIATE THE DAMN THING.

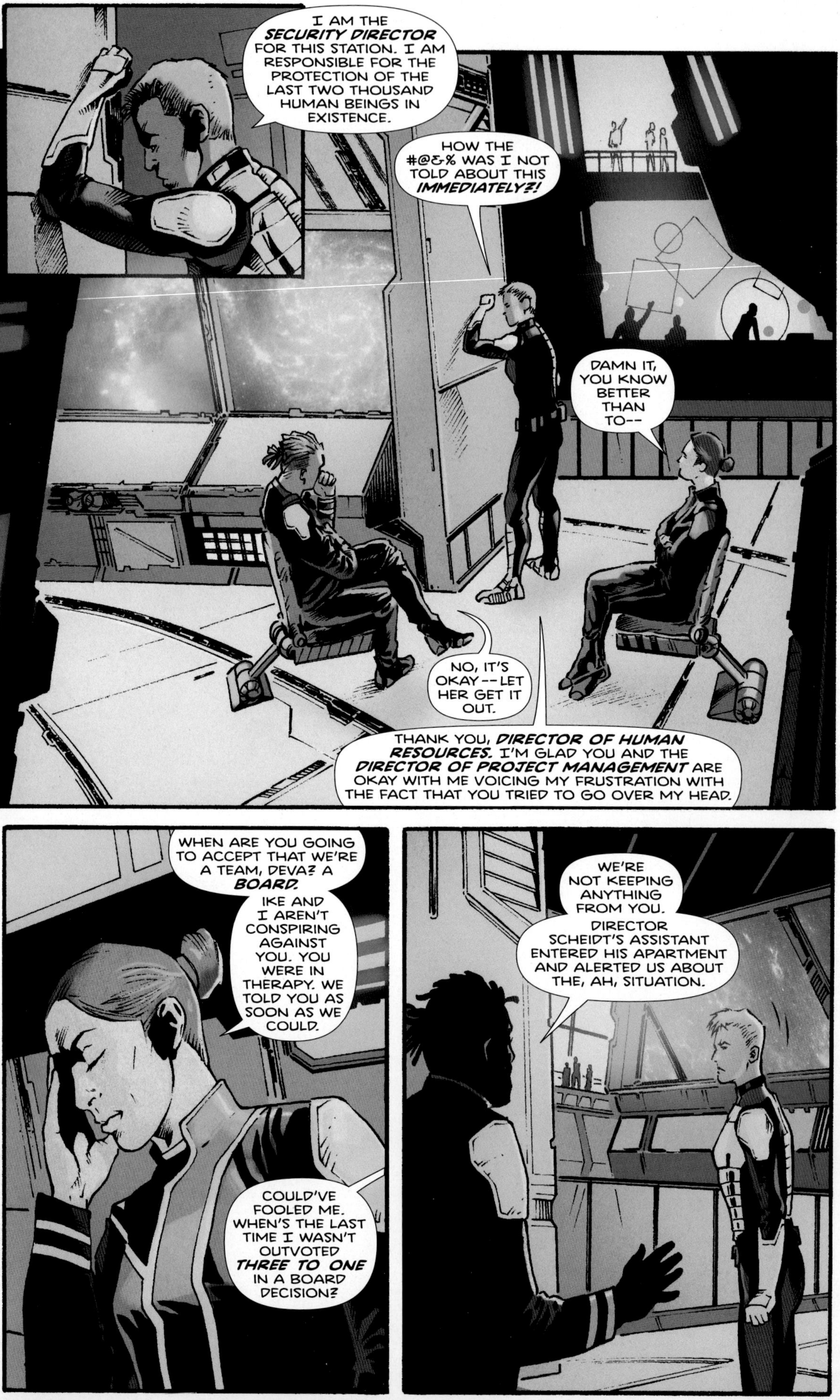
I AM THE SECURITY DIRECTOR FOR THIS STATION. I AM RESPONSIBLE FOR THE PROTECTION OF THE LAST TWO THOUSAND HUMAN BEINGS IN EXISTENCE.
HOW THE #@&% WAS I NOT TOLD ABOUT THIS IMMEDIATELY?!
DAMN IT, YOU KNOW BETTER THAN TO--
NO, IT'S OKAY--LET HER GET IT OUT.
THANK YOU, DIRECTOR OF HUMAN RESOURCES. I'M GLAD YOU AND THE DIRECTOR OF PROJECT MANAGEMENT ARE OKAY WITH ME VOICING MY FRUSTRATION WITH THE FACT THAT YOU TRIED TO GO OVER MY HEAD.
WHEN ARE YOU GOING TO ACCEPT THAT WE'RE A TEAM, DEVA? A BOARD.
IKE AND I AREN'T CONSPIRING AGAINST YOU. YOU WERE IN THERAPY. WE TOLD YOU AS SOON AS WE COULD.
COULD'VE FOOLED ME. WHEN'S THE LAST TIME I WASN'T OUTVOTED THREE TO ONE IN A BOARD DECISION?
WE'RE NOT KEEPING ANYTHING FROM YOU.
DIRECTOR SCHEIDT'S ASSISTANT ENTERED HIS APARTMENT AND ALERTED US ABOUT THE, AH, SITUATION.

YOU MEAN THE INCIDENT IN WHICH OUR *TECH DIRECTOR,* ALVIN SCHEIDT--THE CHIEF TECHNOLINGUIST ON THIS STATION, A MAN CAPABLE OF PRACTICALLY REWRITING THE ORPHEUS' CORE CODE--

SPONTANEOUSLY DECIDED TO ABDUCT HIS NEIGHBOR, JALIL EVANSON, AND YOU ALL WAITED HOURS TO ALERT ME AND THE REST OF SECURITY?

IT'S NOT LIKE HE'S GOT ANYWHERE TO RUN. I'M SURE YOUR TEAM HAS--

LET'S SEE.

SEBASTIAN?

IT'S COLD HERE, DIRECTOR. SPOKE TO THE ASSISTANT WHO FOUND THE SCENE--

"DEFINITE SIGNS OF A STRUGGLE."

"SCHEIDT APPEARS TO HAVE CRACKED EVANSON'S DOOR LOCK. MAYBE CAUGHT HIM UNAWARES?"

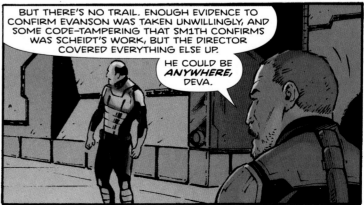

BUT THERE'S NO TRAIL. ENOUGH EVIDENCE TO CONFIRM EVANSON WAS TAKEN UNWILLINGLY, AND SOME CODE-TAMPERING THAT SM1TH CONFIRMS WAS SCHEIDT'S WORK, BUT THE DIRECTOR COVERED EVERYTHING ELSE UP.

HE COULD BE *ANYWHERE,* DEVA.

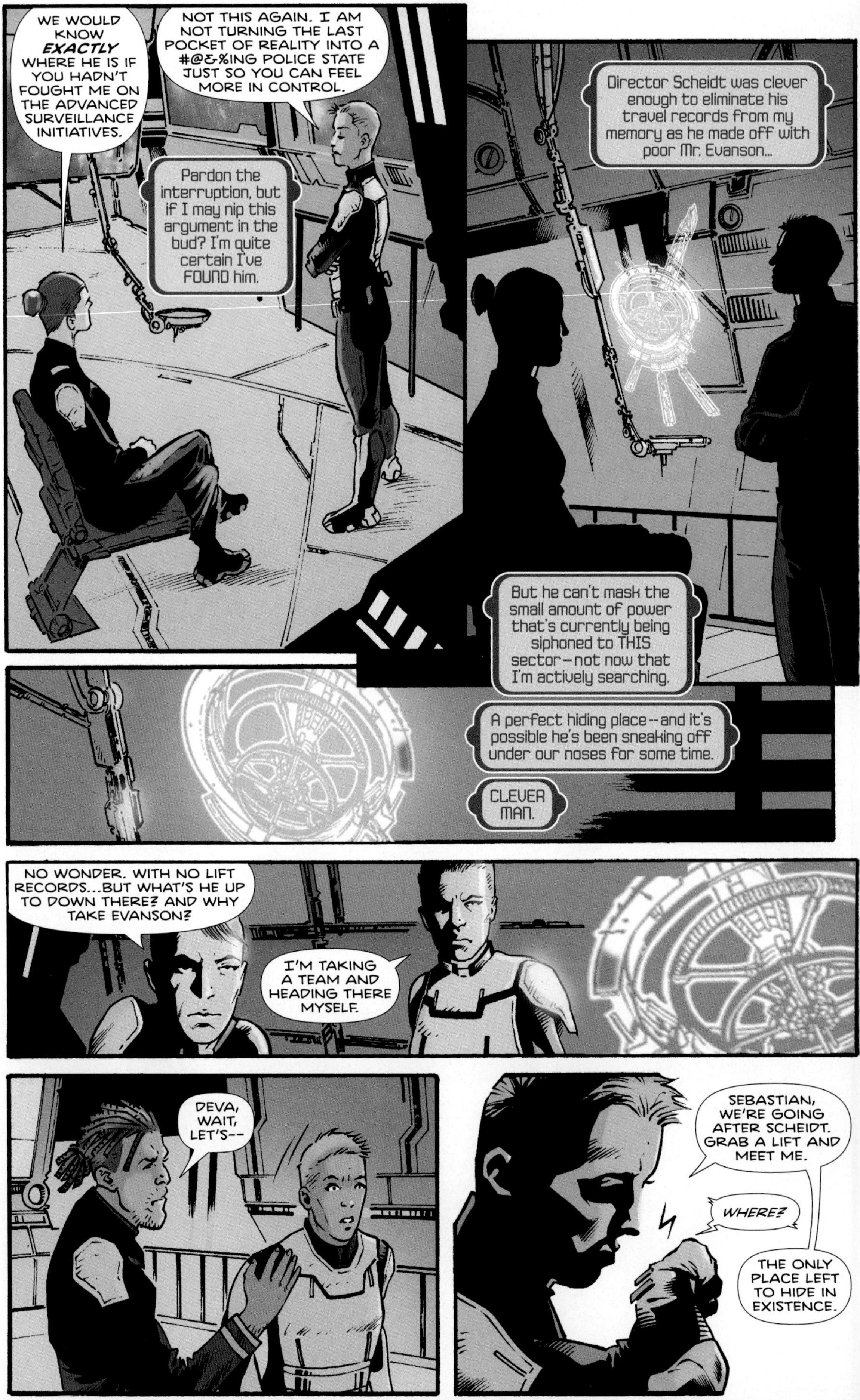

WE WOULD KNOW *EXACTLY* WHERE HE IS IF YOU HADN'T FOUGHT ME ON THE ADVANCED SURVEILLANCE INITIATIVES.
NOT THIS AGAIN. I AM NOT TURNING THE LAST POCKET OF REALITY INTO A #@&%ING POLICE STATE JUST SO YOU CAN FEEL MORE IN CONTROL.
Pardon the interruption, but if I may nip this argument in the bud? I'm quite certain I've FOUND him.
Director Scheidt was clever enough to eliminate his travel records from my memory as he made off with poor Mr. Evanson...
But he can't mask the small amount of power that's currently being siphoned to THIS sector—not now that I'm actively searching.
A perfect hiding place--and it's possible he's been sneaking off under our noses for some time.
CLEVER MAN.
NO WONDER. WITH NO LIFT RECORDS...BUT WHAT'S HE UP TO DOWN THERE? AND WHY TAKE EVANSON?
I'M TAKING A TEAM AND HEADING THERE MYSELF.
DEVA, WAIT, LET'S--
SEBASTIAN, WE'RE GOING AFTER SCHEIDT. GRAB A LIFT AND MEET ME.
WHERE?
THE ONLY PLACE LEFT TO HIDE IN EXISTENCE.

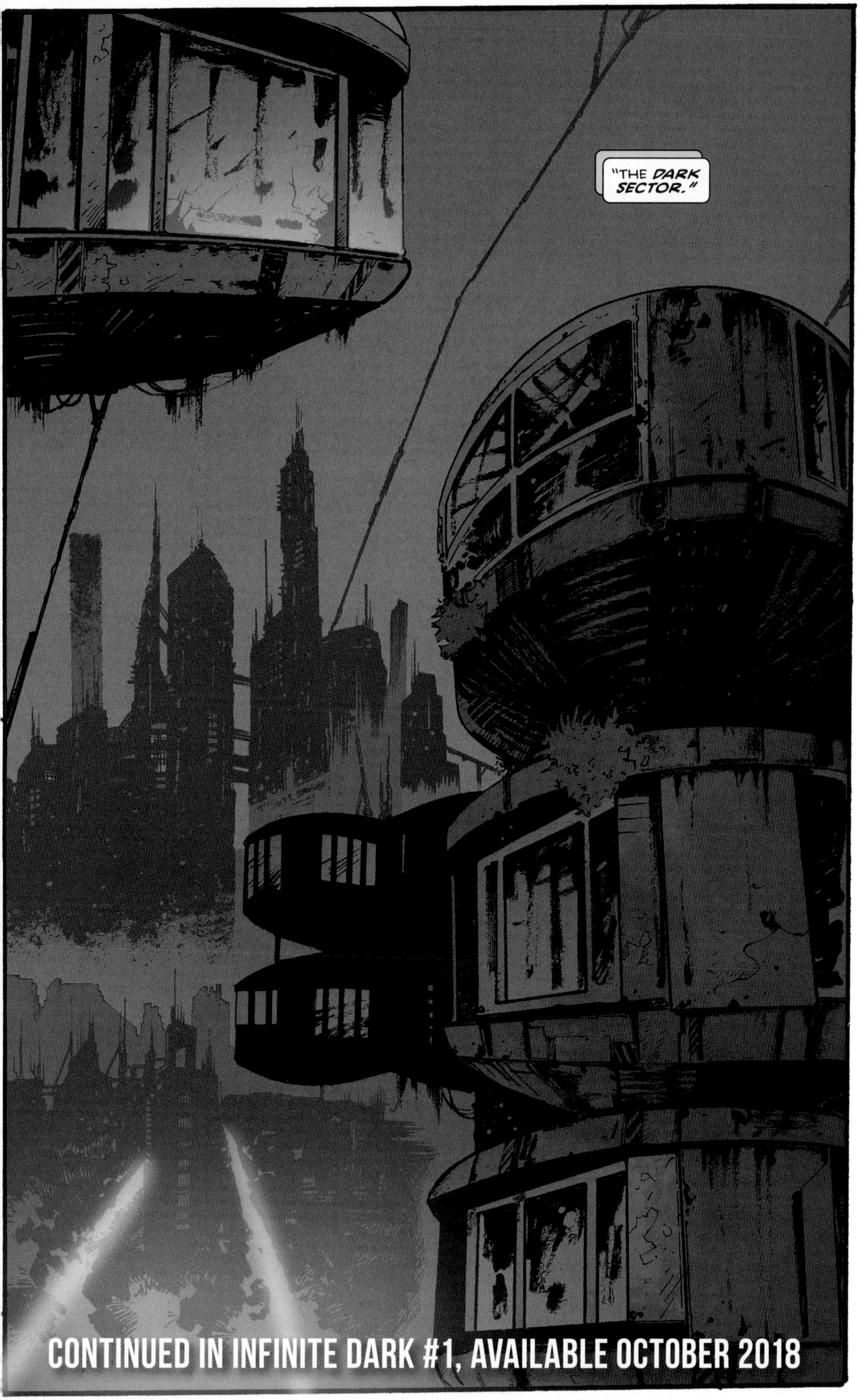
"THE DARK SECTOR."
CONTINUED IN INFINITE DARK #1, AVAILABLE OCTOBER 2018

WARFRAME™

HUMANITY'S DESCENDANTS SCRAMBLE TO SURVIVE IN A GALAXY RIFE WITH CONFLICT.
THE CRITICALLY ACCLAIMED, FREE-TO-PLAY COOPERATIVE SHOOTER COMES TO COMICS.

VOLUME ONE
AVAILABLE NOW
IN TRADE PAPERBACK

STAIRWAY

MATT HAWKINS   RAFF IENCO

Will these scientists find
a stairway to heaven...
or will they unleash
something that
will kill us all?

RAFF
IENCO

STAIRWAY, VOLUME ONE
ORIGINAL GRAPHIC NOVEL
AVAILABLE NOW

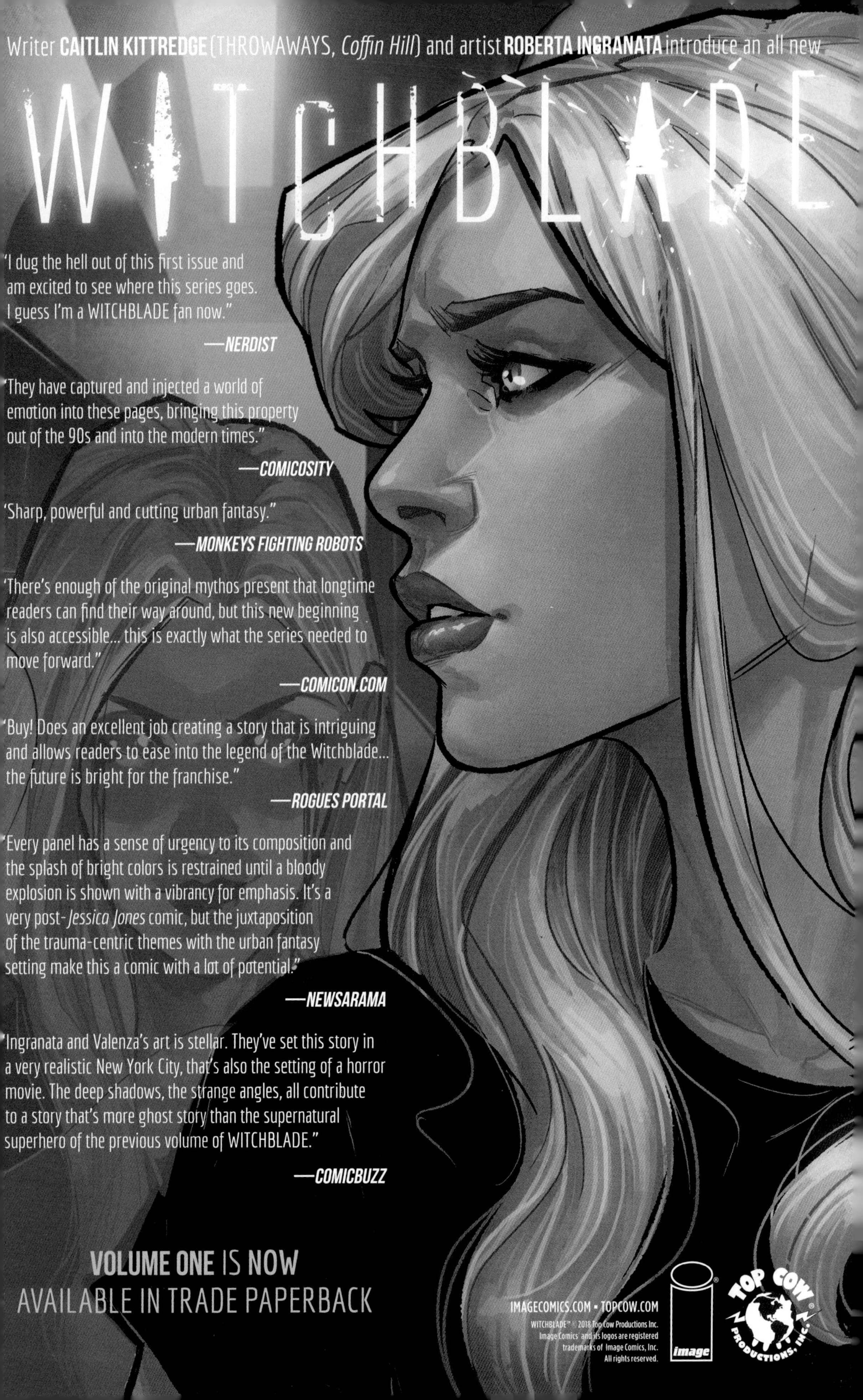
Writer CAITLIN KITTREDGE (THROWAWAYS, Coffin Hill) and artist ROBERTA INGRANATA introduce an all new
WITCHBLADE
"I dug the hell out of this first issue and am excited to see where this series goes. I guess I'm a WITCHBLADE fan now."
—NERDIST
"They have captured and injected a world of emotion into these pages, bringing this property out of the 90s and into the modern times."
—COMICOSITY
"Sharp, powerful and cutting urban fantasy."
—MONKEYS FIGHTING ROBOTS
"There's enough of the original mythos present that longtime readers can find their way around, but this new beginning is also accessible... this is exactly what the series needed to move forward."
—COMICON.COM
"Buy! Does an excellent job creating a story that is intriguing and allows readers to ease into the legend of the Witchblade... the future is bright for the franchise."
—ROGUES PORTAL
"Every panel has a sense of urgency to its composition and the splash of bright colors is restrained until a bloody explosion is shown with a vibrancy for emphasis. It's a very post-Jessica Jones comic, but the juxtaposition of the trauma-centric themes with the urban fantasy setting make this a comic with a lot of potential."
—NEWSARAMA
"Ingranata and Valenza's art is stellar. They've set this story in a very realistic New York City, that's also the setting of a horror movie. The deep shadows, the strange angles, all contribute to a story that's more ghost story than the supernatural superhero of the previous volume of WITCHBLADE."
—COMICBUZZ
VOLUME ONE IS NOW
AVAILABLE IN TRADE PAPERBACK
IMAGECOMICS.COM • TOPCOW.COM
WITCHBLADE™ © 2018 Top Cow Productions Inc. Image Comics® and its logos are registered trademarks of Image Comics, Inc. All rights reserved.
image
TOP COW PRODUCTIONS, INC.

The Top Cow essentials checklist: